MAGDALENA STANHOFF

THE TROUBLE WITH BELONGING

a novel

LING ARTIST

This is a work of fiction. Names, characters, places, organizations, and incidents either are the product of the author's imagination or are used fictitiously. Any resemblance to actual persons, living or dead, events, or locales is entirely coincidental.

First edition

ISBN: 9788396242631

This book was professionally typeset on Reedsy.
Find out more at reedsy.com

To the first reader of this novel, with love.

Contents

The Question

When Kehuan met Niki, he already had all the makings of a lone wolf. He was eight years old, his whole family consisted of one perpetually absent parent, and he had no friends at all.

The isolation wasn't entirely by choice, of course, but it also wasn't something he struggled with, as Kehuan didn't feel he really needed other people so much. He was of the opinion that being alone was his natural state and that it suited him quite well.

Enter Niki, and before he knew it, the notion became obsolete.

As their meeting had been pure coincidence, he sometimes wondered later, when he was much older, what would've happened to both of them had they missed each other on that day?

It was hard to deny certain disasters could've been completely avoided, and many things would've probably gone easier for Niki if she hadn't known him, but he chose to believe that all in all, she was better off as it was. As for himself, each time he lost her, he fought like crazy to find her back, and each time he found her, he swore he would never lose her again, and even if it wasn't possible to keep this promise in the end, at least it answered the question well enough.

And so he liked to think they'd have met anyway, in a different place and different time. After all, their second and third encounters had been also quite accidental, as if they were the spare occasions arranged just in case the first one hadn't worked out.

Normally, Kehuan was a staunch advocate of rational thinking, but he was inclined to make an exception in this matter and to believe that fate had its hand in it all because Niki was the one person he simply couldn't imagine not having in his life.

I

Part One

1

What Was Before

It could be said that Kehuan's problems with belonging had started before he was even born. Not only was he a child of two people of different nationalities, but one of them just couldn't stay put in one place.

His father was Taiwanese, a brilliant international lawyer. He had spent a big chunk of his youth abroad, first living with his parents in London for several years, and then studying in Canada. He'd been into politics since his university days, and worked in this or that capacity at diplomatic posts of Taiwan for many years, moving from one country to another. He put his entire energy into the work, and, being a man of a western cast of mind, strongly opposed the pressure of traditional Chinese culture with its emphasis on familial duty. For many years, his personal life stayed limited to a few very discreet flings, and he was entirely satisfied with this state of affairs, forgive the pun. In the middle of his forties, however, during the time he worked at the embassy in Seoul, he met Kehuan's mother, and the situation changed radically almost in a day.

Lee Soojin worked as a secretary at the embassy, and she owed the prestigious position to her late mother, an immigrant from China, and her determination to educate her daughter in spoken and written Mandarin. Soojin was much younger than Chen Liang, but not so young as to not want to start a family as soon as they sorted out their feelings. The decision carried a hint of rebellion: her living family consisted of a fraternal grandmother and a few aunts and uncles, and they were all less than enthusiastic about the marriage. Chen Liang could have been well-off, good-looking, educated, and successful, but the bottom line was he wasn't Korean, and they were sure Soojin could do better, just as they'd thought about her father some thirty-five years earlier.

Kehuan was born a year after his parent's wedding, and for the next couple of years, nothing interesting happened to them, if one can describe in such cavalier terms the everyday life of a happily married couple raising a healthy child. A significant change took place when Chen Liang was offered a new post in Europe. Soojin had never set foot outside of Korea and was feeling adventurous, and Chen Liang was getting a little tired of her meddlesome relatives, so he accepted the offer, and with the beginning of the new millennium, they moved to Berlin. In these new circumstances, Soojin's Korean-Chinese ancestry wasn't of much advantage, so she gave up working altogether and simply dedicated her time to raising her son. Chen Liang, who had been such a stringent opponent of the traditional family model of life for so many years, was quite content with it and not conflicted at all.

Although this was probably the most peaceful period of Kehuan's childhood, even then he was already alienated from other children. His father earned good money, and despite Soojin staying happily unemployed, they could afford living in a comfortable house in a very good part of the city, but there wasn't much going on around in terms of social life among young children, especially those whose parents didn't know each other. There were no common playgrounds in the neighborhood; each house had its own garden with its own facilities, separated from others by a solid fence and thick barrier of greenery. Children didn't play in the streets either, God forbid. They were invited from time to time to play in each other's houses, and that was that.

Unfortunately for Kehuan, Chen Liang was already doing all his socializing during working hours and had no time to befriend his new neighbors, and Soojin wasn't bold enough to accost people whom she only met at the local grocery store, and whose language she could hardly speak. As a result, Kehuan spent most of his time in the sole company of his mother.

Soojin had a lot of playfulness in her, and she didn't mind spending her days finger-painting, solving puzzles, and building endless variations of spaceships out of Lego blocks. It certainly helped that Kehuan wasn't a difficult child. He was a little serious and smiled too rarely for his mother's satisfaction, but he also didn't make a fuss over small things, like many children. It didn't bother him what he was given to eat or to wear, or if his day was arranged in a different order than he'd expected. He loved learning new things. If something interested him, and Soojin sometimes thought everything interested him, he'd get totally engrossed in it and put all his attention to the one thing, until he understood, or did the task, or solved the puzzle, or finished whatever there was to finish to make him satisfied. He learned at amazing speed, and observing him brought her a lot of pleasure.

Soojin loved books, and they spent many blissful afternoons over classic children's stories from all over the world. They usually read in Mandarin, but she sometimes smuggled in some books in Korean as well, and Kehuan didn't mind, though she had to explain a lot, and it took much longer to go through a story in her mother tongue.

Both mother and son seemed perfectly happy, but at some point, Chen Liang started to worry about Kehuan's social development, and after a lot of fretting over the language barrier, it was decided the boy would go to kindergarten.

* * *

On the day of Kehuan's kindergarten debut, Chen Liang cut his work short—an almost unheard-of occurrence—and returned home just in time for dessert. He entered the kitchen, kissed his wife on the cheek, and then looked at Kehuan at the table and raised his eyebrows.

"Chocolate ice cream?" he asked, feigning confusion. "Is this the end of the world?"

His wife smiled and waved the teasing words aside with a graceful gesture of her beautiful hand. “It’s a special occasion,” she answered. “Kehuan was very brave today. He didn’t cry at all.”

Kehuan glanced at his mum from over his bowl of ice cream, licking the teaspoon, and wondered what she meant. He didn’t recall anything happening during the day that would deserve shedding tears over it.

“Is that so?” Chen Liang asked, very pleased. “Excellent. Since that’s the case…” And he produced the big box of Lego blocks he’d been hiding behind his back.

Kehuan was even more baffled now; his day at the kindergarten really didn’t account for so much fuss. Some children had been a bit too noisy, the soup they’d had for lunch had no taste, and he got a little annoyed when the teacher tried to help him solve the puzzle with panda bears, but none of that bothered him much, and he had no complaints. But since his parents thought he deserved the present, he certainly wasn’t going to protest. He turned over the box, examining the pictures of different constructions proposed by the producer, and decided he didn’t like any of them.

“Can we make a space station out of it?” he asked, opening the set. He took out all the bricks and started to separate them into categories depending on their size and shape. Color wasn’t really important, he decided after a short deliberation. “I don’t know if there are enough pieces,” he noticed a moment later with a slight frown. “I can bring more from my room…”

His parents exchanged amused glances over his head, and Chen Liang, still in his elegant business suit, sat down on the carpet next to his son.

“Let us see,” he said. “Do you have a special project in mind? What are our objectives?”

It turned into a very pleasant evening, which later transformed in Kehuan’s memory into some fantastic, magical event he kept replaying in his head again and again because it was the last happy moment he could remember for a very long time.

Just a couple of weeks later Lee Soojin noticed something wrong about her left breast, and their perfect world suddenly crumbled.

* * *

The few months that followed were forever blurred in Kehuan's memory. He mostly remembered being always the last child to be collected from the kindergarten, which he didn't like so much anymore, and terribly missing his mother, who wasn't there. He knew she was in the hospital, but he was scared, and lonely, and confused by the sudden replacement of Soojin with a very friendly, but completely foreign babysitter, and so he began causing problems.

It started small. Kehuan got touchy and lost his easy-going attitude. He made trouble over things he'd never cared about before and got angry when someone touched his things or a toy he was playing with or sat at his place during lunch. He'd only just started learning German and couldn't properly argue, but he'd caught a few useful insults and used them like a weapon. Everyone was very understanding at the beginning, and even when he proceeded to shout and push, adults were still quite patient, though children began to fear him. But then he started to hit, and kick, and bite, and while the teachers were still sympathetic, the parents gradually lost their goodwill. Kehuan was tall for his age, and he could pack quite a punch.

Chen Liang was more or less aware of the whole situation, though he kept quiet about it in front of his wife. But Soojin's condition kept deteriorating; they'd already tried radiotherapy, and two different types of chemotherapy, but nothing helped while it all cost a lot of money, and he had his work on top of that. There was so much to deal with already that Kehuan's kindergarten brawls didn't seem so important in comparison, so he didn't pay much attention to them until one day he received a phone call from the headteacher who asked him to come and collect his son, and not to bring him anymore. This was a private institution depending very much on the parents and their good opinion, and Kehuan became, at the tender age of five and a half, a bogeyman of the neighborhood, scaring people off with his violent tendencies. Chen Liang tried to parley, but it was too late.

Kehuan returned home, and soon he was bored out of his mind.

His father was basically absent, either at work or in the hospital. The first babysitter, whom Kehuan had finally accepted, had already left by then, and another one took her place, only to quit as well after a few weeks. After that, he didn't really want to get to know any of his babysitters. In the end, they all left, and there was no point.

To be fair, it must be said that most of them started their work with the best intentions, but Kehuan was a singularly unlikeable child those days. He discovered he had a real talent to repel people, and practiced this new skill with a vengeance on everyone he met. He'd caught quite a lot of basic German during his short stint in the kindergarten, but pretended not to understand a word of what was said to him, and ignored all requests and commands. He also learned that most adults were not inclined to hit him, even if he hit or kicked them first, though there were some exceptions. He didn't tell his father about the exceptions, choosing instead to spend more time on his own inside his room or outside the house, and accidentally making the life of his last German babysitter much easier.

That was the time when he really discovered books. During those reading sessions with Soojin in their happy days, he'd already learned quite a lot of Chinese characters, but it wasn't enough to let him read all by himself. Korean alphabet with its limited number of letters was much easier to master, but books written in Korean presented him with a different difficulty: he didn't understand most words.

A lucky accident helped his situation. Chen Liang wanted to buy some audiobooks for Soojin, who didn't have the energy to read anymore, and while his secretary was browsing through the online bookstore, she came across some children's books with audio version added on CD, and in a rare fit of initiative added to the cart a compilation of traditional children's fairy tales.

It wasn't the best choice for Kehuan, but he listened to the CD and read the book all the same, several times, scowling and sneering in turns at the naivete of the stories. After that he did some thinking, and finally initiated contact with his not-reluctant-to-hit-back babysitter, asking for more books with CDs. The babysitter had a problem understanding him and had to consult with his father, but Chen Liang said yes, of course. After that, they reached a truce of sorts: Kehuan kept out of her hair, reading in his room most of the time, and she ordered new books for him every time he asked.

It took him almost a year to shed the audio files completely, and start using dictionaries instead. About the same time, three months after he turned six, his mother died.

* * *

It wasn't really a surprise. Kehuan had known Soojin was going to die, even if nobody ever mentioned it to him. Or maybe people did mention it when they thought he wasn't listening. Anyway, he knew, and he'd already cried over it many times in his room and kicked and bitten many people for it. When it happened, he was sad, but it wasn't such a blow as could be expected because in a way his mum had already been gone for a long time by then.

At the beginning of Soojin's illness, Kehuan had been allowed to visit her in the hospital, and he couldn't wait for those visits, but he quickly became disappointed. His mother didn't play with him the way she used to, and she cried a lot instead of smiling. Later, as her condition worsened, the intervals between their meetings became longer, and finally, Chen Liang put a stop to them altogether because each time Soojin saw her son, she got very depressed afterward. When she died, Kehuan hadn't seen her for several months, and several months is an epoch in the life of a six-year-old. When he was told, he simply thought things weren't going to be so much different from what already was, only now it was clear they'd never change back again.

If Kehuan was grimly resigned and prepared for the news, Chen Liang was not. Soojin had been the love of his life, and he'd been in full denial mode, never allowing himself to even consider the possibility that she could die. When she did, it was a complete disaster. He took leave from work, returned home, took a bottle of whiskey, and locked himself in his study.

Kehuan also kept to his room, and his babysitter wondered if she should go home since the boy's father was present. Chen Liang had left his phone in the hall, and it kept ringing every few minutes, annoying her to no end, until it finally ran out of power and stopped, and the house became eerily quiet.

Her shift ended, and now she was actually supposed to go, but it wasn't sitting well with her to leave the boy alone, with his father locked away and incommunicado. It was true that she hadn't been reluctant to hit Kehuan back, but she still pitied the brat quite a lot. Though it was a relief to not have to deal with him very often.

She stayed in the end, made some simple food, checked up on Kehuan from time to time, and waited until Chen Liang finally emerged back from the study two days later. She bragged to her friends about this sacrifice for years.

* * *

Chen Liang quit his job and went with his son back to Taiwan.

He owned an apartment in Taipei, which he always kept empty, though he'd been told many times that renting it out would be more reasonable. It was on the seventh floor of a high-rise apartment block, and, unlike their former house in Berlin, wasn't located in any prestigious neighborhood. It was also small and cramped, as it dated from the times when he'd just come to Taipei from Canada, and had still been young and moneyless. The place had been a rental back then, but he bought it out some years later, both as an investment and for sentimental reasons. Now it came in handy.

They were living on his savings, and the money was melting away. There wasn't much left after Soojin's long stay in hospital and all the treatments, and Chen Liang was aware they couldn't go on like that forever, but he felt incapable of taking any action. The only thing he seemed to be able to do these days was drink.

He'd always liked alcohol, but kept his drinking habits firmly under control. In those past days with Soojin, he used to content himself with a single glass of whiskey in the evening, after returning home from work.

She'd sit with him in the living room, and they'd hug, and play some music, and talk, and he'd feel good even if his day had been hard. It was all paradise lost now, so he didn't really want to think about it. Everything was bleak, without any prospects of change, and he felt broken inside.

Still, he made some minimal effort to take care of his son. When they arrived, the summer was just beginning, but Chen Liang enrolled Kehuan at a local school for the next school year. He also bought the boy some new clothes, better suited for muggy Taipei weather, and took him to a local store for a new haul of books. That was all. Anything more, like actually interacting with his son, was beyond him at the moment.

Around this time a guy from Soojin's Korean family contacted him. It wasn't any member of the older generation, but some cousin from Busan whom Chen Liang had never met. The man called him several more times during the summer, trying to convince him to send Kehuan over for the holidays, but Chen Liang never agreed. He knew the proposal had its merits, but he had an unfounded, but strong premonition that if he let Kehuan go to Korea, he might never see his son again, and even in his current state of permanent stupor the thought terrified him.

Kehuan had no idea his mother's relative kept trying to invite him over for the summer. He was busy turning himself into a part-time street child.

He was finally able to understand what people were saying around him, more or less, and to communicate with other kids. In the beginning, he was glad about it and eager to socialize, but it quickly became clear that his inability to make friends in Germany had been caused by more than just the language barrier.

Kehuan discovered that he didn't really like other children. He'd spent his early years in the company of books and very intelligent adults, and he couldn't help thinking that children were stupid.

The truth was he had no common ground with most of his peers. The children in the streets didn't read many books, and he didn't understand their games and got quickly bored talking to them. Chen Liang and Soojin had shared the opinion that TV damaged children's brains and should be reserved for adults, so Kehuan had no idea about popular cartoons or anime serials. Any references to characters and plots flew right over his head, and it gave other children the much-needed ammunition: he thought they were stupid, but it turned out it was him who didn't have a clue. And he used strange words sometimes and had a funny accent, and he also didn't have a mother. At this point, things usually quickly escalated from the quarrel to a physical fight because Kehuan was never averse to using his fists these days. He had a lot of anger bottled up inside, and the cork popped out readily on every occasion.

It kept happening along the same lines with every new group of children he encountered, and because he wasn't dim, it came to his mind very quickly that the problem probably lay with him, not them.

That was really annoying. If it had been their fault, he could beat them all up, but Kehuan didn't know what to do when something was wrong with himself. He chose the simplest solution and stopped trying. He just wandered around, making larger and larger circles around his home, and getting to know the whole area: the housing estates, the shopping streets, the marketplaces, the bars, and entertainment zones. It wasn't a particularly bad part of the city, but it had enough of seedy alleys and corners, and if Chen Liang knew where his six-year-old son could be found at times, it's possible he'd sober up on the spot. But Chen Liang had no idea and never asked, so Kehuan walked wherever he wanted.

He observed people and learned quite a lot every day. Even if he didn't try to talk to others anymore, sometimes others talked to him, and every time a new situation unfolded. By the end of the summer he understood that most adults were nice, but some he should definitely avoid. He also found out that some older kids and teens could be truly vicious, and that not every fight was winnable, and how to fight dirty, and when to keep his opinions to himself, and when to run. He returned home every evening tired and hungry, and sometimes there was something to eat, but sometimes there was nothing, as Chen Liang was all about liquids these days. So Kehuan also understood that if he wanted to eat, he had to make sure there was food at home or to eat on the street, and he learned to count money, and not to count money when somebody was watching him because after that there might be nothing left to count.

You could say it was a very educational summer for Kehuan.

* * *

In September, the school started. Chen Liang remembered about it at the very last moment and felt bad because of that, but Kehuan knew about the first day of school anyway because he'd overheard some children talk about it. He even knew he was supposed to wear a white shirt on this occasion, only he couldn't find any white shirts among his clothes, so he gave up and went in a white T-shirt instead. It had a picture of a dragon on it and wasn't entirely clean, but it was the best he could do.

His school was simply the nearest one to the apartment. The old Chen Liang would've never sent his son there, but it wasn't that bad, really. It was just a big, a little shabby, ordinary school in a hard-working, but down on its luck neighborhood.

Kehuan quickly decided he liked school. It gave some structure to his days, which was good, but mainly he liked it because he still had the same voracious appetite for learning. He especially enjoyed math, though the pace was somewhat slow in his opinion. But solving math problems was fun, and he could always solve more if he didn't feel like listening to the same explanations again.

There were more than a thousand children at the school, but he didn't talk to anybody and kept to himself, as usual. Still, he quickly discovered there were some kids who weren't completely stupid, after all. He started to hang around them and overheard some talks about the after-school classes they were attending. That caught his attention. Kehuan wondered what he'd like to learn or practice after school, and decided to consult it with his father, making Chen Liang feel again like a candidate for the worst father in the world award.

Chen Liang wanted his son to be able to learn everything he wished, and in the past, he would've encouraged every interest and ambition Kehuan might have, but now the situation became a little tricky: they were almost out of money. He recognized he really needed to cut down on the alcohol and start looking for a job, but it was all easier said than done. He didn't want to go back to his old work, even if he had such a chance. He felt as if his work at the Berlin embassy had been somehow connected to Lee Soojin's illness and death, and though he knew it was irrational, he was absolutely sure he was done with diplomacy. At the same time, he'd worked in this field all his life, and had no idea what he could do instead.

The next morning after Kehuan had caught him off guard with his after-school classes dilemma, Chen Liang woke up with a slightly clearer head than usual. He took the long-overdue shower and ate some stale egg pancake rolls he'd found in the fridge, trying to remember when he could've gone out to buy them. Then he started browsing the contact book on his phone, in hope that some course of action would present itself, and finally decided to call Liu Wen, an old acquaintance from his university days. They used to be good friends, and the guy was a lawyer like himself, but most importantly, he still lived in Canada. They hadn't talked for years, and Chen Liang hoped Liu Wen wouldn't know his recent history. He didn't want to talk to anybody who'd known Soojin, or even knew about Soojin.

It was a partial success. It turned out Liu Wen did know, and when he started offering his condolences, Chen Liang was seconds away from hanging up on him. But the man kept the condolences short, and soon they were talking about his job as a legal counsel for a construction company, and in the end, Chen Liang didn't find it so hard to ask for advice. Liu Wen promised to think about it and call him back.

Chen Liang didn't really expect anything to come out of it, but a few days later, he received a message saying a relative of Liu Wen wanted to meet with him in Taipei. He'd almost forgotten about the whole conversation by then, as it had happened some three bottles of whiskey earlier, but decided to give it a chance. He dusted off one of his business suits and got on the bus to meet the guy in a downtown restaurant.

Later, he often thought of this meeting as one of the luckiest turnabouts in his life, right after meeting Soojin.

Liu Wen's cousin's name was Chen Xiao, and they both smiled when they first introduced themselves. Chen Xiao had a great smile, which made others feel at ease in his company, and Chen Liang suddenly remembered that he used to be brilliant at interacting with people and made an effort to dig out some of his old charm. Soon it became clear they operated on the same wavelength, despite the age gap and different professional backgrounds.

Chen Xiao was a thirty-something computer whizz with a flair for business. His personal history seemed like a reverse to Chen Liang's: he grew up in Vancouver, and then came to Taipei to study computer science. After university, he'd started a small software company, which began to do well after obtaining a contract with a big client.

The client had several branches in Asia and Europe, and Chen Xiao's company had serviced them all from Taipei so far, but at one point, he decided it'd work better if they had a subsidiary company in Europe. This required a lot of legal work on-site, though, and employing local people. Chen Xiao had found a few potential investors, including Liu Wen, but he had no experience in overseas business, and Chen Liang, with his international lawyer's experience, seemed to him like a godsend. Chen Liang knew of course it was exactly the other way round, but maybe they were godsends to each other, or at least he really wanted to believe so.

Later that day he hesitated for a moment over the bottle of whiskey he was holding in his hand, but in the end, he threw it away. This was his one chance to dig himself out of the hole. What's more, it was also a chance to dig out Kehuan, and that wasn't something he could pass up and forgive himself.

As soon as he shook off the alcohol haze, he took a first sober look at his son and their apartment and felt appalled. He wasn't sure Soojin would recognize her pampered boy in the scraggy, unkempt, scowling creature. As for the place, the less said the better. He couldn't believe he'd let himself live like that. At first, he wanted to do all the cleaning himself—it'd be a fitting punishment for keeping his son in this pigsty—but in the end, old habits won: he hired a local cleaning service, and they did the job. Cheng Liang in the meantime took Kehuan for a haircut, and then for a proper meal, and over dinner, he asked his son what after-school classes he'd like to take.

Kehuan was a little surprised, but he had it all thought out by then. He wanted to take up a musical instrument because he liked music, and English because everybody said it was important, and some martial art because he wanted to be a better fighter, and something to do with computers because computers were cool but he had no idea how to use them, which caused him a lot of grief at school.

His father listened to it all and shook his head, laughing quietly, which stunned Kehuan all over again. A few days later he was signed up for piano lessons once a week, private English lessons three times a week, and taekwondo classes twice a week. Kehuan had expected it'd be Tai Chi, but taekwondo looked really fierce, so he was glad. As for computers, Chen Liang simply introduced his son to Chen Xiao, and if ever there were people destined to meet, they were those two.

Chen Xiao was absolutely enchanted with Kehuan, not because he was an enchanting child—he definitely wasn't—but because he was the smartest kid Chen Xiao had ever met. The problem of Kehuan's incompetence with computers was solved after an hour, and then it was into the land of computer games, the Internet, elementary algorithms, and computer programming for kids. Chen Xiao gave him one of his older laptops and made a point of finding time for him every Saturday, and Kehuan appreciated these sessions a lot.

They lost Chen Liang after the first two meetings. He'd never been particularly interested in technology, or good at it. He felt he belonged to the pre-Internet age, though since he'd started working for Chen Xiao, he'd been on a steep learning curve. But seeing how much his son enjoyed this new experience, he was very grateful to the younger guy, who in many respects understood Kehuan much better than himself.

* * *

Kehuan enjoyed all his new classes very much, but he didn't fail to notice the different levels of importance his father put on each of them. He especially wondered about the amount of time allotted to English lessons. He didn't mind learning the language, since English often came in handy when he was playing online multiplayer games, but he couldn't help feeling a little uneasy, as Kehuan's logical thinking was always stellar.

The bomb detonated in February, just a few days after his seventh birthday.

Chen Liang announced he was soon leaving for Poland, to set about the opening of the company's new subsidiary. He didn't want to transfer Kehuan in the middle of the school year, so his son was to stay with Chen Xiao until June. Then he'd join his father, and after holidays he'd go to an international school in Warsaw.

Kehuan was furious. He began shaking, angry tears sprang to his eyes, and he couldn't even speak properly. He'd just started school. He'd just started his classes. He'd just...started. He felt utterly betrayed and couldn't understand how his father could do it to him.

Chen Liang had expected his son wouldn't welcome the news, but the intensity of Kehuan's reaction gave him pause. He couldn't change the plans, though, as everything had been already set in motion, and besides, working at the subsidiary in Europe was the main purpose he'd been employed for. But it was difficult to explain to Kehuan that all the recent good changes in their life happened on the condition they'd move again, and finally, Chen Liang lost patience and got a little angry himself. He was doing his best, and he was doing it all for his son, and his son hated him for it.

They parted two weeks later in a rather frosty atmosphere, and Kehuan moved to Chen Xiao's place.

It was far away from his old apartment, so even with Chen Xiao driving him to school every morning, he had to get up much earlier to be on time for lessons, which didn't improve his mood at all. Even so, living with his computer guru had its perks: Kehuan could now ask questions about the ICT stuff almost as soon as they popped in his head. The apartment was also much bigger, and he had his own room, at least for the next three months. But he still felt betrayed and resentful.

Earlier, when things had started looking up, some of his anger towards the world evaporated, but now it was all back. He didn't want to go back to Europe and start all over again in another foreign country. He hated his father, and he hated his life. He hated other kids at school as well. He couldn't stand their constant giggling and babbling, and those stupid snots didn't know how lucky they were he had his taekwondo classes where he could hit and kick in an organized way. He hated Chen Xiao, too, because he finally connected the dots and realized the whole exile project was because of this guy and his stupid company, and he felt like a moron for not catching on to it earlier.

Finally, the anger fizzled out and left him empty. Kehuan hardly talked to Chen Xiao at home anymore, and when he was at school, he felt like a hundred-year-old surrounded by gurgling toddlers. From time to time he noticed another hundred-year-old in the crowd, but he never approached any of them. What would it help? Misery wasn't a team sport, and besides, he was leaving soon anyway. Even his after-school classes didn't feel like fun anymore.

Chen Xiao had an enormous flat screen in his living room, and Kehuan spent a big chunk of April and May staring at it, binge-watching cartoons, anime, children's films, and different documentaries his temporary guardian had programmed for him. In those two months he made up for all the popular children's culture he'd missed up on earlier, and now he could probably discuss with a flair all Disney, Pixar, and Ghibli plots and characters, and quote funny lines, only he had no one to talk to, and couldn't care less. On the days he felt rebellious, he went for adult content as well. Most of it wasn't so interesting, and some pieces were downright gross, but he enjoyed action and adventure films, and sci-fi sagas. But it was all just fiction, and reality still sucked.

At the beginning of summer, Kehuan finished his first grade, said goodbye to his piano and English teachers and the taekwondo *sabom*, packed his life into a middle-sized suitcase, and boarded a plane to Warsaw (to Istanbul, really; there weren't even any direct flights to this godforsaken place). Chen Xiao saw him off to the airport, and they parted on more or less good terms.

Kehuan hadn't forgiven him for the exile, but he also hadn't forgotten all the help the guy had offered him. It all kind of balanced out, and Kehuan let it go. He didn't want any drama.

He had to switch planes twice, once in Istanbul and then again in Frankfurt, but it went without a hitch. The professionally smiling flight attendants and ground staff transferred him through the airports, and he slept through most of the long flights. Still, he was already seriously jet-lagged when they finally arrived in Warsaw.

He saw Chen Liang waiting for him behind the sliding glass doors and felt nothing, though in the past months he'd sometimes had to admit to himself that he missed his father, despite everything.

Chen Liang gave his impassive son an awkward hug and they went out of the hall. They took a taxi to their apartment, and Kehuan remained in the zombie mode during the whole forty-minute drive. Then he went to sleep straight away, and it wasn't until the next day that he finally gave his new surroundings a proper look.

* * *

He woke up at four in the morning if the clock on the wall could be trusted, and it was daylight already. The room wasn't big, but it had a big, floor-to-ceiling window on one wall, and Kehuan got up to take a better look.

The sky was pale blue, and he had a view on a wide river, visible behind a road and some trees. He could see thin wisps of morning fog lingering over the water, and the downtown on the other side. To the right, a long bridge crossed the river. Kehuan didn't think the city was as big as Taipei, but it still looked quite big and had a different feel.

He dressed up, unpacked his suitcase, plugged in his laptop, and went out for some breakfast. The kitchen was right next to his room, and he was pleasantly surprised to find actual food in the fridge.

Sometime later his father came to the kitchen as well and sat next to him at the table. Kehuan just ate on, keeping silent, and Chen Liang sighed and asked if he liked their new place. Kehuan said it was okay; with its big windows, toned-down colors and simple furniture it reminded him a bit of Chen Xiao's apartment in Taipei, except this place was much smaller; there were only two rooms. But it didn't matter, as long as he had his own space.

Chen Liang offered to show him the neighborhood, and Kehuan agreed with a smirk. He expected that soon he'd be doing a lot of walking around on his own again, and he didn't really need a guide, but whatever.

They went out of the apartment, and Kehuan saw it was located on the fifth floor of a low-rise apartment block. It was still morning, and the air was drier and much cooler than in Taipei, even though the day was sunny. A light breeze was coming from the direction of the river, but he couldn't see it now. There were a few similar blocks close by, all separated from each other by greenery and lawns. Kehuan didn't recognize the trees, but he was suddenly reminded of their old garden in Berlin, and he felt a pang. He hadn't thought about Berlin for a long time and didn't remember so much of it anymore, but Berlin meant Soojin.

They turned to the opposite direction from the river, and after a few minutes of walking entered a busy street lined with shops, offices, and small eateries. Some places were still closed at this time of the day, and some were just opening. The pavements were wide, and many eateries had tables and chairs outside, though they didn't look like a permanent thing. In Kehuan's eyes, the whole neighborhood seemed rather fancy.

In fact, for all that Chen Liang had been crazy busy with work during those last months, he'd made an effort to make Kehuan's new beginning as smooth and nice as possible. He'd felt bad about the way they'd parted, but there was more to it: he didn't remember many details from the time they'd first arrived in Taipei, but what he did remember made him cringe, and he wanted to make up for it to his son. It looked like they were going to stay in this city for a long time, so he picked a place he thought Kehuan would like, cost be damned.

The apartment he'd rented was within a walking distance from the school Chen Liang had in mind for his son, though it would be a rather long walk. He'd already found an English tutor for Kehuan for the holidays, and also checked that the school offered extra classes on music. He'd even done some tentative research about martial arts for children in Warsaw and was surprised to find many options, including a few taekwondo clubs. All in all, he hoped Kehuan would see it wasn't going to be so bad, really.

After an hour of walking around, they went to the school. Kehuan was a little curious about it. He'd already known they had all lessons in English there, and he thought the two teachers who talked to him wanted to check if he'd manage. They called him Kehuan Chen, which sounded weird because he'd always been Chen Kehuan before, and they accented his name all wrong, but he didn't correct them. Finally, they said he'd do.

After that, his father stayed behind to finish the paperwork while Kehuan took a stroll around the school grounds. On the way back he grudgingly admitted everything seemed all right so far, and since he was still jet-lagged, he went back to sleep as soon as they returned home.

* * *

On the next day, Chen Liang had to go back to work.

It was very telling that he'd found an English tutor for Kehuan but didn't even consider hiring a caregiver or organizing his son's time in any way. If Soojin were still alive, Kehuan would be probably spending his holidays on some fancy theme summer camp, but Chen Liang was clueless in some respects. He'd never been the one who took care of their son when the boy had been younger, and he got so accustomed to Kehuan taking care of himself during that time in Taipei that it didn't even cross his mind that it might not be an entirely normal arrangement.

Kehuan woke up very early again, played online games on his laptop for a while, read a book, and then heard his father get up and leave. He went out of his room then, and while eating breakfast, he thought about what he could do. His English tutor was coming soon, and Kehuan decided to do some city exploring after that. He'd already seen the neighborhood and wanted to take a look at the downtown now, but it seemed a little far. The previous summer he'd sometimes walked for hours at a time, but he was older and wiser now, and besides, on the day before he'd already noticed the bus stops on both sides of that busy street.

The tutor came at nine. He was a university student on holiday, young and upbeat. His name was Tomek, and he told Kehuan to call him by it. He was pleased Kehuan could already speak some English using simple sentences, and they talked for an hour and a half about different stuff: Tomek wanted to know about Taipei, so Kehuan told him some, and Kehuan asked him about Warsaw and the buses, so they opened the map of the city on his laptop, and did some browsing together. Tomek was very interested in the keyboard with Chinese characters; he'd never seen one before. The local websites didn't have Mandarin versions, though, so they had to do all the research in English, which was all right, since it was supposed to be an English lesson. After that Kehuan had no problem with getting a day ticket at the machine next to the bus stop, and he got on the bus and took his first trip around Warsaw.

This was again a summer when he learned a lot. Warsaw was a very different city from Taipei, but some things were exactly the same. There were people who wanted to help him, needlessly, probably because they thought he was lost, and people Kehuan knew at once to avoid. There were many fantastic places, beautiful in a totally different way from Taipei, and there were dirty alleys and nasty-smelling passages as well. The weather could be tricky at times, but after a few surprises Kehuan learned to check the forecast on his laptop in the morning, and he was set. Food was different, too, but he'd never been a picky eater, and besides, he quickly discovered there were many small places with Asian food around if he felt fussy. Though some of them were rubbish.

Kehuan didn't understand the language again, and it was a pain, but the letters were mostly the same as in English and German. He could at least read the names of streets and places, even if he had no idea how to pronounce them, and if he really had to communicate with somebody, his basic English and some gestures were usually enough.

But the most important new thing Kehuan learned was that he was a person of color living in a country of white people.

It took him some time to notice and to realize what it meant because he didn't know to look for the signs at first and didn't speak the language, and of course, it wasn't as if everybody in Warsaw was racist. But there were enough.

He first got the message when he was walking through the park not far from home, and stopped near a playground to watch some kids on the swings. Kehuan wasn't trying to join them; he just liked sometimes to look at other children. But the boys started sneering and shouting at him, and even if he didn't understand a word, he got the gist: they wanted him gone from there, and they thought he was trash.

It happened a few more times, and Kehuan didn't understand the reason for those attacks at first because he really wasn't doing anything when they happened. He made a mistake and asked Chen Liang about it, and it was the first time he saw his father truly angry. Chen Liang wanted to go out and find those punks at once, and it took some convincing to dissuade him from the plan. Kehuan decided to talk to Tomek instead, and he could tell his English tutor felt really bad about it. As if it was his personal fault somehow. Kehuan told him it was all right; he just wanted to understand.

Tomek was a history student, and the topic triggered a lengthy discussion about different strange beliefs some people had about others, and how it sometimes led to really nasty stuff. Like in Europe in the past, he said, and Kehuan, quite curious, did some additional digging on the Internet later and got horrified and fascinated at the same time.

After that he became aware. He noticed when a woman on the bus didn't want her child to sit next to him, and when a shop assistant wiped his hand on the apron after Kehuan's fingers had accidentally touched his while taking an ice cream. He made an effort to ignore it, but it grated on his nerves all the same.

The boys were the worst. The very first group of little nazis he encountered turned out to be his curse. They lived in the same neighborhood, unfortunately, and they were a pack, while he was alone. Kehuan felt seriously tempted to try some of his taekwondo moves on them because after the first few accidental meetings the wretches started to follow him around, and he had to develop some weird strategies to avoid them. He sincerely hoped none of them would be at his new school because it would really suck.

And then September came and the school started, and hallelujah, they weren't there.

Kehuan was in the second grade, and his class had only twenty children in it, which was half of his old class in Taipei. The group was a real mix. There were two girls he'd thought might speak Mandarin, but they didn't (they were both Vietnamese) and a boy from India, a few Americans and Canadians, and children from different European countries, including Germany. And a scattering of Polish children, too. Kehuan learned all this on the first day when their form teacher asked everybody to introduce themselves for the benefit of the three new students in the class.

The lessons were fine. The American and Canadian children had an advantage because of the language, but Kehuan could already tell it wouldn't last. There were other very smart kids, too, who just needed to improve their English. As for math, he was the best again, hands down.

It should be said that Kehuan had made some progress in his social skills since the previous year. He'd already stopped getting into fights because he'd realized that this road usually led to nowhere, and he didn't think anymore that all children were stupid. He'd understood at some point that most of them were simply...more children than himself. But no further change of habits followed this understanding because whatever the reason, the conclusion was the same: he had nothing to talk about with them, and felt no inclination to try. There were better outlets for his energy.

He started training taekwondo again, and since he was tall and strong for his age, and already had some skills, he got placed in a group of older boys, which was really cool.

Then there was music. The music teacher at the school was very earnest about her mission, and she called Kehuan's father to tell him he should buy a piano for his son to practice at home. Chen Liang, who didn't have a clue about music, and had never treated Kehuan's music interests seriously, was surprised and annoyed at the meddling. But the teacher had already found a second-hand acoustic piano for Kehuan, and Chen Liang had only to pay for it, and it wasn't expensive while being of good quality, and it was really important for a music student to have a good instrument. In the end, Chen Liang surrendered. He didn't know how to argue with her, and the teacher unknowingly hit upon the best strategy with him: ask him to pay, and let him forget about the rest.

Kehuan enjoyed his new-old piano very much, not to mention the kick he'd got out of hearing the music teacher bully his father. He'd only heard one side of this conversation, but it'd been hilarious.

Another thing was the after-school computer club. Kehuan hadn't expected much of the shaggy young man with a beard and thick glasses who was a teacher there, but he'd been completely wrong. The guy was just as brilliant as Chen Xiao, except his interests lay in different areas, like computer graphics and animation, and he was also working on this program translating between English and Polish which was supposed to work on mobile phones. It wasn't long before Kehuan started writing codes again under his direction.

Still, his life was far from perfect.

First, he had to study Polish at school, and it was a nightmare. No other language had caused him so much grief. If he could, he'd drop it on the spot, but alas, it was obligatory for all students. So he struggled and cursed, and didn't make much progress at all, and it didn't console him that it seemed just as hard for almost every foreign kid.

But that was a trifle in comparison with the other matter.

The nazi boys had become the bane of his existence: he met them almost every day now. Kehuan suspected following him around was their main entertainment, and wanted to roll his eyes and ask if they really didn't have anything better to do, only he couldn't, of course, because he didn't speak the damn language. The public primary school they attended was halfway between his own school and home, and he had to invent different roundabout routes to steer clear of them. But then it was late autumn, and the weather turned foul, and when winter came, he became thoroughly fed up with it.

* * *

Kehuan was walking home on a frosty February afternoon when he spotted a whole group of the nazi boys standing in front of a small shop. He'd already learned that the more of them were together, the uglier it'd get, so he immediately changed direction and walked through a passage between two buildings into a small courtyard.

A few cars stood on one side, and on the other, there was a swing, a slide, and a sandpit, all covered with a thick layer of snow. Next to the slide Kehuan noticed a snowman, and stared: the small figure, though crudely made, looked unmistakably like Sid, the chatty sloth from *Ice Age*.

Kehuan sat on the rim of the sandpit, gazing at the snow Sid and shivering violently because he'd forgotten his hat and gloves that morning. He took out his phone and took a photo of the snow figure, and was gloomily pondering his options when someone suddenly poke his back.

He turned around swiftly, ready to face his stalkers and finally deliver some taekwondo, but instead, he looked into the strangest pair of eyes he'd ever seen.

They looked like a work of a CGI artist, enormous in a small triangle face, bright and clear like water, and striated with dark blue and gold. The creature the eyes belonged to looked somewhat strange, too. She was tiny—Kehuan was almost certain it was a she—and dressed in several layers of clothes obviously too big for her, with a gray woolen shawl wrapped around her head and shoulders. In the outstretched hand, she held a big metal cup with a lid.

The creature said something in a melodic voice and beamed at Kehuan, who of course didn't understand a word, and for the first time regretted his aversion to learning Polish.

"I don't know what you're saying," he said in his own language and shrugged.

The little girl frowned, fixed him with the gaze of her improbable eyes, and impatiently repeated the same thing, shoving the metal cup in his hands.

Kehuan felt that despite the insulation it was a little warm on the outside. At this point, he was so cold that he didn't think much: he just opened the lid and took a swig of whatever was inside. It was hot, milky, and sweet, and he shivered and drank more, looking at the girl between the gulps. She started to bounce up and down, spinning around at the same time, and chanting one word over and over in her melodic voice, and Kehuan couldn't help laughing. He actually laughed, aloud.

The tiny creature stopped at that, grinned at him, and pointing to herself in a perfect me-Jane-you-Tarzan re-enactment, said very clearly, "Niki".

And Kehuan remembered it forever because, even though he didn't realize it then, it was the moment that separated his life from what was before.

2

Like a Ghost

Niki reminded Kehuan of a young stray cat, small and half-starved, but adventurous. She looked like a cat, with her small triangular face and enormous eyes, which were even shaped like a cat's, and she behaved like a cat, curious, playful, and easily bored. She'd find him when she was in a mood for company, and then she'd disappear when some other idea struck her, and Kehuan soon started to worry that one day she'd get hit by a car, or harmed by some wrong people, like it happened to so many other stray cats, because Niki wandered around on her own all the time, just like Kehuan had, only she was much younger.

That first day she walked with him for some time on his way home, in turns skipping over different shaded pavement tiles or sliding on the fragments where the snow hadn't been cleaned. They were playing a game: she pointed to something, he said the name of it in Mandarin, and then she parroted the words after him. She was like a recording device, perfectly copying the sounds, Kehuan's tone, and even the hitch in his voice when he once tripped over a big chunk of ice. She said the words in Polish, too, and Kehuan also tried to repeat them, but he was nowhere near as good as her.

They both had fun, but after twenty minutes he started to worry she wouldn't find her way back, so at the next intersection he stopped, turned to her, and said, "Go home", motioning with his hand. He half expected she'd protest, but the little girl simply waved at him with both hands, turned around, and ran back the way they came, still skipping and sliding along the pavement. For a moment Kehuan considered walking her home. She looked so tiny, flitting between other people in those ridiculous clothes, and it was already getting dark. But he was half-frozen, with icicles in place of fingers, so he let it go.

Back at the apartment he took a hot shower, ate some noodles left over from the previous day, and sat down to his homework. And then he remembered Niki and started wondering if she got home without any trouble. The longer he thought about it, the more uneasy he felt, and finally, he decided to check up on her the next day after school.

But on the next day, Niki wasn't there, nor on the day after that. Kehuan checked the place a few more times, but the small courtyard was always empty, and finally, he concluded it might not have been her home after all, and there was nothing else he could do.

* * *

About two weeks later he was cutting diagonally across a snow-covered garden square on the longer, alternative route home when he noticed a small snow sculpture standing on one side of the path. It wasn't Sid this time, but Stitch. Kehuan again didn't have any trouble recognizing the character, and he felt a jolt. He hadn't connected the first snow sculpture to Niki before, but now it struck him it might not have been a coincidence the little girl and the snow Sid had been in the same courtyard on that day. He slowed down, looking around among conifers and bushes, and sure enough, there she was.

Niki, covered in snow from head to toe, squatted under overhanging branches of a big leafless shrub, gathering small twigs. She'd lost the gray shawl, and dark, snow-encrusted hair was flowing over her shoulders from under a red woolen hat she was wearing instead. Apart from that, she was dressed like before, in layers of too-big clothes. Kehuan noticed she wasn't wearing gloves, and winced.

A moment later she scrambled up from under the branches and carried all the twigs to a small empty space among a few conifers. Kehuan came up closer and saw that she was putting together some complicated pattern of twigs, conifer sprigs, and snowballs.

Niki raised her head at the sound of crunching snow, smiled brightly, and called, "Kehuan!", and Kehuan felt absurdly gratified that she'd remembered his name.

"What are you making?", he asked in Mandarin, and then repeated the question in English without much hope. The Polish version was beyond him, which annoyed him a little.

She just stared at him without blinking with her alien eyes. Kehuan pointed to the pattern on the ground and asked the question once again, sticking to Mandarin. Niki shrugged and got back to work, but after a moment she glanced at him again, pointed to a few snowballs lying on the ground, and asked something, looking at his hands. Kehuan experimentally made a new snowball and gave it to her, and she smiled and nodded.

After that, their cooperation was established: he made the snowballs and brought her new twigs and sprigs, and Niki put them into right places, though Kehuan for the life of him couldn't guess where the right places were. From time to time she'd order new materials, and he learned Polish words for a twig, a sprig, and a snowball, and some other words, like "give me", and "put it here". He taught her some words in Mandarin in return, and she did the recording device impersonation again.

After about half an hour Niki decided the thing was done. She got up, brushing the snow off her clothes, stepped back, and motioned to him to come over.

Kehuan looked and felt amazed. He had no idea what it was supposed to be, but it was beautiful. They contemplated their work together for a few moments, and then he extracted his phone from the inner pocket of his winter jacket and took a photo because it was definitely worth keeping.

They left the garden square together, and this time he was determined to make sure she'd get home safely. But when they stopped at the nearest intersection next to other people waiting for the green light, Kehuan looked away for a moment, and when he turned back, she was gone.

She was really gone, like a ghost, and he got irritated, first with her, and then with himself because really, how could he have lost her in three seconds flat? But later he learned it was par for the course: Niki was gone whenever she wanted to go, and he lost her in different places countless times.

* * *

Their third meeting brought over a small drama.

It was March already, and the snow had finally melted. Kehuan was taking another detour this day, walking through a quiet residential area near his school, where elegant old houses hid inside the overgrown gardens separated by tall fences and walls. It reminded Kehuan of Berlin again, and he was thinking about Soojin and feeling nostalgic when he heard someone singing in a clear, lovely, and very young voice. It took him only a few seconds to connect the voice to the person, and a moment later he saw her.

Bareheaded and disheveled, she was sitting atop a high wall, with a leg on each side, and singing an upbeat song with great gusto, clapping her hands to the rhythm during some fragments, and waving her arms in the air during others. The wall separated one of the gardens from the street, and Niki was looking down at someone on the other side, who was clapping, and possibly waving, along with her. Her hair was much shorter now, and she looked even smaller, and it took Kehuan a moment to realize it was because she wasn't wearing so many layers of clothes anymore.

As soon as he grasped the whole situation, he got angry with the idiot on the other side. The wall was almost two meters high, and anybody with a shred of common sense would be taking Niki off it right now, instead of clapping with her. He called out her name, and she looked at him over her shoulder and grinned. Kehuan lurched forward, frightened she'd try to jump off, but she did nothing of the sort and just kept singing. He came closer, looked up, and swore, wondering how the heck she got up there, and more importantly, how the heck he was going to get her down without any accident.

She finally finished singing and asked something the person on the other side, and judging from the voice that answered, Kehuan thought it was another girl, but older. Niki stood up on the wall, almost giving him a heart attack, stretched her arms out to both sides, and started walking fast, giggling happily to the other girl. Kehuan followed her along the wall, getting ready to catch her if she lost balance, but then she suddenly took a turn onto the section of the wall separating the garden from another one and immediately disappeared from his sight. The older girl must've gone away as well because when he called out, nobody answered.

Kehuan waited a few more minutes and finally went on his way. He felt irritated and upset, and there was also some other feeling he couldn't name, bitter and burning, and he didn't like it at all. He told himself he wasn't going to worry about Niki anymore, or even think about her.

After coming home he concentrated on his lessons, and then went to the martial arts club and focused on the training. It was all good until he went to bed and tried to sleep because every time he closed his eyes, he saw her sitting on this wall, singing and clapping, and then running away, and not looking at him even once, and this bitter, burning feeling almost choked him.

The next day he woke up in a grim mood and reminded himself firmly that he was done with Niki.

He was running late because he overslept (it was her fault). He washed and got dressed in a hurry, and popped into the kitchen to check the fridge for some quick snack, but there was nothing (he'd been supposed to do some shopping on the previous day, but he'd forgotten, and it was her fault as well). Cursing, he grabbed his backpack, locked the door, and ran down the stairs.

Outside, Kehuan checked the time on his phone and realized he was going to have to run all the way to be on time (damn Niki). So he ran, and because it wasn't a short distance, he got a little out of breath in the middle of it and had to slow down and walk for a minute. And Niki was walking next to him.

It was like magic. He could swear she hadn't been there a moment ago, but she must've been running too—she was huffing and puffing, and laughing at his confusion.

"Nihao, Kehuan," she wheezed out, and he forgot he'd been angry.

They started running again, and Niki escorted him all the way to the school. He slowed down a lot for her, but even then, she had to sit down on the ground at the end. She grinned at him, panting, and waved with both hands, and then Kehuan really had to go in. He was late, of course, but who cared? He felt happy all day.

After that, he decided he wouldn't get upset with Niki, even if she ran away or did the disappearing trick again.

* * *

As days lengthened and trees sprouted new leaves, Niki started to show up around Kehuan more often. He had to admit she was far better at finding him than vice versa. She sometimes waited for him on his way to school in the morning, or outside the school gates in the afternoon, and sometimes she'd appear out of nowhere when he was taking one of his roundabout routes.

They could communicate now about simple things. Kehuan started to put more effort into his Polish lessons at school, and could catch the phrases she said regularly, like "let's go", or "wait", or "I'm thirsty", or his least favorite, "I need to go".

She seemed to like his company, and Kehuan certainly liked hers because Niki was fun. She sang a lot, and she still parroted everything he said with uncanny precision, which always made him laugh. She liked to make things out of nothing, and when she wasn't making anything, she was always running somewhere, or bouncing, or climbing, and following her around often made Kehuan feel as if his head was spinning on his shoulders. But he didn't mind at all.

* * *

The summer holidays were getting closer, and one day Chen Liang asked Kehuan if he'd like to go to Taipei for the summer; it could be arranged with Chen Xiao.

He thought of the proposal as of an olive branch he was extending to his son and expected Kehuan to jump at the chance, but to his astonishment, the answer was absolutely no. This sudden reluctance of his son to visit Taipei was really baffling, considering how much he'd fought against leaving the city the previous year. Chen Liang suspected the boy might still hold some grudge against Chen Xiao. But he was glad.

They didn't spend much time together: he was usually out of the apartment before his son got up, and even in the evening, he was usually still preoccupied with business matters. There were always some late phone calls to make, or some overdue emails to read, or some reports to check. And Kehuan seemed to prefer to spend time on his own, too, even at the weekends. But he was there, and Chen Liang could always poke his head in his room in the morning and look at his boy for a moment, or take him out for a Sunday lunch to one of those small eateries nearby. If Kehuan went to Taiwan for the summer, Chen Liang couldn't go with him, and the last time they'd been separated for so long he missed his son a lot.

Besides, he still hadn't told Kehuan that he'd sold the apartment in Taipei to buy shares in the company. So maybe it was for the best that Kehuan didn't want to go.

* * *

Of course, Chen Liang got it all wrong: Kehuan had nothing against visiting Taipei, he just didn't want to leave Warsaw.

By then he'd already made the leap from having fun with Niki to being worried about Niki. A little of the concern had always been there, from the very first day, but for a long time, the fun prevailed. Perhaps Kehuan didn't want to think too hard about unpleasant things when he finally had someone to play with; he was still a child, after all, even if he didn't consider himself one. But it wasn't going to last forever because deep down he knew very well that many things about Niki were strange, not just her eyes, and he was never one to keep his head buried in the sand for too long. In the end, a small incident decided, as is often the case, and once Kehuan opened his eyes, he couldn't close them back again.

It happened in late April, on a warm spring day. He saw Niki sitting on a bench under the bus stop shelter. The weather was nice, and she looked almost normal in the only slightly oversized T-shirt. She was chatting merrily with some man, and at first, Kehuan thought it was her dad. But then a bus arrived and the man stood up and got on it, leaving Niki behind without a backward glance, and Kehuan immediately knew he'd been wrong, and it hadn't been her father at all.

She noticed him then and bounced over with a happy smile. She wanted to go climb some trees in the park, and before Kehuan had a chance to express his opinion on the idea, she was already running, and there was nothing left for him to do but chase after her, as always.

Niki chose a massive oak for the climbing business, and Kehuan got panicky just looking at it. He was scared again that she'd fall, and this time it wouldn't be some measly two meters, and he also wasn't that keen on climbing the tree himself because seriously, it was gigantic. But Niki was in a gracious mood and agreed to keep to the lower branches, and it was also hard to miss that she could shinny like a squirrel, so Kehuan finally shook off some of his apprehension and started climbing, too. And once he overcame his height anxiety, he started to enjoy the challenge, and they had a great time. As always.

But he couldn't shed the uneasy feeling about earlier, and when they started walking in the direction of his home, he decided it was time for a talk.

Kehuan had recently started carrying with him the old mobile phone transformed into a translating device which he got for testing from the ICT teacher at school, and he used it when he wanted to ask or tell Niki something more complicated. It was awkward because the sentences coming out of the device weren't really sentences, but a jumble of words, and besides, with Niki it only worked one way—she couldn't write yet. But sometimes it was the best option.

He took out the device now and switched it on.

"Who was man on bus stop?" he asked in Polish, reading words from the screen after typing his question in English. He knew he sounded like a moron, but that was the program: no finesse.

Niki shrugged and spread her arms. Of course.

"Why talk to stranger?" Kehuan got edgy now.

"He smelled nice", she answered, smiling serenely. She often commented on things smelling good or bad, so Kehuan understood her words perfectly well, but he still asked her to repeat that twice, and then cursed heavily in Mandarin.

"You smell nice, too," Niki reassured him hurriedly, and he was speechless.

* * *

That night he lay in bed, cataloging in his head all the places where he'd met Niki, some crowded, some deserted. He tried to guess how often she spoke to strangers and wondered if anybody would look for her if she disappeared.

After that he slept badly, plagued by a scary collage of different scenes from the adult films he'd seen, including some aliens abducting people to do weird experiments on them, mixed with the worst of his personal memories from Taipei, and some extra nasty pieces from that research he'd once done on European history. He woke up at three in the morning, covered in cold sweat, and was afraid to fall asleep again. Damn Niki.

Kehuan waited for the nightmares to fade away, and then got up and tiptoed to the kitchen for some water. When he returned to bed, he was ready to do some rational thinking. But after a few minutes, he realized he couldn't decide if his surmises were true, or even realistic, without some background information. He lacked what an adult would call a frame of reference, so he decided to call Tomek in the morning, and prepared a list of questions in advance. The guy wasn't his tutor anymore, since Kehuan had more than enough English at school now, but he was still the person Kehuan contacted when someone's behavior or a local custom threw him for a loop. He considered Tomek his personal expert on all things Polish.

Tomek on his side was a bit entertained by this nomination but willing to help. Though it was a pain sometimes, especially when his phone rang at six-thirty in the morning.

"Are there homeless children in Poland?", Kehuan asked him by way of good morning.

Tomek had to gather his thoughts. The call had woken him up, and his brain wasn't functioning properly yet.

"Hello, Kehuan," he finally rasped out. "Homeless children? I don't think so... Not many, anyway."

"Why not?"

Tomek had a sad feeling he wouldn't be allowed to go back to sleep.

"There's the social care system for such things. Why?"

Kehuan skipped the questions. "Does it happen that children get snatched from the streets? If no one is looking after them?"

"What?!" Tomek looked at his phone, as if he could see Kehuan on the screen. "I don't know. I guess, sometimes..."

"What happens then? Are there organ harvesting gangs in Poland?"

Tomek was wide awake now. "Organ harv—How do you even know such words??"

Kehuan decided to switch to a different line of inquiry.

"Where are the children who don't have parents?"

"In orphanages, mostly. And some children get adopted or placed with special families. Listen, have you got any problems?"

"If a child walks around alone all day, is it because she's from an orphanage?"

"Not necessarily. Some teens—"

"What if it's a very young child?"

There was a pause. Then Tomek asked slowly, "Kehuan, are we talking about some particular case?"

Kehuan briefly considered explaining about Niki, but finally said, "Just asking."

"I'd say with a young child it's most probable the parents don't look after him or her properly."

"Yeah, I thought so," muttered Kehuan. "One more thing. Why would someone wear too big clothes all the time?"

"It's a fashion statement? They are hand-me-downs?"

"What's that?"

"When someone gives away their old clothes, and someone else wears them…"

"Right. Thanks."

"Wait, Keh—"

Kehuan hung up. What Tomek had said confirmed his own suspicions, and he needed to think some more.

Niki was a mystery, and many things about her just didn't compute. He'd met her over the months in many different places, quite distant from each other, but he'd never seen any adult around to look after her, not even once. On the other hand, she'd had this insulated cup with something hot inside the first time they'd met, and he also knew already that Niki wasn't starving, even if she looked as if she was. She often had a sandwich or an apple with her, and always tried to share her food with him, though Kehuan suspected it wasn't so much out of the goodness of her heart as because she simply wasn't a big fan of eating. She wasn't dressed properly, but even in winter, when she'd often played in the snow for hours, she'd never seemed to be freezing—maybe except the hands. He supposed whoever wrapped her up in all those layers knew what they were doing, even if it looked terrible. Also, he'd noticed that every time they walked somewhere together, at a certain point she'd turn around and go back, as if there was a place she needed to return to. Kehuan was sure all those little pieces belonged to the same picture, and he was determined to solve the puzzle.

Because they didn't meet every day, it took some time before he figured out that Niki could be found around the same locations on the same days of the week. It was a big step forward, but Kehuan also realized she'd have probably shared with him this piece of information long ago if they only could properly talk, and it gave him the boost to finally start learning Polish in earnest.

In June, the summer holidays started, and he could follow her around all day now. From that point, it didn't take him long to solve the puzzle, and it all turned out very simple in the end.

* * *

On Thursday morning, in the first week of the holidays, he was wandering around that quiet residential neighborhood near his school because this was the area where Niki was on Thursdays. He turned a corner and saw her walking in his direction, hand in hand with a slim teenage girl dressed in pale blue jeans and a black hoodie.

Kehuan was immediately reminded of the bus stop guy incident, and he got testy, but as they came closer, he hesitated. The teenager looked a lot like Niki, with a thin, pale face, dark hair bound up in a knot at the top of her head, and similar alien eyes.

"Hey, Niki," he said.

"Nihao!", answered Niki brightly, and then immediately turned to the older girl and said, "It's Kehuan," and the teenager looked at him, unsurprised, nodded, and smiled faintly.

"Hello, Kehuan," she said in Polish.

Kehuan was taken aback. It was obvious she knew him, or at least knew about him, while he had no idea who she was, though he had a strong suspicion.

He knew the right word, so he asked, "Sister?"

But Niki hugged the teenager's leg and said very fondly, "Mama."

Kehuan stared. Then he checked the word on his translating device, though there couldn't be any mistake, really. He knew it, of course, and besides, it sounded almost the same in every language.

He was totally baffled. In his mind, mama was a woman like Lee Soojin, lively and cheerful, but mature. This girl was nothing like that. Now he could see she might not be a teenager, but she was still very young, like some of his babysitters back in Berlin, and she didn't seem very joyful, either.

They started walking together, and Kehuan was so distracted by this unexpected family revelation he didn't recognize at first the familiar fragment of the street with the tall wall, but it was exactly the place where they stopped.

Niki's mum rummaged in her big denim tote bag and took out a bunch of keys. She opened the gate, and they entered the front garden, and then she opened again the front door of the house, and they came into a very nice-looking hall. The place seemed empty.

She took off her shoes, put her tote bag on the small table, and looked at her daughter.

"Are you hungry?" she asked, and Kehuan understood the simple phrase. So far so good.

Niki shook her head, as expected.

"Do you want some water?" Miracle of miracles, Kehuan still understood.

Niki nodded, and they moved to a luxurious but very messy kitchen. Niki's mum looked around and pursed her lips, and then took out a glass from a cupboard and filled it with tap water.

"Do you want some, too?" she asked, and Kehuan realized she was talking to him. He shook his head. He had already recovered from the initial shock and was shifting into the investigation mode again.

The young woman took back the empty glass from Niki and put it on the counter. Then she turned back to her daughter and started talking in a serious and somewhat admonishing tone. Kehuan had a feeling he could guess what she was saying, but he asked Niki about it anyway when they went out to the big garden behind the house.

"To stay close, and not to talk to strangers," answered Niki truthfully, confirming his suspicion.

Niki's mum had brought out sandwiches for both of them later, and then she returned again to the house.

"Why don't you stay in the apartment with her?", he asked Niki as they were sitting on a swing, eating.

He was asking all the questions in Mandarin because he'd recently discovered that Niki understood much more of what he said in his language than he did of what she said in hers. So unfair.

"She has to clean it," she answered in Polish, "and it's boring. Do you want my sandwich?"

There were still some gaps in the picture, but Kehuan managed to fill them during the next few days.

Niki's mum's name was Alina, and she told Kehuan to call her by it, reminding him of Tomek. She cleaned a different apartment on each day of the week, and since all of them were big, it usually took her whole day. Kehuan wasn't surprised when it turned out each of the apartments was close to some places where he'd previously met Niki, but it was also clear the little cat did plenty of wandering around them.

"You know Niki walks a lot?" he asked Alina one day next week, feeling like a snitch. He'd started preparing his questions in advance, at home, so he wouldn't have to use his translating device all the time, though it still came in handy.

Alina sighed and nodded.

"Why won't you tell her to stay put?"

At that, she laughed ironically. "You try to tell her to stay put," she replied. Sadly, Kehuan had no problem understanding her meaning.

The next day he went with them to their place and understood some more.

Niki and Alina lived in an apartment on the last floor of an old tenement house, on the opposite side of Kehuan's school from his own home. The houses along the street were all run-down and battered, and the apartment was a dump, to tell the truth.

What surprised Kehuan most was that they didn't live in it alone: there was a very old lady, too, and she occupied one room, while Alina and Niki lived in the other one, which was also a kitchen.

He started thinking again and prepared a new list of questions.

"Why not leave Niki with grandma when you work?" he asked Alina.

"She isn't any grandma. She's our landlady."

Kehuan had to check the meaning of the word, and then asked again, "But she can take care Niki, no?"

Alina winced. "Not really. She forgets."

"Forgets what?"

"Everything."

And it was the truth. Kehuan soon realized the apartment looked like a dump mainly because the old lady, just like Alina said, forgot literally everything. She scattered her stuff all over the place and forgot to close the door, and sometimes she'd put some food in a pot on the stove and leave it there, or spill milk or sugar and forget to clean it up, and every time he came around, she behaved as if she'd never seen him before, though he'd introduced himself five times at least. She was senile and unsteady on her feet, and Kehuan had to admit leaving Niki under her care might not be the best idea.

So he thought some more.

"Don't you have family?" he asked Alina. "Where's your husband?"

She looked at him with a wry twist of her mouth. "You are like a bulldozer, you know that?"

Kehuan shrugged.

"No husband. Or family," she said, and he dropped it. He remembered that family matters could be a touchy subject.

Also, he had another question on his list.

"Why not put Niki in kindergarten?" he asked without much enthusiasm. Kehuan's own kindergarten memories weren't the best, to put it mildly.

By then Alina had started to treat him as a friend of sorts, and didn't seem to mind his nosiness very much; he rather had an impression she was amused by the whole interrogation, but at this question, she clammed up.

"I can't," she said, and that was all Kehuan could get out of her.

In the meantime, the weather turned really hot, and it wasn't so much fun now to spend time in the streets, or even in the park, especially in the middle of the day. Even Niki became listless and tired with the heat. They often tried to wait out the worst hours inside whichever apartment Alina was cleaning, but it was only so long they could stay there. At most places there were people present, working, or resting, or doing other stuff people do at home, and Niki and Kehuan were in their way. Alina kept shushing and hushing them until she had to send them out again. Out of all the places where she worked, only that one from the first time was always empty and had its own garden, and Kehuan and Niki didn't have much choice unless they wanted to stay at the girls' place, which was a dump.

And then, one day when Kehuan was walking home in the evening, he had his Eureka moment.

"Can I take Niki to my place?", he asked Alina the next day.

Alina considered. "Where do you live?", she asked warily.

Kehuan told her his address.

"It's far," she said.

"I walk her back in evening." Kehuan had thought it all out, and the plan was perfect if he could say so himself.

Alina wasn't convinced. "Niki's trouble," she told him. "Won't your parents mind?"

Kehuan almost blurted out it was no problem at all since there was no one at home all day anyway, but luckily his inadequate Polish didn't allow for such a blunder.

"No problem," he just said instead. "Is fine. I look after her, I promise."

And maybe because Alina was tired of the whole situation, or maybe because she saw Kehuan really could and would take care of Niki, she agreed.

* * *

The first time Niki came to Kehuan's place, she was enchanted. She got especially enamored with the big gray beanbag Kehuan kept next to the floor-to-ceiling window in his room. She wriggled her way into it and just stayed there, changing position every minute, and giggling happily every time the beanbag rearranged itself around her body. Finally, she stopped fidgeting, and just lay in it, gazing through the big window at the river and the trees, the blue sky with a few feathery clouds, and the city skyline in the distance. Kehuan felt a little smug that she liked his home so much.

Then she saw the flat screen in the other room and wanted to watch a film. Chen Liang had long ago given up the no-flat-screens-for-children policy, and Kehuan had his own accounts on several online movie channels. He browsed the Polish one now, and chose *Spirited Away*, wondering with an inside grin which of the characters she'd make out of snow next winter. After that, they went out and strolled down to the river because Niki wanted to see it up close.

They scrambled through the thick greenery and found a slim strip of sand by the water, hidden from the view by the shrubs and overhanging branches of trees. They spent some time there, shadowed from the sun, making a round rosette mosaic out of different colored pebbles. Kehuan took off his tennis shoes and paddled in the shallow water, picking up the pebbles, and Niki pushed them into the wet sand, putting the geometric pattern together. They had the routine down pat by now. They could hear voices of other people nearby, and children yelling and giggling by the water, but they were hidden away from prying eyes and alone, and perfectly happy.

After that, they got hungry and decided to return home. Back at the apartment, Niki helped Kehuan make scrambled eggs and toasts, but she didn't want to eat much, as usual. Niki's "hungry" was a very relative concept.

Then she wanted to watch *Spirited Away* once more, only in Mandarin. Kehuan, a little amused, found the version for her, and while she was watching it, he went to his room to read a book.

Late in the afternoon, the heat eased up a little, and they went out again to play in the small park nearby. Niki saw the swings at a distance, and she hopped excitedly and grabbed Kehuan's hand, pulling him in their direction. A moment later they were taking a turn around the small newsagent's shop into the park alley.

And there were the nazi boys.

Kehuan could kick himself for not thinking about it in advance. The park was their usual stomping ground, and it was easy to predict they could be there, but he'd somehow forgotten because lately he'd been spending time with Niki and Alina in different parts, and hadn't seen his stalkers for two weeks.

There were three of them today, including the meaty blond boy who seemed to be their ringleader. They looked a little surprised at first that he had company, but after a moment the usual taunts and insults commenced. And while Kehuan still didn't understand most of what they were shouting (though he could catch their drift), Niki understood every word.

She frowned in surprise at first, and listened for a moment, and then her triangle face flushed with anger. She swiftly climbed up the nearest bench and struck a pose with her thin legs slightly apart and matchstick arms crossed on her chest, glowering at the boys with her CGI eyes. They fell silent for a moment, eyeing her combative stance suspiciously, and Niki seized the chance: she took a deep breath and loudly barked out a short string of words.

The boys' mouths fell open, and a young woman walking by with a pushchair stopped in her tracks and looked at Niki in outrage.

"What language!" she chided.

Kehuan smothered a laugh. He had a feeling he'd caught Niki's drift as well.

Niki just rolled her eyes, and the woman shook her head, disgusted. But then she turned to the boys and said a few sentences in a tone suggesting she wasn't much impressed with them either, and they scrammed in a hurry.

Niki jumped down from the bench, and they went to play on the swings, and every time Kehuan remembered the dumbstruck faces of the nazi boys, he felt a giggle bubble up his throat. Niki was the best.

* * *

Alina worked on Saturdays, too, and Chen Liang got quite a shock when he entered his kitchen at ten o'clock on Saturday morning, still wearing pajamas, and found his son folding origami frogs in the company of a thin, dark-haired girl half his size kneeling on one of the kitchen chairs. Chen Liang made a startled sound and dropped the empty plastic bottle he was holding in his hand, and they both looked up in sync, long black eyes and round blue eyes wearing the same expression of surprise and slight annoyance.

He quickly retreated to the bathroom, and when he entered the kitchen again, showered and properly dressed, it was empty. The new collection of origami creatures of different sizes and colors was sitting on the windowsill.

He made himself a cup of coffee and stood next to the window, looking at the paper animals. They were made of pages of old magazines and weren't all frogs: he could also recognize a rabbit, a lizard, and a cat, but the others were anyone's guess. He picked up a few of them in turn and examined them closer. They didn't look like proper origami work to his amateur eyes: not even two were the same, and they were folded up in a haphazard way, lacking symmetry, which made some of them look as if they were in the middle of a jump or some other move. He put the animals back on the windowsill and went about his breakfast.

While eating, he contemplated this new development. He was almost sure it was the first time he'd seen Kehuan play in harmony with another child, so even if the choice of company seemed to him a little eccentric, he wasn't going to ruin his son's newly discovered social life with untimely criticism.

Two hours later they were back, and the little girl beamed at him brightly before following Kehuan into Chen Liang's own room. He observed them unobtrusively as they made themselves comfortable in front of the TV with drinks and snacks, and watched two episodes of some anime, snorting and exchanging short comments in a bizarre mix of two languages. It was obvious this wasn't their first meeting, or even second or third, and Chen Liang shook his head, mystified all over again.

Later they moved to Kehuan's room and closed the door, and Kehuan started to play some melodies on the piano. After a moment, the girl sang along in a bright, clear voice, and in no time they were making some new melody together, bantering and interrupting each other, and every so often bursting with laughter.

Chen Liang listened with disbelief to the exotic sound of his son's happiness and promised himself to be the best and most accommodating host ever to the little girl.

Some time later he ordered takeout at the nearby eatery, and when the food was delivered, he knocked at the door to ask them to come to eat.

Kehuan scowled at the intrusion, but he was hungry, as always these days, so he ushered Niki out of the room, and they joined his father in the kitchen for the meal. Niki didn't eat much, but she smiled at Chen Liang a lot. Kehuan could tell his father was very curious about the guest but didn't want to pry too much; he just asked about her name, and how old she was, and if she lived nearby. It piqued Kehuan no end that Chen Liang had no trouble with asking all those questions in Polish, and he swore to himself he'd master the accursed language, even it was going to kill him.

* * *

Since the family presentations were out of the way, Kehuan and Niki could spend together as much time as they wanted. But halfway through the holidays, Kehuan started to check the date on his phone more often and to worry about what was going to happen with Niki when it was time for him to return to school. It wasn't really his responsibility, of course, but he'd already realized by then that Alina, even if she wasn't exactly the neglectful parent he'd thought her to be at the beginning, had no chance to take proper care of her daughter.

Unexpectedly, help arrived the same way as before, in the person of Chen Xiao.

The company in Warsaw was doing well and acquiring new clients, and both Chens were eager to grow their business some more, so Chen Xiao came to Warsaw at the end of July to stay for several weeks. He was always the one to overview the business and technical aspects of the company work, while Chen Liang tackled legal matters and PR; they were a good team. But they had also become good friends by then, and since Chen Xiao wanted to meet Kehuan again, he dropped by their place almost first thing after arriving.

This day Kehuan decided to try to cook something. He was fed up with sandwiches, it was raining buckets outside, and his father wasn't home, so they couldn't order takeout, as local eateries didn't want to accept delivery orders from a kid.

Niki was all for the new challenge, so they browsed the Internet for some easy recipes, and checked the fridge and kitchen cupboards for the ingredients, and finally decided to make spaghetti with tomatoes, bacon, and eggs. It wasn't very complicated, and went mostly well—they only burnt the bacon a little. Niki unexpectedly turned out quite useful with the kitchen stuff; she told Kehuan her mum did some cooking from time to time in their room slash kitchen, and Niki liked to help. She also invented on the spot a chant about eggs, bacon, and tomatoes, including rhythmic banging with wooden spoons on the pots, and performed it repeatedly with her usual fervor while Kehuan kept nervously checking the time, trying not to overcook the spaghetti.

They'd just started eating when Chen Liang and Chen Xiao entered the apartment. Kehuan saw them through the kitchen door and froze for a moment at the sight of his old computer guru. Chen Liang watched his son with some tension, but the boy got up at once and came to say hello, visibly glad to see Chen Xiao. They followed him into the kitchen, and there was Niki.

Chen Liang felt slightly abashed; he forgot to mention to the guest this small detail about their household. Chen Xiao did not seem to mind, though. He greeted Niki as if she was his favorite niece, and when he additionally gave her his winsome smile, Niki was charmed. She immediately offered him her portion of spaghetti, which made both men laugh and Kehuan roll his eyes. But Chen Xiao was very impressed that the offer was made in Mandarin, and a little intrigued.

He talked to Kehuan for some time, pleased that his protégé seemed to have adapted well to his new environment, but at the same time, he kept observing Niki, who was wriggling on her chair, jumping down and climbing up again, and walking around the kitchen, as if sitting in place for five minutes was beyond her capabilities. Her plate was still almost full when she declared she was done with it, and Chen Xiao thought it was no wonder she looked as if a small breeze could topple her over.

Chen Xiao liked children, and he had a true talent for interacting with them—befriending Kehuan with the giant chip on his shoulder was enough of recommendation. He was also much more observant about them than Chen Liang, and noticed at once some things about Niki which his business partner missed all summer.

"I like your shirt," he told her sincerely. The flannel shirt did look nice: it was well-made, if not new, and the color suited the girl's lovely eyes. "But isn't it a bit too big?"

Kehuan immediately threw him a dirty look, which didn't escape Chen Xiao's attention.

"It is good," answered Niki seriously. "Is me too small."

He had to smile at that.

"That's because you don't eat enough," he told her. "You have to eat much more to fit such an excellent shirt."

She looked a little unsure, as if she didn't understand exactly what he said, and turned to Kehuan instead. She said something to him in a different language, and he nodded and went out for a moment. Chen Xiao realized she'd been making an effort to speak Mandarin on his account, and felt honored.

Kehuan returned after a moment with two pencils and a piece of paper and sat at the table. Niki immediately joined him. She observed keenly as he wrote a Chinese character for cat. He showed it to her, saying the word aloud, and she squealed with excitement, grabbed the other pencil, and pulled the piece of paper from under Kehuan's hand. After staring at the character for a moment, she started coping it carefully. She wasn't paying any attention to the order of strokes and wasn't as much writing the character as drawing it.

Chen Liang, who had just returned to the kitchen, glanced curiously and clicked his tongue.

"Are you teaching her Chinese writing?" he asked Kehuan with disbelief, "Because she's doing it all wrong, you know."

"Nah, it's just for fun," Kehuan answered. "There was a Chinese version of the cooking instruction on that packet of spaghetti we used, and she got curious. I promised I'd show her some characters after dinner."

Chen Liang asked his son to tidy up the kitchen, and Kehuan started loading the dishwasher.

Niki in the meantime finished copying the character and was now drawing a cat next to it. It was a very simple drawing, as could be expected from a child of her age, and yet she managed to capture the features of the animal surprisingly well. When she finished, she turned around and poked Kehuan unceremoniously with the pencil.

Chen Xiao half-expected an angry reaction from the boy, or at least the usual scowl, but Kehuan turned round without protest and simply asked, "What word now?"

Niki thought for a moment and said a word in Polish, and Kehuan wrote the character for wolf.

"Why wolf?", asked Chen Xiao with interest.

"We watched *Princess Mononoke* two days ago," Kehuan said with a little smile, "and now she says I'm her wolf."

Chen Xiao chuckled; it was quite an apt description.

After that afternoon he reflected that the little girl was, in her own way, just as interesting a child as Kehuan. But Chen Xiao came to Warsaw for business and didn't have much spare time, and it's quite likely he wouldn't even see Niki again if not for the wasps.

About a week after his visit, Kehuan and Niki were playing on the big meadow near the river when Niki accidentally stepped on a wasp nest in the ground. She didn't know what happened until they started to swarm around her and sting, making her flail and scream. Kehuan, who was a few steps behind, jumped to her, grabbed her hand, and pulled her away from the nest, and they ran. The wasps didn't follow them for long, but Niki was wailing in pain, and Kehuan's heart was pounding like crazy because he could already see the multiple red marks on her legs and arms, and one on her collarbone, and the beginning of swelling.

They ran to the apartment, and he took out all the ice packs he could find in the freezer and put them on the worst stings, but the swelling was getting worse every second, and Niki started to feel nauseous. Her face went as white as a sheet, and Kehuan panicked. The situation was far beyond the scope of his experience, so he grabbed the phone and called his father. The call went to the voice mail, so he hung up and thought furiously.

Alina didn't have a phone, and running with Niki such a long way was out of the question. Kehuan decided to call the emergency service, but just before he dialed the digits, he remembered that Chen Xiao was now in Warsaw. He called his Taiwanese number, heard the recorded message, and hung up again, calling himself a moron. Then he took a deep breath to calm down and called the office number this time, and finally was transferred to Chen Xiao, who immediately drove one of the company cars to their place, bringing with him a doctor and a nurse from the private health care clinic the company had a contract with. They gave Niki a shot and painkillers, and she finally got better.

Chen Xiao offered to drive her home then, and Kehuan had to do some explaining why it wasn't a good idea in the middle of the day. Instead, they went to the apartment where her mum was working.

When Alina saw Niki, she got so shocked she almost fainted, and when Chen Xiao saw Alina, he got quite shocked as well. He took her for some schoolgirl at first, just as Kehuan earlier. But Chen Xiao was an adult, and he saw other things Kehuan didn't pay attention to. He noticed how pale and worn-out Alina looked, and how despondent she was, and after driving her and Niki home, he also took a good look at their place. And because he was a kind man, he started meditating about the present life and future prospects of both girls, struggling to survive in this world where the only help they'd received so far were some hand-me-down clothes and babysitting service offered by an eight-year-old boy.

He visited them again, and later met with Alina alone several times, and they talked. It wasn't easy because she didn't speak English well, and they had to resort a lot to that translating device he'd borrowed from Kehuan.

In the beginning, she wasn't very eager to talk to him, either. But she'd carried her burdens completely alone for a long time, and Chen Xiao had that special something that made people feel at ease, and trust him, and after a few meetings, he finally heard Alina and Niki's full story.

And since he had his own difficulties as well, and also some unfulfilled dreams, at some point it all started to fall into a new pattern in his head.

* * *

At the end of August, when the holidays were almost over, Kehuan woke up at night at the sound of quiet voices in the apartment. He got up and walked to the bathroom, and on his way back he glimpsed his father and Chen Xiao sitting at the kitchen table, engrossed in a serious conversation.

Kehuan didn't want to eavesdrop, and he was just going to turn around and go back to his room when he heard Niki's name, and then Alina's. He immediately paused and stood quietly on the other side of the wall next to the kitchen door, listening keenly.

"...and the girl isn't even a Polish citizen," Chen Xiao was saying.

"Wait, she's not Polish?!" Chen Liang sounded just as astonished as Kehuan felt.

"Well, it's a little complicated. Her family at home was apparently Polish minority—she's even got some documents for that. She says she feels Polish, too, and wants to stay here, but she still has the Ukrainian passport."

"How long has she been in Poland?"

"About ten years now, she said. She came to Warsaw with her older sister, and went to school, but dropped out later when she got pregnant."

"Where's the sister now?"

"Alina doesn't know. She left a couple of years ago."

"And Niki's father?"

There was a short pause, and Chen Xiao must've made a gesture or a face, because Chen Liang simply said, "I see."

"She said she wanted Niki to have Polish papers, so she hasn't registered her anywhere. She hoped she'd be able to get the citizenship at some point, and then Niki would get it automatically as well. I think it was the sister's idea, actually."

"Not a wise move. But Alina should be able to apply for citizenship at this point," said Chen Liang. "Especially with those documents about her ancestry. She's been living here for years, speaks Polish fluently, she works, has a place..."

"Yes, but all the jobs are undeclared. She has no contracts or insurance, nothing. The same thing with the room they live in. No papers."

"That complicates things."

"And the worst problem is with Niki. This child is like a ghost, she doesn't legally exist. She hasn't even had any vaccinations, since she's not in the public health care system..."

"So what, she's never been ill?"

"I asked the same question. Alina said she took her for private visits a few times, but she has no money to do it often. And she's scared to death someone will get interested, and they'll come and take Niki away from her."

"I'm surprised it hasn't happened yet."

"I chatted yesterday with our HR lady, asked some general questions. She said Polish social services aren't very proactive. They don't have enough people and resources. They'll intervene when they get a tip, or when something happens that'll draw their attention. I guess Niki's flown under their radar so far."

"Alina's lucky Kehuan didn't summon an ambulance on that day," Chen Liang observed. "It would be a mess."

Kehuan felt a little lost at this point. He thought he needed to do some research on the Internet again.

"So, I've been thinking," said Chen Xiao after a moment in a different tone. "I offered to register Niki under my name."

The silence that fell after that was profound. Kehuan was stunned as well.

"Why?!"

"They could really use some help, those two. And I've thought about it a lot already, for quite a long time. About adopting a child."

"You could marry and have your own children in the future."

"That's not going to happen."

"You are still young, you know..."

"It's not a matter of age," said Chen Xiao firmly, "I just won't."

There was another lengthy silence, and then Chen Liang said again, very softly, "Oh. I see."

Kehuan had no idea what fascinating discovery his father had just made to sound so staggered, but it didn't matter at the moment. He wanted to hear what was going to happen to Niki.

"But she needs to come into existence first for you to be able to register her," noticed Chen Liang after a moment, businesslike again.

"Yes. She needs to appear in the legal system somehow, with as little noise as possible."

"I'm afraid it can't be done without putting Alina in a tight spot," Chen Liang pointed out.

"No," Chen Xiao agreed. "At least not completely over the table."

"Damn," said Chen Liang quietly, and Kehuan couldn't decide if his father sounded outraged, scared, or awed. They both fell silent again.

Kehuan was fuming with impatience. All those pauses in the conversation were really maddening.

"So, I thought it would be best to register her at the embassy. Is it possible?"

"Yes, but they'll ask some questions, since the child is, what, five years old?"

"Almost. She'll be five in October. I hoped you might help with the questions a little."

"I guess..." Chen Liang meditated for a moment. "But then Niki will have Taiwanese papers. Is Alina all right with that?"

"As long as she can stay here with her. I promised I'd help with the citizenship. Then she'll be able to get Niki Polish documents, too."

"Help how?"

"I have to go to Taipei soon, but I can keep the apartment. I'll be coming more often now, anyway. I'm going to ask the landlord to employ Alina as my, say, housekeeper, and to sign a legal contract with her. Then she'll have a decent place to stay and a job at once, and papers to prove it."

"Two birds with one stone. Clever."

Kehuan agreed. But then, Chen Xiao had always been a clever guy.

"I understand you aren't going to marry her..."

"I'd rather adopt her as well if it was possible. She's still a kid."

"But I'm wondering," Chen Liang spoke again after a short pause. "How did she even give birth to that child, without filling any papers?"

"Better not ask."

"Right."

There was another pause, and then Kehuan's father suddenly chuckled.

"You know, it's kind of ironic."

"What?"

"Rich European people import and adopt Asian orphans all the time, legal and illegal ways. But I've never heard about it going the other way round. We could hit Guinness book with this stunt."

This time they both chuckled, and Kehuan decided to retreat.

He lay down in his bed, pulled the blanket up to his chin, and thought with an immense sense of relief that he could finally stop worrying now and that Chen Xiao was a great guy. And then he smiled and fell asleep.

3

Chen, Veronica

Since Chen Xiao was a man of action, he put the plan into practice without any delay.

First, he magically conjured up some medical paper stating Niki's birth and then used it to obtain a backdated birth certificate. Chen Liang preferred not to inquire by what means and at what cost both documents had been procured, but he helped Chen Xiao and Alina concoct a credible story of their earlier acquaintance and lost contact, after checking first the age of consent in Poland, so they wouldn't accidentally land the guy in hot water. Chen Xiao used to come to Poland for business from time to time before creating the subsidiary company, and they managed to match the dates more or less, though Niki became a prematurely born child in the process; it was that or change her birthday, and Alina didn't like the second option. Chen Liang declared himself Chen Xiao's distant cousin and confirmed their version of events at the embassy. It passed because there were no obvious obstacles or reasons to investigate, and also because Chen Liang, as a former member of the diplomatic corps, was deemed trustworthy. He felt bad about all these lies but told himself it was a rare case of lying for a truly good cause. After that they just had to wait for the documents, and then Niki would finally be able to properly exist.

In the meantime, the girls moved to Chen Xiao's new apartment. After thinking it over once again, he decided the one he'd used in summer would be too cramped with the three of them in it, and switched to a bigger one, with three bedrooms and a nice living room, located in a walking distance from Chen Liang's place—that is, walking distance as Chen Xiao understood the term, which meant five minutes on foot.

Alina was a little intimidated by the grandiose of the place, as she was more used to cleaning such spaces than living in them, but Niki had no qualms. Invited to choose her own room, she immediately went for the one with the biggest window. She didn't have a view on the Vistula River, like Kehuan, but on a small garden square on the opposite side of the street, but she declared it was almost as good.

Alina was like a new person now—she smiled much more. After consulting it first with Chen Xiao, whom she started to treat as an older brother of sorts, she gave up most of her cleaning jobs. She still kept the most profitable two, though, because she didn't want to sponge off him too much, as she said. He was already providing them with a home and paying for all Niki-related expenses. They didn't have to sign the housekeeping contract after all. Cheng Liang had a short conversation with Alina's long-time employers, and her jobs became legal in a trice. He also convinced her to enroll in evening classes at an adult high school. She wasn't very enthusiastic about it but could see the merit of getting a high school diploma.

One day at the beginning of October, a few days before Niki's fifth birthday, they all gathered in the new apartment to see the newly issued documents.

"Name write different in Polish", noticed Alina sulkily, inspecting the passport and pointing to the line where it said 'Chen, Veronica'. Her English was still rather lame.

"So her name isn't Niki?!" Kehuan exclaimed at the same time. It was hard to say which of them sounded more offended.

Niki, who had been hopping around the apartment on one leg, threw Kehuan a sheepish look.

"I think it doesn't matter so much," said Chen Liang in a conciliatory tone, answering Alina, "It sounds the same. And the English spelling may be actually a better idea since the surname isn't Polish either."

Alina looked as if she wasn't entirely convinced, but nodded with resignation.

"But look, now she can go to kindergarten," Kehuan consoled her with a smirk, and she snorted at that, tousling his hair.

Chen Xiao had to leave soon after that. He was planning to return to Warsaw in a few months, both for business and to spend time with Niki and Alina again. Still, constant traveling between Warsaw and Taipei didn't seem a reasonable option in the long haul. He was thinking about finding someone to take over the management of the Taipei company from him, especially because it was now smaller than the European subsidiary, but it was going to take some time. Before leaving, he asked Chen Liang to keep an eye on Alina, which his friend promised to do, and reminded Kehuan to look after Niki, which earned him a particularly contemptuous glare.

Soon after that, Niki indeed went to kindergarten, but not for long. She turned out to be a very problematic candidate for organized childcare because she was accustomed to complete freedom. Whenever she felt bored, or an interesting new idea popped up in her head, she'd leave the group during a stroll in the park, or walk away from the playground, or sneak out of the kindergarten building, and no amount of talk could convince her that all the restrictions were there for her own benefit and safety. Kehuan, who came round to the girls' place almost every day after school, got a lot of entertainment out of listening to Alina trying in turns to persuade, coerce or cajole Niki into stopping treating kindergarten like a pit stop. Alina could hear the trumpets of doom when she got summoned to the headteacher's office several times for a serious talk, but she was helpless. Finally, about three months after her kindergarten debut, Niki was declared unfit and got kicked out from the noble institution, just like Kehuan earlier. It didn't trouble her at all, but Alina was another story.

"I don't know what's so funny," she said testily when Kehuan heard the news and kept guffawing about it every five minutes. "What am I to do with her now?"

Kehuan knew she'd promised Chen Xiao to take proper care of Niki, so he said mercilessly, if not very grammatically, "You look after her your own, what other?"

"But I have work, and school!" whined Alina. "And you have no idea how hard it is to keep tabs on her."

Kehuan grinned with vengeful satisfaction. "You don't say..."

"Now I'll have to run after her all day long," she went on grumpily, not picking up on the irony, "and she has such crazy ideas like you wouldn't believe..."

At that, he laughed so hard he had to sit down.

Alina meditated for a moment, chewing at her upper lip.

"You'll need to help," she ordered in the end. "Or she'll be wandering around on her own again. You wouldn't like that, would you?"

Alina, just like Chen Liang, never seemed to remember Kehuan's true age, and tended to treat him as if it was closer to her own than her daughter's. In her defense, Kehuan was tall and looked older than he really was, and he very rarely behaved like a child. He didn't like being treated like one, either, and never tried to rectify the situation. And so they split the supervising duty between the two of them, though Niki still had to spend some hours on her own on the days when Alina went to work. Kehuan talked to her very seriously, and she finally agreed, without much enthusiasm, to stay in the apartment and not to go out without him. He used the ultimate weapon and told her Chen Xiao would be really upset if she did, and that worked at last; Niki adored Chen Xiao and didn't want to get in his bad books.

Around that time Kehuan finally made his peace with the Polish language. He was now improving by leaps and bounds, and it was mainly thanks to Alina. When the thick layer of weariness and dejection finally cracked and fall off, underneath she turned out to be a very chatty and sociable girl. She was thrilled to have a surrogate family, and if Chen Xiao had become the mostly absent big brother she didn't want to disappoint, and Chen Liang got the role of a wise and distinguished uncle, Kehuan was the ever-present annoying younger sibling she could complain to, banter with, and press into doing her chores. And since they saw each other all the time, Kehuan understood and spoke more Polish every day without having to resort to his translating device, which he hated from the bottom of his heart by this point.

It was interesting, however, that his conversations with Niki tended to veer more and more into Mandarin. It certainly wasn't because Kehuan tried to impose his mother tongue on her; it was actually the other way round. Perhaps because she was so young, or because she had a truly excellent ear for music, or maybe it was just a talent on itself, but Niki imbibed the language like a sponge. After a year of playing with Kehuan, watching films, and listening to stories, she could speak it quite well. But more importantly, Niki loved speaking Mandarin, because in her head it was the secret language of her family.

"Why do you keep speaking Mandarin with her?" asked Chen Liang one Saturday, after listening to Kehuan and Niki's animated discussion about how Pippi would fair if she met the Monkey King. "It doesn't make much sense. You should teach her English instead."

Kehuan shrugged. "She likes Mandarin, so we do it her way," he answered.

"Yes," Niki piped up, smiling brightly. "And I like the pictures for words, too. It's fun."

Chen Xiao had sent her for Christmas a set of brushes for traditional Chinese calligraphy, together with a booklet with some basic characters and writing instructions. Chen Liang had to show her how to hold the brush and make different strokes because Kehuan was hopeless at it, and now she practiced writing with great zeal, the more complicated the character, the better. Niki was a great fan of visual expression, and she thought representing each word with a beautiful little picture was a wonderful idea. Learning the Latin alphabet necessary for reading and writing in Polish wasn't in her opinion even half as entertaining.

Chen Liang shook his head in faint exasperation. Niki was a permanent riddle to him, even more than his own son.

"If she's going to attend your school, English would be much more useful," he said, speaking to the boy again because Niki had left the kitchen to bring some new stories from Kehuan's room.

"Maybe she could have lessons with Tomek," Kehuan suggested. He basically agreed with his father, but in his book, Niki's wishes held at least as much importance as any practical arguments.

"Good idea. I'll talk to Alina."

But Alina turned out unexpectedly resistant to the idea of Niki learning English and attending the international school. Chen Liang couldn't understand her doubts at the beginning.

"It's a very good school," he explained patiently. "She'll have first-rate teachers and multi-cultural environment, and they have many excellent after-school classes, too. Music, for example. There's this really dedicated music teacher. Doesn't she love singing?"

"She can sing every place," Alina answered mulishly. "Why she go to school where lesson in different language? She's Polish."

And that was the clue. Chen Liang finally realized she was apprehensive about too much foreign influence in her daughter's life. Alina's long-standing plan was to stay in Poland with Niki, and while she was deeply grateful to Chen Xiao for all his help, she was also a little anxious, perhaps without even realizing it, that one day he'd want to take her child away.

Chen Xiao came for a few weeks in February, and also tried to persuade Alina, but seeing her stress, he promptly dropped the subject. He agreed with Chen Liang about the advantages of the international school, and he was willing to send Niki there, even if it was expensive, but he didn't think it was worth fighting with Alina over it. He just wanted both girls to be happy.

But Niki got enrolled in the school after all. It was Kehuan who convinced Alina, and he needed only one sentence.

"Why not want Niki go to my school?" he asked her one day when the three of them were sitting together on the carpet around the low coffee table in the living room. Alina was watching some ski jumping competition on Chen Xiao's traditionally gigantic flat screen, Kehuan was doing his homework, and Niki was sitting next to him, practicing Chinese calligraphy again.

"What's so great about that school that everybody keeps yapping about it all the time?" Alina asked peevishly.

"I am there," replied Kehuan, right on target, "and I can look after Niki if she's there, too."

And just like that, it was done.

So Tomek got hired once again as the Chen family's English tutor, and he fell in love with Niki at their first meeting. They had so much fun together during these so-called lessons that Alina and Kehuan, banned to the living room, rolled their eyes in shared irritation as they listened in affronted silence to the peals of laughter coming from Niki's room. Alina was miffed because Tomek never said more than three words to her beyond the polite greetings, and Kehuan because he'd discovered he didn't like it when Niki had too much fun with other people without him.

Sadly, Kehuan's own social life at school was in the same state of virtual non-existence as always, though not for the lack of opportunities. His old classmates gave up on him long ago, but the school had quite a lively rotation of foreign students. This year there were again new kids in his class, and in September some of them had made friendly overtures in his direction.

First had been the curly-haired girl.

"Hi, my name's Amy," she'd said to Kehuan in the first week of school, sitting at the desk next to his right before the start of the math lesson. "I'm from Glasgow."

Kehuan gave her a short nod. The girl was still looking at him, obviously waiting for something, so he grudgingly muttered, "Hello."

The math lesson began. While the class was struggling with the order of operations, Kehuan solved much more advanced problems assigned to him individually by the teacher, and the girl kept glancing in great awe at him and his notes.

"You are so good at math," she said earnestly after the lesson, "I wish I was better."

"You would be if you looked more into your own notebook," replied Kehuan reasonably, and she didn't try to speak to him again.

Two weeks later a similar situation occurred with the slim black boy. Kehuan had no idea where he was from, but he thought the boy was called

Dale. Or maybe Dave. Something like that.

"Don't you like art?" the boy asked him in the middle of the art lesson. Their easels stood close to each other, and Dale, or Dave, was looking with a frown at Kehuan's almost empty sheet of paper.

"I like art."

"But you haven't painted anything yet."

"I don't like to paint."

"Do you prefer to draw?"

"No."

"What about sculpting? Mr. Burnes said we're going to sculpt next time."

"No."

"But you said you liked art..."

"I like to look at art," said Kehuan. Really, this guy was slow.

"Oh. You mean you aren't good at it?" guessed the boy, and smiled with pride. "I'm quite good, I think."

Kehuan looked at the boy's work sitting on the easel next to his own and examined it for a moment, tilting his head to one side.

"I know someone who's much better," he said truthfully, and another one bit the dust.

* * *

One Friday evening in the middle of March, Kehuan was putting away his gear after coming back from the taekwondo training when Chen Liang knocked at the open door of his room. Kehuan eyed him warily, as his father hardly ever intruded on his privacy.

"I've got news," Chen Liang said gravely, leaning against the doorframe. "I got a call from that cousin of your mother, Seong Joonho."

Kehuan had to dig in his head a little, but then he remembered. He'd received greeting cards from someone of this name for his last two birthdays.

"That guy in Korea?" he asked, just to make sure.

"That guy from Korea," corrected Chen Liang, sounding like a martyr.

"He's here."

"He is? Why?"

"He's an automotive engineer or designer, I don't remember, some hotshot specialist in automotive anyway, and he's just got transferred to this new factory they opened near Warsaw."

Kehuan just waited. He knew it wasn't the end.

Chen Liang sighed and continued, "He's got a contract for the next two years, so he also brought his family. They want to meet."

Kehuan groaned.

Chen Liang looked at his son and stood upright, clearing his throat. He told himself he wasn't behaving in a very pedagogical way and tried for a more optimistic tone. "It's only natural they want to get to know their relative. I think it's nice of them."

"You think nothing of the sort," answered Kehuan morosely. "I can see it. All right, I'll go. But only once, right?"

"God, I hope so," said Chen Liang with a feeling, giving up the pedagogical approach.

Two days later, in one of the private dining rooms of a posh Korean restaurant in Old Town, Chen Liang threw a quick surreptitious glance at his son. Kehuan was contemplating the other side of the table with raised eyebrows and a sardonic twist to his mouth. Chen Liang stifled an inappropriate urge to laugh and reflected with remorse that he really wasn't giving his boy a very good example, but Lee Soojin's relatives had always tended to set his teeth on edge.

"Mr. Chen Liang, we've talked a few times on the phone, but I am pleased we can finally meet in person", said a handsome, roundish man in his forties, and gave him an amiable smile and a bow. He was speaking in Korean. "I am Seong Joonho. Let me introduce the family: my wife, Kim Haneul, and her sister, Kim Hana. This is our oldest son Seong Taejin, and these are our twins, Taerim and Taeyeon, and our niece, Yoon Sori."

All the Koreans on the other side of the table, including two identical little boys, smiled politely and bowed when the head of the family mentioned their name. Chen Liang watched it with suppressed amusement, thinking wryly that the meeting was evidently unbalanced. Their side of the table was severely underrepresented.

"It's a pleasure," he said to the whole row of people, "I'm Chen Liang, and this is my son, Chen Kehuan." His son nodded once and curved his lips for a moment, which was probably meant to suggest he was cram full of warm feelings.

They all sat down, and after a moment of awkward silence Chen Liang's professional habits kicked in, obligating him to make some small talk. He switched to English and started asking neutral questions about their journey and first impressions of Warsaw. The exchange was rather stilted, and he noticed that Seong Joonho's wife wasn't taking part in it, though her sister said something from time to time.

The food finally arrived, thank goodness. It was going to be a long dinner.

Kim Haneul said something to her husband, and he nodded. Then he addressed Chen Liang again, "We had some doubts about leaving Korea because of the children. We were concerned about their education here."

Chen Liang felt his son stiffen next to him, and he also wasn't much impressed. Really. Poland wasn't a barbarian country. Well… Maybe a little, in certain aspects. But education wasn't one of them.

"Can you make some recommendations about schools?" asked Seong Joonho hopefully.

"Certainly," Chen Liang replied drily. "We can't allow your offspring to suffer from ignorance, after all." Next to him Kehuan almost choked on his *kimchi*, and the younger woman on the other side of the table hid an amused smile.

"What about Chen Kehuan's school? Are you satisfied with it?"

Chen Liang didn't have to look at his son to feel his instant reluctance, but there was no way around the question, so he gave them the name of the school and added a few sentences of description.

"It sounds good," said Seong Joonho. "I think maybe we'll visit it on Monday and have a look."

Chen Liang thought it was going to be a costly option with so many kids, but it wouldn't be a polite thing to say.

But Seong Joonho seemed to have read his mind somehow, or maybe his own thoughts simply ran along the same line, because he remarked, "I guess it won't be cheap, but my company promised to participate in the costs of schooling."

Chen Liang once again counted all the children on the other side of the table and felt a certain amount of respect toward his wife's cousin. The guy had to be brilliant at his job.

* * *

After dinner, Kehuan went out of the restaurant for a moment. The March day wasn't very warm, but he needed a break from the strained conversation and all the stagy smiles. He wanted to go home and read a book in peace, or better yet, to drop by Niki's place and watch her draw. Or to cook something with her and listen to a new crazy kitchen chant. He sincerely hoped all these little snots wouldn't land in his school. Seriously, it'd drive him crazy if he had to deal with them every day. He felt a sudden sense of kinship with all the Polish people walking around; they certainly weren't a lot prone to smiling without a solid reason.

"There you are," said someone behind him. He turned around and saw the oldest of the Soeng boys. He looked about Kehuan's age.

The boy sat next to him on the bench.

"I'm Seong Taejin," he said. He was speaking in Korean, and Kehuan had to consciously analyze his words in his head. Using the language was like trying to navigate through a dense fog a landscape he might've seen once or twice, but could hardly remember.

"I know," he replied. He wasn't deaf, after all.

"I thought maybe you haven't caught all our names," said Taejin, grinning. Geez.

"I know you all Tae-something," answered Kehuan, groping for the words and struggling to put them in the correct order in the sentence. The similar names business seemed ridiculous to him: were their parents really that uncreative?

"Me and my brothers, yes," Taejin clarified, and added with pride in his voice, "It's a tradition in Korea." Then he noticed Kehuan's little smirk, and asked in a sharper tone, "Something's funny?"

"Your names," answered Kehuan. "And the tradition."

He studied the look of stunned affront on the other boy's face and felt better.

"We're family," Taejin started again. His smile looked more careful now, and he didn't sound so overly friendly anymore.

"I know," Kehuan repeated with exasperation.

"But I don't think we look much alike."

They examined each other. It was true: apart from more or less the same height, there were no similarities. Kehuan was paler, with long black eyes and a hint of wave to his hair. Taejin's skin had a golden tone, his eyes were the color of dark amber, and his hair was straight and glossy. The easy-going smile looked as indigenous to his friendly face as the scowl to his cousin's.

The mutual perusal gave Kehuan time to form his answer.

"We not are close family," he said.

"How old are you?" asked Seong Taejin after a short pause, sounding official now.

"Nine." Kehuan's birthday had been a month earlier.

"I'm eleven," announced the other boy, and his smug tone suggested some further ramifications of the fact, but Kehuan had no idea what he meant.

"So?" he asked without much interest.

"I'm older. You should speak up to me," Taejin told him, and it sounded as if there was 'duh' somewhere in this sentence.

Kehuan remembered there was a thing about different ways you were supposed to talk to people in Korean.

"I've got a better idea. Let's speak English," he suggested in English, "and problem solved."

It was evident Seong Taejin wasn't happy with the proposal, and a moment later the reason became clear: it was his turn to struggle with words now.

"School is all right? Your school?" he asked finally.

"It is, but you'll have problems there if you don't improve your English, and fast," Kehuan told him with a smirk.

After that, the other boy had nothing else to say, and they returned to the restaurant. Ten minutes later Chen Liang and Kehuan said goodbye and left.

"Are they really going to come to my school?" asked Kehuan on their way home.

"I don't know. It seems their children aren't very advanced in English, so maybe not. But I gave them Tomek's number, you know."

"You didn't!"

"Sorry."

* * *

Three days later, Kehuan cursed under his breath at the sight of Seong Taejin entering the classroom after their form teacher. He half expected the guy to announce to the whole class that he had a relative here, right there in the third row next to the window, but mercifully it didn't happen. His cousin simply introduced himself, said he was from Busan, South Korea, and bowed a little. A few children snickered, but most were smiling, probably because the newcomer's handsome face once again wore this wide, friendly grin.

Kehuan wasn't sure if Taejin had noticed him when he'd first entered the classroom, but even if not, he must have later, during the recess. But his cousin didn't try to approach him, talking instead to other boys and girls in the class. His English was atrocious, but the easy-going attitude seemed to gain him friends in no time. At lunch he was already sitting with a large group of other kids, laughing at some silly jokes.

Kehuan noticed them the moment he entered the canteen. He collected his food, sat at an unoccupied table, took out a book, and while eating, he focused on analyzing Euclid's algorithm for calculating the greatest common divisor of two numbers. Five minutes later he didn't even remember Taejin existed.

It looked as if both of them made up their minds to completely ignore each other, but in fact, Seong Taejin was very interested in his elusive and arrogant distant cousin. First of all, Kehuan was family, and the importance of that fact was so deeply ingrained in Taejin's way of thinking it was reason enough to try to befriend even the most repelling and ill-mannered individual. But he didn't really think Kehuan was that horrible. Actually, after the first wave of indignation and annoyance had passed, he felt amused and a little impressed by his cousin's bluntness. He also noticed quickly that Kehuan, even if aloof and distant from what was happening around, was still one of the best students in the class.

But Taejin had his pride as well, and besides, he had been admitted to the school on the condition that he'd quickly improve his language skills. He was struggling every day on every lesson, and all his energy went into catching up with this new reality where he'd been suddenly converted from Seong Taejin the top student to Taejin Seong the dimwit. He hated the feeling of lagging behind and had every intention of climbing to the top again, as soon as possible.

* * *

A few weeks later on Saturday morning Kehuan came to the girls' place, and was told by stressed-out Alina to go and find Niki, and to get out of her hair; she had some tests next week, and final exams at the adult school getting closer, and she needed to study. Kehuan felt a little irritated she once again had no idea where her daughter was but decided to let it go under the circumstances, and just went out to look for the wandering cat.

He knew all Niki's favorite places now, and after about half an hour he found her on a small playground near his school, close to that house with the high garden walls where Alina still worked on Thursdays.

Niki was riding on a swing, counting loudly, and on her both sides two other children swung along, looking at her with anticipation. Kehuan could see all three of them were working hard to sway their swings as high as possible, and he wasn't surprised in the slightest when a moment later, at the highest point, Niki cried, "Ten!", and flew through the air with flailing arm and legs, and then landed in the sandpit some four meters away. The other kids followed after her with loud battle cries.

"Rima! Yeona! Quit it!" someone yelled behind him.

Kehuan turned and saw Soeng Taejin observing the scene in front of them with an exasperated expression on his face, hands on hips. Surprised, Kehuan took a better look at the boys shaking the sand off their clothes next to Niki, and sure enough, they were the identical twins from the Korean restaurant.

"They'll knock their teeth out if they aren't careful," he told their big brother in English.

He wasn't much concerned about Niki because he'd seen her perform that stunt many times before and knew she always landed on her feet, like a real cat, but he felt somewhat obliged to issue the warning since she seemed to be the initiator of the game. Still, he didn't feel charitable enough to struggle with Korean.

He half-expected Taejin to react with alarm or anger, but the other boy simply nodded, and answered in his own language without much agitation, "Oh well. They're still mostly baby teeth, anyway."

So. Not so stuck-up, after all. Kehuan relaxed.

Niki had a new idea now, and she was explaining it to the twins, gesturing with both hands toward the seesaws on the other side of the sandpit.

"They don't understand Polish," Kehuan called to her and walked up closer.

Niki beamed and waved at him. She turned back to the boys and started explaining her idea once again, this time in Mandarin. The twins, slim, pretty, and taller than her by some ten centimeters, stared at her without blinking.

Kehuan grinned, amused. "Niki, you dork," he said. "They aren't Chinese. They're Korean."

Niki gaped at him incredulously, and then turned back again and surveyed the boys in silence. She looked as if she couldn't believe her bad luck.

He chuckled, and heard Seong Taejin say next to him, "I knew you could do it."

"Do what?" Kehuan asked warily.

"Smile," replied Taejin, and snickered when his cousin immediately lost the grin and returned to his usual scowl.

Niki in the meantime managed to get over her disappointment. She had certain experience with such situations, after all, and there was an established course of action: she pointed to herself in the well-practiced gesture, took a breath… and suddenly stopped. She turned around, looked at Kehuan, and after a moment of careful consideration turned back to the twins and said, "Hi. I'm Chen Veronica."

Kehuan snorted again.

"Is that your sister?" asked Taejin, eyeing Niki's obviously Caucasian features.

"Nah, that's just Niki," answered Kehuan. Then he said to the cat, "Hey, let's do it."

They ran together to the seesaw, and Niki climbed to the top of it on one side while Kehuan stood on the other end of the beam, propped on the ground. Then they started walking along the beam towards each other, and after they swapped sides in the middle, the seesaw started to tip to Kehuan's side again. After a moment it gathered momentum and hit the ground with a loud bang. Both of them managed to stay on top of it, and Niki giggled happily.

All three Korean boys came closer to watch their maneuvers. Taejin looked simply amused, but the twins were completely mesmerized.

A moment later they climbed the other seesaw, trying to copy the exercise. They were very evenly matched, though, and it wasn't so much fun this way, so they called Taejin to replace one of them, and after a moment even their big brother was having fun with the game. They all switched partners several times after establishing a rule that who fell off the swing was the loser, and had to give up his spot to another person.

After that day Taejin started to talk to Kehuan at school between lessons and to sit with him in the canteen. Kehuan still wasn't very friendly, but he usually strove to answer him in Korean now, and Taejin treated it as a sign of his cousin coming around. In fact, Kehuan made the effort to speak Korean just because he associated the language with his mother, and felt certain pleasure using it. But after a few conversations he had to admit Taejin wasn't so bad, and talking to him was even fun sometimes.

They also started meeting quite often outside the school, willing or not, because the twins were completely smitten with Niki and wanted to play with her all the time, to Kehuan's great displeasure. In his opinion, he had dibs on chasing her around, and on having fun with her as well.

But then one day something happened, which made him finally accept the notion that having a few friends or relatives around could be of some use.

* * *

It was May already, but the weather suddenly turned cold and unpleasant again, which apparently was some kind of a regular seasonal occurrence. Kehuan was crossing the small garden square near the girls' place on his way back from the training when he noticed in some distance ahead Niki and the twins standing on the path.

Something was off. He couldn't tell what was happening because the path bent a little, and the shrubs on its side obscured part of his view, but Niki's posture looked distinctly hostile, and Taeyeon and Taerim stood very still behind her, alertly watching something in front of them that Kehuan still couldn't see. He hastened his steps, and then he heard them.

The nazi boys, again. Kehuan didn't have so many encounters with them this year. After that memorable meeting last summer, they almost stopped pestering him. Niki had told him it was because of that young woman back then: she'd warned the boys she'd tell their parents if they kept bullying other kids. But now three of them were here again—though without the blond ringleader—and this time they had something to say to Niki. Kehuan didn't need any translating device anymore to understand they were disgusted with her because she played with "yellows" all the time, or to catch the ugly names they called her. Niki, despite her upright stance and clenched fists, seemed close to tears.

Kehuan leaped forward, and he was just a few steps away from the whole group when Taerim and Taeyeon glanced at each other and finally decided it wasn't a normal conversation, and both took a large step forward, standing next to Niki with sinister expressions on their pretty faces. They were much smaller than the three boys in front of them, but then from the opposite end of the path their older brother came running, and he and Kehuan stepped behind Niki and the twins at the same time.

The nazi boys gaped at all of them for a moment, and then turned around and beat a hasty retreat.

"Those little shits," Taejin spat furiously. "It's a pity they ran away. I'd love to talk with them a little."

"In what language?" asked Kehuan, watching Niki as she breathed deeply and unclenched her fists. He was still angry, too, but also astonished to discover that Seong Taejin, under his easy-going attitude and ever-present grin, had quite a temper and that he'd managed to diagnose the situation accurately without understanding a word.

"I need no language. I do taekwondo, you know."

"So do I."

"Seriously?" Taejin sounded at once surprised and slightly offended. "But you aren't Korean. It's a Korean sport."

"So what?" Kehuan had recently started to get kicks out of riling his cousin up. "You play soccer. You aren't British, are you?"

Taejin laughed.

"And besides, my mum was Korean."

They all walked Niki to the apartment and ended up watching cartoons together. Later, she wanted to show them her room, and Taejin was very impressed with all the pieces of Chinese calligraphy hanging around on the walls. He wrote the *hanja* for his name with a ball pen, and Niki took out her brushes and calligraphed the characters in black ink on a sheet of thick off-white paper. It looked really cool, and Taejin took the card home, to put it on his bedroom door.

After that day even Kehuan couldn't deny they'd all become friends. Or something like that.

Unfortunately, Taejin had caught a nasty cold during that spell of bad weather, and he didn't come to school for a week. By then he and Kehuan had already exchanged phone numbers, so he texted his cousin on Friday morning with a request to borrow his notebooks. He asked Kehuan to give them to Yoon Sori.

Kehuan had never talked to Taejin's other cousin before, though he glimpsed her from time to time around at school. She was a very girly girl, always dressed in some frilly skirts, pink blouses, and with bows in her hair. Ugh. But since Taejin asked, Kehuan went to find her, and to inform Sori he didn't have all the notebooks on him.

"I can go with you after lessons and take them," she offered, not looking at his face. Kehuan thought she had to be shy, but her English was much better than Taejin's.

He considered. The notebooks were actually at Niki's, but he planned to go there after school and take her out to play, so it wasn't a problem.

"All right," he answered. "I need to feed the cat anyway."

* * *

Contrary to Kehuan's impression, Yoon Sori wasn't shy at all, but this cousin of her cousin always intimidated her. She privately thought he was a very pretty boy, but every time she saw him, he wore a particularly disdainful or impatient expression on his face.

As they were walking to his place, she felt nervous and tongue-twisted all the way, which was completely unlike her, as Sori was normally a very quick-witted girl. But her companion didn't say a word to her, and he seemed to be thinking about something else.

They finally stopped in front of an old, elegant tenement house, and entered it directly from the street. Sori followed Kehuan up the wide stairs to the big double door on the second floor, which he opened with a key.

While she was looking around the long hall with several tall white doors on both sides, Kehuan put away his backpack and called out, “Niki!”

Sori waited for the cat, but there was none; instead, a moment later a little barefoot girl appeared in the door at the far end of the hall, holding a long painting brush in one hand. She wore her dark hair in a ponytail and was dressed in a loose white T-shirt with a picture of a dragon.

They started talking in Chinese, and Kehuan ushered her into the kitchen on the left side of the hall, leaving Sori alone. A few minutes later they were back, Kehuan with a few notebooks in his hand and the girl in a blue hoodie now, and with a sandwich instead of the brush.

While Kehuan was locking the door behind all of them, the little girl turned to Sori, looked up at her curiously with large, bright eyes, and said in English, “Hello, I’m Chen Veronica”.

Kehuan laughed under his nose, and Sori was momentarily distracted by how different his face looked with the amused, indulgent look on it.

“Hello, Veronica,” she answered politely and smiled at the little girl; it was hard not to. “I’m Yoon Sori.”

“We’ll walk with you, after all,” Kehuan told her, impassive again. “Niki wants to visit the twins.”

The Seong family, together with Yoon Sori and her mum, consisted of seven people, so they’d rented an entire house for the time of their stay in Warsaw. It was located quite close to the school, and Sori thought on the way it hadn’t been necessary for her to walk all the distance there and back to get the notebooks, after all. But she didn’t complain.

They went inside, greeted enthusiastically by the twins. A moment later Taejin, still coughing, walked down the stairs and joined them in the living room. And while Kehuan was explaining to him the material from the last days at school, switching from Korean to English and back, Veronica, Taeyeon, and Taerim quickly established a makeshift obstacle course around the living room and started chasing one another in a circle. Each round included skipping over the cushions they’d put on the floor, crawling under the coffee table, jumping between four chairs standing in a row, and bouncing on the big green sofa. Veronica loudly chanted some rhythmic incantation, and Sori's younger cousins cackled like two crazy hyenas. Sori observed this deranged performance with horrified fascination, glad that her aunt wasn't there to witness the desecration of her usually pristine living room. What baffled her additionally was the complete lack of any reaction from Kehuan and Taejin, which made her wonder if this was perhaps some kind of a norm for those three when put together.

"They are like these terrible triplets from Tom and Jerry," she finally noticed to herself.

Kehuan and Taejin raised their heads from over the notebook, turned to look at Niki and the twins, and snorted in unison.

"You're right," Taejin admitted. "I never noticed it before."

Kehuan just grinned, still watching the naughty trio, and Sori felt proud of herself. It was worth having the house transformed into a bedlam.

* * *

By the end of May Alina had finally passed all her exams and was relaxed and approachable now. She had already applied for Polish citizenship sometime earlier, and was ecstatic about it, even after learning that the procedure might take a year or more. A sad thing which happened around this time was the death of the old lady from the girls' old place. Alina, who used to visit her from time to time, went to the funeral, but she didn't want to take Niki or Kehuan with her.

She finally had time to play with her daughter again, and they went back to cooking and baking together, often singing in the kitchen on such occasions. Kehuan joined them regularly. He enjoyed making the food, not to mention eating it, but he also liked to listen to them sing because they both had lovely voices.

At the beginning of June, Chen Xiao flew in from Taipei again and visited the international school together with Alina, to enroll Niki for the first grade next year. It wasn't really necessary because she could stay at home one more year, but she wanted to go. The twins were starting school in

September as well, and besides, Kehuan was there.

Chen Xiao had come with a ready plan to take the girls for a two-week vacation at the seaside, and they were going away in a few days. Alina was over the moon. For all the years she'd lived in Poland, she'd never visited the coast or any other touristic destinations; she'd been on a few short trips with her class at school, but they'd never gone far from Warsaw. Niki was totally hyped, too, but Kehuan still had lessons at school and couldn't go with them, and he felt really sore about it.

On the departure day, Chen Xiao brought the company car, a black SUV, to the street under the apartment. A colleague at the office had suggested they should drive at night, to avoid heavy traffic and the worst heat, and it sounded like a reasonable option, all the more so because there wasn't a motorway on the route, and it was going to be a seven-hour journey mostly on local roads. In the afternoon Kehuan helped them carry down all their suitcases and bags, and pack them into the trunk, marveling and complaining aloud about their number. A little later Chen Liang came over after work, and they all ate together. It was already getting dark outside when Chen Xiao with the girls finally hit the road.

Back at home, Kehuan texted Taejin, and they played an online game for an hour until Taejin's mother entered her son's room and told him to go to bed. After that Kehuan read a book, and it was almost midnight when he finally went to sleep, so he was totally disoriented and very groggy when his father woke him up in the morning, shaking his arm and speaking in a low, quivering voice, "Wake up. Kehuan, wake up, wake up."

Kehuan opened his eyes halfway, glanced at the big window, and saw it was still very early; he could recognize it now just by the kind of light flowing into the room. His eyes started to close again.

"Listen to me, Kehuan. Something happened. Wake up and listen, something happened."

Kehuan opened his eyes again, fighting the sluggishness. He saw Chen Liang's face, pale and stricken, and the frantic note in his father's voice finally registered with him, sending an icy shiver down his spine.

He sat up. The meaning of the words now penetrated as well, and when he groped to put them in some context, all his thoughts suddenly spun and jumbled, and for a short moment, his mind went completely blank.

Then it started working again, and he asked in an alien voice, "Where's Niki?"

4

Not All Right

They were more than halfway through the journey when Chen Xiao started to feel a little tired.

He enjoyed driving, and the road was almost empty. It was already well past midnight, and they were traveling now through a sparsely inhabited area. There were mostly forests around, and the summer night was clear, with no clouds or rain. He'd found a program on the radio playing soul music, but kept it low not to wake up the girls sleeping on the backseat head-to-head, Niki in the child seat, and Alina propped against its side. Chen Xiao looked at them in the rearview mirror from time to time and smiled to himself, feeling content and at peace with his life, like he hadn't felt for a long time.

Finally, the late hour caught up with him. At first, he fought the sleepiness, but his concentration started to waver, and the GPS device said there were still three hours to go. He decided to take a break, and when he spotted a long hard shoulder ahead a few minutes later, he pulled over and stopped the car, and then opened the door to step outside.

The night was warm, the sky clear, and he could see the stars, but no moon. A dark meadow bracketed the road from both sides, surrounded by the black walls of the forest in some distance. He could hear a night bird and some crickets.

The back door clicked and Alina went out of the car, yawning.

"Where are we?" she asked.

"I don't know how to pronounce it," Chen Xiao replied, and she giggled.

He took out the road atlas and showed it to her, using his phone as a torch. "We passed this town some time ago."

"Kościerzyna," she read aloud.

"If you say so."

They heard a sound of a car behind, and as it got closer, its headlights illuminated the road and the meadow on both sides of them for a moment. The car passed, and its taillights gleamed in the dark for a while before dimming in the distance. The night was dark and quiet again, except for the crickets.

The door clicked the second time, and Niki jumped out as well.

"Hello," she said with a big smile.

"I think I need to take a short nap", announced Chen Xiao, tousling her hair. "My eyelids keep drooping."

"You can sleep in the back, we are awake now anyway," Alina offered.

"Good idea," answered Chen Xiao.

He opened the door, took out Niki's child seat, and put it on the ground next to the tire. Then he got inside and stretched out on the backseat, pulling over himself the light blanket the girls had used before. A moment later he was asleep.

Alina and Niki crossed the road and used some bushes as a cover for the toilet business, which was rather redundant since the road was completely empty. When they got back to the car, Alina opened the trunk and took out a bottle of water and a hoodie for Niki, who was a little cold despite the mild air.

"Want to stretch your legs a little?" she asked her daughter.

Niki nodded and walked off the hard shoulder onto the meadow behind it. She jumped a few times in the thick grass and started walking in circles, taking careful steps because she could hardly see in the dark and the ground was uneven.

Alina leaned against the back of the car and looked up at the night sky. What a view. She couldn't remember the last time she'd seen so many stars.

Niki was making bigger and bigger circles in the meadow, and was hardly visible now, even in her white hoodie, so Alina called, "Don't go too far!"

Her daughter raised a hand and waved at her.

Some car was coming again, and judging by the low, rumbling sound, it was something bigger. Alina looked at the road and saw the approaching headlights and the black silhouette of a truck without the semitrailer. It was slowing down now, but still going quite fast when the lights started to veer to the side. She froze, and when the breaks groaned and the tires screeched, she had just enough time to turn her head toward Niki in the meadow, and that was all.

* * *

Chen Liang was listed on both Chen Xiao and Alina's phones as an ICE contact, and the police reached him early in the morning. They'd arrived at the scene of the accident at the crack of dawn, after the SUV, lying on its side in the meadow, had been spotted by the driver of a delivery van passing by. Chen Xiao was still inside and alive, though in critical condition, and he was transported to the hospital at once. They also found Alina, but she was beyond any help.

The police didn't see anybody else, or any other vehicle, and it was Chen Liang who told them there'd been one more person they needed to look for. The child seat hadn't been found at the beginning; it was light, so it had flown quite a long distance away from the car, and the meadow was covered with the morning fog when the rescue services first got there. As soon as they learned about Niki, they started searching for her, and quickly found the seat, but not the child.

When Chen Liang woke Kehuan up, it was to tell him he had to go to the police station, and then to the hospital, which was over three hundred kilometers away, in Danzig. But he also told his son at once all the facts because the scale of the disaster didn't allow for any mitigation.

A few hours later Niki was still missing.

By then the police had examined the site and the SUV and analyzed all the clues. They said the SUV had been parked and hit by a truck, which hadn't been moving very fast at the moment of the collision. They thought the truck driver had wanted to park at the hard shoulder as well, and probably didn't notice the black SUV in the dark because Chen Xiao hadn't switched on the parking lights. Also, they were almost sure Niki hadn't been in the crash, which was good, of course. But they had no idea where she was. The accident happened in the middle of nowhere, and there were big woods around, which local officers and foresters started combing at once. There was also the possibility she'd been taken from the site by some other person, possibly the perpetrator, who also hadn't been found so far.

The police notified the Ukrainian embassy about Alina, and Chen Liang declared he'd arrange the funeral. He also contacted Chen Xiao's family in Vancouver, to inform them about the accident and the fact that their relative had already undergone surgery, after which he was still unconscious, but stable. Then he returned to Warsaw. It was late at night, and he was dead on his feet.

Kehuan was waiting for him, and for a few minutes, they sat together in the kitchen in silence. Chen Liang had been calling his son all day with updates, and there was nothing new, and nothing else to say. Finally, he told Kehuan to go to sleep and did the same.

* * *

An hour later, Kehuan was still lying in his bed with his eyes wide open, staring at the ceiling. Finally, he realized there was no point staying in bed. He got up, walked up to the big window, and stood there for a while, staring at the river, the black outlines of the trees, and the distant lights of the downtown. Then he sat down in Niki's favorite beanbag.

He thought about Alina and felt numb; during that last year she'd become a true friend, and it was hard to believe she was really gone. He thought about Chen Xiao, and hoped wholeheartedly he'd get better soon; he was one of the few people Kehuan considered family. But mostly he thought about Niki. He remembered how he'd used to worry in the past that something bad would happen to her, and the different times when she'd disappeared on him, and how he'd got annoyed at her for doing the ghost trick again, and at himself for losing her. He'd believed it to be history because for that last year Niki had always been someplace where he could easily find her. But now he was suddenly back to the point where he had no idea where she was, and if she was well, and if she'd ever return. Every few minutes he realized it anew, and each time something inside him clenched painfully.

He didn't fall asleep until early morning, and when his father came in a few hours later and woke him up, Kehuan looked so terrible that Chen Liang, alarmed, put his hand on his son's brow and asked with a frown, "Are you all right?"

But Kehuan was as far from all right as one could get, and he also had a feeling that unless Niki returned soon, safe and sound, he'd never be all right again.

* * *

Alina's funeral was three days later. Apart from Chen Liang and Kehuan, only three other people showed: an older teacher from the adult school and two young women who later told them gloomily they'd been Alina's classmates.

On other fronts, the situation wasn't much changed. Niki was still missing, the police still hadn't found the perp, and Chen Xiao was still in the hospital. But he started regaining consciousness, and even if it was only for a few minutes at a time, it was a great relief.

The next day Liu Wen flew in from Canada. He was going to take Chen Xiao to Vancouver, as soon as the doctors allowed such a move, but he had also some issues to discuss with Chen Liang.

Firstly, Liu Wen said, his cousin's condition was serious enough to prevent him from doing any work for an unpredictable amount of time. Apart from the ruptured spleen, which had been removed during the operation in Danzig, he had a severe spine injury, which could end up with quadriplegia. At the same time, there were both companies to manage, one in Taipei, and one in Warsaw. Liu Wen had some shares in both, and he also represented several other members of the family who invested in the businesses. He declared they didn't have a problem with Chen Liang taking the wheel, as long as the matters went smooth. He also asked Chen Liang very politely if he could take care of the apartment in Warsaw and Chen Xiao's belongings in it, and Chen Liang agreed, though he felt he really had enough on his plate already.

But the other lawyer still had one more subject to broach.

"We didn't know about the girl," Liu Wen said, looking at him steadily. "Is she really his daughter?"

"He registered her under his name," replied Chen Liang, dodging the question.

"Yes, I have no quarrel with this fact. But is she indeed his biological child?"

Chen Liang could see the other man already knew the answer. As Chen Xiao's close relative, he'd probably been aware of his sexual orientation for a long time, and perhaps of his ruminations about becoming a parent, too.

Still, the decision to reveal or not all the facts to his family belonged to the man in the hospital bed, so Chen Liang simply answered, "You'll have to ask this question to your cousin."

Liu Wen nodded and said, "He seems to be to coming to more often. I hope we'll be able to talk to him tomorrow."

They were, though it could hardly be called a real conversation since Chen Xiao wasn't able to utter a word. But they established with a few factual questions that he understood what was being said, and could make some decisions by nodding and shaking his head. It was apparent even this much effort exhausted him.

They went through all the questions related to business, and he gave the empowerment to manage both companies to Chen Liang. He also agreed to be transferred to Vancouver, which was understandable—his whole family was there. Interestingly, Liu Wen didn't ask any questions about Niki, after all. When everything was decided, he got up and went to talk to the doctors about the possible date of transport, leaving Chen Liang alone in the room with the patient.

Chen Liang noticed that Chen Xiao was looking at him intently, visibly distressed, and he wondered suddenly if it was possible that nobody had told the man the news yet.

"Niki..." Chen Xiao mouthed, and Chen Liang sighed and explained the situation, trying to sound optimistic, which was really difficult under the circumstances.

Chen Xiao closed his eyes for a moment. Then he opened them again and stared at him, waiting, and it became unavoidable.

"Alina's gone," Chen Liang said quietly and then watched with sorrow as two tears formed in the man's eyes and leaked to the sides of his head.

Liu Wen took his cousin to Vancouver one week later. Before their departure, Chen Liang had to swear to Chen Xiao several times that he'd continue looking for Niki, and promised to inform him immediately about any progress in this matter. But the truth was there wasn't much he could do.

He had now a double load of work and responsibility on his shoulders, and besides, he wouldn't even know where to start if he tried to perform the search himself. All he could do was contact the police every day for an update, and they kept looking, but it'd been already more than ten days, and apart from the working assumption that the girl had disappeared together with the perp, they had nothing. At some point, Chen Liang started to consider hiring a private investigator if the police didn't make progress soon because he really had to find Niki, not even so much for Chen Xiao as for his own son.

Kehuan was like a wounded animal these days, better not to be approached. He returned to school after the first three days after the accident because his father insisted on it, but he avoided people even more than before, and literally growled at other kids if they came too close to him, and blew up if they didn't retreat at once. Even Seong Taejin, though sympathetic and full of good intentions, preferred to stay away, and other children were downright scared of Kehuan now. Chen Liang had already received a very polite, but also very concerned call from the school headteacher, and was seriously worried the situation from the Berlin kindergarten was going to repeat itself. It was a good thing the school year ended in another week.

* * *

On the first day of the school holidays, Chen Liang received an unexpected call from Seong Joonho, who wanted to meet. Chen Liang didn't have time for social visits, but the man said it was about Kehuan, so he went, and got completely sucker-punched when Seong Joonho, after a few minutes of obligatory small talk, straighten up and announced, "My wife and I would like to invite Chen Kehuan to go with us to Korea for the summer."

Chen Liang almost laughed. It wasn't funny, really, but he still felt wryly amused when he imagined the Seongs, with their polite talk, smiles, and bows, trying to domesticate Kehuan in his present feral state.

"Thank you for the offer," he answered at last, "but I don't think it's a good idea."

"Why not? My son told us Kehuan has been in a bad mood lately. He said a cousin went missing, is that right? Taejin wasn't sure."

"More or less." Chen Liang didn't elaborate.

"It's a terrible situation, and I'm sure your family is doing everything possible to find the child, but Kehuan can't really help with it, can he?"

"No, not really," Chen Liang agreed.

"So why not distract him with a trip?"

Chen Liang sometimes felt that despite his long and successful past carrier in diplomacy, he had more in common with his son than he normally thought. Right now, for example, he was severely tempted to punch Seong Joonho in his roundish belly.

"I have to come back after two weeks, but my wife is planning to take the children to Jeju later. It's a beautiful place. They'll have a great time..."

"I'm sure they will," Chen Liang said a little impatiently, "but Kehuan won't go."

"Maybe you could consider allowing—"

"I meant he won't want to go."

"But if you decide he should, he certainly will."

Chen Liang again felt close to bursting with a mirthless laugh. Instead, he said with as much courtesy as he could still muster, "Thank you for the offer, but not this time."

* * *

Two more weeks passed until something finally changed on the search front.

Chen Liang was still in his office that evening when he received a call from Liu Wen. This morning—it was still morning in Vancouver when they talked—Chen Xiao, who was still in the hospital bed and incapable of any movement, but finally able to speak, asked Liu Wen to check his email, and they found a message from the Taiwanese embassy in Warsaw with a carefully phrased question about Chen Xiao's daughter, whom they remembered registering almost one year earlier.

Chen Xiao became almost incoherent with nervous excitement. They called the embassy right away to explain the situation, and in return heard the news: a Caucasian girl of unknown parentage and nationality, about five years old, had been staying for some time in the child service shelter in Amersfoort, the Netherlands. Now some new clue emerged, indicating the girl might be actually Chinese or Taiwanese. Both embassies in the Hague were contacted first, but nobody was looking there for such a child, so they passed the message to other diplomatic posts in Europe, and when the Warsaw Taiwanese embassy received the memo, they wondered... Chen Xiao almost burst into tears after hearing that, though of course, it could have been another child, not Niki. But what were the odds?

Chen Liang contacted the embassy for the details, and then went home to pack a small suitcase. He planned to set off for the Netherlands on his own early in the morning, but when Kehuan heard the news, there was no stopping him from coming as well, and he wanted to go at once. He finally agreed, very reluctantly, to wait until the next day because his father announced sternly that he really needed some rest before driving for twelve hours.

The next morning, Chen Liang looked at Kehuan's feverish eyes and tense face and felt suddenly terrified of what would become of his son if this trip ended with a fiasco. But he still let him go.

They didn't talk much on the way, despite the long drive, but it was obvious both of them kept pondering and wondering, and finally, Chen Liang decided it had to be said.

"It might not be her," he told his son. "Niki can speak English well enough to tell them her name at least, and that she lives in Warsaw."

"I know," said Kehuan. "But maybe she didn't think about English. Maybe she tried talking in Mandarin instead. "

"It's possible," Chen Liang admitted. "That would explain why they thought she was Chinese."

"Why didn't they send a photo? We'd know at once."

"Child protection, they said."

They arrived in Amersfoort late in the afternoon. The embassy had already contacted the shelter, so they were expected by the director of the place, a tall middle-aged woman.

"We couldn't find out anything about her until a few days ago," she told them as they walked together to the playground in the park, where the younger children were playing at the moment. "It was quite a mystery. She was found one day at a gas station near the ring road, and the police put her here because they had no clue where she came from."

"Didn't she tell you anything?" asked Chen Liang. They were now walking across a bridge over the canal, and the playground was already visible ahead, behind some trees. "Not even her name?"

The woman gave him a speculating look. "She doesn't speak," she said.

Chen Liang stopped, and she stopped as well. Kehuan, who'd been a few steps behind, came closer.

"I see you weren't told about that," the director remarked after a moment. "That's why we didn't know where to look for her family or guardians."

Chen Liang's heart sank a little.

"So why did you think she was Chinese? Or Taiwanese?"

"One of our childcare assistants is from Chongqing. The children were doing a painting activity a few days ago, and she noticed the girl painted some Chinese characters. The assistant tried to talk to her in Chinese, but didn't get anywhere."

"Chongqing. They have a different dialect there, I think."

"Maybe, but as I told you, she doesn't speak at all."

"Which characters?" asked Kehuan suddenly.

"Some symbols for animals, I think," the woman thought for a moment. "Cat? Wolf as well if I remember well."

Kehuan ran.

The playground was quite big, and the children were scattered all around it, and he ran from the swings to the slides, and from the slides to the sandpit, and then to the big jungle gym in the middle, but he couldn't see Niki anywhere. The director was talking now to the childcare worker standing in the middle, and the young blond woman pointed to a low, gnarled tree on the fringe of the playground, and a small figure hunched on one of the big boughs hanging low over the ground.

Kehuan sprinted towards the tree, and there she was. Straddling the branch and propped on one arm, she was tracing some lines on the bark with a small stick in her other hand.

"Niki," he said.

Niki raised her head and looked at him. She looked a little different, her triangular face impossibly thinner, her hair longer, her mouth straight and unsmiling, but the CGI eyes were exactly the same. Only he wasn't sure if she recognized him because her expression didn't change much; she just sat there and stared at him, without a word.

So Kehuan grabbed hold of the branch with both arms, swung his legs up and around it, and pulled himself up on top of it. He sat astride the bough, in a mirror pose to hers, and leaned closer, examining her face.

"Are you okay?" he asked.

Niki went back to tracing the lines in the bark with her stick.

"Hey," he tried again. "Niki. It's me."

When she looked up this time, he was almost sure she recognized him; she frowned, and there was a gleam of some emotion in her eyes.

"Let's go back home," Kehuan said. He'd been talking in Mandarin before, but now he repeated in Polish, "Let's go home."

Niki watched him for another moment, and then she dropped the stick and climbed down to the ground. Kehuan jumped down after her and turned around only to discover they had an audience: his father, the director of the shelter, and the young blond woman all stood close by, observing the scene with rapt attention.

"That's the most of reaction I've ever seen from her," noticed the young woman, and the director nodded in agreement.

Chen Liang produced Niki's passport and his own, and the document he received from Liu Wen, giving him the power of attorney in all matters concerning the girl, and followed the director to her office to sign all the papers.

In the meantime, Kehuan and Niki sat on the chairs in the corridor outside the room. She was quiet and didn't really look at him, but when he told her how clever it'd been of her to draw those Chinese characters, a ghost of a smile appeared on her face.

When they left the shelter, the night had already fallen. They found a small B&B, had a quick meal, and went to bed; Chen Liang was dog-tired after the whole day of driving.

In the middle of the night, something woke Kehuan up. He opened his eye and saw Niki sitting on her bed, chin on knees, hugging her legs and gazing at the window with her eyes wide open and luminous in the moonlight. He walked up and sat next to her.

"Can't sleep?" he whispered. She glanced at him and shook her head.

So he moved closer and threw the blanket over both of them, and they sat together in silence. Kehuan couldn't remember falling asleep, but when he woke up in the morning, she was lying next to him, curled up into a tight ball.

* * *

The journey home went mostly in silence again. Chen Liang felt odd talking to Kehuan as if the girl wasn't there, but it was just as strange trying to talk to her because she hardly showed any reaction. He wondered if she even heard what they were saying.

Besides, he was preoccupied with his own thoughts. He felt relieved they'd finally found her, but was already thinking ahead, and feeling uneasy about how he was going to cope with this whole new configuration.

When they'd last talked with Liu Wen, he had a distinct impression the other lawyer expected him to take responsibility for Niki if she was found; there'd been no word about sending her over to Canada. Chen Xiao was certainly in no shape to take care of a child right now, but Chen Liang was sure he'd have mentioned such a possibility if he had the support of his family in this matter. Which obviously wasn't the case.

On the other hand, even if sending Niki to Vancouver was an option, Chen Liang didn't think it would be a good idea, seeing what condition the child was in. Not to mention how Kehuan would react to such a proposal. It seemed Niki was with them to stay, which meant numerous complications, and he needed to work out some reasonable solutions, and fast.

* * *

Niki heard what they were saying, of course. But lately, it'd been really hard to concentrate on what was happening around, and time seemed to be ripped up into small pieces, jumbled together in a strange mosaic of unrelated events.

It had started on that meadow.

It was very dark, and she was walking around in a spiral, counting her steps and listening to the sound of the crickets. Mum called out to her, so she looked up and waved.

She was sitting in a cabin of a moving car, very high over the ground, and watching the road ahead as it emerged from the pale morning fog, and someone was breathing next to her in loud gasps.

A young man was sobbing loudly, wiping his face every few seconds with both hands. His shoulders shook and she felt sorry for him, so she patted his arm and tried to say "It's OK," but every time she opened her mouth, it felt as if someone put a hand around her throat and squeezed, and no sound came out at all.

A bald older man with an agitated face was leaning over her and speaking in a harsh voice, but she didn't understand a word.

She was standing in front of a gas station shop, waiting for mum and Chen Xiao, and she was hungry.

She was sitting on a chair in a big room. There were many people around, most of them in uniforms. A telephone kept ringing, and she was really, really hungry.

She was at a table in a room with yellow walls, and there were other children as well, and a plate of soup in front of her. She'd been so hungry a moment ago, but now after eating a few spoons she couldn't swallow any more. Her throat squeezed up, and she felt nauseous.

She was playing in the park and thought Kehuan would surely like to climb that jungle gym with her, but he didn't come.

She was sitting on a bed. Other children were breathing quietly in the dark, but Niki couldn't sleep because something frightening happened in her dream, only she couldn't remember what.

They were in the dining room with yellow walls, and a new lady was distributing the bread rolls. She had black hair and a nice face which reminded Niki of Chen Xiao, so she smiled at her.

They were playing in the park again, and she wanted to take a walk along the canal and see if there were other bridges over it, but Kehuan had said she shouldn't walk around on her own, and she was afraid mum would come when she was away, so she stayed.

A woman in the uniform was talking to her again, and Niki realized now she was a police officer. The woman started speaking in English, and Niki finally understood a little. She liked the way the police officer had braided her hair. Niki wondered if she could do it with her own hair as well.

She woke up at night again, and went to look for mum, but then she remembered it was this place for lost children, and mum wasn't here. She really wanted mum to come and get her at last.

They were painting, and Niki took a brush and wrote 'cat', and thought about Kehuan, and wrote 'wolf' as well. The black-haired woman with the nice face looked at the symbols and spoke to her, and what she said sounded somewhat familiar, but not really. Niki wanted to answer, but then remembered her throat wasn't working properly anymore, so she gave up.

She was looking at the tree bark on the bough. The tree wasn't so big as that oak they used to climb with Kehuan, but the bark had a nice pattern.

Kehuan was finally there. He said, "Let's go home," and it was an excellent idea. Kehuan's father was standing next to the tree, too, and Niki wanted to say hello, but her throat was still out of order. Mum and Chen Xiao weren't there.

They were all in a car, and Kehuan's father was driving. Niki was tired, so she put her head on Kehuan's shoulder and slept.

She woke up, and she was in Kehuan's room, in his bed. She saw him asleep on the floor next to the bed, on a blanket. The sky behind the big window was deep blue, but it was getting paler. Niki tiptoed to the beanbag, sat down, and watched the Vistula River as the sky turned lighter, and the water started to glimmer in the sunlight. She decided to go home and check if mum was up.

She was walking through the garden square near their home, and it was already very warm. She thought it'd get really hot later, and it was a good thing she and Kehuan didn't have to stay outside all the time now. She entered the house and climbed the stairs to the second floor, but when she rang at the door, nobody answered, so she sat down on the steps and waited. Some time later Kehuan came and said, "Niki, she's not here. Let's go," so she followed him back to his home. They had rice with vegetables, but she couldn't eat much.

She woke up at night and felt frightened, but couldn't remember why. Kehuan woke up, too, and sat with her in the beanbag. He put a blanket on both of them and fell asleep after some time, but Niki couldn't. She went to the kitchen to drink some water. It was getting light. Kehuan's father came to the kitchen, too, and got startled at the sight of her. It was a little funny, so she smiled at him. He made a toast for her, but she could eat only half of it.

She saw on Kehuan's phone it was Thursday, so she went to the house with the tall wall. She climbed the wall and sat on it, and watched the garden and the house. Then Kehuan came and climbed the wall next to her. After a moment, he said, "Let's go on the swings", and they went. Niki loved to swing, and it was fun, but then she remembered she wanted to wait for mum. But Kehuan said, "No, Niki, she's not there," and they went to his home again.

Kehuan's father went with her to meet someone, and Niki knew at once the lady was some kind of a doctor. She'd already met a similar person in that house for lost children. The lady doctor spoke to her, but Niki was engrossed by one of the pictures hanging on the wall. They all had the same name on them, but this one's frame looked as if it was made of connecting wings of birds, and Niki wanted to try and draw it later in her room. But they again went back to Kehuan's place instead.

She decided to go check that apartment near the shopping street where mum used to work earlier, though she didn't really think mum would be there. The lady in the apartment remembered her, but she said she hadn't seen mum for almost a year. So Niki went to this small courtyard nearby and made a sand dragon in the sandpit. A little boy helped her make the dragon's scales out of pebbles and blades of grass. Then Kehuan came and took her to his place.

* * *

Kehuan was having a hell of a summer. Literally.

When he woke up in his room on that first day and Niki wasn't there, he panicked at first, but then started thinking, and it wasn't so hard to guess where she went. He was relieved Chen Xiao's old apartment seemed to be empty because he wasn't sure how the situation would go if a stranger opened the door for Niki.

It wasn't difficult to follow her during the next days either because he'd figured out how her mind worked, and if she sneaked out without him noticing, which of course happened all the time—she was still Niki, after all—he just had to check the places where Alina used to work, and Niki's favorite playing grounds around them. He'd never minded following her around in the past, and it wasn't a problem now. Other things were harder.

He felt as if he was trying to keep alive some small, injured creature, too young and weak to survive on its own.

She didn't speak, and he was getting really worried she'd never say a word again. In the beginning, he sometimes had an impression she tried to, but later it was as if she'd decided it wasn't worth the effort.

She moved around like a sleepwalker and didn't hear most things people said. He was afraid again she'd get hit by a car because she didn't pay much attention to the street traffic either, and wouldn't the irony of the fate just suck, under the circumstances.

She couldn't sleep. He knew because they both slept in his room, Niki on his bed, and he on the mattress his father got him on the second day after they'd returned from the Netherlands. Every time she woke up now, he woke up as well. But he usually returned to sleep soon afterward, and he knew she didn't; instead, she'd fall asleep in different places during the day for an hour or so, sometimes more than once, when her body gave up from exhaustion.

She hardly ate and looked skinny and sickly. Kehuan tried to feed her a little as often as possible because she couldn't swallow much food at one go. He'd once tried to convince her to eat more for dinner, and she started gagging, so he knew it was no use.

At times he wondered how long they both could go on like that and felt afraid, but after a few weeks, he noticed some small signs of progress: she seemed to be more aware of what was happening around, and always recognized him now. But he wasn't sure if it could be called the light at the end of the tunnel yet.

* * *

That afternoon Kehuan walked around for hours, looking for Niki, and he was getting really anxious. He'd already checked all the regular places, and Chen Xiao's old apartment, and then went back home thinking maybe she had returned in the meantime, but she was still MIA. In the end, one more possibility occurred to him, and he ran to check that street with the old, dilapidated houses where Alina and Niki used to live with the forgetful old lady.

As he was passing the school, somebody called his name, and when he turned around, he saw Yoon Sori on the other side of the street, in a pink summer dress and with an ice cream in her hand. She waved at him, so he stopped for a moment, waiting for her to cross the street.

"Hello, Kehuan," she said in English. He remembered that Sori, unlike her cousin, never tried to press him into speaking Korean. "Where are you going?"

"I need to check one place," he answered. "I'm looking for Niki."

"I'll go with you," she offered.

Kehuan didn't answer and just started running again. If the girl wanted to tag along, she'd have to keep up. He didn't expect she really would, though, and was a bit impressed when she simply threw away her ice cream in the nearest bin and started running as well, in that dress and dainty sandals.

A few minutes later they reached the street, just as gloomy and dirty as Kehuan remembered. He found the right house and entered the gate, and then climbed up the rickety stairs to the fourth floor, two steps at a time, with Yoon Sori on his heels. And there was Niki, sitting on the last step, hugging her legs with both arms, with her head lying sideways on her knees. It was a depressingly familiar sight for Kehuan, but the girl behind him made a quiet sound of concern.

He sat next to Niki, and when she looked up at him, it suddenly struck him how broken-hearted she looked. She didn't seem oblivious or absent-minded, like in the previous days; her bright eyes were wide open and very aware. And then they suddenly turned glassy, and two fat tears gathered and spilled over on her cheeks.

Kehuan put his arm around her shoulders, and she began to cry in earnest. After a minute she was sobbing and gasping, and shaking all over, so he pulled her closer and put his other arm around her as well. She leaned her head against his shoulder and cried until she could cry no more. Then she just sat there, limp, and an occasional sob spasmed her thin body. Finally, she went quiet, and Kehuan realized she'd fallen asleep.

All this time Yoon Sori had been standing two steps below, watching the whole scene with sympathetic eyes.

"What now?" she asked in a low voice, looking around with visible and rather understandable distaste. "We can't stay here."

"Help me put her on my back," said Kehuan.

In the end, he didn't need much help because Niki weighed about as much as could be expected from a bunch of twigs. But it was still a long way from that place to his home, and when they went out of the tenement house, Niki fast asleep on his back now, he felt somewhat grateful when Sori proposed, "Let's go to our place. It's closer."

The Seongs' house seemed empty, and when Kehuan was climbing up the stairs behind Yoon Sori, puffing a little, he suddenly realized something.

"Are you all back yet?" he asked after getting Niki off his back and putting her on the bed in Sori's room.

"Huh?"

"You went to Korea, right? Have you all come back?"

"Oh, no. I didn't go with them," answered Sori, sitting on a swivel chair next to her desk.

Kehuan sat on the floor and leaned back against the bed. He could hear Niki behind him, breathing steadily in her sleep.

"Why not?" he asked.

"My mum got a new job, and I didn't want to go without her," explained Sori, propelling her chair around, and added without any encouragement from him, "She works in the tourist information center in Old Town."

"Sounds cool."

Sori smiled and nodded, and added after a moment, "And mum said it made no sense to waste money on plane tickets to Korea when we just got to Europe."

Kehuan smiled a little. A reasonable attitude.

"We went to Cracow last week," she continued.

He felt momentarily jealous; he hadn't been anywhere outside Warsaw yet, and he'd been living here for two years.

"Was it nice?" he asked.

"It was wonderful!" Sori gushed, and Kehuan winced internally. "Mum said she'd take a week off in August, and then we'll go somewhere else. Maybe to Danzig, and to the seaside."

Kehuan's heart squeezed a little and he didn't comment. He turned his head away, and then something captured his attention.

"Do you play the violin?" he asked. He got up to look at the instrument and then inspected it with interest.

"Yes, since I was five," answered Yoon Sori, and Kehuan heard that note in her voice which told him it was something important to her.

"I play the piano," he said, "but not that well."

"Really?" Sori sounded surprised.

He shrugged and added, "Niki sings really nice." Then he remembered Niki hadn't made a sound since the time of the crash and felt like a moron. And then he also realized with a pang it was one more thing to mourn if she never opened her mouth again.

Niki woke up an hour later. She was a little groggy, but didn't show any inclination to cry again, to Kehuan's relief, and seemed still aware of everything around her, which made him suddenly hopeful. Maybe she'd finally get better now.

Yoon Sori offered them orange juice and some fruit. Niki ate half a peach and was full, but when the older girl tried to persuade her to eat some more, she smiled. She seemed to really like Sori, and the observation suddenly gave Kehuan an idea.

"Come round to our place tomorrow," he told the older girl. "Bring your violin."

* * *

The next morning Kehuan lifted the fallboard of his piano, feeling nervous. Niki was in the kitchen, drawing something on a big sheet of paper he'd given her earlier.

"There's this song," he said to Yoon Sori. "I'll play it for you, and see if you can catch the melody." And he started playing one of the songs Alina used to sing when she cooked with Niki.

Alina had been a fan of oldies, but Kehuan had always thought she had good taste. He'd even learned to play several of those songs. The one he wanted to try now was one of his favorites: it had a wistful, gypsy-like melody in the stanzas and a dynamic chorus, and funny lyrics to boot. But most importantly, Niki liked it as well.

He played the melody twice, and Sori nodded; it was catchy. She checked the pitch and started playing. First, she faltered and made mistakes, but after he played it for her again, and she practiced some more, the melody flowed smoother and more confident.

Kehuan noticed Niki just behind the door, peeking inside.

"Let's try it together, okay?" he said to Yoon Sori, trying not to look at the little cat.

"All right, but go slow. I'm still learning it."

They played it in a very slow tempo from the beginning, and then a second time again. Normally Kehuan would consider the exercise fun in itself because Sori was really good, but right now all his attention was on Niki in the doorway.

She stepped inside, and when they started the song once again, this time closer to the original tempo, she began to hum along with them. Yoon Sori turned and beamed at her, still playing the violin, and Niki sang.

She mumbled the words very quietly at the beginning as if she couldn't remember them well. But she loved to sing, and it had always been as simple and easy as breathing for her, and once she started, there was no stopping it: her lovely voice unfurled suddenly like a ribbon freed from a snarl, and Sori's eyes opened wide in amazement. She stopped playing, but

Kehuan went on, and Niki sang like only she could, in that bright, effortless voice which always sounded as if she was laughing with joy underneath, and perfectly in tune.

The song ended. Yoon Sori put down the violin and started clapping with a big smile on her face, and Niki burst into tears.

But even as she cried, she also smiled a little, so Kehuan got up from the piano, went to her, and said quietly in Polish, "Cześć, Niki."

And Niki answered, "Nihao," and it was enough for now.

5

A Practical Solution

Chen Liang had to go to Taipei for some time because running the original company remotely from Warsaw turned out just as tricky as he'd expected, and their people there were running around like headless chickens. But there were also things happening in Warsaw he needed to be here for, as they were in the middle of business negotiations with an important new client. Chen Liang had always approached his work very seriously, but right now he felt enough was enough, all the more so because there was their family life to organize as well, with its own plethora of different problems.

For example, he had no idea who was supposed to stay with the children when he went away to Taiwan for a week, and what's more, such business trips were going to happen regularly in the future.

Also, the children had three more weeks of holidays left, and then Niki was supposed to start first grade. Until last week he was certain there was absolutely no chance to go through with this plan, but then all of a sudden she started talking again, finally. In the beginning, he tried to speak with her about the accident and to find out what had really happened to her, and how she'd ended up in the Netherlands. But she never answered any of his questions, and in the end, the psychologist told him to leave it alone. She said Niki had to decide on her own when she was ready to discuss it.

Chen Xiao called him every few days to inquire about his adoptive daughter, but he'd only recently learned all the facts. Earlier, it had been like some unamusing drama between them: Chen Liang hid from his friend how bad a condition Niki was in when they brought her back from the Netherlands, and he was able to keep it secret because Chen Xiao didn't want to talk to her, so she wouldn't get upset with how bad a condition he was in after the crash. He only found out she'd been unable to speak for weeks when it was already history.

They still hadn't talked yet. Chen Liang could tell facing Niki was a daunting prospect for Chen Xiao, and Niki for some reason never asked about him. The psychologist wasn't sure why, but her advice was the same as before: give the girl more time.

Anyway, now that Niki seemed a little better, Chen Liang was inclined to go with the original plan and send her to the first grade. The old pro-school argument was as valid as ever: she'd be under care for a substantial part of each day, and Kehuan could keep an eye on her, too. But on the other hand, Niki was still far from well. Her sleep patterns didn't improve much, and Chen Liang often had the impression she had to put a lot of effort into actually hearing and understanding what people said to her, which didn't bode well for her school career.

And there was also the question of the afternoons. He worked until late every day during the week, and Kehuan was starting fourth grade this year, which meant new subjects, new teachers, more lessons, and more studying. Even if his son didn't protest, Chen Liang didn't think it was fair to charge him with the additional task of looking after the younger child all the time.

Another problem: they couldn't stay in the same apartment much longer. They didn't even have a living room, and Kehuan's bedroom was too small for the two of them. There was no space for another desk, and the boy couldn't sleep on the floor forever.

The last problem was the easiest to solve. As for the rest, Chen Liang had been thinking about it since they'd come back from the Netherlands, and he actually had a solution in mind, and a very practical one, he just wasn't decided yet if he was willing to put it into action.

For now, the most urgent matter was finding some childcare for the week he was going to spend in Taipei.

Unexpectedly, this problem solved itself without any effort on his part. In the middle of the week, out of the blue, he received a call from someone called Kim Hana. The name rang a bell, but he couldn't place it in a context at first.

"I'm the sister-by-law of Seong Joonho," the woman on the phone explained helpfully, obviously aware of his confusion. "We met once in April."

The younger woman in the Korean restaurant. The one who seemed to possess some sense of humor.

"Ah yes, of course. How can I help you, Ms. Kim?"

"Actually, I thought maybe I could help you a little," said Kim Hana, and it sounded as if she was smiling. "On Sunday, my daughter and I are leaving for the seaside for ten days. I know you are very busy, and Sori wanted me to invite Kehuan and Veronica to join us."

Several things took Chen Liang by surprise in this speech. First, she knew not only his son but also his ward. Second, her daughter—a kid of the same age, and a girl at that—seemed to be friends with Kehuan. (Maybe it wasn't that strange; there was Niki already, after all. But he'd always felt Niki was a special case.) Third, Kim Hana was willing to take care of two extra kids, on her own, for ten days. The whole proposal was so on time it sounded suspiciously close to a miracle.

But he also felt certain unease at the thought of the travel, even if it was completely irrational, so he asked, "Are you going by car?"

"No, we're taking the night train to Danzig. We're going to stay there for two days, and then to take a coach to Łeba, to see the sand dunes."

It sounded like an enjoyable trip, and Chen Liang felt a little irked; he had no chance in hell to do anything like that in any predictable future. But at least his immediate problem was solved, and he wasn't going to look the gift horse in the mouth.

"It's a very kind proposal, Ms. Kim," he said gratefully. "You'll indeed help me tremendously by taking them with you."

And since she sounded like a person who wouldn't take offense at a direct question, he asked, "How did you know I needed a hand?"

"Veronica told me. When she visited Sori a few days ago, she said you had to go to Taipei for a week."

Niki. So she did hear what was being said around her. Maybe there was more hope for this child than he'd thought.

* * *

Kehuan and Niki loved the seaside. They'd liked Danzig, too, but they were both city kids, and it was just another city, even if very old and splendid. But the sea, the wide sandy beaches, and the pine forests were something new and fabulous.

After Danzig, they went to the national park near Łeba, where the main attraction were enormous sandy dunes. Niki immediately wanted to do what all children did there: roll down from the top to the bottom, and she and Kehuan tumbled down from the highest dune three times. Meanwhile, Sori and her mum just sat at the top, talking and laughing between themselves, and Kehuan noticed the sight made Niki feel forlorn, so when they reached the top again, he took her by the hand and said," Let's go," and started walking in the direction of the sea. The older girl and the woman got up at once and followed after them.

Kehuan liked it about those two: they seemed to get most things right off, without any bothersome explanations. After that day at his place when Niki started talking again, Sori asked him what was wrong with her, and when Kehuan said, "Her mum died," she didn't have any other questions.

After the trip to the dunes, the original plan was to stay in Łeba, but it turned out very crowded, and Kim Hana wanted a quieter place. She promptly made a few phone calls to some friends at the tourist office in Warsaw, and ten minutes later they had an address of a pension in a much smaller seaside village on the other end of the national park.

The moment they arrived, Niki wanted to go exploring. She had a soul of a wanderer, and the endless sandy beaches were her idea of heaven. The weather was nice, but it wasn't hot because of the constant wind, and here she could walk, and walk, and walk for hours, barefoot on the wet sand, with Kehuan next to her, and stare at the horizon without having to talk to other people. On the way, they could skip together over the foamy waves, and make sand reliefs or pebble-and-shell mosaics every time a new inspiration struck her, and when they had enough of going forward, they could go back a different way, through the pine forest stretching along the coast, where the air smelled of resin and dry sand.

Kehuan sometimes wondered how far Niki would go if he wasn't there to remind her that they needed to turn back sometime. But he loved these walks as well. The wind, the continuous rumble of the waves, and the clear circular line of the horizon were a great background for thoughts, and he solved many interesting math problems on the way.

Yoon Sori and her mum went with them sometimes, but they usually returned earlier. Sori had brought her violin with her and practiced playing it every afternoon, and her mum turned up to be a very active person. If she wasn't swimming in the pool in the nearby hotel, she rode the bike rented at the pension, or played beach volleyball with some random people. In the evening she often went for a jog, sometimes dragging her reluctant daughter with her as well, and Kehuan thought with wry amusement this was probably why Sori could run so well when necessary.

He and Niki also tried riding bikes and had a lot of fun with it. Sori couldn't believe they'd never done it before. Kehuan could remember riding a tricycle when he'd been very young, but it'd been ages ago, and riding a regular bike was a completely different story.

Several times they played a board game at the end of the day, where you had to grow crops, and trade with other players, and build villages and roads. Kehuan found it surprisingly engrossing. He won the game almost every time, but Niki managed to win once, too and was very proud of herself.

There was only one rainy day when they had to stay at the pension. Sori was bored and wanted to experiment with some new hairstyles, and her mum tried to help but wasn't good at it at all. Kehuan, who was reading a book, and Niki, painting with the new watercolors Kim Hana bought for her in Danzig, raised their heads now and again at their snorts of laughter, usually caused by Sori looking particularly weird or her hairdo falling completely apart. After twenty minutes Niki volunteered as a new model, and soon she was snorting and giggling together with them.

And then it was time to go back, and Kehuan knew he was in Yoon Sori and her mum's debt forever.

* * *

By the time the children came back from the seaside, Chen Liang had already returned from Taipei and made his decision.

Funnily enough, what tipped the scale was a tooth, or rather a toothache. It tormented him for several days during the business trip, so when he came back, the first thing he did was make an appointment with the dentist. But when he pressed the disconnect button on his phone, it suddenly occurred to him he had no idea when his son had his teeth checked up last time. It was one of the things Lee Soojin used to take care of, and Chen Liang asked himself how many other parental duties he'd been neglecting for years, without even realizing it, and felt like a complete failure of a father, again. And then he made up his mind.

On the day the children returned from their vacations, he got Kehuan alone.

"So here's the thing," Chen Liang started, "I don't have enough time to properly take care of you and Niki, and I'm afraid I'm not doing a great job of it."

"It's not that bad," Kehuan reassured him, a little baffled.

"I don't even take you to the dentist."

"You don't have to," Kehuan answered, perplexed by the strange turn of the conversation. "We have a dentist at school."

"Really? Oh. That's good. But anyway… I think I require some help, and I decided I need to marry."

If his father declared that he needed to clone himself or take a six-month-long holiday on Mauritius island, Kehuan would be less dumbfounded.

"What?!"

"I'm planning to marry. Niki needs a mother, and so do you, honestly speaking."

Kehuan considered.

He was absolutely certain he needed nothing of the kind. He'd had a mother once, but she was gone, and he'd learned to deal with life on his own, end of story. But maybe his father was onto something about Niki. She'd definitely enjoyed Kim Hana's company at the seaside, and while Kehuan was willing to look after her the best he could, some things were beyond him. Like experimenting with new hairstyles, for example.

He kept thinking and quickly came to the conclusion that Chen Liang wouldn't have started the topic if he hadn't already had a particular candidate for the job in mind.

"So who are you marrying?" he asked, striving to keep his tone level. He might not like it, but that wasn't the point. "And when?"

Chen Liang gaped at his son, feeling at once thankful for his no-nonsense attitude, and saddened by it. When had his boy grown up? Wasn't he still a child? But it was already said, and now it just needed to get done as well.

* * *

Kehuan was right, of course: Chen Liang did have a candidate for the job. Anna Grabowska had been working in the Warsaw office of the company from the start, which meant well over two years now, and all this time he'd been aware she was interested in him.

Anna was a tall, good-looking woman in her mid-thirties, with wavy brown hair and warm brown eyes. When she smiled, Chen Liang sometimes saw in her face a shadow of resemblance to Lee Soojin, which probably was the reason why he treated her in a softer manner than most people. She seemed genial and well-mannered, and he liked talking to her sometimes in the break room, over a cup of coffee.

Because she was his employee, and also his junior by almost twenty years, at the beginning he hadn't even considered anything, despite all the signals she kept sending him. Later he felt tempted a few times; he'd never been a prude, and she was an attractive woman. But what he had in mind was a few dates and possibly some casual sex, and Anna had very different expectations. She was on the lookout for a permanent partner, and the moment Chen Liang realized it, he abandoned any designs.

After he'd brought Niki from the Netherlands, though, he started thinking about Anna along different lines. He invited her for lunch a few times, and for dinner once, but it didn't feel right to pretend to romance her when his motives were so depressingly mercenary, and he was still undecided. But then that bloody toothache came, and at the end of August he made up his mind.

Chen Liang strove for honesty whenever it was possible, so he laid his cards on the table at once: need for help, two companies to manage, two children to take care of, enough money, not enough time, and the attraction between them to glue it all together. Anna listened carefully and then asked a few questions about Niki—she'd known about Kehuan already, of course—and her eyes opened really wide at the news the girl was a daughter of Chen Xiao. Chen Liang skipped the details, and once again made it sound as if he and his business partner were related, which was a lie he'd already told or implied so many times he almost believed it himself by now.

She didn't seem daunted by his proposal, such as it was, straightforward and unromantic, but then she stumped him with a condition of her own.

"I don't mind looking after the children," she declared with a warm smile. "In fact, I like children very much. I'd like to have one of my own, too."

This required some consideration, so Chen Liang suggested they both needed a little time, and their meeting ended at that.

He didn't really want more children. He was fifty-three, had a son he loved and was proud of, and any procreative ambitions he'd ever had were already fulfilled. But he felt he'd have to cave on this. It was clearly important to her, and understandably so.

And in the end, what would one more child change in the grand scheme of things? They certainly wouldn't starve because of that, and it was Anna who'd bear the burden, literally and metaphorically, so it was only fair to leave the choice to her. And so he said yes to her condition, and that closed the deal.

* * *

"Think again, Anna," said Renata, who'd come to Warsaw for a few days to visit her mother and younger sister. She sounded upset. "He's a foreigner."

"So what?" Anna answered, shrugging. "I don't mind." She smiled. "Honestly, I think he's even more interesting because of that."

"But it's not just that he's a foreigner, you know," Renata persisted. "It's that he's from a completely different culture. You have no idea what you're getting into."

"Oh please. He's not some Islamic extremist, Renata. Besides, he's lived in Europe for years."

"But he's not European, and doesn't look like one..."

"I didn't know you were such a racist," Anna scoffed, displeased. "We live in the twenty-first century. Wake up."

"I'm not," said her sister defensively. "But there are people around who'll treat you differently if you marry a Chinese, even among your friends. Mark my words."

Anna dismissed the warning with a wave of her hand. "He's very good-looking and can be really charming. They'll come around."

"I doubt our mother ever will," Renata told her somberly. "I'm serious."

Anna sighed, immediately subdued. Their mother had thrown a real tantrum when she'd heard about her marital plans. She plain refused to even meet Chen Liang, ever, and then listed all Anna's previous boyfriends by name, in chronological order, asking dramatically time after time why it couldn't be one of them. It wasn't as if nobody else had ever wanted to marry her, she said angrily.

It was true, but none of those guys had shown any real promise, and Anna wasn't going to repeat her mother's mistake, and work her fingers to the bone all her life to keep in style some lazybones. She'd never wanted just a man. She wanted a man of success, and that was a much rarer bird to find. And here he was, finally.

Unfortunately, her mother didn't understand that, and their stormy discussion ended with her bursting into bitter tears and declaring she'd never talk to her younger daughter again if she went through with the marriage. Anna was sure it was just theatrics, but it was still very depressing.

She'd hoped at least Renata would be on her side and felt very disappointed now with her disgruntled reaction.

"And he's so much older than you," her sister started again, "and a widower..."

"Better than a divorcee," Anna noticed dryly. "Don't you think?"

"I'm not sure," Renata countered. "With a man divorced, at least his previous wife isn't a competition. In all probability, they can't stand each other. But if the wife died..."

There was some sense to Renata's words, and Anna felt uneasy for a second, but then a new thought cheered her up. "But he wants to marry me. That counts for something. He proposed of his own initiative."

"Because he needs a nanny for his kids."

"There's more to it. He's got feelings for me, he's just not open enough to confess them," Anna was sure of that. "And you know I like children. I don't mind."

"Have you even met them yet? They may be total brats."

"We're meeting this weekend. Keep your fingers crossed."

* * *

Chen Liang was determined to find a bigger place to live for all of them before the end of the school holidays, and at the last weekend of August, he had a few options lined up to check. They agreed with Anna it'd be a good occasion to introduce her to Kehuan and Niki, and on Saturday morning they all met at the entrance to the first of the places.

Anna greeted the children with a charming smile. Even dressed in casual clothes, she looked elegant, and Chen Liang noticed Niki gaze at her dreamily. He suspected the girl was appreciating the combination of the colors of the clothes or some such because she certainly didn't pay much attention to the introductions. Kehuan was reserved but polite, which was probably the best Chen Liang could expect of his misanthrope of a son.

They had three places to visit: a two-level apartment near the big park, a semi-detached house very close to the international school and to the Seongs' place, and an apartment with a fantastic view on the Vistula River, but from the opposite side, as it was over the bridge, close to the city center. After they toured them all, Chen Liang invited them for lunch in a sushi restaurant near the last place and asked for opinions.

"I like the house," Anna answered at once, excited. "The neighborhood looks classy. And there's the garden, too."

Chen Liang looked at Kehuan, and Kehuan looked at Niki, who was completely engrossed in studying the grassy design on the plate the waitress put in front of her a minute ago.

"Which place did you like, Niki?" Kehuan asked in Mandarin. His father cleared his throat, so he glanced at him, and then repeated the question in English.

"I like place with big windows," answered the cat. Of course.

"But which one? By the river, or near the park? They both had big windows."

Niki gave him a slight frown and meditated for a moment. "You like river," she said.

"Yes, but it's far from our school. We'd have to take the bus every day."

"But it's very close to your taekwondo club," Chen Liang interjected, "And you have training three times a week."

"But Niki doesn't. And school is five times a week."

"But isn't the house really close to your school?" chimed in Anna, sounding hopeful.

Kehuan didn't answer and looked at Niki again. She was back to studying her plate.

"Niki?"

"Park is fine, too," she said distractedly.

Kehuan nodded, and Chen Liang said, "The park it is, then."

And to Anna's bewilderment, that was the end of the discussion. She decided to be gracious about it, though, since it didn't matter that much; the apartment near the park was gorgeous, too.

She surveyed the children again. The girl was dressed in a blue T-shirt which couldn't belong to her—it was evidently a few sizes too big. She was wearing it with leggings, and it didn't look bad, but still.

"Are you sure it's your shirt, honey?" Anna asked.

The girl didn't react, but Chen Liang followed Anna's eyes, and his face flushed.

"Why are you wearing Kehuan's clothes, Niki?" he asked.

The girl woke up at that and gave him an apologetic smile. "All my are small," she answered. "I don't like small T-shirt."

The boy chuckled at that. So he was capable of looking and sounding warm and amiable, after all. Thank God.

"Has she really grown out of all her clothes?" Chen Liang asked incredulously, obviously trying to hide his discomfort.

"I think so. She checks my closet every morning for T-shirts," answered his son, smiling at the girl again, and then shrugged. "It's OK, most are too small for me, anyway."

Anna could recognize an excellent occasion. Here was her chance to make friends with the children.

"Maybe we could go clothes shopping together in the afternoon," she suggested. "The beginning of school is an important occasion."

Chen Liang, whose parental incompetence had just been brutally exposed, nodded meekly. But then he remembered he'd planned to drop by the office for an hour or two and asked if Anna could take kids to the shops on her own.

"No problem," she answered with a radiant smile, and he felt a sudden surge of optimism. Maybe it all would work out just as he'd hoped.

* * *

Anna took Kehuan and Veronica to her favorite multi-label clothes store. She expected to have a good time choosing clothes for them. They were both attractive children, the boy especially, tall and long-limbed, and with that distinct coloring. The little girl had great eyes and nice hair, but she was way too skinny, and gap-toothed at the moment.

The trip did turn up entertaining, but it didn't go the way she'd anticipated.

Veronica enjoyed clothes shopping, but she didn't need much advice. She had her own opinions on what she liked: she shook her head on girly pinks, and stayed away from all things elaborate and fancy, and went for simple forms and strong colors. She seemed to like her clothes loose and flowing, and slightly oversized, and Anna made a mental note to remember it.

Kehuan was another story. He presented an ultimately pragmatic approach, and once he'd tried on one pair of jeans, and they fit, he declared he'd take two pairs of those.

"Why won't you choose a different model for the second pair?" suggested Anna, amused. "Or at least a different color?"

"These are good," he answered indifferently. "I just need two pairs."

"Blue is nice," observed Veronica, looking at the jeans in his hands, "but black is nice, too."

And Kehuan put away one pair of blue jeans on the shelf and picked up the black ones instead.

Anna watched the strange dynamics between those two with growing fascination. Kehuan went for some T-shirts next, but he didn't want to try on any of them and just checked the size by putting a tee next to his torso. He almost took several identical pieces again, but then seemed to think better. He turned and asked the girl a short question in what Anna guessed must have been Chinese, and she immediately looked around and picked out four different T-shirts for him, and then also a hoodie, a sweater, and two shirts. Kehuan just stood there and waited while she heaped all the clothes in his hands. It didn't even look like the classic case of an undecided male needing advice. Kehuan never asked Anna for her opinion and didn't seem to really care what his cousin chose for him. Though maybe that wasn't entirely true because later Anna noticed him look with certain appreciation at the pile of clothes he was carrying.

Finally, they were done, after Anna had picked a few things for herself as well, and moved to the cash register. And that was when she suddenly realized that Chen Liang hadn't given her any money. For a moment she felt hot and a little nauseated, but then she guessed he must've simply forgotten, and decided to pay for everything by herself; he'd certainly reimburse her later. Just as she started groping in her bag for the wallet, praying there was enough money in her bank account to cover it all, Kehuan stepped forward, produced Chen Liang's gold credit card, and paid for everything, including her own purchases.

Anna had a problem wrapping her head around the whole situation, and she later called Chen Liang about it.

"I gave him the card because I thought you'd feel self-conscious if I gave it to you," he explained, sounding rather self-conscious himself. "We aren't married yet, after all."

"But what if he'd lost it?!" asked Anna, still appalled.

Chen Liang laughed. "He wouldn't," he assured her. "Kehuan understands money, you don't need to worry."

In Anna's opinion, no ten-year-old understood money, and she started to mull over the strange dynamics between the father and the son as well. It was official: the Chens were one peculiar family indeed.

* * *

The Seongs were back, and on the first day of school Kehuan and Niki ran into them in front of the main school gate. Sori said hello to both of them, Taejin gave Kehuan his usual grin, and the twins stepped next to Niki without any fuss, and they all went in.

There were no lessons on the first day, just the opening ceremony, and when everybody received their lesson plans, the students were released home, so an hour later they all met again at the front gate. The early autumn weather was mellow and inviting, and since it was still before noon, they decided to go to the park.

It was the one with Niki's favorite oak, and Kehuan wasn't surprised when the cat, who hadn't been talking much so far and seemed a little detached again, suddenly said, "Let's go climb," and marched in its direction.

After so much time of following her around Kehuan was totally cool with climbing just about anything, and he watched with uncharitable glee as Taejin's jaw dropped at the size of the tree, and then his face started changing colors when he imagined and digested the possible implications.

The twins had no such misgivings. As soon as Niki pulled herself up on the first branch, still in her pristine white blouse and dark blue skirt, they followed after her with their typical enthusiasm and lack of reservations.

Their older brother watched them in grim silence, visibly torn.

"After you?" said Kehuan, motioning to the oak, and the hint of mockery in his voice was just enough to propel Taejin into action.

He looked once again at his younger siblings, already several branches up the tree, and finally started climbing as well, copying their technique. He didn't look very comfortable and kept looking down every few seconds.

"Are you coming?" Kehuan asked Sori, but she just smiled and shook her head, and sat below the tree on her folded jacket.

So he jumped up to get hold of the lowest branch and followed after the rest.

"Rima! Yeona! Stop now! Don't go any higher" Taejin yelled anxiously somewhere above.

Kehuan snickered. He'd always had the impression the twins were two little fiends in angelic disguise, who'd happily do each and every crazy thing Niki suggested, and then some more.

Still, he decided to be magnanimous and show some mercy.

"Niki, stop!" he called.

He couldn't see her now but heard an answer after a moment.

"Why?!"

"Because someone will break a leg or an arm if they fall down!"

Niki answered something unintelligible in a displeased tone, but a moment later he saw her again as she climbed down a few branches. She nestled comfortably in the place where a thick bough grew out of the main trunk. They all reached her a few minutes later and settled around, each finding their own more or less secure and agreeable spot.

"Now what?" asked Taejin edgily, holding to his branch with a white-knuckled grip.

Kehuan snickered once more. He was glad Taejin was back. He had someone to rib again.

Niki shrugged. She leaned her head against the trunk and started humming some melody, switching to singing when she remembered the words. He caught something about being like a moon, and autumn. His Polish was good enough for everyday stuff, but understanding poetry in any form was still far beyond his level of competence. It definitely sounded like another of Alina's favorites, but he didn't know it and was completely thrown when at some point the twins started humming the melody together with Niki. Those three really were like some weird spiritual triplets—the little devils had nice voices, too. Taejin didn't protest anymore; he just sat there and listened, quiet and uncharacteristically solemn.

Sori must've heard the melody as well from her place under the tree because as soon as they went down, she said to Niki, "I'll work out the accompaniment."

Niki beamed at her and bounced forward in the direction of the pond, and Kehuan felt happy. It was a truly beautiful day, the park looked magnificent in the autumn sun, and she was one step closer to all right.

* * *

The new apartment took up the entire last floor of a modern block standing separately at the end of a row of old tenement houses, and it had an extra part in the story addition at the top of the building. It was airy and uncluttered, and when Anna walked around it once again, she didn't mourn the semi-detached house any longer.

"How shall we split the bedrooms?" asked Chen Liang.

There were four: two on the main level, on the opposite side of the hall than the open space of the living room and the kitchen, and two upstairs, each set with their own bathroom.

Anna considered. When they had a baby, it'd be more comfortable to stay on the same level as the kitchen, but on the other hand, they'd have more privacy upstairs, and they could set a rule the older children couldn't venture there without permission.

"I think we should take the upper level," she offered, and waited to see if her opinion would be overruled again, but nobody objected.

Kehuan turned to Niki and asked, switching to Mandarin, "Which room do you want?"

The building was built on an oval plan, and one of the bedrooms on the main level had a shape of a semi-circle with three tall windows on the curving wall, facing east. The other room next to it was smaller, and an ordinary rectangle, but it had an enormous window taking up the entire long wall opposite the door, with a spectacular panoramic view to the south, towards the city center. Kehuan discovered he could glimpse a sliver of water in the distance, behind all the buildings and trees that separated this place from the river.

"You take the big window," Niki told him generously. "I'll take the round room."

"You sure?" Kehuan knew she generally held on to the principle that the bigger her windows, the better.

"Just put the beanbag there," she answered. "For me."

As if he didn't know that.

Anna listened to them talk between themselves and wondered if she'd have to learn Chinese as well. Maybe it wouldn't be necessary. Chen Liang didn't seem to mind them communicating in English, and the boy spoke it very well, too. The girl would get there in time as well, she already had the basics.

Anna was somewhat confused about the status of Veronica in their household. In the beginning, she'd thought the girl would be with them only temporarily, but it didn't look that way now, since they were going to furnish the room for her. She had no idea what was really happening with the girl's father; everybody at the company knew the big boss had been in some accident in June, but nobody had heard any details.

Anna was quite curious about Veronica's origins, too. She'd already asked around and learned that Chen Xiao had never been married, and Chen Liang had been very vague about the relationship between his cousin and the girl's late mother. Veronica didn't look Chinese, but her Mandarin sounded fluent while her English stuttered, so Anna guessed the girl must've been living with her father so far.

A few days later she felt like an idiot after hearing Veronica sing in the kitchen.

"Was Veronica's mother Polish?" she asked Chen Liang when he returned home in the evening.

"Yes," he answered succinctly.

"So what happened to her?"

"She died in the accident," said Chen Liang, and before Anna had time to even think about sharing this juicy tidbit with her colleagues from the company office, he added in a stern tone, "Please keep it to yourself, Anna."

"Of course," she agreed hastily, and that was the end of the conversation.

Chen Liang didn't like the snoopy note in Anna's voice, all the more so because they'd agreed with Chen Xiao to keep the seriousness of his condition a secret from the company grapevine.

He talked to his partner regularly, and Chen Xiao's condition improved enough to allow him to get involved in the business again, in a limited scope. The tentative prognosis was he should be able to eventually regain the use of his upper body, but probably not his legs, and even this much progress was going to take months of rehab, if not years. Chen Xiao was going to stay in Vancouver for it, and apart from all the complications it meant for their business, there was the matter of Niki.

They'd finally talked, the two survivors of the disaster. Chen Xiao decided to bite the bullet and face his adoptive daughter through Skype, and Niki didn't protest, though she looked a little uneasy. Chen Liang and Kehuan left them alone for the talk and didn't know how it went exactly, but they must've been able to reconnect somehow, despite the loss and grief they both struggled with because Chen Xiao told them later that he and Niki agreed to talk once a week from now on.

Later he also told Chen Liang alone that he had every intention of bringing Niki over to Vancouver, but it'd have to wait until he became more or less self-sufficient. Chen Liang told him not to worry, and to leave the girl in his care without any qualms.

He was well aware he wasn't being completely honest with Chen Xiao on this subject, but he didn't know how to tell the guy, especially in his current state, that he needed to leave the girl in Warsaw so Kehuan would stay human.

For now, though, everything was settled.

* * *

Two weeks into the term Chen Liang started receiving phone calls from the school.

The first one was from Niki's form teacher.

"As you are aware, all our students have lessons of Polish," she said, "but the foreign students learn separately from the local children, for obvious reasons."

"Yes, of course."

"We put Veronica in the foreign group since she's been enrolled as a Taiwanese student, but she seems to speak Polish quite well ..."

Chen Liang felt like face-palming.

"It's been a mistake," he said. "She should be in the native children's group, of course."

"Oh. The documents say—"

"Yes, I know, but Veronica's Polish, like her mother. Her citizenship status is pending."

"I was told by our school office that her mother was Ukrainian."

"She was Polish," repeated Chen Liang firmly, remembering Alina's struggles to shake the status of a foreigner.

"All right then. We'll just need you to sign the permission to move

Veronica to the other group."

The next call was from Chen Liang's old friend the music teacher.

"Ms. Mazur," he said with a smile after hearing her greetings, feeling a bit nervous already, and amused at himself for feeling nervous. "What can I do for you?"

"Mr. Chen, I can't tell you how happy I am that we have another of your talented children in our school."

Chen Liang raised his brows and said cautiously, "Oh?"

"We have a policy here of not involving first graders in any after-school classes, at least during the first term, to give them time to settle..."

"Sounds reasonable."

"But I was walking along the school corridor yesterday, and accidentally heard the first-grade class sing, and your girl has such an amazing voice I really had to contact you at once..."

Chen Liang almost snorted. He'd already heard from Kim Hana the popular story about the music teacher prowling the school corridors at the beginning of every new year and eavesdropping at the classroom doors to fish out new musical talents.

"What's your suggestion, Ms. Mazur?" he asked politely.

"Would you agree for Veronica to attend our music club? I know it's against this rule, but I really think she'd benefit—"

"I agree," he interrupted. "If Niki's willing."

"Oh yes, I've already talked to her. I assure you—"

"I trust you," Chen Liang hastily assured her back. "Is that all?"

"Well, yes, I only need you to sign the permission paper..."

Then it was the form teacher again.

"Mr. Chen, I have some matters to discuss with you."

"I only have a few minutes now, Ms. Piontek," Chen Liang warned, checking his watch.

"I'll be quick, then. Firstly, we have a new PE teacher at our school. He is a gymnastics coach, and he's recruiting children from the youngest classes for his new sports club section. It's apparently better with gymnastics to start training as early as possible."

"Does Niki want to sign up?"

"She's an active child, a little overactive sometimes, I'd even say...Very agile, too."

"Let her attend if she wants to," said Chen Liang impatiently. He really had only a few minutes left to his next meeting and wanted to look through his notes before it started.

"We need you to sign—"

"Oh for God's sake!" he exploded, and immediately regretted it. "I'll call you back later, all right?"

But he forgot, and it was Ms. Piontek who called him once more a few days later.

"Mr. Chen, I'm really sorry I have to disrupt your day again."

Chen Liang groaned and thought it was a good thing he was getting married to Anna in a few weeks. Then she'd take over all the tedious calls from school, and he might actually be able to concentrate on his work again.

"I'm sorry I forgot to call you back, Ms. Piontek."

"It's all right, I know you're busy. But I do have two more matters to discuss with you."

Chen Liang felt he owed her for earlier, so he resigned himself to listening to her for as long as necessary.

"First, our art teacher would like Veronica to attend his extra classes..."

"Could we simply assume I agree to all extra activities Niki wants to take up, and be done with it?"

"I'm afraid we still need your signatures in the papers. But you can sign them all in one go, during the parent-teacher conference next Tuesday."

What?! Really, they had it in for him.

"But there's a more important issue," the teacher went on, and the slight note of entertainment disappeared from her voice.

Chen Liang sat straighter. He had a feeling the funny part of their conversation was over.

"Veronica has serious problems with focusing during the lessons. At times she seems to withdraw completely from what is happening in the classroom..."

Oh yes. Here were the dragons.

"I also noticed she doesn't interact much with other children. Maybe apart from the Seong boys, but they are cousins if I understand correctly?"

"Something like that," he muttered.

"And her brother of course. Kehuan's such a caring boy."

"He is?" That was the first time ever Chen Liang heard this word applied to his son. It flummoxed him even more than the fact that Kehuan somehow managed to become Niki's brother at the school.

"Oh yes, he checks up on her quite often during recesses. But what I meant to say is, I'm concerned with Veronica's behavior."

"I understand, Ms. Piontek."

"Maybe we could discuss the situation with our school psychologist after the parent-teacher conference."

Chen Liang sighed. There was no avoiding it: all the things he had planned for the next Tuesday afternoon would have to be rescheduled.

* * *

If she was pressed to say if she liked school, Niki would be in a bind.

She loved the music club, where she could meet with Kehuan and Sori, and other musicians from different classes, and practice with them for the school concert planned for the next month.

The art classes were absolutely fantastic, too, and the art teacher was the first person who gave her some useful tips about how to draw or paint using different techniques, and how to plan her compositions better, and how to choose the best materials for what she wanted to create.

And she also liked the gymnastics club and was glad Rima and Yeona were there as well because it was always fun to spend time with them. In the beginning, they'd been doing all exercises on the mats only, but lately, some new equipment turned up in their gym, a balance beam among other pieces, and she loved it to bits.

The regular lessons were sometimes interesting, too. But it was hard to concentrate for so long every day and stay still at the same place for what felt like an eternity. And on some days, she was really tired and struggled to even stay awake, especially if she'd waken up in the middle of the night again and couldn't go back to sleep after that.

During the recesses, she often felt a desire to find a place to hide away or to go wander on her own around the city again. But it wasn't now like when she'd been in kindergarten last year. She was older now and understood better how it all worked.

Kehuan often found her and kept her company, and when he wasn't there, the twins usually were, and sometimes Sori would come to talk to her, too, and while Niki was generally trying to avoid other kids, especially in big numbers, having the familiar faces around made it all a little easier.

She was meeting every week with this special teacher at school who was supposed to help her pay better attention in classes, but it wasn't working that well. Good thing they'd been mostly learning letters and numbers so far—she already knew them all and could do her homework without much help from Kehuan or Anna.

Anna was living with them now, and that was another thing Niki wasn't sure how she felt about. Sometimes having Anna around was nice. In the morning she'd help Niki comb and braid her hair, and she cooked for them in the afternoon, which was good because Kehuan was always hungry now. Anna also checked if their clothes were clean and their rooms tidy, and that wasn't a bad thing either.

But she often looked as if she was annoyed with them both, and Niki wasn't sure why. And she could tell Kehuan wasn't keen on his stepmother, and since that was the case, Niki was wary of her as well. She didn't like staying at home alone with Anna, so when Kehuan went to his taekwondo club three times a week, she got into the habit of going with him. She sat there on the wooden floor under the wall bars, reading or drawing in her sketchbook while he practiced with Seong Taejin and some other kids, mostly older boys, though there were a few girls as well.

Niki sometimes joined them for the warm-up and stretching, but she didn't feel any inclination to participate in the proper training, which was all about fighting other people. But she could see Kehuan loved that part: he almost vibrated with energy while practicing all those strikes and spinning kicks, deadly focused on each exercise. There was some violent grace to it, almost like a dance, and she kept drawing him in her sketchbook time after time.

* * *

At the beginning of November Chen Liang took Niki and Kehuan to visit Alina's grave. It was a tradition in Poland to light candles and bring flowers for departed relatives and friends on All Saints' Day, and he wanted to observe it.

Niki has never been to a graveyard before, and at first, she thought it looked nice, illuminated by thousands of shimmering vigil lights, with the graves decorated in abundance with asters and chrysanths. But when they were standing at mum's grave, looking in silence at the three small flames of the candles they'd lit for her flickering in the wind, she suddenly felt very lonely and scared. It was difficult to take in that mum was really there, in the ground, under the gray stone slab. Was it heavy? Was it dark in there? Was it very cold? Could mum somehow feel Niki standing there, so close to her? Imagining it made her throat close up again, and she was afraid to speak, in case the words got stuck for good again.

When they returned home, Niki went straight to her room and hid in the space between her bed and the wall, squeezing herself into the corner. She pulled the blanket over her head, and then sat in the dark, pressing cold hands to her chest, until she heard some rustling.

She poked her head out from under the blanket and saw Kehuan sitting next to her on the floor. He looked a little uncomfortable in the tight space because his legs were much longer than hers. The room was dark, but he was reading a book casting light on it with his phone. When he noticed that Niki was looking at him, he said, "Let's make dinner".

So they went to the kitchen, and made their favorite spaghetti with tomatoes, bacon, and eggs, even though Anna had already made something else earlier. Anna got irritated with them again, and this time Niki at least understood why and was sorry. But she felt better all the same.

* * *

Anna had been a part of the Chen family for a few months, and she was getting a little disheartened, mostly because she didn't feel like a part of the family at all.

Chen Liang hadn't been joking when he'd told her in August he had loads of work and no time. She didn't realize the scale of it back then because she saw him almost every day in the office. Now, after she'd quit work, they only met late in the evening and on Sundays. On Saturdays he usually was at home, but occupied with work, having transformed the second room next to their bedroom into a home office.

This was something she felt chagrined about, too: it was supposed to be the room for the baby. Chen Liang said he'd vacate it at once if necessary, but there was no need for the time being: she wasn't even pregnant yet. Sadly, it was true. Anna really hoped it'd happen soon. She felt bored and lonely in the big apartment, left on her own most of the time.

There were the kids, of course. But they spent a big part of every day at school and on some afternoon classes. During the weekends they usually hung out with their cousins, and even if they were at home, it wasn't as if they wanted to socialize with her.

In the beginning, she'd tried really hard to make them like her, but nothing changed much. She had no idea what Chen Liang had meant when he'd said she'd have to take care of them, unless it was washing and ironing their clothes, because those two did everything on their own, and didn't seem to welcome any help or company, and certainly not hers. Kehuan was always his aloof and reserved self, and he never chose to speak to her unless asked a question, and Chen Xiao's daughter was beyond strange. She behaved as if she lived in an alternate universe, and most of the time didn't even notice Anna, even if they were in the same room.

She felt so down. Her mother still refused to see her, and talking to

Renata on the phone just deepened her frustration. The only thing her older sister seemed to have to say were the endless creative variations of "I told you so," and it wasn't what Anna wanted to hear right now. She needed someone to cheer her up and to tell her all would be fine. But there was no one. Renata's bleak predictions came true: Anna's friends and acquaintances were quickly melting away.

Her company colleagues had been the first to go: they didn't seem to feel comfortable around her anymore after she'd married their boss, and she'd been completely alienated in the office. She quit the job in the end; it wasn't as if she still needed it.

As for her older friends, some snickered behind her back at her choice of a husband, commenting that she must've been really desperate. Others, probably jealous of the sudden dramatic upgrade of her living standards, accused her of gold-digging. And of course, there were also those goodhearted people eager to relay to her all the stinging comments, just in case she hadn't heard them yet, or didn't feel bad enough already.

Anna really hoped she'd have a baby soon. It would change the balance of their family situation at once: she was sure Chen Liang wouldn't ignore his own child, and he'd certainly start paying more attention to her, too. And perhaps Kehuan and Veronica's attitude would change as well when a new baby arrived. They might be difficult children, but they weren't really bad, and they certainly cared for each other.

And even if all these hopes proved futile, at least she'd have someone of her own, who'd love her unconditionally and never cast her away.

II

Part Two

6

No Big Deal

Anna woke up at half past seven. Her husband was in Taipei this month, and normally she'd have slept much longer with nobody moving around in the room next to hers, but she was thirsty, and as soon as she opened her eyes, she felt the beginnings of a migraine.

It was only to be expected, she thought sullenly, seeing how she'd cried half the night, and drunk some wine to boot. Staying in bed all day looked like the most attractive option, but right now she needed to go to the bathroom and drink some water. She sat up with a moan and waited out the wave of nausea, glaring at the row of books about pregnancy, child-rearing, and children's psychology sitting on the bookshelf in front of her bed. Then she picked her cardigan from the floor and shrugged it on, getting to her feet.

When she opened the door, she heard voices downstairs in the kitchen, talking and laughing. The fridge door slammed, and Anna winced; her head was throbbing already. She must've asked Kehuan not to do slam the door like that a hundred times at least, but so what. She felt stinging in her eyes, and she clenched her teeth. Stupid hormones.

After visiting the bathroom she sat on the stairs, waiting for them to leave the apartment. She couldn't stand to see them right now. Veronica would look sorry for her, and Kehuan completely indifferent, and she didn't know which upset her more.

Though Kehuan's present behavior should be probably considered progress from the previous years, Anna reflected ironically. She'd sometimes thought the not-even-ten-year-old boy from the time when they'd first met had been more mature than the unstable ball of animosity and resentment he'd become in his early teens, bad-tempered and short-fused all the time, snarling at people and mouthing off acidic remarks.

He'd even happened to berate Veronica sometimes when she received another bad mark at school, and he had to explain to her yet again the same math or science problem. But as soon as anybody else expressed the slightest criticism towards the girl, he blew up, as if he had the monopoly on telling the brat off.

As if he was the one who had to answer the calls from the school, or to sit at the umpteenth meeting with the form teacher and the school psychologist, trying to conjure up a magical solution that would make Veronica pay attention during lessons, or remember about homework, or at least stop cutting classes, dragging along the Seong twins in the bargain. The last issue involved the additional bonus of having to sit next to outraged and puffed-up Kim Haneul, aka Madame Seong, which was a very doubtful pleasure. It had all been on Anna, and the only person who'd ever expressed any gratitude was Chen Xiao.

But Veronica was hailed an art prodigy and a music talent, and she was also a member of the school gymnastics team, and they wouldn't expel her from the school even if she was as thick as a brick, which she wasn't. It would be just nice, Anna commented regularly, if she could show her brilliance in some important subjects as well.

"What are you going to live off? Art? Music? Do you know how hard it is?", she'd asked the girl one day, trying to get through to her with some real-life arguments.

Kehuan heated up at once. "Hard or not, some people do it," he said cuttingly. "And if it doesn't work, she can always find a loaded husband, and live off him."

That one earned him a rare reprimand from Chen Liang, but not even a very severe one.

"Something's wrong with what I said?" Kehuan asked his father with heavy sarcasm, and there was no reply, to Anna's bitter chagrin.

"And leave Niki alone, all of you," the boy continued crossly. "She'll manage. If nothing else, she can speak five languages."

Starting in grade four, each student at the international school had to choose a new language to learn, apart from English and Polish. Kehuan took a shortcut and chose German since he'd already had some basics, and when it was the girl's turn, Anna suggested the same, so he could tutor her if needed. In this one case the precaution turned out completely unnecessary; after three years it was Veronica who could tutor him.

And then there was also Korean. It had taken Anna some time to realize that when the Soengs came over, they weren't talking with her stepson in the same language which Kehuan and Veronica used between themselves. When she'd finally worked it out, she became curious, since these kids were supposed to be Kehuan's relatives. It would be simple to ask Veronica about the language, but she wanted to get to the bottom of it all, and so she found that box with old photos and a few letters and documents in her husband's closet.

She'd known he'd been married before, of course, but it was a completely different thing to know the bare fact, and to stare at the photo of much younger, blatantly happy Chen Liang holding hands with a beautiful, pregnant woman. Anna felt her heart bruise just thinking about these pictures. But at least now she knew which language her unruly ward learned to speak so well simply playing with her friends.

So Kehuan had been right to some degree, but it didn't change the fact that during the primary stage of her education Veronica basically crawled from one grade to another. It finally got a little better last year, when she was in the last, sixth grade.

About the same time, Kehuan's temperament started to cool down at last, but Anna wasn't sure it was really a good thing. She would never say that aloud, but she found the present Kehuan somewhat intimidating. He was already as tall as his father, though still very lean, spoke now in a deep, smooth, dispassionate voice, and his face didn't show any softness anymore, at least not in her presence. Anna sometimes thought she'd actually preferred the nasty, temperamental kid he'd used to be to this emotionless android she had to deal with lately.

Finally, the main door slammed, and they were gone. She leaned her head against the wall and felt the stupid tears leak out from under her closed lids. Time to get up and find some painkillers.

* * *

"Be nice to Anna," Niki admonished Kehuan on their way to school. "I heard her cry at night. I guess it didn't work again."

Kehuan shrugged. "I've no idea why she keeps it up. It's been so many times already I can't even count."

"It's not your call to count. If your father agrees, and she wants to try…"

"I'm not so sure father's going to agree again. I heard him say it was last time."

They fell silent. Anna was a difficult subject.

"Did you wake up at night again?" asked Kehuan after a moment.

"So have you decided if you're going to take part in the concert?" asked Niki at the same time.

"Maybe. Jason keeps pestering me."

They both chuckled.

Kehuan didn't know how it happened exactly because it certainly hadn't been by design, but when Niki had come to the school and to the music club, he'd come by a few additional, well, sort of friends.

It was mainly Yoon Sori's fault. Niki didn't play any musical instruments, and she was paired from the beginning with different instrumentalists for all school performances. Sori, who was a very sociable girl, and quite popular, quickly introduced Niki to her two good friends from the same grade, musicians as well: Mauricio de Silva and Jason Sullivan. And since Niki started meeting with them regularly, so did Kehuan, by default.

While Mauricio attended the state music school for the piano in the afternoons, just as Sori did for the violin, and also played several other instruments, wrote his own pieces of music, and wanted to become a professional music arranger in the future, Jason was just a very average amateur guitarist. But he was a true social butterfly and the chief mingler at the school. During the working meetings of the music club, when they discussed repertoire and configuration of performers for each new event, Jason always opted for big multi-instrumental arrangements, because he was generally of the opinion that the more people, the merrier.

Right now they were in the middle of the debate about the Christmas charity concert, and Jason wanted Kehuan to play, because then Mauricio could ditch the piano and do the lead guitar, and with Jason himself as the second guitarist, and Sori on the violin, and Aneta on the cello, and Ridhaan on the drums, and a whole crowd of people doing the singing, it would be just perfect.

Kehuan still liked to play the piano at home and to make music with Niki, but he rarely got involved in school events. He didn't think he was that good, to begin with—no comparison at all with Mauricio, of course—and he didn't have so much time to spend on the rehearsals. He did a lot of programming for the ICT club, and now also for Chen Xiao, and was preparing for a big math competition apart from that, and he still had his training. But Jason was hard to shake, and Kehuan could tell Niki also hoped he'd join them, so he decided to yield this time.

Close to the school, they met the Seongs, and Taejin fell into step with them while the twins followed behind.

"Are we still on for the swimming lesson tomorrow?" Taejin asked, glancing down at Niki.

She nodded, and Kehuan frowned. "What swimming lesson?"

"Taejin's going to teach me to swim," she answered, sounding a little confused. As if she'd expected him to know about it already. "On Saturdays."

"You are?" Kehuan couldn't remember hearing about it before. "Good idea. She can't swim at all."

"I know," said Taejin with a peculiar note in his voice, and Kehuan eyed him narrowly. But his cousin didn't add anything else, and neither did the cat.

"Yeah, let's do it," Kehuan said, turning the idea over in his mind. "Should've thought about it earlier. What time?"

He'd learned to swim in middle school, when they could choose to have PE at the pool twice a week, and he'd enjoyed it a lot, though he'd never got to be as good at it as the Seongs, who'd all been swimming regularly since kindergarten. But Niki didn't go to the pool; she did the gymnastics training instead.

Taejin wasn't answering, so he asked impatiently once again, "What time, man?"

"Ten," his cousin replied finally.

They were already at the gates, so Kehuan reminded Niki, "I'll come to eat with you later," and she nodded with a smile.

Food was still a bit of a problem with her. Even after such a long time she wasn't able to eat much at one go. At home, they cooked for themselves regularly, but Niki wasn't a fan of the school canteen, which was usually very busy. She preferred to take some snacks to school in her backpack, but more often than not they rode back home with her in the afternoon because she forgot about them during the day. So the best solution they'd worked out over the years was someone eating together with her as often as possible, and it had become a sort of a game among their friends, with bragging rights, who'd manage to squeeze more food into the cat. But she was still as thin as a rail; it was difficult to get enough nutrition in this system, what with the gymnastics and all the other stuff she did.

They split into different buildings then, as Kehuan and Taejin were in the high school now, and Niki stopped and waited for the twins to catch up to her.

She was glad Kehuan had said yes to the concert, and she was looking forward to the swimming lesson tomorrow, too, but then Taeyeon murmured, "Harpy alert, level three," and she lost a little of her good humor at the sight of the three girls approaching the entrance to the building from the opposite direction.

She glanced at the twins. They'd both put on the expression of long-suffering martyrdom, and Niki snickered. Time to put up the shields.

* * *

Kamila Bartnik had a deeply ingrained appreciation of self-reliance, as well as equality and justice, and Veronica Chen grated on her nerves like you wouldn't believe, since the very first day she'd laid eyes on the girl.

Kamila had come to the international school in the middle of the last year of primary school, and it hadn't been an easy start. But she was ambitious, and hard-working, and yes, very self-reliant as well, and firmly believed she could do anything if she only put her mind to it, so after a few months, she was at the top of the class. And Veronica Chen was at the very tail-end, but everybody still treated her like a princess.

It was hard to believe what that girl could get away with.

She slept in the classroom, regularly. She played hooky, also regularly. Homework, forget. She often behaved as if she didn't see or hear other people, and Kamila was sure that after half a year of them being in the same class Veronica had no idea what her name was. It was irritating as hell, and she couldn't understand why their other classmates tolerated it, and not only that: most of them seemed to really like the annoying girl, for no apparent reason. And it was only the tip of the iceberg.

Let's take the food nonsense. Kamila didn't get it: a whole bunch of people seemed to consider it their duty and pleasure to feed the girl all day long. There were the two Korean brothers from their class, who usually went MIA together with her, and Sori Yoon from the third grade. Veronica's brother, of course, and his best friend, who'd both come from the other building and found her during recess just so they could jam some rice balls down her throat. As if it wasn't already ridiculous enough, just a few days earlier Kamila witnessed Jason Sullivan, of all people, try to cajole the princess into eating some cashews in the middle of the rehearsal, as if the girl was five and couldn't decide on her own if she was hungry or not, for god's sake.

Then there was the cult. Veronica was a talented artist, and all right, but the amount of fawning she received both from their art teacher and from other students over every new piece she created was disgusting. And the same went for her singing.

Here was where their interests really clashed because Kamila could sing, too, and so did her best pals, Marlena and Ola, and that was why they'd joined the music club. But everybody there also thought Veronica Chen was all that, and she was designated as the soloist for every event, while the three of them were eternally relegated to the choirs or the backing vocals. It was totally unfair.

* * *

"So shall we sing the carols, or Christmas pop standards?" asked Ms. Mazur for the third time.

They had a problem with coming to an agreement because of their different backgrounds. Since it was a Christmas charity concert, the people from catholic or protestant families, like Jason and Mauricio, and most of the Polish kids, and also Elena, the Romanian girl whose family belonged to the orthodox church, opted for the carols. But there were also atheist students at the club, and a few Buddhists and Muslims, and they weren't crazy about the idea.

On the other hand, nobody was keen on doing the omnipresent Christmas pop songs, even if they didn't have any religious connotations, because they all agreed they were fed up with them. Niki certainly was.

"Look at it from a different angle. Carols aren't just religious songs," the teacher reasoned. "They are important pieces of culture in many countries."

"Still," said Ridhaan, who was Hindu. "Ms. Mazur, with all due respect, I'd prefer not to have to sing any Ave Marias and Christ-is-the-lords."

Ms. Mazur shook her head and chuckled, and Kamila raised her hand.

"What if we do carols," she said, "but those which aren't so serious and prayer-like."

"For example?" asked Elena with interest.

"Take 'I saw three ships'."

"There's still Mary and Christ in it," noticed Jason.

"Yes, but the lyrics don't have much to do with the biblical story. They are completely idiotic, honestly speaking."

That elicited some gasps from the three British students present and muffled snorts of laughter from others. That was Kamila in a nutshell, Niki thought. Brilliant and crude at once.

"But are there even more carols like that?" asked Ridhaan doubtfully, considering the compromise. "In different languages? Because that was the original idea, yes?"

"'Los peces en el rio'," said Mauricio. "Spanish. Also completely idiotic."

More mirth sparked across the room.

"Let's brainstorm," said Ms. Mazur. "All idiotic carols that come to your mind, let's make a list. Jason, write them all on the board."

A lively discussion followed, and Niki's attention drifted away. She noticed Kamila grin at something Ridhaan said to her, and once again regretted how things were between them because that girl was awesome. Crazy smart, and funny, and self-confident, and she also had a nice warm voice and a good ear for music. Unfortunately, she hated Niki's guts.

Niki understood it, at least partially. She'd actually tried many times to cede the main vocal to other people, and she could tell Kamila and her friends really longed for some recognition. But the music club was a democratic institution governed by its members, and while the teacher supported her arguments, most students were of the opinion that fairness had nothing to do with it—the soloist parts should be done by the best singer, and that's that. Niki thought they were all influenced by Mauricio, the music club's president for the last three years.

"Forget it, Niki," he told her each time she spoke up, "they'll live. No big deal."

Mauricio was an obsessed artist, and the only thing he cared about was creating the best music possible. He wasn't bothered at all by such minor issues like hurt feelings, slighted ambitions, and trodden upon toes.

Niki saw Kehuan enter the room, and she grinned. This concert was going to be fun.

* * *

In the middle of November, when the rehearsals for the Christmas event were already in full swing, Chris Morton appeared at the school.

Chris wasn't enamored with the fact that he had to start at a new place in the middle of the year, but his father had just got this new job, and they'd just moved to Warsaw from Dublin, and it couldn't be helped. One good thing was, he'd already met a great guy from the school. Their fathers used to know each other as boys, and as soon as it turned out they were going to work together now, the Sullivans invited the Mortons over for a family dinner.

Jason was older than Chris by a year, but he was easy-going and friendly. They chatted about different things, and then the conversation drifted towards music. And when Jason said that he played the acoustic guitar, and also showed Chris the electric guitar he'd got for his last birthday, Chris, very excited, shared with him his long-cherished idea to start a band.

"I'm at the music club at the school already", Jason replied, not as impressed with the plan as Chris had hoped.

"But I bet it's all very traditional there," said Chris disdainfully. "We had something like that in Dublin as well. Kids singing in a choir and all that. What I have in mind is a band: electric guitar, bass, keyboard, and drums."

"But it's more fun with other instruments, too," Jason objected. "And a choir isn't always a bad thing—"

"Yeah, yeah," Chris said impatiently, "but if we had a band, we could play what we like, you know? Not what a teacher gives us..."

"We basically play whatever we want at the club. Our teacher gives us free hand."

Chris was already regretting he'd even started the topic. The guy was hopeless with his music club.

"But I get what you mean," Jason said unexpectedly. "It'd be something a little different. What's your instrument?"

"The bass," Chris said proudly. "We'd need a keyboard player, too, and a drummer, and a good lead vocal. Unless you sing?"

Jason shook his head. "Not well enough."

"Me neither. But maybe we could organize an audition at the school.

What do you think? Will it fly?"

"Yeah, sure. There are many people who are good... And there's this one girl with the amazing voice, only I don't know if she'd be interested."

* * *

On his first day at the school, Chris was surprised by how multi-national the student body here was; he hadn't expected that. Jason was showing him around, muttering funny and informative comments.

"That's Sori Yoon over there, from my class," he said at a certain point, and his voice suddenly became all warm and taffy-like. "She's a violin fiend."

An Asian girl with a cute round face, surrounded by a group of friends, smiled from a distance, producing two dimples, and Chris nodded. "Nice."

The girl must've heard her name called then because she suddenly turned around and made a few steps to talk with two guys, also Asian, who'd just entered the school hall through the main door. Chris noticed that their appearance caused some stir among other students, which wasn't surprising. They were kind of hard to miss, both taller and older than other kids here, and good-looking to boot.

"Who's the brooding hero?" he asked, nudging Jason.

"Kehuan Chen," Jason said. There was distinct hero-worship in his voice now. "An ICT hotshot, and a math genie."

"For real?" Chris eyed the guy curiously and grinned. "A nerd, eh? I thought maybe he'd dropped by to commit mass murder or something."

"Yeah, well. He isn't too friendly."

"And the smiley face?" Chris watched with fascination as the crowd of students parted in front of these guys as they moved along the school corridor. You needed some presence to evoke a reaction like that.

"Taejin Seong. Looks harmless, but don't tease the tiger. He's got a temper, and he does martial arts. Chen as well."

"They aren't brothers, are they?"

"Cousins. They're in high school, actually, I wonder why they came. To see Niki, probably..."

Before Chris had time to ask who Niki was, Jason pointed to a small clutch of girls in the intersecting corridor, next to the lockers. "Ola, Marlena and Kamila. Come say hello, they all sing."

Jason introduced him to the girls and then ran off after the cute Asian violinist, leaving Chris to his own devices.

* * *

Chris liked the trio. They were all buoyant and pretty, especially Kamila, the reddish blonde with an impertinent face and great hazel eyes. All of them were also very interested in doing the audition for the band, and he felt smug; he'd been right they didn't have anything like that here.

But then, even as he was talking to them, he noticed that another girl go out of a classroom and walk down the hallway.

Chris stared as she came closer, very slim and graceful, and somehow completely isolated from all the people around. He thought she looked like an adolescent elf lost in the human world, in that flowing white shirt, with enormous blue eyes and thin face, and the long, long hair, braided on both sides at the top of her head and then let loose, a dark waterfall cascading down her body. He couldn't stop watching, entranced, and when she was only two steps away, and her eyes touched him for a brief moment, his stomach clenched. But she'd already moved past him and round the corner, disappearing from his line of view.

"Who's that?" he asked the girls, pointing with his chin.

They shared a meaningful look, and Marlena said dryly, "The princess."

"Don't expect her to notice you," Kamila added in a tone of friendly advice. "She doesn't see ordinary mortals."

Chris didn't believe them. The girl looked a little strange, but not haughty or arrogant at all. He'd had some experience with pretty, haughty, and arrogant, as he'd had a year's worth of crush on someone like that at his old school.

"Is she in your class?"

"Yes, but seriously, don't waste your time."

When the first bell rang, he walked them to their classroom and waited by the door. Two minutes later the elfin girl appeared, with a piece of sushi or something similar in her hand.

"Hi, I'm Chris—" Her eyes moved over him as if he wasn't there, and she didn't even slow down as she passed him and entered the room.

Kamila was already inside, but Ola and Marlena roared with laughter at his stupefied expression.

"Told you," Ola said unmercifully.

Chris felt his face go crimson with the hot wave of humiliation and anger. He'd promised himself when he was leaving Dublin that he'd never allow anybody to treat him like dirt again, and here it was.

But this time it'd be different. This time he wouldn't let any pretty girl walk all over him, no matter what.

* * *

"Did you see that guy gawk at Niki like a moron?" asked Taejin, sounding cross, as they were walking back to the high school building.

Kehuan had seen and been annoyed as well, but now he was rather taken aback by his cousin's strong reaction.

"Do you know him?" he asked after a moment. He didn't, but that was a given: he wouldn't recognize ninety-nine percent of the people from the school if he met them somewhere else.

"No, he must be new. I bet Jason will know." It sounded as if Taejin was planning to investigate the new boy, and Kehuan felt amused.

"You don't have to go there with me every time, you know," he remarked after a moment.

"It's cool."

Something had changed about Taejin's attitude towards Niki, and Kehuan didn't know when and how, and why it happened, and he also wasn't sure how he felt about this change. In the past Taejin had often been at odds with his younger brothers' honorary triplet because he'd blamed Niki for all their risky ideas and wayward behaviors, which of course was complete rubbish. He also used to complain that Niki and Kehuan were constantly joined at the hip, which forced him to spend too much time in her company.

Not anymore.

Kehuan noticed it for the first time in September, when he saw Taejin contemplate the piece of art hanging on the wall over Kehuan's bed. It was Niki's previous year's production, but each of them claimed they had a share in its creation as well since they all gathered materials for it during the holiday.

After that first year when they'd gone back to Korea for the summer, the Seongs changed tack. Maybe they'd realized Kim Hana was onto something when she said there were enough fascinating places in Europe, or maybe it was simply the considerable cost of the plane tickets for five people. Anyway, they stayed in Poland for the next vacation, and they visited many other places in the following years: Ireland and Spain, Croatia and Norway. But Kim Hana and Yoon Sori developed a routine of spending one week every year at the Baltic seaside, and they usually took the Soeng boys, Kehuan and Niki with them. And during that holiday one year ago Niki decided to make something to commemorate this tradition.

For the whole week, she'd collected all pieces of driftwood she could find on the beach, as well as shells and rare pieces of amber, and demanded that everybody did the same. They obeyed, though Taejin grumbled about it every day. Then she brought all this loot home, to Anna's great displeasure, and spend a month or so tying the driftwood together with pieces of white cotton string. Nobody had any idea what it was supposed to be until one day Niki asked Kehuan to help her hang the whole construction on the wall over his bed, since she didn't have any free space left on the walls in her own room. Kehuan remembered the sense of wonder he felt when they put the thing up, and the driftwood suddenly transformed into a suggestion of a wave crashing forward from the wall into the room. During the next weeks Niki strung up on it all those shells and pieces of amber she'd bullied them into gathering, and when she finally declared it ready, everybody who saw the structure was in awe.

Taejin was a frequent guest in Kehuan's room, but that day in September he'd stared at Niki's creation as if it had been his first time seeing it.

Finally, he turned to her and said, "Niki, you have to make something like that for me, too."

Kehuan's hackles went immediately up, but Niki, sitting with her sketchbook in the beanbag next to the window, didn't even raise her head and just made a non-committal sound.

"I still have that card with Chinese calligraphy you once made for me," Taejin spoke again.

At that, she finally looked up and beamed at him, and Kehuan felt irked even more.

This year they'd started high school and moved to the other building. Taejin was very satisfied with the promotion, so the first time Kehuan had gone to the old place to have lunch with the cat, he hadn't expected his cousin to follow. But he did follow, and he kept coming every time now, and Kehuan couldn't escape the funny feeling that Taejin suddenly seemed to like Niki's company very much.

If it were anybody else, he'd think the guy fancied the girl and was trying to get together with her. But it was Niki, who was twelve, apart from other things, and Seong Taejin, who'd known them both for years and wasn't suicidal, and so it was a riddle.

But not of the enjoyable kind.

* * *

Even if Kehuan couldn't pinpoint the date of the change, Taejin himself could, and without any problems, because it happened on the day when Niki almost drowned.

This year in August Kehuan went for two weeks to Vancouver to Chen Xiao, who wanted to include him in his new programming project on big data. Niki didn't want to go, though she'd been invited, of course. She still wasn't completely comfortable with seeing Chen Xiao. This one time when he'd come to Warsaw three years ago, finally able to move his wheelchair by himself, she'd been stressed out and unsettled in his presence all the time, and after some debates with the psychologist, her adoptive father decided not to push her.

So Kehuan went to Canada alone, and Niki in the meantime joined Kim Hana, Sori, and the Seong boys on their trip to the lake district. They didn't bother with any fanciful accommodation, and just put up two tents on a small campsite at the high bank of the lake.

On the second day, Kim Hana and the twins ventured on an expedition to the nearest village to bring some food supplies, and Sori wanted to read a book, so Taejin and Niki went down to the lake to take a swim on their own.

Taejin had been going to the swimming pool every week since he'd been five, and he could swim like a fish, so it didn't even occur to him that Niki might not know how to do it until she lost the ground under her feet while they were horsing around, and started flailing, and choking, and panicking, and pulling at his hair trying to get hold of something to keep her head over the water. Niki looked like a skinny little thing, but she was a gymnast and had quite a lot of strength, and fear made her thrash and fight furiously. Taejin barely managed to drag her to the shore.

They both fell down in the shallow water, Taejin on his back, and Niki on her side, and lay there gasping. She was completely limp, and he was too exhausted to move her further away.

"You… okay?" he finally managed to wheeze out.

Niki just moved her fingers.

A few minutes later Taejin sat up. For a moment he watched her long dark hair undulate in the shallow water and then felt goosebumps rise all over his body.

"You didn't say you couldn't swim," he said in an accusatory tone.

"I didn't know I couldn't swim," she answered, and flopped over to her back, sprawling her arms to the sides.

Taejin just snorted at that and turned his face up to the sun. His heart started to quiet down. Then a sudden thought struck him, and he groaned.

"Kehuan's going to kill me," he said, not joking.

Niki sat up, too. For a moment they looked at each other in silence, and then the corners of her lips twitched, and her large crystalline eyes glittered mischievously.

"Let's keep it a secret," she said in a low voice, giving him a conspiratorial little smile. "Nothing happened, after all. No big deal."

Taejin got a sudden glimpse into what she'd be like in a few years, and his heart skipped a beat. Right on the heels of this first revelation came another one, that it was fun to have secrets with Chen Veronica.

"All right," he said, gazing at her with a feeling of a groundbreaking discovery. "But I think you need to learn to swim."

"So you teach me," said Niki carelessly, wringing water out of her hair with both hands, and his heart skipped another beat.

Taejin had hardly ever talked to her before without Kehuan being around, and during that week he felt more and more perplexed by his own earlier obtuseness. Niki was one of a kind, and the more time he spent with her, the more bewitched he was. He never forgot her age and was well aware it wasn't the time to start anything now; it would be crass. But he was determined not to let anybody beat him to asking her out in the future.

When they all met again back in Warsaw, he realized philosophically it would be only a matter of time before Kehuan noticed something. Later, he also understood his best friend's dismay and wariness and didn't hold it against him. Taejin had a younger female cousin as well, as close as a sister, and he eyed each guy who approached Sori with the same distrust; it was his role, after all.

But he was sure it was all going to work out in time. He had only the best intentions towards Niki, and sooner or later Kehuan would see it as well.

* * *

The Christmas charity concert was just around the corner now, and bigger or smaller rehearsals went on almost every day.

In most schools it wouldn't be such a serious affair, just some children singing carols before Christmas, but the international school wasn't normal in many aspects, and parents were one of them. They were all a very ambitious lot, with big expectations of their kids, and they paid plenty of money for the school and had equally big expectations of all activities carried out there.

In other words, if the school was doing a charity concert, the parents didn't mind shelling out some extra cash, but they wanted to see their kids in a professionally organized affair with top-level performance.

And so there were special people responsible only for the technical aspects, like the sound system and the lights, and others to rearrange the scene between songs when the makeup of the performing group changed, and there had also been a serious discussion about what the dressing code for the musicians and the singers should be, and a whole separate business of organizing a café outside the concert room.

Mauricio de Silva was responsible for the entire music arrangement, and he'd been a little nonplussed in October when Niki came to him with the idea of including in the event a group of kids from the youngest grades of primary. She'd thought the children's voices would go well with the Christmas motive.

Mauricio had been skeptical.

"They can't sing well yet," he told her, shaking his head. "Most of them are completely out of tune, and they don't listen when you correct them." He'd tried it one time in the past and given up very soon.

"I'll practice with them," she insisted. "They can be a choir just for a couple of pieces."

"Niki, it will ruin the songs."

"It won't," she said stubbornly. "I'll ask Ms. Mazur to draft only those kids who are willing to work hard. It'll be great, you'll see."

Mauricio rarely listened to other people in matters related to music, but Niki was an exception, and he gave in. It didn't mean he was completely rid of his reservations, but she turned out as good as her word, and in December he had to admit the ten kids who'd persevered through the whole ordeal were an adorable element of the performance.

It was also very funny to watch them with Niki, all of them staring at her with devoted eyes and following her around like little ducklings trailing behind their mother-duck. The girl was so withdrawn that she looked at a complete loss now about what to do with this new tail she'd accidentally acquired.

Mauricio was totally in love with both Chens, in several different ways. He'd had a good old crush on Kehuan for years, and Niki was his muse, but what he loved the most was watching them together.

He'd never understood how other people weren't fascinated by it. Separately, each of them was an oddball. They were always out of sync with the outside world, Kehuan aloof and forbidding and Niki lost somewhere in her inner space. But as soon as they got together, they both metamorphosed: Kehuan talked and grinned, and laughed, and Niki was suddenly awake, and when she was awake, she literally sparkled.

So Mauricio always did whatever he could to have them both in his productions, and was delighted it'd worked out this time. It had been a good idea to enlist Jason's help on it.

* * *

In the meantime, Chris Morton's music band endeavors weren't going so well.

They'd already held an audition for instrumentalists, but he wasn't thrilled with the results. Jason had assured him he'd have his pick since half the students at the school played this or that musical instrument; all kids here did lots and lots of extracurricular stuff. But most people who turned up for the trials were quite young, and even the older ones weren't very good.

"I don't get it," he grouched to Jason. "Don't you really have anybody better here? You said there were many."

"Yes, but they're already very busy," Jason explained patiently.

They both fell silent for a moment, each preoccupied with their own thoughts.

"The vocal trials are on Friday. Do you think they'll go better?" Chris asked, somewhat disheartened.

"You know what," interrupted Jason, "what you need is some good PR, my man."

"Yeah?"

"Yeah. I'll ask some of my pals from the music club to come and give you support on Friday."

Chris rolled his eyes. He was seriously fed up with all the mentions of the music club.

"If Mauricio shows up, for example," Jason continued, unaware, "it'll send out a message that it's something to be in on."

"All right, all right," Chris conceded, motioning with his hand. "Go ahead. If it helps..."

The audition took place on Friday afternoon in the assembly hall, where all school plays and concerts were held. It looked like a regular concert hall, just a smallish one, with a proper stage at the front, theater seats in descending rows, no windows, and a ramp of lights under the ceiling. Chris thought it was a rather overblown setting for the level of skills he'd had to do with so far, but the school was loaded, and so were most parents, so he guessed they could afford it if they wanted to see their offspring look like professionals, even if they didn't sound like ones.

People started to trickle in a few minutes before the start of the trials, and he saw Ola and Marlena come in, so he went to say hello.

"Where's Kamila?" he asked.

"She's not coming," Marlena answered. "Something came up at home."

"But we're here," Ola chirped enthusiastically, dragging him by elbow towards the stage. "Go get things started."

* * *

Mauricio was sitting in one of the middle rows, watching Jason on the stage and the new boy, who hadn't registered on his radar so far. Jason said the guy was driven and played the bass well enough, but Mauricio had been crazy busy lately and hadn't had time to check him out yet.

The boy was quite good-looking, with messy brown hair and brown eyes, and a cocky smirk on his face. Perhaps the last feature didn't bode so well for his career here, but Mauricio was inclined to give him the benefit of the doubt.

There were many younger kids present already, the hopeful prospects for the music band, he guessed, occupying the front rows.

He heard the top door open and looked back to see Ridhaan and Elena come in, and a moment later Kehuan Chen with his best friend. Mauricio felt the usual little flutter in his chest. Seriously, the guy was gorgeous. They all raised hands in a greeting, and he motioned them to sit next to him, but Sori entered right then, with her violin case hung over the shoulder, and she came down the few steps to talk to them. A moment later Taeyeon and Taerim Soeng also made an appearance.

Mauricio smiled. He hadn't seen much of those two this autumn. They used to be regular guests at the music club in the past, as they often sang backing vocals for Niki, but right now they were undergoing the voice mutation, and both screeched like old doors. Out of commission for the time being. He guessed they'd heard Jason entreat Niki to come, and decided to tag along. Ah yes, Taeyeon even had her backpack slung over his shoulder, so she couldn't be far behind.

Sori with Elena, Aneta, and Ridhaan came to sit next to him, and the Seong boys all went down and sat together at the end of the third row. Kehuan remained on the steps.

The lights over the auditorium dimmed down, and the audition started.

* * *

Chris had to admit that Jason's PR action brought great results.

He couldn't see much of the auditorium now because the big room was dark, the stage the only part of it properly lit, but he'd seen earlier there were a lot of people present. There were also many candidates for the audition today, some actually not half bad. He was already thinking about redoing the trials for instrumentalists as well.

The side door at the bottom of the auditorium opened, and through the rectangle of light in came Veronica Chen.

Chris had seen her many times since that memorable first encounter a month ago, and unfortunately, he hadn't been able to completely recover from the enchantment she'd cast over him. She was still lovely in his eyes, and since he'd heard from Kamila the girl could sing quite well, he was also a little curious about it. But he couldn't stand her at the same time because she'd never once looked at him, though he'd been in their classroom many times, and she really didn't pay much attention to other people either, except for the two identical pretty boys who seemed to be there to entertain her and provide her with food. Veronica Chen was exactly as bad as Kamila had told him on the first day, and he got angrier every time he saw her.

And now, what, she came to do the audition for his band? He didn't think so.

Chris stood up from his chair at the edge of the stage, where he'd listened to the candidates while Jason had played the accompaniment for them, and marched down the few steps.

"You don't need to stay," he told the girl, loud and clear.

She looked up at him with surprise, and then turned around, like an idiot, to check if maybe he was talking to somebody else standing behind her. Freaking princess.

"I said you don't need to stay for the audition," Chris reiterated crossly. "I don't need anybody with your attitude."

"Do you know me?" she asked, bewildered.

"Chris, what are you doing?!" he heard Jason's frantic whisper behind his back.

"I don't need to know you," Chris spat with all the disgust and chagrin he'd brought over from Dublin. "I've met people like you before."

"People like me," Veronica echoed slowly, and Chris suddenly realized the dark assembly hall had become deadly quiet.

He turned around and looked at the stage. The boy who'd been preparing for the audition when she came in was now standing there with his eyes bulging, jaw hanging open, and the microphone dangling from his limp hand, and behind him, Jason had risen from the chair and was gaping at

Chris with horror-stricken eyes. The silence was deafening.

And then there was the sound of measured steps descending in the dark from the top of the unilluminated auditorium. A few seconds later a tall black figure emerged from the darkness behind Veronica, and when Chris saw the face of the person at her back, the air around him froze over. A half-forgotten memory resurfaced, and he heard Jason's voice in his head say "Kehuan Chen", and his own laughing words that the guy looked as if he was considering mass murder.

He didn't look that way now. He looked as if he was absolutely ready to immediately commit just one, very individual homicide. He glowered at Chris with furious, pitch-black eyes, his face hardened in a malevolent snarl, and Chris involuntarily took a step back, and then another.

Chen snorted contemptuously, grabbed Veronica's hand, and spoke to her in a low voice, "Let's go, Niki."

Her fingers tightened on the guy's hand and she simply turned around, and then they both walked out of the room through the same door she'd entered, without one backward glance.

Chris heard a noise behind him then, the clap of the seats folding, and when he wheeled round, there was what looked like a whole row of people standing up and looking daggers down at him. But no, there were really just three of them, the two identical pretty boys from Veronica's class and another one, older and bigger, but still similar enough. Chris had another déjà vu and heard Jason say in his head, "Don't tease the tiger," and he felt a little weak in the knees.

"Who's the idiot?" asked lightly one pretty boy.

"Chris Moron, I think," said the other one.

"Never heard a better name," noticed the first one with a smirk, and Chris heard snickers fly around the room.

"Let's go," rumbled the older guy darkly, echoing Chen, and they all walked past Chris and out of the room. Right behind them was the cute Asian girl Jason liked, with several other people.

There were more sounds of folding seats. The top door opened as well, and people started walking out, one after another, and when he turned back, he saw that the younger kids at the front who came to be auditioned were talking among themselves and also gathering their stuff.

It was like a nightmare. Chris had already grasped he'd blundered in a big way, but he only understood how big when he saw Jason walk off the stage, with his guitar already packed in the case.

"Jason..." he started, uncertain.

"Do me a favor, and don't talk to me ever again," Jason answered coldly, and a moment later he was gone.

The room was empty.

* * *

The charity concert was one week later, right before the Christmas break.

Chris sat in the audience, waiting for it to begin, and wondered for the hundredth time how he could have been such a dummy. About Veronica Chen, he could actually trace the path his mind had traveled, and he put a lot of blame on Aileen back in Dublin, and even more on the trio from Veronica's class. What infuriated him most was that they were still on good terms with everybody, while he'd become the school pariah. Some people were probably aware that Kamila, Ola, and Marlena bore some grudge against Veronica, but those girls knew the lay of the land much better than him and treaded carefully. And he, like a fool, had swallowed everything they'd said, and never tried to cross-check the facts or make sure if antagonizing the elfin princess would be prudent, or even safe.

How could he have missed, for example, that the guy he'd witnessed on the first day part the sea of students like some freaking Moses, and the lovely girl he'd followed to her classroom shared the same family name? They didn't look alike at all, that's how, though it was a thin excuse. Everybody here apparently knew they were half-siblings, or something like that, and was the only idiot who'd missed the memo.

Another thing. There was only one Korean family at the school; he'd heard many people refer to them as the Korean clan. So how could he have not realized that the popular girl Jason was so smitten with, the guy who was Chen's best friend, and the obnoxious twins from Veronica's class were all related? And they did look alike to boot, so he couldn't even use this excuse in their case.

But he'd also been a total dumbbell about the whole thing with the music band. He'd come to the school from another country, and assumed, just because he didn't know anything about this place, that he would be a celebrity here. Jason had tried to tell him, but Chris didn't listen. He'd never once tried to meet any of those people Jason mentioned in such complimentary tones. During that last week he'd made up for a lot of his previous ignorance, and every new crumb of information he gathered made him want to kick himself.

The concert was about to start, and Chris looked around. He'd hesitated a lot at home if he should even come today, but curiosity won. He'd been interested, for example, if they'd be able to fill up the hall. He needn't have worried: right now some kids were carrying inside additional folding chairs, to put them on the walkways for all those people who didn't have seats. After a moment, the lights over the auditorium began to dim, the room quieted, and the stage lit up, with chairs, music stands, and some instruments already there.

Kamila entered the stage, looking great in a red dress, and the audience clapped. Chris ground his teeth and promised himself they'd get even one day.

She said a few words of welcome, and then the musicians appeared, all guys in white shirts and black pants, and all girls in red dresses. Chris could name them all now.

The middle-sized boy with unremarkable face and dark hair who was just taking the guitar in his hands was Mauricio de Silva, the main honcho of the infamous music club. The beanpole with the shaggy mop of blond hair next to him was Jason, of course, and Chris felt a pang of regret yet again.

The dusky guy behind the drums was called Ridhaan Khatri, the willowy girl with the flute was Elena Negreanu, and the roundish, smiling girl with dark blond hair and the cello was Aneta Markowicz from Chris's own class.

Next to her Sori Yoon had just started tuning her violin to the sound of the piano, and when Chris checked the pianist, the sight sent a very unpleasant chill down his spine because he turned out to be nobody else but Kehuan Chen. Could it get any worse?

It could, he decided ten seconds later, when the singers went out, and Veronica Chen in a flowing red dress took the position at the very front of the scene. She looked much more there today when she turned her head back for a moment to smile at the band. Chris, who was sitting on the far end of his row and could see the scene at just the right angle, noticed also that extra grin she sent to her homicidal maniac of a brother back at the piano.

So she could sing well enough to be the soloist, he noted dully. Let's hear it, then.

They'd just finished tuning the instruments, a short pause ensued, and the concert began, and Chris Morton was finally able to comprehend the full extent of his idiocy.

It was the best amateur performance he'd ever heard. The music arrangement of the well-known carols was inspired, all the instrumentalists and singers were really good, and Yoon and Khatri were plainly brilliant. It was also obvious they'd put a lot of work into it because their collaboration was perfect; Chris could appreciate it well as another musician.

And Veronica Chen sang like an angel.

He almost burst with bitter laughter when he remembered how he'd kicked her out of the audition. But then he realized that he hadn't, not really, because she hadn't been there to do the audition, to begin with. She'd just come to show her support, at Jason's request. Chris had never felt so crestfallen and mortified in his entire life.

The last song was some Polish carol he'd never heard before—he didn't know any Polish carols, exactly speaking—and there was now the entire crowd of people on the stage, singing in parts, including a group of young children at the front of the scene, who looked a little unnerved by the large audience but did surprisingly well. Veronica stood and sang together with them. In this last song, she only did a solo for the ending line of each chorus, but it was enough to make his heart squeeze every time.

After it was over, applause raised the roof. People stood up at once, which was only to be expected when they cheered for their kids, of course. Chris heard loud whoops and whistles behind him, and he turned round to see all the Seong boys just two rows above, standing up as well and clapping like crazy with wide grins on their faces. There were several smiling adults next to them, who looked like family.

And then his eyes fell on a good-looking, brown-haired woman in her forties, still down in the seat. Her hands lay limp on her lap and she was staring at the stage with glassy eyes, and Chris thought with mean satisfaction that apparently, there was one person in the assembly hall today who was just as miserable as himself, after all.

7

Pay the Price

Niki broke her right wrist in late spring of the first grade of middle school. It happened during the gymnastics training, and it hadn't been the first injury she'd sustained over the years, but this one turned out really pesky.

Her hand was put in a cast up to the elbow for six weeks, and she couldn't even write at school. Actually, she had no quarrel with that particular effect of the accident and secretly thought it could even be considered the silver lining in the whole situation, but she wasn't able to draw or paint either, and that was a completely different story. And when the cast finally went off in June, it turned out her right hand wasn't working exactly as it should, so she spent the entire summer getting physical therapy and doing all kinds of exercises, and trying not to panic.

Kehuan stayed in Warsaw as well. He said he had no problem with skipping the annual taekwondo summer camp because he was getting too old for such outings anyway. And he declared there was no real need for him to go to Vancouver either; his collaboration with Chen Xiao went well enough through the Internet.

But there was also that camp in the mountains in preparation for the international math competition for which he qualified in the spring, and the competition itself, and Niki tried to convince him to stick to at least this one element of his plans.

Kehuan just shrugged and told her that math was the same everywhere. He exchanged email addresses with some guy he'd met during the national finals, and simply solved at home all the math problems the guy sent him from the camp. As for the competition, he said he didn't really care about it. After the finals, he already had a guaranteed place at any university in Poland he'd like to go to after school.

"Chill, Niki," he told her when she kept fretting over it, "I can always do it next year if I really want."

"You'd have to go again through the eliminations, and semifinals, and finals," Niki knew very well it wasn't as simple as he made it sound.

"So what?" Kehuan answered loftily. "You think I can't do it? Piece of cake."

Niki still had her doubts, but in the end, she was glad he'd stayed. If he went away, she'd be left alone with Anna, which was a rather scary prospect.

This year the Seongs had decided it was time to visit their homeland at last. The only ones who didn't go to Korea were again Kim Hana and Yoon Sori, but those two were on Crete, where Kim Hana landed a seasonal job at some campsite.

And Chen Liang was once again in Taipei.

He'd been spending more and more time there. Niki had a suspicion it wasn't so much because the company business required his constant presence as because his relationship with his wife, on a downward slide for years, had lately reached its all-time low. Since that day last autumn when he'd declared that enough was enough and he wouldn't agree to any more IVF, their home had turned into an additional ring of hell, where Chen Liang was being constantly punished for his deadly sin of giving hope and taking it back, and Niki and Kehuan were being punished together with him, as guilty by association. But while Anna always showed a certain level of caution with Kehuan, Niki was a much easier target for her blasts and barbs.

"Stop moping," Anna had told her impatiently in June. "It's your own fault. You can't be an artist and a gymnast at the same time. You didn't listen, now you pay the price."

It had been a rather elaborate version of the traditional "I told you so", with an extra seasoning of smug satisfaction, and Niki went out and walked around for two hours after that, though the weather on that day wasn't very nice.

She knew Kehuan stayed with her precisely for that reason, but also to keep her spirits up through the wearisome rehab. And it worked, too, because when he said it would be all right, she believed him without reservations. After all, he'd never lied to her, or let her down.

In the end, it became a lot like that very first summer they'd spend together, years ago, with plenty of wading in the shallow water on the sandy banks of the Vistula River, and walking around the city for hours. Of course, now they came up with many ideas that hadn't crossed their mind when they'd been children, like visiting art galleries and going to summer concerts in the parks, and to the swimming pool, and making day trips to different interesting locations around Warsaw. And all in all, it turned into wonderful vacation.

* * *

In August, Chen Liang finally returned. Niki guessed he couldn't stay in Taipei forever. (Well, technically he could, but the Polish company also required some overseeing from time to time, and Kehuan was here, of course). Unexpectedly, Chen Xiao also flew in from Vancouver for a week. He was able to travel more now, but he didn't come to Warsaw too often because he knew it still disturbed her a lot.

Niki remembered how she used to adore him as a child. She still admired him and was eternally grateful for everything he did for her, but it was an ordeal to face Chen Xiao, every time. In his presence, she always felt jittery and antsy, and scared, as if something terrible was about to happen. She understood it was irrational, just a case of a really bad association, but the reaction was hard to overcome.

And there was also this little voice that whispered quietly in her ear every time she saw Chen Xiao, "Your mum would be alive if not for him."

She didn't believe it on a rational level. It wasn't true, and it wasn't fair, and she was determined not to listen to that voice, but it was still there.

Niki sometimes had the impression her adoptive father could guess quite a lot of her complicated emotions, and she felt even worse because of that, but there was no trace of reproach in the way he treated her. He was always his kind and supportive self.

Chen Xiao liked visiting her room. He once commented with a fond smile it was like looking around inside her head, and he was probably right.

There was the wall bar on the left side of the door, where she always did her stretching and strength exercises, and sometimes hung off it upside down for some time without any particular reason, just because. Then there were the easels and the big table in the middle of the room, and the tall chest of drawers between two windows on the half-circular wall opposite the door, which contained her drawing and painting supplies, and all that junk she kept collecting and bringing home and then using for her works. On the right sight of the room was her bed, and a clothes rack next to it, with the clothes appropriate for the current season, while the rest was hidden away in a closet. There were also two big speakers of the sound system on both sides of the room because Niki liked her music in good technical quality. And all the walls were covered with watercolors and pastels, and pencil sketches, and Chinese calligraphy, and various funny pieces she'd made from different materials over the years.

Overall, it was quite messy, not like Kehuan's place, which was always super-tidy, half-empty, and kind of impersonal. Even so, Niki liked his room very much, with its giant panoramic window, the piano, and all things organized in a very Kehuan-like, no-nonsense logical order, with no unnecessary clutter at all, except for the driftwood structure on the wall over his bed.

But he seemed to enjoy her chaotic space just as much, and it was a routine thing for him to bring over his laptop or math notes and do his work at the big table while she was drawing on the other end of it, or making some new piece of craftwork on the floor, and music flowed from the hi-fi equipment and wound its magic around both of them.

Niki never minded Kehuan's presence in her room, and Chen Xiao had an open invitation as well, but other people were a different story; only a few were welcome. Unfortunately, some still came in, invited or not.

It was the last day of Chen Xiao's visit, and she was laying the table for dinner in the living room when she noticed Anna pass through the door on the opposite end of the long hall. Niki put down the stack of plates and followed after her, and was about to enter the room when she noticed inside Chen Xiao in his wheelchair. He was turned towards the wall on the right side of the door, where her bed was, and Niki immediately knew what he was gazing at. She stopped, uncertain, and then heard Anna's voice.

"What are you looking at, Chen Xiao?" Anna asked. "Ah, Veronica's self-portrait."

Chen Xiao kept silent for a moment. "It's not a self-portrait," he finally answered. "It's a portrait of Niki's mother."

"Oh," Anna said, slightly abashed. "I've always thought there was something off with this picture." She paused and then spoke again, evidently curious now, "She looks very young here. Is it... correct?"

"It's not my place to tell you about Alina," Chen Xiao replied in a cooler tone.

"Whose if not yours?" Anna asked in a baffled tone.

"Has Niki never talked to you about her mum?"

Anna laughed harshly. "Wrong question," she said. "You should've asked, 'Has Niki ever talked to you?'"

"And why is that, I wonder?" Chen Xiao asked.

"She talks to nobody," Anna answered defensively, "except Kehuan."

"That's not true," he objected at once. "She talks to Kim Hana quite a lot."

"Oh, Kim Hana," Anna sneered. "Of course. The favorite confidante of every Chen alive."

"I wonder if your communication with Niki might go better if you took a nicer tone with her, Anna."

"Believe me, I've taken a nicer tone with her many times," Anna answered, irritated, but still polite. If it had been anybody else, not Chen Xiao, the gloves would've been off long ago, Niki thought. "I know she's your precious daughter—"

"She is my precious daughter," said Chen Xiao, crisp and clear. "I'd like you to remember about it."

"I do," Anna said after a moment, subdued. "But let me tell you, it's really hard to be nice to someone who most of the time doesn't even notice your existence."

Niki couldn't deny there was some truth in this statement, and promised to herself she'd try harder for some positive communication with Anna. After all, most of what Kehuan's stepmother said to her and about her was true, and it could be interpreted as an expression of concern if only the form wasn't so virulent and hurtful.

But Niki wasn't ready to discuss mum with her, or with anybody else, and had enough of their discussion, so she made the last few steps with deliberate noise and entered the room.

"We've made chicken and peas risotto," she announced. "Would you like to come and have some with us?"

* * *

The Seongs returned at the end of August, right before the start of the school year, and so did Yoon Sori, and they all came over on the last day of the holidays.

"How's the hand, Niki?" asked Taejin as soon as they all sat down on the semi-circular terrace outside the living room.

"Better." She stretched out her right arm and made several circles with her fist. "Almost good." She turned to the twins and added apologetically, "But no more gymnastics. Sorry, guys."

"Yeah, we gathered," Taeyeon answered gloomily. "Can't be helped, I guess."

"You'll get fat now, woman," Taerim added, and everybody chuckled.

While the others were watching Sori's photos from Crete, Taejin and Kehuan went out for some snacks and cold drinks.

"Sorry we went away," Taejin told his cousin. "Our mother wouldn't change her mind, no matter what."

Kehuan nodded, looking untroubled.

"Niki was really down in June," Taejin observed. "It's good she recovered so well."

"Yeah."

"So was it hard?" Taejin asked.

"It was," Kehuan answered. "She had to do a lot of stuff to get this hand working again." He sounded proud of her.

"I know, but I meant..." What Taejin was trying to ask was a different question, but he didn't know how to phrase it without annoying his cousin too much. "Staying here all summer, just the two of you. Was it hard?"

"Why'd it be hard?"

"Weren't you bored, you and Niki?"

Kehuan didn't answer. He was looking up at the sky with an odd smile on his face. "So how was home sweet home?", he asked at last, changing the subject.

Taejin made a funny face. "Strange," he said. "It'd been seven years, you know?"

"And? Has it changed much?"

"Not that much," Taejin answered. "But I'd forgotten how some things were over there."

"How?"

"Well, different. Very... traditional."

"Isn't it a super modern country?" asked Kehuan curiously.

"Sure, if you mean technology and stuff. But our family there..." Taejin groped for the right word. "Ah, it's very hierarchical, I guess." He winced a little.

"I thought you were fond of hierarchy and tradition," his cousin reminded him, sounding amused.

"I thought so, too," Taejin admitted. "Don't know why it gets on my nerves now."

"You got spoilt."

"I did?"

"Travels broaden the mind," Kehuan cited. "You've traveled too much, my friend, or maybe for too long, and your mind became over-broadened."

Taejin chortled. "Is it even a word?" he mused with a grin. "What does it mean?"

"It means now you'll have to make an effort to appreciate your roots," Kehuan told him with a lopsided smirk.

Taejin thought about it for a short while. "If my mind got over-broadened, what about you?"

"Oh, me," Kehuan replied sarcastically. "My mind is an open space, you could say. With the wind howling."

"So can you appreciate your roots?"

"What roots?"

* * *

In September Niki told the gymnastics coach at the school thank you and goodbye. They both had tears in their eyes, but he understood, as she'd always been very upfront about her priorities. He didn't even try to convince her to take the risk with her hands again.

This year the charity action at school included a theater play in December, staged by the drama club, and an art exhibition with a sealed-bid auction in January, and Niki was going to take part in that second event, of course.

During the summer she'd been doing Chinese calligraphy again, to exercise the injured wrist, and now she decided she'd paint a series of watercolor posters featuring different animals, and use the black ink and the calligraphy brush to draw partial outlines of their bodies and to accentuate some lines. The style would match the Chinese characters she was also going to place on the posters.

She did some experimenting first, with the materials and the tools, and the order of the whole procedure, and finally decided to do the ink drawing and calligraphy first and to put the watercolors over it.

It proved to be a time-consuming process. For each poster she had to outline the whole picture lightly with a pencil first, to know where to use the ink, and to erase the pencil marks later. Then she had to wait because the permanent ink needed time to dry properly before the watercolor could be applied. And if she finished painting and wasn't happy with the end result, she had to start from the very beginning because watercolor was an unforgiving technique, which didn't allow for many corrections.

"Niki, have you become a wildlife buff?" Yoon Sori asked her one day in November when she came over and found Niki watching on her laptop a documentary about tigers. "Or is it some research for school?"

Kehuan, who'd let her in a moment earlier and was now sitting back down to his own computer at the other end of the table, scoffed at that. "You must be joking," he said. "She just wants to draw a tiger."

"But why to watch a whole film?" asked Sori, intrigued. "Are you even interested in all these details?"

"Don't get tricked," Kehuan spoke again. "She isn't listening to a word they say in it."

Niki threw at him a piece of crumpled paper. "I don't need to listen, just to watch."

"But why?" Sori was even more puzzled. "Isn't it enough to look at some photos?"

"No," Niki said firmly. "If I don't know how they move, I can't draw them properly."

"In that case, maybe you should listen to the narration, too," Sori suggested. "Habits can be important, too."

Niki gaped at her for a moment. "You're right," she said, switched off the music in the room with a remote, and then stopped the film and started it from the beginning.

"Now you've done it," Kehuan told Sori, resigned. "She won't get to her homework before midnight at this rate."

Niki muttered some very unflattering and not entirely quotable comment about homework in general, and now it was Kehuan's turn to throw back at her the same ball of crumpled paper.

Yoon Sori didn't have much free time, what with all the regular studying, the music school classes in the afternoons, and practicing the violin every day, but she loved coming over and spending time with them. For her, there'd always been something very magical and alluring about this place, in how it looked and sounded, and even smelled, and in the way time flowed here. Sori supposed she wasn't the only one feeling this way, as Taejin was a frequent guest at the Chen's as well. He sometimes stayed so long that his mother would call to summon him home in the evening.

Sori's aunt wasn't thrilled with how much time all her sons spent with the Chens. Even when Kehuan finally grasped the whole concept of different levels of speech in the Korean language and started using them more or less properly, there was always something vaguely disrespectful about his attitude, as Kim Haneul often pointed out with displeasure. As for Niki, her verdict was even worse: the girl was strange, unruly, and a poor influence on her boys. She was very aggrieved that all she could do was set some time limits on their meetings outside the school. Any proposal of cutting the ties with the Chens completely earned her a lecture from her husband about family obligations, and from her younger sister about understanding and acceptance.

Sori often thought that the deepest and truest reason for Taejin's frequent visits at the Chens' might be very similar to hers, and felt sorry for him, and also happy that her own mum didn't have such objections.

* * *

The music club this autumn was a much more relaxed place since they didn't have any big affair to organize and stage. Everybody played or sang just for fun, and Mauricio de Silva found the ever-changing configuration of musicians present on different days quite diverting. It was an excellent occasion to experiment with various styles and music arrangements. He noticed, though, that their last year acquisition, Chris Morton, better known as Chris Moron, wasn't so happy about it.

They'd accepted him in the end. He'd apologized to Niki, first thing after the Christmas break, and to Jason as well, and then came and apologized to very amused Mauricio, who had no idea why he got included in it as well, but neither was inclined to give his absolution so easily. Nobody was very enthusiastic about taking Moron in, but Ms. Mazur appealed to them to give him a chance, and Niki said okay, so they finally agreed.

The boy managed to patch things up with Jason after some time, and he was still trying to create his dream music band. But though there were always some free vocalists around, waiting for a chance to shine, good instrumentalists were harder to lure in. Mauricio knew Chris was observing Ridhaan Khatri with covetous eyes, but all his overtures in this direction stayed without success so far. Moron even dared ask once, very carefully, if Mauricio himself wasn't interested in joining him as a keyboard player. Mauricio just laughed at him. He often thought the boy had better be careful if he didn't want to lose his teeth.

The Seong twins were back at the club, for example, with their brand-new baritones, and they watched him like two hawks. Their older brother also sometimes dropped by to listen to a jam session when Niki was singing, and Mauricio thought to himself that Moron didn't have a long life in front of him unless he stopped following the girl around like a tormented shadow. He was like spellbound: wherever Niki went, a few minutes later Moron appeared as well, and it'd been fun to watch at the beginning, but quickly became annoying as hell. But he vanished into thin air every time Kehuan Chen showed up, which was proof he had some basic survival instinct after all.

And Kehuan came round quite often because he seemed to like observing Niki's struggles with her pygmy choir.

All ten of those little first graders from the last winter Christmas concert signed up for the music club this year, and their parents submitted an official petition to Ms. Mazur to assign Niki as their mentor. If that wasn't a hilarious development, Mauricio didn't know what was. She'd looked so comically baffled and daunted when she'd first heard about it that he'd been sure she'd decline the request. But she had much more time now after she'd dropped the gymnastics training, so she agreed in the end, and he was glad. The kids were almost as good at making her awake as Kehuan.

* * *

The art exhibition took place after the Christmas break, in January, and it was just as professional an affair as the school concerts and theater plays, with the printed catalog of all available works, the bidding auction, and the unavoidable café.

On the last day of the exhibition, Kamila Bartnik was walking around the high school hall turned art gallery and gazing at the works. She loved visiting art galleries, and the event at their school was pretty cool. All the exhibits were displayed on special frames and stands around the central hall of the high school building, and along the adjacent corridors. Of course, there were some pieces created by younger students as well, though it wasn't as if every submitted work had a chance to be included: they had to have been approved first by a special commission consisting of the art teacher, two parents of artistic profession, and two student representatives from the art club. No kidding.

There were a lot of people milling around, and Kamila had already walked the whole exhibition twice this afternoon. She was just waiting now for a good moment to take one more look at the most besieged part of the hall, which contained the series of eleven animal posters by Veronica Chen.

Damn, but that girl could paint.

Kamila disliked her just as much as ever, if not more, because to all the grievances Ola, Marlena, and herself used to hold against her now they could add another one, of having one rabid Chris Morton hound their every step and make their life as difficult as possible. As if it was really their fault that he'd made such an idiot out of himself last winter.

But she could dislike the artist and still admire the art, and Kamila wanted very much to look at those posters once more before they were sold and disappeared from the hall. Since the exhibition had started two weeks ago, she came to look at them every day. If she had the money, she'd buy one, but with so many people interested it was certain the pictures would reach prices completely out of her modest range.

They were really exquisite. On each of them the calligraphed Chinese character took up one entire corner, and the watercolors were extraordinary, each picture in its own palette of colors. But there were also some things about those posters that kept niggling at her since she'd first laid her eyes on them.

For example, why those animals and not others? She'd thought at first maybe they were the Chinese zodiac signs, but that wasn't it. A wolf and a cat. A snake and a peacock. A bear. A tiger. Two monkeys and a fox. A black swan, a dog, and a chameleon. Why were they even grouped this way? She'd asked some kids from the art club, and they said they were displayed according to Veronica's own suggestions.

Why were all animals shown in the light of the day, and only the wolf was depicted on the dark background of the night sky? Why did all posters contain just one animal, apart from the monkeys, which were two? Why were all animals moving, but not the cat, which was asleep, with its legs and tail hanging lazily off a tree branch?

She finally managed to squeeze through the throng of people and moved slowly from one picture to another. There was another thing bothering her about the animals, but it was even harder to define. Some of them just looked eerily familiar, as if she'd seen them already, but where and when?

"Hello, foxy," murmured a warm baritone behind her, and she didn't have to look back to recognize the voice of one of the Korean twins from her class. "Looking at your portrait?"

Kamila was just going to deliver some witty comeback, but as she once again glanced at the picture in front of her, the words withered, unspoken. Did the fox really look a little like her, or was she just confused by the wild suggestion? No, it was ridiculous. It was just an animal, and besides, why would Veronica paint her of all people? And yet, she couldn't turn her eyes away from the poster.

The boy behind her chuckled quietly.

"Don't sweat it," whispered another voice in her other ear, sounding exactly the same. "You look great here, as always."

She whirled round to face them, but they were already gone.

* * *

Kehuan went to the auction office to place the bids.

In the past, the school used to hold traditional English auctions, with all their drama, but they'd switched to the Vickrey system for the last two editions. It had been first proposed by a knowledgeable older student interested in economics, and everybody was happy with it because it turned out to be much easier to organize, and quicker.

Chen Xiao, who'd already heard all about the exhibition, asked Kehuan to buy one of the posters for him. He didn't mind which one, he said, and named a high sum of money to offer on his behalf. Of course, it didn't mean he'd have to pay what he offered; since it was a Vickrey auction, the winner would pay the amount of money equaling the second-highest bid.

Which meant Kehuan could bid really high himself, too.

He'd seen all those posters come to life in Niki's room over the last four months, one after another, and he'd known for weeks he wouldn't allow anybody else to lay hands on those two pictures. The rest, he didn't care. They were all beautiful, of course, but they were just works of art in his eyes and nothing else. But those two were personal.

And so he divided in half all the money he'd earned during the last year and a half writing codes for Chen Xiao, and added twenty percent more to it, and placed two identical bids in two closed envelopes. He didn't really think the final price would go anywhere near this level, but better safe than sorry.

He wondered where Niki was. Earlier he'd spotted her at the higher landing of the staircase, watching the exhibition and the crowd of people from a distance.

"Who's the author of those pictures?" asked an energetic-looking woman in an elegant jacket, showing the screen of her phone to the girl behind the desk. "Can you give me the name? And some contact details, if possible?"

"Why are you asking?" asked Kehuan, who'd been about to leave.

"I've got an Internet store selling interior decoration," the woman explained. "Posters are popular, and I think reproductions of these could sell quite well."

"The original works from our exhibition are just being auctioned, and can't be used for such a purpose," recited the acne beleaguered teenager running the office in a perfectly professional tone.

"She's right," Kehuan told the woman. "But if you're interested, the artist could probably make some new pictures for you. If you come to an agreement about the conditions, of course."

"Very well," the woman agreed with an amused smile and switched on the address book in her phone. "Can I have the contact details then?"

"The name's Veronica Chen," said Kehuan, and rattled off his father's phone number, thinking with an inner grin that he just couldn't wait to tell Anna about this meeting.

The results of the auction were published an hour later, and Kehuan took all three posters home the same evening.

"I don't know why I even bothered bringing them to school," said Niki, who was walking next to him, eyeing with a frown the big flat package he carried in his arms. It was very unwieldy. "If you'd told me you wanted them, I'd have given them to you without any stupid auction."

"But I wanted to buy them," Kehuan answered, trying to grab the frames in a more comfortable way. "You made them for the auction, it was only fair to pay the price."

"But it's a total waste of your money," grumbled Niki, and added, "Put it sideways, we'll carry them between us."

Kehuan shipped Chen Xiao his poster the very next day, and he hung the wolf and the cat over the piano in his room.

"They look good here," said Niki, a little surprised, while they were both standing in front of the pictures, contemplating the end result. Kehuan nodded, feeling smug.

Taejin came a few days later and saw the posters as well.

"Man, how much did you give for them?" he asked, awestruck. "Jason told me his mum wanted to buy one and offered quite a big sum, and nothing."

"Be quiet," Kehuan said, irritated, and checked the door.

Taejin smirked.

"Are you scared your little sister will learn how much money you paid for her own productions?" he asked, entertained and ticked off at the same time. "You two are a riot."

"Niki's not my sister," Kehuan told him for what felt like the hundredth time.

He wondered why some people never seemed to hear those words, and didn't like his conclusions at all.

* * *

At the end of May, the school organized a trip to the south of the country for the students of middle and high school. The twins couldn't go because of some gymnastics competition, but the rest of them signed up for it.

They spent the first day touring Cracow, and it turned out to be a fabulous city, much older than Warsaw and completely different in character. The only annoying thing where the crowds of tourists everywhere.

The next morning, they set off in the direction of the Beskid mountains to do some hiking. It was a lovely day, sunny, warm, and very summer-like already. The trail started in a valley, and the first part of it was very easy, as they were walking along a dirt road rising gently towards the wood-covered slopes. But after half an hour the trail entered the forest, and the road turned into a path, winding up at a much steeper angle over tree roots, moss, and stones, and the climb became more of a challenge, especially for those kids who weren't very sporty.

There were several meadows on the way where they could take a break, waiting for the stragglers to catch up. At one of these stops, Kehuan found Niki among the middle-schoolers, so they could have a snack together, and he wasn't surprised at all when she declared enthusiastically it was her kind of fun. Walking and walking, and walking some more, up and down and up again, what's not to love, he thought amused, eating a sandwich and listening to the complaints of other kids around them, apparently unafflicted by Niki's vagabond disorder. But as he gazed at the ranges of forest-covered mountains stretching out in every direction, he had to admit he enjoyed it as well, very much.

In the early afternoon, they reached the mountain shelter below the summit, in the middle of an enormous meadow with even more spectacular views. Everybody had dinner on the wooden terrace outside, and then a small group of volunteers decided to hike up to the top, while the others rested around in the grass, sunbathing and joking, and taking photos. After that, there was just the walk down to their lodgings for the night.

It was a complex consisting of one bigger building with the kitchen and the dining room, and several long bungalows, located in a place where the trees of the forest gave way to yet another vast grassy meadow, interspersed with some shrubs and big clumps of bilberry bushes. The place was still on the slope, but on its gentler part already, close to the bottom of the valley, and there were many paths winding around, with benches made of big logs.

After the boys put their stuff in one bungalow, and the girls in another one, everybody scattered around. The daylight lingered long at this time of the year and the weather was beautiful, so people were hanging out in pairs and small groups, talking and laughing.

At a certain moment Jason, who never forgot to take his guitar if there was any chance at all for a social gathering, brought it out to the meadow and started playing, and soon there was a whole group of students sitting around him and singing messily. After some time Mauricio intercepted the instrument, and the party became even livelier. It was the last real day of the trip, since the next day after breakfast they were returning to Warsaw, and everybody wanted to make the most of the remaining time.

The sun had already set and the sky was gradually turning to darker shades of blue, but the air was still warm and balmy, and a few people decided to stay longer on the meadow, even when somebody brought the news about a buffet supper available in the main building, and Mauricio and Jason went to eat, together with most of the boys.

It was such a beautiful night, with myriads of stars visible in the sky, unobscured by any tall buildings and far away from the light pollution of a big city. The music was over now, most people had left, and the meadow quieted down. At the retreat of the noisiest invaders, the night creatures could finally go out, and some ten minutes later the crickets started chirping.

And that was the moment Veronica Chen picked to completely freak out.

* * *

Kehuan was eating supper with Taejin and Jason when he heard his name called. He turned and saw a younger girl he didn't recognize halt right next to their table.

"Kehuan," she repeated in an agitated tone, "something's wrong with Veronica."

He was on his feet before he knew he was going to stand up. Taejin rose from his chair as well.

"What happened?" Kehuan asked, striding out of the dining room.

"I don't know. We were all on the meadow, singing. Everything was fine. Then most people left to eat, and suddenly she was... I don't know... wheezing, and swaying..."

Kehuan started to run but slowed down again when he realized the girl was still talking.

"We thought maybe she had belly cramps, you know, because she was clutching her stomach, but she wouldn't answer when we asked, and started whimpering..."

They'd just rounded the corner of the second bungalow, and there was suddenly Yoon Sori, who caught his arm at the elbow and said, "She's already inside."

Kehuan stopped. His heart was pounding, and he told himself very sternly to calm down and think. It always worked, right? Think.

"What's wrong with her?" he asked finally.

"How is she?" asked at the same moment Taejin, who turned out to be right behind him.

"I don't know," said Sori, worried and unnerved. "Ms. White is with her. She said it looked to her like a panic attack."

"Panic attack."

"At the beginning, we didn't know if she was ill, or hurt, or what. She was hyperventilating and looked really pale, and clammy. Then she fainted—"

"What?!"

"But only for a moment, she was back in a minute..."

"Can I come in?" Kehuan asked impatiently.

"No," Sori answered, "the girls inside are going to bed. But I think she's already better, really. She said nothing hurt."

They all sat down on a long wooden bench next to the wall. A few minutes later the teacher went out to talk to them.

"Kehuan," she said, "do you know what could have happened to cause such a reaction?"

He'd been thinking hard for the last few minutes, but he had no idea.

"It looked like a classic panic attack, and they usually have a trigger," the teacher explained. "I thought maybe you knew."

"No," he said, and then added somberly, "But she had some... hard moments in the past."

"I realize that," said the teacher.

Yeah, he guessed. He supposed all teachers at the school knew. That was probably why so many of Niki's transgressions and strange behaviors had been overlooked over the years.

"All right," said Ms. White. "She's in bed now, anyway. I'll talk to the school psychologist when we return. Veronica met with her regularly in the past, didn't she?"

"Yes, but not recently," answered Kehuan.

"Maybe she'll need to go back to it," the teacher noted soberly.

After that she went inside, taking Sori with her. Kehuan and Taejin also went to their bungalow, already dark and full of sleeping boys.

"Kehuan," said Taejin quietly when they went to the bathroom to brush their teeth, "what happened to Niki back then?"

Kehuan didn't answer.

"I'd really want to know," said Taejin. "It looks like it's important."

"Oh, you want to know," mocked Kehuan, his voice suddenly a low growl. "And because you want to know, I have to tell you?"

"I'm not trying to be a busybody," Taejin made an effort to sound as non-aggressive as possible. "I care for Niki, too, you know. I really do."

Kehuan was silent for a moment, and when he finally answered, the growl was mostly gone.

"She never talks about it," he said. "Not with Chen Xiao. Not with my father. Not with me. So even if I wanted to tell you, I can't because I don't really know."

* * *

Niki was standing in the middle of the meadow. It was a lovely night, dark and starry, and the crickets were chirping. Mum was right there, next to her, and Niki wanted to grab her hand, but the next moment she was already in a distance, calling, "Don't go too far," and there was the rumbling, and the wheezing, and the screeching, and then she was suddenly sitting in her bed in the dark room, gasping for air.

Around her other girls were stirring.

"What was that?" somebody asked in the dark, and she recognized Kamila's sleepy voice.

"Someone screamed," answered someone else.

"Sorry," Niki croaked and started groping for her shoes next to the bed.

Some girls grumbled, some giggled, and after a moment they all quieted down again. She put on the shoes, trying not to make any noise, found her hoodie, and walked out of the room.

* * *

In the morning, Marlena and Ola went out for a walk. Yesterday during the supper they'd heard Taejin Seong ask Kehuan Chen if he'd like to do some jogging in the morning, but it was before all the commotion with Veronica. Still, they wanted to check if they wouldn't meet their guys somewhere around. But they found her highness instead, fast asleep on a log bench under a big pine tree.

"Oh great, our drama queen," Marlena said scathingly.

"Drama princess," Ola corrected with a smirk. "All ready and waiting to be wakened up with a kiss."

They both really had it up to here with Veronica Chen, and there was more to it than just the infuriating situation at the music club.

They'd had a crush on the two older boys for two years, having divided them between themselves at the very beginning, so they wouldn't encroach on each other's territory. You could even say Ola and Marlena stalked them a little, kind of. Kehuan didn't have any social media account, but Taejin did, and he posted many photos of himself and his best friend. They downloaded them all, and knew everything about their guys, and liked to discuss how dreamy they looked, and what new gossip they heard about them from the high school girls. They felt quite possessive of them. But every time Kehuan and Taejin appeared around, there was the nauseating princess with her attention-seeking antics, as if her brother and cousin had nothing better to do but take care of her all the time. Just look at that whole performance last night. Disgusting. And people bought into it, too.

They observed the sleeping girl for a moment.

"That's this bench where I ruined my shirt yesterday," Marlena noticed, pointing to the smears of pine resin marking the log. "The idiot will be all sticky when she wakes up."

They noticed it at the same moment: the golden drop of resin in Veronica's dark hair. They exchanged a gleeful look. Oh, it was going to be hilarious.

Ola looked up at the crooked trunk of the pine tree, bending from behind over the log bench. Different teenage guests of this place had used it to carve their names in the bark, together with other meaningful inscriptions, and the trunk was sweating resin in many places.

"Are you thinking what I'm thinking?" Marlena asked quietly.

"Yeah."

Ten minutes later they heard some noise, but it was just Kama.

"What are you doing, guys?" she asked curiously.

"Shh," whispered back Marlena. "Helping nature."

Ola snickered.

Kamila looked closer, and her heart lurched. Veronica Chen was sleeping on the log bench, and her long hair, spilling all over the place, was dotted with multiple golden-brown drops gluing the dark strands to the wooden surface.

"Are you insane?" she hissed. "Do you want to die?"

"Ah, don't be a spoilsport," Marlena said. "Nobody will know."

Kamila watched, transfixed, as Ola used a small stick to carefully transfer another drop of resin from the trunk, and then waited patiently until it dripped over the hair.

Suddenly there were voices somewhere close.

"Evacuate," Marlena muttered, but a few girls from the high school had already walked out from among the trees at a brisk pace.

"Breakfast is in five minutes in the dining room," called the girl at the front of the group. "You'd better hurry before the guys gobble all the food."

"Ah, she's here," said Sori Yoon, sounding relieved, and Kamila watched with a sense of fatalistic impotence as the lovely black-haired violinist crouched in front of the bench and carefully shook Veronica's arm. "Niki, wake up."

The girl opened her large eyes and stared at her friend for a moment, still groggy, and then tried to sit up, only to drop right back on the bench with a quiet yelp.

"What's the matter? Are you feeling unwell?" asked Yoon Sori with concern, but just a moment later she saw the cause of the problem and cried out in dismay.

Veronica clasped her hair close to her head with both hands and struggled to get up again, but in vain. Sori Yoon was saying something quickly to her in a hushed voice, but the girl didn't seem to hear her at all. With the pale face and wild terrified eyes, panting and thrashing, she looked like some small animal wrestling to escape from a trap.

In the meantime, the group of girls around them swelled to a small crowd, and now a few guys appeared as well. People were talking and gesturing chaotically, trying to explain to the newcomers what was happening.

Somebody had already run off to summon a teacher.

"Go find Kehuan," said Sori to one of her friends, and Kamila nodded to herself, unsurprised. The situation was unfolding precisely according to her worst predictions.

A moment later the older PE teacher was there. He took one look at the resin-incrusted hair and the panicky girl and ordered the nearest student to quickly bring scissors from the kitchen. Then he came closer and inspected the hair once again. He started talking to Sori and her friends, looking more suspicious with each passing second.

Three minutes later Kehuan Chen came running, with Taejin Soeng and the boy with the scissors right on his heels. Now almost all the students were around. Kamila noticed Sullivan and de Silva, and Morton, all looking aghast and watching the whole circus with wide eyes.

Chen saw his sister strapped to the bench with her own hair and stopped dead.

"Who?…" he said in a voice that made all that swarming crowd suddenly stand still.

Kamila raised her hand. "It was us," she said, "Ola, Marlena, and me."

Next to her one of the girls gulped loudly.

"Mr. Agostini," said Kehuan Chen, his voice crisp and deadly calm, "will you please take those dumb cunts out of here before I kill them."

There were a few muted snickers, and the disconcerted teacher looked for a moment as if he wanted to object, but then quickly motioned at the three of them to move.

Kamila marched down the slope, with silent Marlena and Ola behind her, thinking hard. She really liked the international school. The program was ambitious, the standards high, and she enjoyed its climate, valued the teachers, and was friends with most of her classmates. But now she was absolutely certain that unless she immediately and miraculously found some way to make up for this birdbrained stunt, her life at this place was over.

They entered the empty bungalow and sat on their beds, facing each other.

"Why did you say that?" asked Ola sullenly.

"Why did you do that?" asked Kamila in turn. "It was so crass."

"Don't you hate her, too?" Marlena reminded her defensively.

"Even so. That girl has some serious issues," Kamila answered. "Didn't you see her yesterday?"

"Drama," scoffed Ola. "Fainting and screaming in the middle of the night. Give me a rest."

"Yeah, she'd do anything to become the center of attention," Marlena agreed.

"People can't control their nightmares," said Kamila, starting to lose patience. Didn't they see they went far too far? "And she left and stayed outside not to disturb your beauty sleep."

"Whose side are you on?" asked Ola, outraged. "You threw us to the wolves."

"I did you a favor," Kamila told her, wondering at their shortsightedness. "He was preoccupied at the moment. He'd find out later anyway, and then he'd skin you alive."

"Who, Mr. Agostini?" asked Marlena incredulously.

"Kehuan Chen, you idiot," Kamila answered. Really, they were unbelievable.

"Nobody would have known if you'd stayed quiet," said Ola furiously, rubbing at the very telling resin smudges on her fingers, and Kamila was astonished to see tears in her eyes. "It's all your fault."

Kamila nodded to herself again. Talk about scales falling from the eyes. Or maybe rather armor plates.

* * *

Kehuan kneeled in front of the bench and looked closely at Niki's face. She was breathing in quick shallow gasps, her face pale and her large eyes unfocused.

"Niki, listen to me," he said quietly in Mandarin. "It's all right. It's all right."

She looked at him and seemed to calm down a little.

"I need to cut your hair." He showed her the scissors. She watched them with panicked eyes, and her breathing accelerated again.

There was no chance in hell to unstick the hair from the wood without ripping half of it out of her head, and even if he managed to do it somehow, there was a lot of resin all over it. Time for a new hairstyle.

"Listen," he said, as the thought suddenly conjured up a distant memory. "How about a little new image experiment?"

He took the scissors, grabbed at his own hair, and snipped the whole chunk off, trying not to slash his scalp in the process. He heard a loud collective intake of breath around them.

Niki looked at his hand clutching the cut hair, and her lips suddenly twitched. Good.

He grabbed another handful and cut again, noticing with the corner of his eye Mauricio de Silva cover his mouth with a hand.

"How do I look?" he asked her, cutting on rapidly.

"Funny," she said in a raspy voice and giggled weakly. "Really... wacky."

"Your turn," Kehuan said, and she nodded. "Don't move your head."

And he started the carnage.

* * *

Two hours later they were all on the bus, on the way back to Warsaw.

Taejin turned in his seat again to look at Kehuan and Niki on the other side of the aisle. His cousin was sitting on the outside, but he'd turned his face away, to the window, and Taejin could only see it in profile, severe and unsmiling. Kehuan's hair looked really weird, cut haphazardly and sticking out in all directions in uneven, short clumps. He sat motionless with both his arms around Niki, who'd fallen asleep against his chest. She looked even smaller and thinner than usual with her own hair hacked off in an equally chaotic manner, though not exactly as short.

What was bothering Taejin right at this moment wasn't so much the hair as the way they were sitting. Not very sibling-like, he thought, feeling inexplicably annoyed.

Yoon Sori moved around in her seat in front of him, and called quietly, "Kehuan!"

Kehuan turned his head away from the window and looked at her, raising his eyebrows.

Sori showed him her phone. "My mum made an appointment for both of you with her hairdresser," she said, keeping her voice low. "You can go there right after we arrive." She looked for a moment at sleeping Niki with affectionate eyes, and then added, "You know what, I'll go with you."

And since they'd spent all their childhood together, and knew each other inside out, Taejin understood at once what she meant. "Me too," he said.

Because annoyed or not, he still had their back in this whole preposterous affair.

* * *

The story of Veronica Chen's hair made rounds on the social media and students' group chats over the whole weekend, together with a ten-second-long recording of Kehuan Chen cutting off his own hair, ending rapidly with Taejin Seong's voice snarling, very appropriately, "Cut it out, dude." So when Niki entered the school on Monday, nobody looked surprised with her new image, though people still stared a little. She guessed it couldn't be helped.

She entered the classroom, sat at her desk next to the window, and observed with quiet exhilaration all the reactions ten minutes later, when the twins came in, their hair now just as short as Kehuan's and Taejin's. And it turned into a real pandemonium during the long break, when Sori dropped by with some *kimbap*, and showed off her new short bob as well.

Niki had convinced her to stop at that. Her own hair was more of a pixie cut now, which was the only possible option after the massacre Kehuan had to commit on it, but there was no need for Sori to sacrifice even more, though Niki appreciated the gesture very much.

But even she gaped in shock when after the next lesson Kamila Bartnik arrived, fashionably late, with her hair shorn almost to the skin.

The twins almost fainted at the sight.

"What have you done, woman?" Taeyeon groaned, horrified. "Has nobody told you fox fleece jumpers are out of fashion?"

"Shut up, pretty boy number two," Kamila told him unceremoniously.

"So am I pretty boy number one?" asked Taerim hopefully.

"You are pretty boy number two, photocopied," she answered. "Now get out of the way, I need to speak with Veronica."

Niki noticed Ola and Marlena near the door, watching the scene morosely, and wondered if the trio had a falling-out. In any case, the hair of those two was still as long as before the trip.

"Veronica," said Kamila, looking her straight in the face, "I apologize for my part in this idiocy."

Niki had no idea what to say to that, especially because so many people were watching. She really hated big scenes like that.

"And I'm sorry for being a bitch to you earlier, too," Kamila continued, without paying any attention to the muttered comments flying around the classroom. "I was wrong. I didn't see very clearly at the time."

"You didn't have to do that," said Niki at last. "You look terrible, honestly speaking."

"I know," the girl agreed, unfazed. "It's how it works."

"How what works?" Niki asked, curious.

"Learning from your own mistakes," Kamila replied, and Niki didn't have to consult with the twins, nor ask Kehuan for his opinion to decide at once that the mouthy redhead was already forgiven.

8

Unlocked

"How do you even fall asleep in the middle of a biology test?" asked Kamila, genuinely mystified, on the way out of the classroom. "It's some talent you've got, girl."

"It is a special skill," Veronica agreed, rubbing her eyes tiredly. "But if you'd like to master it, I can give you some tips. Try staying awake from two o'clock in the morning, three nights in a row, and it should do the trick."

Kamila decided to shut her mouth at that. She was aware now there were many things about Veronica Chen she hadn't known in the past, and still didn't know. The two of them didn't even talk that often. After all, they hadn't magically become friends after the scare-hair affair in May, they'd just stopped being enemies. But Veronica was an interesting person for sure, and since their undefined relationship was still a work in progress, Kamila was quite curious about what it would become in the end.

Marlena and Ola were long gone now; they'd never returned to the class after the holidays. Any cases of bullying were treated very seriously by the school, so a few days after the memorable trip the parents of all involved sides had been summoned for a meeting with the headteacher. Ola and Marlena's mothers arrived in a huff, threw a big tantrum over the words Chen used in regard to their daughters, and stunned everybody with a bold attempt to make that insult into the main issue of the whole case. Kamila's own mother had been at once shocked, amused, and a little impressed with that tactical maneuver, but it didn't work, of course, what with Chen senior being a very outspoken lawyer, as it turned out. And the girls didn't have any life at the school after that, just as Kamila had predicted. Peer ostracism can be a scary thing, and they weren't able to take the pressure for long.

The additional, a little ironic side effect of all the fuss was that Kehuan and Veronica Chen, that pair of perpetual outsiders, unintentionally set a new trend at the school. Even if Chen never bothered with social life, most people recognized him, and Veronica held the status of a quirky and reclusive, but very talented artist. Sori Yoon and Kamila herself, on the other hand, were both popular girls and quite influential, and Taejin Soeng also had lots of friends. Not to mention the twins, with their sports stars rep, gymnasts' bodies, and angelic faces. So maybe it wasn't so surprising after all that short hairstyles became a very fashionable thing among all students, at least for some time.

Back to the present situation, though, Kamila had a different observation to comment on.

"Classroom narcolepsy aside," she said to Veronica, "kudos to you for staying put for the whole two months. What's changed?"

"We all need to get accepted to the high school," answered the girl with a wry smile. "Yeona and Rima's mother will have conniptions if they cut school again this year."

"I guess it's no fun to ditch on your own," Kamila mused. She'd never skipped an hour of school in her life without some life-threatening condition. Her mother wouldn't stop at conniptions.

"Actually, it's even more fun," confessed Veronica, smiling impishly. "But I don't usually—"

"Ah, you hurt our feelings, Nik," said a male voice behind them. "But since we're on the topic, maybe we should forget math today and check out this new pool—"

"I'm not covering for you again," Veronica replied firmly. "I promised Taejin I wouldn't do that anymore."

"Wait a sec," said Kamila, feeling that she was missing some critical detail here. “Are you saying you’ve been taking the blame for those two all this time?!”

“Why are you so surprised, foxy?” asked the second twin, falling into step with them on her other side. He looked very amused with her indignation. “Niki’s a protected species. But we, ah, we are so endangered, and nobody cares for our survival...”

Both girls snorted simultaneously, and they all walked out of the school building to catch some fresh air.

* * *

On Friday evening Kehuan went to the local gym to play basketball with Taejin and a few other guys, as had become their custom lately. But this time, as soon as they started bouncing and passing the ball, two strangers came up and asked if they could join in.

They both seemed oddly familiar, and when Kehuan looked closer, they turned out to be nobody else but two of his former stalkers, aka nazi boys—though he’d long ago agreed not to use this term anymore. They recognized him as well, and there was a moment of awkward silence as they all stood still, staring at each other. And then the big blonde guy grinned and stretched out his hand.

“I’m Marcin,” he said. “You kicked my ass once.”

Kehuan smirked at that. “I remember,” he said.

It had happened in the first year of middle school. After staying low for some time, the nazi boys started pestering him again then. Kehuan didn’t bother with changing his routes anymore. He just recorded them a few times with his mobile, and then ignored the idiots, hoping they’d get bored with this shit at some point. Instead, they decided to waylay Niki and Yoon Sori on their way home. They’d seen them together too many times, and concluded correctly they’d get to him better this way.

Kehuan and Taejin had stayed behind that day because Taejin had something to discuss with other boys from the soccer team, so Kehuan saw it from afar. Sori was walking on the sidewalk while Niki balanced on the low wall running next to it, and then suddenly, the meaty blond boy appeared from around a corner with a few of his cronies, and they stopped in front of the girls. The guy said something to Niki, striking a distinctly aggressive pose, and all of them guffawed. Niki, still on the wall, turned to face him and answered, but Kehuan was still too far away to hear her words, though he was running already. The blond boy looked furious. He suddenly stepped closer and yanked at the strap of her backpack, and Niki lost balance and fell down from the wall, landing on her side on the ground.

Kehuan saw red.

He didn't even remember later how he'd got there. Punch to the side of the face, block, front elbow to the ribs, and the meaty guy swayed on his feet. Kehuan sent him down with a kick to his side, but there was another one right behind him now, so he stepped to the side and raised his left forearm rapidly without turning, hitting the guy in the face with the back of his fist. The third asshat jumped at him from the right, and Kehuan spun round and planted a hook kick to his jaw, and the guy went down as well, hitting the low wall first before collapsing on the sidewalk. Someone shouted behind him, so he twisted again, but it was only Taejin, delivering a perfect jumping front kick to the last nazi boy still standing. Thirty seconds, and all of them were moaning on the ground, clutching at their faces and ribs.

The next day they both got summoned to the headteacher's office.

"The school received a complaint," she said. She was a stern, no-nonsense lady in her mid-fifties, and many students were scared of her, but Kehuan always appreciated her direct approach. "We were told you attacked some students from the public middle school yesterday after lessons."

"We didn't, Ms. Pawlik. I saw them attack Niki, and we had a fight over that," Kehuan replied, bending facts just a little.

"Taejin?"

"That's true, Ms. Pawlik," his cousin confirmed at once.

"And why did you get into it as well?" she asked, watching him closely.

"I was concerned," Taejin explained earnestly. "I saw there were four of them, so I wanted to make sure Kehuan and the girls wouldn't get hurt."

Kehuan lowered his head to hide a smirk.

The headteacher decided then to confront the two versions of events and invited over the principal of the public school, as well as all the participants of the incidents together with their parents. Taejin had been a little nervous about the meeting—his folks didn't take lightly any summons from the school—but the whole thing lasted half an hour.

The father of the meaty blond boy started from a high tone, pointing to his son's face, bruised and swollen, and listing the other boys' injuries, some visible and some hidden under their clothes, while Kehuan listened and studied said injuries with the deep satisfaction of the job well done. The other parents were very indignant, too, but he needed only to take out his phone and play his recordings to the enthralled audience to turn the tables completely. The father of the meaty blond still tried to quarrel, but when it was revealed that the fight had started because his son had hurt a younger girl, even he didn't have much to say anymore.

The only thing Kehuan got reprimanded for was using the expression "nazi boys".

"You don't understand what this word sounds like in the ears of Polish people," the headteacher of the public school said mournfully. "It's an outrageous insult."

"I'm sure Kehuan wouldn't have used the word if the boys hadn't behaved like out-and-out racists," noticed Ms. Pawlik, who was Polish as well, and Kehuan liked her even more after that.

And now the meaty blond guy was standing in front of him, five years older, with his hand extended.

"We were such dumb shits back then," he said regretfully. "I hope your girl is fine."

Kehuan took this hand in the end, not because he was so eager to make friends, but because he thought that if any progress were to be made, he probably needed to budge a little, too.

They played basketball with Marcin and his buddy, and from that day the guys started coming regularly to the games. Apparently, some people needed to have the snot beaten out of them to see the light.

* * *

In February Kehuan turned eighteen. In Poland, it meant becoming a legal adult, even if in Taiwan he'd still need two more years to be recognized as one.

On the day of his birthday, he stood in front of the panoramic window in his room, contemplating the winter city landscape outside, and thinking about what being an adult really meant for him.

The same major change had happened to Taejin six weeks earlier. (That was the real age difference between them; when they'd first talked as children, his cousin had adhered to the traditional Korean system of counting age). To celebrate his birthday, Taejin invited fifteen or so of his friends to a pub, and they all had a big debate about what they wished to change in their life as newly minted adults, or adults-to-be.

"Man, I'd like to go out without having to report later what I did minute after minute," said Jason.

"Yeah, ditto, and to have to declare each time when I'm going to be back," someone else chimed in. "And then if I'm three minutes late, my mother's in hysterics."

"I want to go on vacations with my girlfriend," said Bartek, a Polish guy from their class. "But noooo, that could lead to sex, God forbid. My folks would rather have me do drugs than have sex."

That evoked a lot of mirth.

"Just keep them in the dark, man," Jason advised him gleefully.

Taejin, who'd led his entire life tucked closely under the wings of his loving, protective, and extremely controlling parents, had his own grievances.

"I'd just like to choose myself where I'll go to college, and what I'm going to study," he grumbled. "And to meet with whomever I want without my mother making faces and setting time limits."

Kehuan smirked. That last complaint probably referred to himself and Niki.

"Forget college," Mauricio de Silva said bitterly. "I'd just like my folks to hear me when I'm telling them I'm gay, and not explain each time that I'm still young and will surely grow out of the rebellious phase..."

People laughed again, but Kehuan didn't. He had his own experience with people never listening to what he was trying to tell them, and in his opinion, preconceptions weren't really funny.

"They think they know everything better," grouched Marcin, the blond ex-nazi boy. "My father always goes on and on how I haven't seen anything yet, don't know what people are really like, yadda yadda..."

"I want to stay," said Ridhaan dejectedly, and a little off-topic. He'd already had a few beers. "Let them all move away. I want to stay..."

Ridhaan had a Polish girlfriend and was very much in love, but his father had just been assigned a new post, and his family was going to leave the country as soon as the school year ended.

"Forget it," Jason told him sagely. "You'd need your own money for that."

The whole party ended with everybody drinking themselves into a highly philosophical and utterly cheerless stupor (some illegally, since they were still minors). That is everybody except Kehuan, for whom alcohol had little allure after what he'd lived through with his father.

As for that whole conversation, it held no real relevance to him. If being an adult meant going wherever he wanted and doing whatever he wanted without anybody paying attention to it, he'd been an adult since the age of six. If it meant having seen the ugly sides of life, getting disillusioned about human nature, and getting rid of too much trust, it'd happened about the same time. If it meant working and earning money, he'd grown up three years ago. And if it meant choosing by himself the person he wanted to be with, or staying where she was, he'd just love to hear somebody tell him he couldn't.

But did it all really mean he was an adult already? He wasn't sure. His life had run along different lines than that of Taejin and his friends, and Kehuan had other gaps to fill.

He'd been dragged across half the globe several times as a child, but it took Kim Hana and her holiday invitation for him to be able to look at the sea for the first time, at the age of nine.

He'd learned to swim when he'd been fourteen, some five or six years later than most of his classmates, and only because the school provided the opportunity. He had a strong suspicion about what might've happened to make Taejin teach Niki to swim so diligently for the last two years, and a cold shiver traveled down his spine every time he imagined the situation, and himself in it instead of his cousin. Would he be able to save her, or would they both have drowned instead?

He could count on one hand all the times he'd celebrated his own birthday, and so he never remembered others'—for him such things didn't hold any importance. Yeah, he knew Niki's, but that was something else. Basically, he had little interest in other people, and no social skills at all, and it probably was a limitation as well, but he wasn't sure it could ever change.

He suspected there were many other deficiencies in his upbringing which he'd discover in time. And there were also those suppressed parts of his mind and closed-off aspects of his personality, which he'd kept intentionally this way, even if it wasn't possible to switch off the functions of his body. He supposed he couldn't and wouldn't want to stay like this forever. But it still wasn't the right time for the change, not because he was completely uninterested, or unaware, or too young, but because Niki was all of these things.

* * *

Chen Liang also meditated a lot about his son becoming an adult.

When did it even happen? Just yesterday Kehuan had been that combative little boy who hated everybody, and now he was, well, this unfriendly young man who tolerated a few people. It surely could be counted as big progress? Or maybe not.

But still, Chen Liang felt their situation changed, and perhaps it was time for him to finally solve the problem of his unfortunate marriage.

Over the years he'd started thinking of it as a failed project, launched on a faulty premise. It never worked the way he'd planned, and neither the way Anna had wanted; he'd realized early on that their hopes and intentions had been incompatible from the very beginning, despite all his efforts to make things clear. Maybe if she'd got pregnant and had this child she'd pined for so much, things would be different, but the reality was what it was.

Chen Liang had often beaten himself over this fiasco, especially when he'd observed the constant skirmishes between Anna and Kehuan, and her callousness towards Niki. Perhaps he should've waited and watched her longer with the kids, or have made that offer to a different person, like Kim Hana. But no, it wouldn't have worked, either, because Kim Hana would've never agreed to begin with. She was a completely different person from Anna, optimistic and full of energy, and perfectly content with her busy life and single status; it was one of the reasons why they were such good friends, after all.

Anyway, it was too late now to repair anything, and as the children grew up, he lost the incentive to even try. He just wanted to end it in a possibly painless way and then forget about it. He was sixty-two and was starting to feel the burden of the years of relentless work paired with constant stress. He often felt tired now, even in the morning, and his breath sometimes shortened without any particular reasons; he wasn't getting younger, and simply wanted some peace.

But right now Anna was going through one of her periods of despondency, spending her days in bed and avoiding other members of the household, so it wasn't a good moment for the change. He'd have to wait a few months until she'd enter again the phase of wrathful belligerence, which he was sure would happen, as her moods had followed the same tiresome sinusoid for years.

* * *

On a drizzly spring day, Taejin jogged out of the school building and saw Niki in her blue raincoat some fifty steps ahead, already near the main gate. Her usual shadow was trailing ten steps behind, and Taejin grimaced with antipathy. That boy was hopeless.

Lately, the twins had entered the phase of unending, though ever-changing romantic affairs, so Niki often walked home with Kehuan and himself, and Sori. But today Kehuan was at some ICT students conference, and Sori was luckily in a hurry, running directly to her music school, and Taejin didn't want to miss the rare occasion to spend some time with his girl alone.

Before he had time to catch up with Niki, Moron suddenly quickened his pace and drew level with her. Taejin could see the pathetic boy started speaking now, so he shot forward and a moment later was right behind them.

"... and I know it," Moron was saying, and Taejin detested the pleading note in his voice, "but how come you're so chummy with Kamila now?"

"What's that to you?" Niki asked impatiently.

"What she did was so much worse, and you've forgiven her," said the boy, sounding aggrieved. "Why can't you forgive me?"

Really?!

"Kamila apologized and made amends," Niki answered, "it's all in the past."

"But I apologized, too," complained Moron. Whiny, whiny.

"You don't even know what you did wrong," Niki told him haughtily, and Taejin grinned. His girl had a spine.

"I do," Moron assured her. "I was rude to you at the audition, and you are a wonderful singer..."

"What if I couldn't sing at all?" asked Niki, tilting her head to the side. "Would it be all right then?"

The boy looked puzzled.

"There were many people there who gave you hard time later," she mused, "and you wanted to play with them. So you had to apologize."

"I didn't have to. I really felt bad."

"Because you made a public faux pas. What if nobody heard you? Or if nobody cared about me? Would you have apologized then?" Niki pushed.

Moron was quiet for a moment. "Perhaps," he said finally, sounding as if he didn't believe it himself.

"I highly doubt it," Niki told him disdainfully. "And that's why I don't like you."

Hit and sunk, as they say.

"Now excuse me, I'd like to talk to my friend," she added, turning around and waving at Taejin.

Moron looked back as well and stopped cold. Taejin smirked at him and jogged up to Niki, falling into step with her.

"You're a slayer, Niki," he told her with a grin, switching the conversation to Korean. "He's dead."

"He's so self-centered it makes my teeth ache," Niki answered irritably. "And he follows me everywhere. It's maddening."

"I think he really likes you," said Taejin. She couldn't stand the guy anyway, so he could be magnanimous.

"Perhaps, but does it mean I have to like him back?" she asked rhetorically.

Taejin was quiet for a moment. The drizzle had stopped in the meantime, and Niki pushed back the hood of her raincoat, baring her chin-length dark hair.

"Promise me something," he started, and she looked at him with her crystal eyes and nodded, smiling. His heart melted a little. "If I ever do something bad, just tell me, so I can apologize at once," Taejin went on earnestly. "You're scary when you hate someone."

Niki laughed. "You never do anything wrong," she assured him. "It's always me and the twins who get in trouble. You're the big brother who bails us out every time."

That was true, and Taejin smiled, feeling his face warm up. It felt good to hear her use the word "big brother", which in Korean wasn't applied only to siblings but could refer to an older male friend, and a boyfriend as well. Niki didn't call him that normally, as her Korean lacked cultural nuances. She simply addressed them all by their names. But he thought it would be nice to hear the title more often.

"And Sori's our big sister who'd defend us even in front of a firing squad," Niki added fondly. "You're both my heroes."

By the firing squad, she probably meant his parents, and unfortunately, she wasn't far off.

"And what about Kehuan?" Taejin asked with interest.

"What about him?" Niki sounded a little perplexed, as if her own brother didn't belong in this conversation.

"Doesn't he protect you as well?"

"Of course he does," said Niki, looking at him strangely. "Always."

* * *

Kehuan and Taejin passed their final exams with flying colors and submitted their papers to the university of technology, Kehuan for computer science, and Taejin for power engineering. And Niki and the twins got accepted to the international high school, which was enough of success for them, and then everybody could enjoy the well-deserved holidays.

Niki decided to finally go to Vancouver this year. Chen Xiao was beyond happy about her change of heart and promised she'd be able to do whatever she wanted there without him breathing down her neck. Kehuan was going as well, and he was looking forward to showing her around the city.

But first, they all went together to the Beskid mountains for a week, to hike again, for the first time without any member of the older generation supervising them.

"But what if you freak out again, Nik?" asked Taerim on the train, sounding hopeful instead of concerned.

The twins had missed the whole affair last year, and they were forever chagrined about it. So much fun, and it had all happened without them.

"Then you'll have to hug me and stroke my head, saying 'there, there, all will be fine'," Niki answered tartly. "But I'll do my best to keep a lid on it."

"But have you got any idea what brought it on last time?" asked Taejin anxiously. "Because if you knew, it'd be easier to avoid it."

"I do," answered Niki, surprising everybody, including Kehuan. "There were several things at once, but I think the crickets were the final straw."

"Crickets?"

"Big open space. Uneven terrain. Darkness. Starry sky. And crickets."

"That's a very specific setup," Kehuan observed. "If it all has to happen at once, eliminating it should be easy enough. But if you only need some elements..."

"I think one or two elements won't trigger it," Niki told him, very confident, and he realized she must've been thinking about it a lot. "It all happened in the past already, separately. The crickets are the worst. I hate this sound, it's so spooky."

"You've got some seriously bad karma with insects," Kehuan noticed.

"Why?" Sori asked curiously, and Niki launched into the story of the mass wasp attack from the time when she'd been five.

In the evening they arrived in the mountain village at the end of the railway tracks, and Kehuan and Niki went out for a walk.

"You remember now," Kehuan said, and it wasn't a question.

"For the most part," Niki admitted. "There are still some blanks. But after that freak-out, my head kind of unlocked, and I started to have more coherent dreams, and to recall more and more. Earlier it was all so mangled."

"Want to tell me?"

"It was mostly like you thought," Niki answered, shrugging.

Kehuan hadn't told Taejin the whole truth on that day in the previous year: they had talked about it with Niki, just a couple of times. He'd tried to reconstruct the events, but since she had huge gaps in her memory and crucial details were missing, it was all hypothesis and guesswork. And Niki wasn't keen on those conversations, so he quit them.

"That guy who crashed into them saw me near the car, and put me in the cab of his truck," she said now.

"Why?"

"He didn't want me to see—" she stopped short, and there was a moment of loaded silence.

Kehuan hesitated, but in the end, he didn't ask. If she'd wanted to tell him about it, she would have.

"Then he drove away from there," she went on after a moment. "I think he panicked."

"Sure he did," Kehuan muttered. He thought he'd like to meet that driver, even now.

"I heard him talk to somebody on the phone later. His father, I think. There was something wrong with the papers of the truck, something wasn't valid—"

"The technical check perhaps?"

"Maybe, I don't know. Anyway, he was scared to death, and totally out of it, crying and stuff..."

"Is that why he drove you out of the country?"

"It wasn't him. He left me at some service station—told me to go to the toilet. When I went out again, I didn't even remember about him. I looked for Chen Xiao's car, but of course, it wasn't there. This part is still quite foggy."

Kehuan's heart squeezed. "So what happened next?" he asked after a moment.

"There was a parking lot with a lot of trucks, and I saw one that looked like that guy's. I remembered him then. The door was open, so I got inside."

"Why?"

"I think I hoped he'd take me back to mum and Chen Xiao."

"But it was a different truck," Kehuan guessed.

"Yes."

"And the second guy took you to the Netherlands?"

"By accident. I was cold, so I got under some blankets on the bed behind his seat, and fell asleep. He didn't notice me until much later."

"Anything else happened?" Kehuan asked, and waited, tense.

He hoped it was all; it was bad enough. But the police had wondered, and his father and Chen Xiao also wondered for years. There was room for so many additional calamities in this enigmatic history.

"Nothing else. He dropped me at another gas station and fled, and then the police came. Someone from the staff must've summoned them."

He exhaled quietly.

"Funny, but I didn't even realize at first I was in a different country," Niki added, smiling wryly. "I was so confused I thought I couldn't understand what people were saying to me because I couldn't speak."

Kehuan really wanted to hug her at this moment. He felt so sorry for that lost, hurt, frightened child who still hid inside her, peeking out from her eyes from time to time. But she wanted to appear strong, so he didn't.

"Let's go back," Niki suggested, sounding a little uneasy. "I can hear these wretched bugs again."

He hadn't notice before the sound of the crickets in the fields on both sides of the road. It must've been hard for her in summer, every year.

"Niki," he told her with genuine pride. "You are one tough cookie."

* * *

Niki was really getting better.

She still had nightmares from time to time, but they weren't so frequent now as right after that panic attack last year, when she'd woken up drenched with sweat almost every night.

She went to Canada with Kehuan in the summer, and it became a little easier to be around Chen Xiao, too. She wasn't so anxious in his presence now, though it still didn't feel comfortable, and she put a lot of work into mending their relationship during these three weeks. Chen Xiao was such a great guy, and he seemed so happy to have her there, and he'd certainly drawn a short straw with her as his adoptive child.

She could eat better now as well and hoped it would help her body finally catch up with her age. All girls in her new class at the high school looked like young women already, with breasts and hips and stuff, only she was still the same stick insect.

Kamila especially was a real goddess, and it was great fun to watch the twins when she was around: their eyes unfocused and glazed over each time she entered the classroom or came up to sit down for a chat. And they weren't the only ones to follow her every move; Kamila had admirers galore.

Niki wasn't longing for multiple admirers. The one she had was already driving her up the wall. She just thought it'd be nice to look more like a real girl because another result of her head clearing up was that she'd started to pay more attention to what was happening around her. And one of the things that had never registered with her before, and of which she became painfully aware now, was how many attractive girls were interested in Kehuan.

He sometimes waited for her in front of the school gate after lessons, on the days his classes at the university ended early enough, and it was hard to miss all those seductive looks, and giggles, and whispered comments flying among the female students every time he appeared. Niki was certain his college classmates were equally captivated, and probably able to express their interest in more mature ways. She sometimes wondered how she'd feel if he decided to act on it one day, and started dating some university girl. But it was better not to imagine such things. Her chest constricted at the idea alone.

"Your brother still has a fan club here," noticed Kamila one day. "I've just overheard in the canteen a very lively discussion about his possible preferences."

"Kehuan isn't my brother," Niki replied, irritated.

Kamila looked at her askance. "Yeah, sure. So what's the family relationship between you?"

"There's none," said Niki.

"Seriously?!" Kamila was dumbfounded. "Then why do people always say you are siblings? Or cousins?"

"I have no idea," Niki answered testily. "Probably because we have the same surname."

Kamila shook her head. "There's more to it," she said. "You live together, right?"

"Yes, but I don't think many people really know it." Niki braced herself for the next obvious question, but the redhead veered in a different direction with her analysis.

"But he always hung out with you a lot when he was still at the school," Kamila was saying. "And growled at other people who approached you, and if they weren't nice to you, he'd bite their head right off."

"I don't know why everybody always treats Kehuan like a rabid dog," said Niki, annoyed even more with this description.

Kamila glanced at her again with curious eyes. "So it's like that," she said contemplatively.

Niki felt her cheeks warm up, and she chose not to answer.

"It must be hard to listen to those geese, in this case," Kamila noted soberly. "But why don't you…?"

"Have you seen him?" asked Niki. "Have you seen me?"

"I have," Kamila answered. "You are both quite decorative. Where's the problem?"

"Kehuan's all grown up," Niki said, astounded that she was discussing it with anybody, and with Kamila at that, of all people. "And I…"

"Ah," said Kamila. "The force of habit. He may be too close to notice, but you're changing, girl."

"You think so?"

"Definitely," Kamila confirmed. "And I think you need a short break from each other, to change perspective."

"You want me to sign up for Finland," guessed Niki, resigned. "I should have known."

"Haven't you been thinking about it anyway?"

"A little," Niki admitted.

A lot, she should have said.

For the last several years the international high school had been collaborating with a bilingual school in Lahti, and every year a number of students participated in the exchange, going there for a few months. You needed to write a good motivation letter to get accepted, and Kamila had already submitted hers and was constantly egging Niki on to do the same.

And Niki was tempted. There were several areas of the collaboration, and one of them was arts and crafts, and she was in love with the things they were doing there, especially the woodcraft.

But to go away for several months… Strange. Scary. Lonely.

* * *

"What are you making?" asked Kehuan, looking at a big wooden plank tinged with blue wood stain and bristling with a forest of tiny nails. So this had been the source of all that banging noise for the last two hours.

"Cotton snowflakes," said Niki, who'd just started winding the white cotton twine around the nails, her brow puckered with concentration.

Kehuan looked closer.

"Have you come up with these patterns by yourself?" he asked with interest.

"Only the big one," she answered, focused on her work. "The smaller ones are from the website. There were more, but not good."

Kehuan looked at the screen of her laptop. There were indeed multiple sketches of snowflakes there, and he could see at once why some of them were off.

"What's wrong with them?" he asked, studying the patterns, curious what she'd say.

Niki looked up at him. "The motif should be the same on each level, just proportionally smaller," she explained. "But those others have a little different motifs on different levels."

"You've chosen only those which are built according to recursive algorithms," Kehuan specified. "Niki, how on earth is it possible you had problems with math in primary school?"

She shrugged and examined the results of her work with a slight frown.

"What language is it?" he asked, checking the screen again.

"Finnish," she said, and hesitated for a moment, as if she was going to add something, but got back to work instead.

Kehuan watched closely as she was weaving the twine around the nails in the complicated pattern. He could see already it would be splendid. It would look great in the living room, over the couch, but Anna didn't want any child art, as she called Niki's creations, in the common parts of the apartment. Stupid, in his opinion, but it was Anna.

"Where are you going to put it?" he asked, eyeing the plank dubiously. There was no free space big enough on any wall in her room.

"Maybe I'll just give it to Taejin when it's ready," Niki answered, untroubled. "He's been nagging me for months to make something for him."

Kehuan immediately felt a strong aversion to this idea.

"Put it in my room," he offered. "I've got a good place for it over my desk."

"Don't you have enough of my pieces there already?"

"Nope. These are fractals what you are making here," Kehuan told her with a grin. "They belong in my space, and nowhere else."

* * *

Niki went to Finland.

It hadn't been such a hard decision in the end. She'd talked it through with Kehuan, and he'd been a little surprised and wary at the beginning, but when she showed him the things people were making in that school in Lahti, and let him read her motivation letter, he changed his mind and told her she should go.

As for her personal worries, Niki adopted a fatalistic approach. She couldn't make her body change faster by willpower alone, and time was flowing the same way everywhere. No point in wasting it on useless fretting.

Ironically, as soon as she arrived in Lahti, she got her first period, finally. But it suddenly didn't matter that much because her new reality was really cool and very absorbing. Kamila was there with her, and the twins, who'd shocked everybody at home when they'd also submitted their letters, and then fought a long and bloody battle with their own mother to be allowed to go.

Each of them was staying with a local host family, and Niki loved hers to bits. The parents were totally laid-back and friendly without being nosy, and there were three young kids at home, always eager to sing with her. She was teaching them to draw and paint and was learning in turn from their mum how to cook different local dishes.

They arrived in Lahti in January, in the middle of the winter, and what a winter it was! Niki had never seen so much snow in her life, the temperature at night regularly dropped to minus twenty degrees and lower, and daylight hours were so short that they left home in the dark to get to school, and returned again in the dark after the lessons. But in time the days got longer, and they were learning kick-sledding and cross-country skiing, and ice-skating, and it was a real revelation; ice-skating was Niki's new favorite pastime. Though a perilous one again, unfortunately.

"Hey girl, I've got something for you," Kamila told her one day. "I can't take your squabbles anymore."

Just a few days earlier she'd had to listen to Niki and the twins' raucous and profanity-loaded argument about how it made no sense for someone to drop gymnastics due to potential injuries, only to take up ice-skating next.

Kamila reached inside her bag and took out what at first looked like a pair of black fingerless mittens, but under closer inspection turned out to be very solid-looking wrist guards.

"That's a fantastic idea," said Niki, beaming at the redhead. "You're a genius."

"Sure I am," Kamila answered airily. "Just remember to wear them to the ice rink. And draw me a nice picture of a fox as a thank you."

* * *

Kehuan had never thought four months could drag so long.

Niki called him almost every day on Skype, and looked and sounded so happy and vibrant that he felt really glad she'd gone there, or so he kept telling himself. Honestly speaking, his first reaction had been "no way in hell". Chen Xiao had given his permission at once, though, so no help from that direction; Kehuan would have to be the bad guy himself. But when he read this letter of hers and saw her animated face when she was explaining to him enthusiastically some woodcraft designs he didn't really care for, he just couldn't tell her not to go. But without Niki life got somewhat dull over here.

He went to his classes, of course, even if some of them were for kindergarteners in his opinion, and he could easily give the lectures instead of listening to them. He was thinking about starting a second faculty next year, probably mathematics. Chen Xiao sent him regularly new tasks and problems to solve, too, and they were more challenging and educative than all the courses at the university, not to mention more profitable.

Apart from that he read books, and played basketball with the guys on Friday evenings, and trained at the martial arts club, and met from time to time with the old crowd to play music together, and it was all good, as always, but somehow lacked any real flavor, like even the most beautiful landscape on a sunless day would lack brilliance and warmth.

But at least she called regularly and entertained him with stories about her life in Lahti.

"I've started drawing a comic story," she told him in the middle of February, after wishing him a happy birthday. "The first episode's ready. I'm going to hang it in the corridor at school."

"Cool," Kehuan answered, grinning. "What's it about?"

"There's this girl who wants to be on the school hockey team, but it's only for boys. And her best friend is a boy who wants to be a fashion designer, but is afraid people would laugh at him."

"Do they pretend to be each other?" he guessed. "Swap places?"

"Of course they do," Niki answered cheerfully. "Pretend and swap."

"Haven't I read something similar before? Or watched?"

"All stories have been told already thousand times," Nik told him, unperturbed. "We just shuffle around plots and characters, and then pretend they're something new."

"True," Kehuan laughed. "Let me know if the kids like it."

"Will tell you tomorrow."

He was sure her drawings were great, even if the story wasn't very original, and wasn't surprised when the next day she told him it was a great success.

"I'm drawing the second episode now. Enter super arrogant hockey star, who can't stand this wimp in the team, and the noble team captain who protects his new player. Oh, and a spoilt but pretty female cousin of the girl, who wants to be a fashion model."

"Plot thickens," Kehuan commented, amused. "But I'd like to see the first part. Send me a photo, will you?"

"Sure," she promised. "How are the classes?"

"Still kindergarten level," he said dismissively. "I hope it's just the first year."

"It's your own fault," Niki said, parroting Anna. She'd never lost that recording device talent, and it still made him laugh, every time. "Who told you to have studied all this advanced stuff already? Now you pay the price."

The next day she sent him the photo of the first episode of the story, and the pictures indeed were great, but they also had a strange, beguiling quality to them which he hadn't expected. The ink outlines, disconnected and unfinished, were not completely aligned with the pastel-colored images, and it gave the whole thing a dreamy feel, not comic-like at all. The dialogues were minimal: the whole story was in these illustrations.

"Niki," he said the next day, "could you start making those pictures on separate smaller sheets of paper, and scan them for me?"

"Sure, but why?" she asked with interest.

"I'd like to publish them on the Internet, as a webtoon," Kehuan explained. "What do you say?"

"I don't think this can really qualify as a webtoon," Niki said doubtfully. "Graphic wise, I mean."

"Yes," Kehuan agreed. "That's what's interesting about it."

So she started drawing each scene on A4 paper and sending him the scans regularly, and he was amused by how absurdly wrapped up in the story he soon became.

"Are they in love?" he asked her curiously four weeks later. "Aapo and Taimi?"

"Not with each other," Niki answered. "Can't you tell? Aapo has a crush on the model girl, and Taimi on the hockey star."

"The arrogant guy?" Kehuan made sure, surprised. "Not the team captain?"

"Nah, girls always go for the bad boys," she informed him sagely. "The captain's too nice."

He chuckled, leaning back in the beanbag.

"But do you know, people started sending me suggestions what should happen next," said Niki. "I get like five new messages every day."

"Ignore them," Kehuan told her resolutely. "It's your story. Let them deal with it."

* * *

That weekend he went to a party with Taejin and some of his buddies.

His cousin had always been one for social life, but Kim Haneul had kept him on a very short leash before, and while many of their classmates partied devotedly through entire high school, Taejin had been a good boy then. Now that he was in college, and his mother had finally loosened up the restraints, he decided it was time to make up for all the deprivation. And since Taejin always needed company for everything he did, he kept hassling Kehuan to go with him to this or that party almost every weekend.

Kehuan went several times, but he felt totally out of place on these occasions, and every time he was bored out of his mind after half an hour. Each party developed in a similar way: lots of alcohol, plus some extra stuff from time to time, inconsequential chattering giving way to noisy chaotic discussions as the drinking went on, followed by occasional dancing or some risqué games, with obligatory canoodling in the dark corners towards the end.

This time the shindig was in a private house of some guy from Taejin's faculty. The place was big and there were forty people present at least, and Kehuan watched with exasperation and the usual feeling of incompatibility as the party advanced through the typical phases. At some point he decided to find Taejin and tell him he was leaving; if he didn't, his cousin would be miffed again the next day.

He was walking along the corridor on the second floor, checking different rooms for Taejin, when a girl walked out from the bathroom on unsteady feet.

"Hello," she crooned, staring at him with a sultry smile. "Were you looking for me?"

"No," Kehuan answered, veering to the right to avoid her.

"I saw you watch me before," the girl purred again, moving in his way. "I liked it."

He had no idea what she was talking about, but this was another reason why he wasn't crazy about these parties: there were always some females on the prowl, looking for a hookup, and even though Kehuan did his best not to notice them, his body sometimes did the noticing for him, and it only unnecessarily complicated things.

"Excuse me," he said curtly and shoved her aside. The girl swayed on her feet and braced herself against the wall, giggling.

He'd earlier bumped into Mauricio de Silva in the kitchen, in the company of a girl whom he vaguely remembered from the music club, and Taejin, who had still been with him at that stage of the party, looked quite taken with her. So Kehuan wasn't really surprised now when he opened the door to yet another room and saw his cousin and the girl smooching enthusiastically in a big armchair.

"I'm leaving," he said and waited until Taejin lifted his head from the girl's neck.

Kehuan smirked and raised his hand in goodbye, but since Taejin stayed motionless and kept staring at him with suddenly sobered eyes, he made a rotating gesture with his hand, encouraging him to go on with what he'd been doing, and closed the door.

He walked back along the corridor and down the stairs, and three minutes later left the house after finding his jacket on the overloaded rack in the entrance hall.

Outside he saw Mauricio, sitting on the steps and smoking a cigarette.

"I had no idea you smoked," Kehuan remarked.

"Only at the parties," Mauricio answered, looking at him with a peculiar smile. "Running already?"

"Yeah," Kehuan sat down next to him for a moment. "There's no fun in watching people drink themselves stupid and then screw around."

"Oh, I can't agree with that," Mauricio contradicted sarcastically. "There's a whole industry out there, making heaps of money off people watching others screw."

Kehuan chuckled at that, and Mauricio grinned at him.

"Made you laugh," he noted with satisfaction. "Good for me."

Kehuan didn't answer.

"Where's your bestie?" asked Mauricio.

"Busy," Kehuan told him with a ghost of a smile.

"Sure he is," Mauricio snickered. "With Elena, huh?"

It happened rather often with Taejin these days. Along with parties he'd discovered sex, and since he was a really handsome guy, and knew how to talk to girls to make them smile, he never seemed to be short of eager partners.

Kehuan was actually glad of it. Before, he'd had that growing suspicion that Taejin was interested in Niki, and it had been like a thorn under his skin, requiring intervention. He'd been deliberating, very reluctantly, talking to his cousin and setting things straight, but Taejin had never really said anything, and Kehuan wasn't keen on being the first one to open this can of worms. But lately, he'd come to the conclusion that he must've been wrong; Taejin wouldn't be acting like that otherwise.

They sat in silence for a moment.

"How's Niki?" Mauricio asked at last.

"Good," Kehuan answered, and smiled. "Ice-skating. Learning woodwork. Singing in a choir."

Mauricio raised his eyes to the dark sky. "In a choir. With that voice. Don't they have a clue about anything in that tundra?"

Kehuan chuckled again.

"Speaking fluent Finnish already?"

"Halfway there, I suppose," Kehuan answered, amused.

"When's she coming back?" Mauricio asked.

"End of May," Kehuan said and sighed involuntarily.

Mauricio watched him for a moment with pensive eyes. "You're so lucky, you know," he said quietly at last. "The two of you."

Kehuan glanced at him, taken aback. He rather wouldn't use this word to describe himself, and it definitely didn't apply to Niki.

But then he thought about it some more, considering everything Mauricio didn't say, and finally admitted, unabashed, "Yeah, I guess we are."

* * *

"How have you been?" Kehuan asked Sori in April when he dropped by at the Soengs' place. "Stressed out much?"

It was her turn to take the final exams, and they were just a few weeks away now.

Sori smiled dolefully. "You have no idea," she said.

"Don't listen to her," Taejin interrupted. "She's been cramming like crazy for months. She's going to do great."

Kehuan had no doubt about it. Sori had always been the most dutiful and diligent of them all.

"So where are you going to enroll?"

"Music university, here or in Cracow. But I have to pass entrance exams first."

"I met Mauricio a few weeks ago, at that party," Kehuan remembered. "He didn't look particularly overworked."

"Appearances," Sori answered, shrugging. "He's quite nervous, actually, and can't decide if he's going to stay in Poland for college or go back to Spain."

"Niki will be sad if he leaves," Kehuan noticed and then realized that he'd miss the guy as well. Who'd have thought?

"How's Niki?" asked Sori with a fond smile. "I heard from the twins she's become the mascot of the school hockey team over there."

"What?" Taejin laughed. "How come?"

"Taeyeon said the boys from the team have been teaching her some ice-skating techniques, and she's apparently drawing a comic story about them, and they all just love her."

Kehuan didn't feel amused at all. In fact, he felt very unamused. He stayed for a few more minutes and hurried back home, not to miss her daily call.

"Niki," he growled as soon as their Skype connection was established. "Is that comic story about you?"

"What...?" She was evidently caught off guard. "Huh?!"

"That comic story you are drawing. Is it about you?" Kehuan repeated impatiently and realized that he sounded a little deranged.

"How can it be?" Niki wondered. "I'm not interested in fashion that much, and have no clue about hockey."

"But is there an arrogant hockey star on the school team?" asked Kehuan before he could stop himself.

Niki started giggling. "Several, actually," she told him drolly. "Some of those boys are such prima donnas like you wouldn't believe, heads swollen like hot-air balloons."

It didn't really sound as if she particularly liked any of them, and Kehuan breathed a quiet sigh of relief.

"But why?..." she asked, sounding curious now.

"Forget it," he told her hastily. "So how was your day?"

He thought about it some more later. He'd overreacted, of course. Niki was still very young, and she wasn't interested in anybody this way, and it would probably take a few more years before it changed.

Kehuan sometimes wished that time flowed faster, or that the age gap between them shrank miraculously. But he could wait, as long as it would take.

* * *

They were coming back in the last week of May, just before the end of the school year in Finland. Kim Hana was going to collect the twins from the airport, and she offered she'd pick up Niki as well, and drop her at the apartment on their way home.

On the day of their return Kehuan was so edgy he couldn't concentrate properly on anything, and finally went out to take a walk along the river; he felt pathetic sitting in his room, all impatient and jittery. He walked for a long time, keeping himself from glancing at his watch, and when he finally checked the time, it'd become quite late, so he ran back home at top speed.

And there was Niki in his room, standing next to the big window and gazing at the city landscape outside. She turned around at the sound of his footsteps.

She was wearing narrow blue jeans, a snug black tee, and an unbuttoned white shirt, which looked as if it could have come from his own closet, though he knew it hadn't. Kehuan had seen her dressed like that countless times, but now all of a sudden he wanted it to be his shirt, which was a really strange first thought.

She was a little taller, though still medium height, and not so skinny anymore, just very slim. But her body lost that childlike androgenic shape it used to have; the changes were subtle, but the delicate curves of hips and waist, and breast and shoulders were pronounced enough to make it now unequivocally feminine.

Her dark hair had grown out a lot, reaching to her collar bones, and her triangular face was the same as always. But at the same time, it was completely different.

When Kehuan looked at Niki, he always saw the eyes first because they were the most dominant feature of her face. That was still true, only now those large cat-like eyes seemed to have acquired some new siren quality he'd never picked up on earlier.

And then there was her mouth. He'd often looked at it, to check if Niki was happy or down, or tired, or ready for some mischief; her moods had always been right there in the corners of her lips, and he could read them without fail. But he'd never noticed before how lush and beautiful those lips were.

As he was staring at her, Niki smiled brightly, and this smile changed her face even more, transporting her far away from the land of childhood into some new uncharted territory, and all the areas of Kehuan's mind which he'd kept half asleep, closed off and disconnected, suddenly blazed to life and unlocked with an earsplitting crack.

III

Part Three

9

In a Haze

Kehuan had never thought living together with the person you were in love with could be so problematic.

In the past, he'd never imagined any particular details of the transformation his relationship with Niki would need to undergo to change from this precious but undefined thing it used to be, where people commonly mistook them for close-knit siblings, to a real couple. He'd just always assumed, rather ingenuously, that with time everything would naturally fall into place. But it didn't happen like that at all because what he'd somehow failed to predict were two critically overlapping problems: his own overwhelming reaction to Niki turning into a young woman and her still being fifteen when it happened.

It was the end of spring when she returned from Finland, and in just a couple of weeks, the temperatures soared to above thirty degrees. This meant she was now moving around the apartment in shorts and tank tops, with hair in a ponytail and arms and legs bare, lithe and slender and unbearably lovely. Kehuan sometimes thought with no small amount of self-pity mixed with black humor that the weather was obviously in cahoots with the cat, current fashion, and his own hormones, all of them blithely conspiring to drive him utterly crazy because he really couldn't let himself forget this one itty-bitty detail. She. Was. Still. Fifteen.

In the beginning, he felt at sea about how to treat Niki now; there was such a giant gap between what he wanted and what was acceptable. It didn't help at all that they were alone at home most of the time, or as good as alone. Chen Liang spent much more time in Taipei than in Warsaw these days, and he was absent all summer, and Anna was like a specter, present but nearly undetectable.

Last winter his father had talked with him about their family situation.

"The Warsaw business has been running well without much interference from me for a long time already," he told Kehuan. "We've got good people here. And you're an adult now, and don't need me all the time, do you?"

Kehuan bit his tongue before he said the acidic words that had sprung to his lips.

"I've got shares in the Taiwan company as well," Chen Liang went on, unaware, "and I prefer to spend more time at home now. I'm not getting younger."

Kehuan was astonished his father still considered Taiwan home, after traipsing all over the world for decades, but whatever.

"I'm not going to move to Taipei," he felt obliged to state. "Just so you know."

"I don't expect you to," his father told him tiredly. "I know your life is here for now. We'll see what happens when you finish college."

Kehuan was tempted to say it was him who'd see what happened then, but decided to let it go. "What about Anna?" he asked instead.

"We're going to divorce," Chen Liang said. "But she'll live here at least until Niki becomes an adult. Chen Xiao wants someone to keep an eye on her, and Anna can still represent him at school, if necessary, so it's more convenient to keep things as they are for now."

Kehuan had his own opinion about Anna's capabilities and usefulness, but he had no problem with her staying at the apartment, not anymore. They'd ceased fire long ago. He felt some pity for her, to tell the truth, now that he was old enough to better understand the discrepancy between her early expectations and what his father had had to offer in that botched attempt at marriage. But it didn't mean they had a good relationship, or any kind of relationship, really: she stayed on the upper level of the apartment when she was at home, and ate mostly out, so they sometimes didn't see each other for a week. Kehuan had no idea what she did with all her time, though he had certain suspicions based on the number of wine bottles in their garbage bags for glass. He'd never understood why anybody would choose to squander their life away like that, but it wasn't his business, and besides, he didn't really care.

Niki had a little more interaction with Anna since she made an effort to talk to her from time to time when Anna showed herself in the living room. Kehuan was surprised she bothered.

But anyway, Chen Liang was absent and Anna as good as absent, so it was basically just Niki and him around, and it quickly became clear that the whole situation was fraught with perils. He decided it was best to stick to their earlier routine as much as possible and try not to rock the boat too much. Which meant touch-limited-to-minimum policy, and constant struggle with himself.

But even as he struggled, he was incredibly happy. She was here at last, and so much better now, and he could finally spend time with her, and have fun again. Sunlight was back in his life, and every new day burst with colors.

The classes at the university were already over before the final exams, and Kehuan went to the international school almost every day in the afternoon to pick her up. Sometimes when she walked out of the gate, there were other people with her: the twins, that redheaded girl she'd mindbogglingly befriended, or the dimwit boy who'd once snubbed her in the assembly hall, but they prudently made themselves scarce at the sight of him.

He and Niki walked home together, making detours, as she was as much a wanderer as always, and he didn't mind, as always. She'd often climb on a curbing wall in the park to walk on it doing cartwheels, handstands, and back walkovers, as if it was a balance beam; she'd obviously long forgotten her anxiety about a possible hand injury. In the meantime, he carried her bag, and they talked about something funny that happened at school, or about what he was currently doing for Chen Xiao, or the latest book one of them read, or why it was sometimes better to use oil pastels instead of dry pastels, or how AI was supposed to learn.

At home they cooked regularly again, and Niki would sing her current favorite song, dancing around the kitchen, or chant and bang on the pots as if she was still five, and he'd listen and stare and laugh, and completely forget about what he was supposed to be doing, so their food would boil over or burn, but who cared?

In the evening he usually came with his laptop to her room, and while he was trying to work, or to study for his finals, she'd be painting with watercolors or calligraphing with black ink, or scoffing and cursing at her homework, and distracting him as much as humanly possible.

Every few days they went shopping together, and each time they laughed themselves silly with some goofy games, like a contest who'd throw more stupid and unnecessary things into the cart, or who'd be able to ride farther on it up the supermarket aisle, or who'd find a product with the most obscure purpose and come up with the most absurd explanation what it was supposed to do. One day they met some people Niki recognized from school, who just stood there and gaped at them before they finally scurried away, muttering among themselves and throwing back suspicious glances. But again, who cared? Not Kehuan, for sure.

* * *

At the end of June, Soeng Taejin passed the last of his finals at the university, and it was as good a pretext as any to meet in the evening with some friends in his fav bar. Kehuan had promised to come as well, and Taejin was glad. They hadn't had much time to hang out lately.

He was putting on a clean shirt when Sori called from the hall, "Kehuan's here!"

Taejin jogged down the stairs and saw both his cousins standing silently near the front door, listening to the raised voices coming from the living room.

"—have the right to hate him, but you cannot hate your whole country because of one scoundrel," his mother was saying agitatedly.

"It's not about Yoon Kwangshik," answered his aunt. "It's about our mother, and the whole family, and the neighbors. There's this whole culture over there of condoning such things—"

"Am I not Korean? Isn't my husband?" asked Taejin's mother passionately. "Haven't we always supported you through all of that?"

"You have, and you know I'm grateful..."

"Don't be grateful, just be reasonable!"

"Let's go," said Taejin morosely, and looked at Sori. "Are you staying?"

She hesitated, still looking towards the living room with a slight frown, but in the end, she shook her head.

"What was that about?" asked Kehuan once they all stepped outside.

"The biannual debate 'to return, or not to return'," Sori answered with a wry smile. "They should record it and just play it every two years, and spare their vocal cords."

"What's the stance of the rest?"

"The twins are all for staying," said Taejin. "But father will go with mother's decision, and mother would've gone back years ago if not for aunt."

"What about you two?"

"I'm staying, of course," said Sori at once. "With mum."

Taejin kept silent for a moment. "Hard to say," he said in the end. "I mean, on the one hand, I'd prefer to stay, too. College, people, everything. But on the other hand, we can't live here forever."

"Why not?" A typical Kehuan question.

"Because this isn't our place," Taejin said, sounding more confident than he felt.

"Where is our place? Busan?" asked Sori sulkily.

"Probably. South Korea, anyway."

"You've lived here longer than there," Kehuan noticed. "You sure?"

"No," Taejin admitted. "But a person needs to have an allegiance, you know."

"I don't know," Kehuan answered with a shrug.

"Oh come on. I know it's a bit complicated in your case..."

"No, really?"

"But you must have some sense of belonging," finished Taejin with conviction. "Deep inside."

Kehuan didn't answer.

"I'm going to visit Elena," said Sori, and seemed to wait for some reaction, but since neither of them spoke, she sighed and added, "Have fun."

Taejin felt his face burn at the mention of Elena. They'd dated for a few weeks in early spring before he ended things, and their parting hadn't been pretty.

"So if your parents decide to go back, you'll just pack and go as well?" Kehuan restarted the conversation after saying goodbye to Sori. "With no regrets?"

"Even if I wanted to stay, they won't let me," Taejin answered irritably. He'd been worrying about it constantly for the last few weeks. That regular debate got very fierce this time.

"You're an adult," Kehuan reminded him, amused. "Live your own life already."

"I don't see how taking my parents' wishes into account means I'm not living my life," Taejin said defensively. It was an old conflict of opinions between them, and apparently unresolvable. "But even if I wanted to go against their will, I depend on them for now."

"So do something about it," Kehuan told him impatiently. "Go find work."

Yeah, as if it was that easy. Not everybody was born a genius programmer.

"I don't have enough free time—"

"Just cut partying and chasing after girls," said his cousin dryly. "You'll have plenty of time at your disposal."

"I don't do that anymore," Taejin answered quietly, feeling pathetic.

He wasn't proud of himself and his deeds over the previous several months; there were many things he'd erase now if he could. But what was done was done, and in the end, he hadn't done anything that horrible. It was just that some temptations were hard to resist, and he was nineteen and single for now, after all. But Kehuan didn't get any of that, being the cold fish that he was, and completely devoid of any human impulses.

"What's Niki doing?" Taejin asked, and twitched with alarm when Kehuan suddenly turned in his direction, pinning him down with a hostile glare.

Oh damn, wrong move.

"I haven't seen much of her since they all returned from Finland," he added hastily. "No problems at school?"

"No problems at all," his cousin answered, still regarding him with slit eyes.

They were there, thank goodness.

"Let's go in," Taejin said meekly. He wondered if there would ever come a time when he'd be able to discuss Niki with Kehuan without fearing for his life.

* * *

One week later, Kim Hana took them all on the traditional seaside trip.

They didn't have much luck with the weather this year: some cold front had come right before their arrival, and the sky was overcast all the time, with heavy clouds hanging low and leaking rain every ten minutes, and strong wind turning momentarily into a gale. The sea was stormy, with high waves crashing incessantly against the empty shore. People sat in their lodgings, cursing and asking each other whose idiotic idea it had been to choose the Baltic seaside for their holiday destination.

But Niki didn't mind the cold and the wind, as she'd become kind of weather-resistant after those few months in Finland, and Kehuan was probably the only person on the entire coast who was grateful for the nasty conditions. He preferred not to think too much about how he'd react to Niki in a swimsuit, and even less about how he'd react to other people looking at Niki in a swimsuit; the additional present his befuddled brain decided to bestow upon him now was complete intolerance for other males staring at her for longer than three seconds.

So they went every day for the usual long walks and sometimes didn't meet any other people for hours. It was just the two of them, the gray, stormy sky, the wind, and the roaring sea. Perfect.

* * *

Taejin went out of the holiday apartment to buy some snacks; the general agreement was to play board games in the evening since they'd had so much fun with it the previous day.

He was looking forward to sitting next to Niki again, and listening to her squabbles with the twins, glancing surreptitiously at her ethereal profile, so at odds with her droll comments. She was still very young, but every time she laughed it did something funny to his insides. He realized he was smiling just thinking about her now, and wondered if she was still drawing, or if she'd be up for some swimming at the pool. The only problem was avoiding Kehuan, who'd lately become more of a watchdog than ever.

He finished shopping and went out of the small minimart. The weather got even worse today, the rain almost horizontal now, and Taejin ran back as fast as it was possible in the gale. He went inside and took off his raincoat and shoes, listening to Sori playing her violin in the other room. That girl didn't understand the concept of vacations. She'd already taken the college entrance exams, so why not give it a rest for a week? Though it was no hardship listening to Sori; she played like a pro, or rather she was a pro already.

"Where's Kehuan?" he asked the twins, sitting on opposite sides of the table over a game of chess.

"Out," said Taerim.

"Out where?"

"Out there," answered his younger brother. "Walking with Niki to the end of the world."

Taejin looked out through the window as if he hadn't just returned and seen a moment ago what it was like outside.

"Are they crazy?" he asked with disbelief.

"Yep," Taeyeon said. "She's crazy. He's crazy. Perfect match."

"Yeah, I guess they are family, after all," Taejin agreed, chuckling.

There was a moment of silence. He looked towards the table and saw both twins watching him in a contemplative manner.

"Brother," said Taeyeon at last. "Has it ever crossed your mind that your perception of reality may be the tiniest bit skewed?"

"Skewed how?" he asked with an unpleasant feeling that his naughty younger brothers were poking fun at him again.

"Skewed beyond repair," Taerim answered, shaking his head at Taeyeon, and they both returned to their game of chess.

* * *

As soon as they returned to the city, the heat was back, of course.

Sori was walking in the park near the Chens' apartment, hoping to meet Kehuan and Niki around. She was ecstatic today, having just learned that she'd got accepted to the academies of music both in Warsaw and in Cracow. She needed only to make the final decision now where to enroll.

It wasn't really a difficult choice. Cracow was fabulous, but taking the entrance exam there had been rather a contingency plan than anything else since she didn't have any real intention of leaving Warsaw. Her mum was here, for a start, as was the rest of the family. Kim Haneul had agreed in the end to stay in Poland for the next two years. She'd sworn it was absolutely the last time, but it made sense: this way, the twins could finish high school and Taejin do his bachelor's degree without any complications.

But even if Sori never talked about it to anybody, and hardly admitted it even to herself, the most important reason for her unwillingness to move away was the fact that Kehuan was here, too.

She'd liked him for so long, and sometimes thought he liked her, too. They often talked, and he was always very polite to her, while he rarely paid any attention to other girls. But that was all, and Sori had been wondering for some time if she should perhaps show some initiative. It wasn't in her nature exactly, but Kehuan was such an introvert she doubted he'd ever make the first step if she left it to him.

Speak of the devil, right at this moment she noticed him in some distance, sitting under that giant oak tree with his back against the trunk and reading a book. She left the path, smiling, and started walking in his direction, and was maybe twenty steps away when she noticed Niki as well, lying next to him on some piece of clothing stretched on the grass, asleep. Nightmares again, probably. Poor poppet.

Kehuan raised his eyes from the book and looked at the sleeping girl for a moment. Then he put the book away and lay down on the grass next to her, propping his head on one hand. He reached out with the other hand and started playing with her hair, carefully winding it around his fingers, and clearly trying not to wake her up. His languorous eyes fixed on Niki's serene features, and his face wore a strange expression, somehow tender and predatory at the same time.

Sori stood motionless, staring at the intimate scene with a feeling of complete disconnection from reality. Was it really Kehuan? Was it really Niki?

Maybe she was reading too much into it—

Kehuan let Niki's hair slip away from his fingers and hesitated for a moment. Then his hand moved again, and he touched her lips very lightly with one finger.

Sori turned around and fled before she had time to make any conscious decision.

Half an hour later she shut the door of her room and sat down in the swivel chair. She put her head against its back and span slowly around. Her face was burning.

Was it possible she'd seen it wrong?

No. There was no mistaking the look on his face.

So it only left the question, how had she missed it for so many years? Because her intuition was telling her now that what she'd seen under that oak tree wasn't anything new; it was something very, very old.

She closed her eyes.

That boy who'd always looked so grim and unapproachable when she was watching him from afar, suddenly chuckling warmly as the little girl with bright eyes said, "Chen, Veronica".

The same young boy, his eyes bleak, putting his arms around the girl crying her heart out on the seedy stairs lit with a dirty light bulb.

Little Niki, walking along the edge of the water with her eyes on the horizon and hair flowing in the wind, and Kehuan, watching her, only ever her, and saying to Sori, "You go back, we'll walk a little further."

Niki saying sharply, "He's much better than all of you put together!", the burly blond boy taking a step forward, and Kehuan running full tilt towards them, shouting something furiously in Mandarin.

Niki with her hair stuck to the log bench, trembling and gasping, and Kehuan kneeling next to her and cutting at his own hair with cold determination.

Those posters in his room, which must have cost a little fortune, and she was suddenly absolutely sure the money hadn't come from his father.

Stupid, stupid, stupid. Where had her intuition been earlier, for all the years she'd been blind? It was as clear as a day and always had been.

So it was only curiosity, not hope, which made her walk out of the room and find her mother downstairs, in the kitchen.

"Mum," she said, "what is the family connection between Chen Liang and Chen Xiao?"

Kim Hana dropped the lid she'd just lifted to check on whatever was bubbling inside the pot. "Why are you curious, honey?" she asked, obviously playing for time.

"Just tell me."

There was a moment of silence. Her mum picked the lid from the floor. "They aren't related," she said at last. "They're just friends and business partners."

Sori wasn't even surprised. "Why does Niki live in their house, then?" she asked in a wooden voice.

"Chen Xiao was seriously injured in this accident when her mother died," Kim Hana answered, watching her closely, "and later it stayed like that because it was... expedient, I guess. For some reason, Niki wasn't able to live with her father."

"Why have you never said anything?" asked Sori desperately, and her eyes filled with tears.

"Oh, honey," her mum breathed, dismayed, "what happened?"

"Nothing happened," said Sori, smearing the tears on her cheeks with one trembling hand. "I've found out what an idiot I am."

Kim Hana put both her arms around her and hugged her close.

"You're not an idiot," she told her affectionately after a short pause. "You simply made an error of judgment."

"But why?" Sori asked miserably.

"Kehuan is such a lovable boy," said her mum quietly. "I think it was very easy."

"Kehuan, lovable?" Sori snorted, and then sobbed. "If aunt could hear you..."

"Yes, well, your aunt's never seen him very clear," answered her mum with a peculiar smile. "But we both know he's gorgeous. And frighteningly smart. And he does martial arts, too."

Sori started giggling through the tears.

"Not to mention he's very loyal, and honest, and responsible," added Kim Hana more seriously. "And he's always been nice to you when he's nice to very few people. That's what led you astray, probably."

Sori nodded, feeling wrung out. "I think I'll go to the college in Cracow," she said.

* * *

Kehuan was wondering how long he could go on like this before he went insane.

He still remembered that time in his early adolescence when he'd struggled with the first tidal wave of hormones. How he'd detested it, all these instant reactions he had no control over, that porno slide show flashing in his mind without any logical connection to the reality around him, the dreams, the need to touch himself, the sudden disobedience of his own body, the bewildering rebellion of flesh. He'd been angry all the time then.

Of course, he'd understood the biological reasons for it all, but it took some time before he managed to develop some acceptable strategy and regain a certain measure of control. He'd always known there was only one girl he wanted in his head, but Niki had been very much a child at the time, and he'd kept her strictly apart from it all, on a conscious and subconscious level. In the end, the solution his brain picked was making his erotic dreams very impersonal and abstract, and animalistic at the same time, the bodies in them faceless and featureless, or no real bodies at all, just some fragments of them. It was his own version of mind over matter, crude perhaps, but operational, and he finally accepted sexual drive as yet another physical need: he got hungry, he got thirsty, he got tired, and now he also got horny, and there was no point in attaching to it any non-existing meaning. And with time his body became much easier to manage, too.

But it was all in the past now, any semblance of control up and gone. Now suddenly all his dreams and fantasies had a face, and a voice, and that one particular shape, and a completely new level of intensity, and so much meaning he sometimes choked on it. He lived in a haze, and this touch-limited-to-minimum policy was getting harder to maintain every day.

In August they were both supposed to go to Vancouver for two weeks, but Kehuan canceled his flight at the last moment. He got cold feet when he started to wonder what such a smart guy as Chen Xiao would see when they both appeared in front of him together.

Niki was very puzzled by his sudden decision to skip the trip, but he convinced her to go without him, and then tried to use the time alone to rebuild his weakened morale. Instead, he ended up constantly fretting over the possibility that she might not come back, which was no real possibility at all.

Seriously, he was going crazy.

* * *

Niki returned as planned, of course, and they went for a stroll along the Vistula on the next day.

"Have you heard about Sori?" she asked him. "She's already left for

Cracow. She called me on Skype three days ago."

"I heard," he said.

"I had no idea she was planning to go away for her studies."

"Yeah, it was a little out of the blue," Kehuan agreed. "But she's always liked it there."

"She'd better come home often," said Niki, sounding forlorn, and Kehuan suddenly realized she was probably going to miss the older girl quite a lot.

"Maybe she wanted to try living on her own," he told the cat. "I get it."

"But why? She's got such a great relationship with her mum," said Niki wistfully.

"But this way she could finally give Taejin the slip, and his mother," Kehuan said, and she snorted at that, as he'd hoped she would.

They sat on the grass close to the edge of the water. The summer was coming to an end and it wasn't hot anymore, so there weren't many people on the riverbank, even though the day was sunny. Kehuan looked at Niki's triangular face, so close to his at the moment. Her smooth cheeks had taken on the healthy summer glow, and her hair reached shoulder blades now. He noticed some lighter strands in it, golden brown mixed into the shiny mass of dark brown, a present from the sun. She was looking at the river, and Kehuan's eyes snagged on her long eyelashes, dark, but tipped with gold as well. He gulped and looked away.

"How was Vancouver?" he asked after a moment and felt a little embarrassed with the guttural sound of his voice

"Good," she answered, smiling. "It grows on me. I went hiking two times with those friends of Chen Xiao, to the Alice Lake and to Lynn canyon. I love that the mountains there are so close to the city. The ocean, too."

"So what, going to move now?" Kehuan asked, smiling as well. He'd pondered this option so many times when she'd been away that he had it all figured out already.

Niki stared ahead at the river. "Chen Xiao tries to talk me into applying to the university there," she said finally. "But I don't know." She looked at him questioningly with her CGI eyes.

"Why? Vancouver's cool."

"You wouldn't mind?" she asked, watching him closely.

"No," he answered, shrugging. "It'd be actually easier to work with Chen Xiao if I was there."

Niki's face lit up and her eyes sparkled like diamonds, and Kehuan suddenly felt very pleased with himself, even if he wasn't sure what he'd said exactly to evoke such a reaction.

"We'll see," she said. "There's still plenty of time."

And then she leaned against him, putting her head on his shoulder.

They'd been sitting close to each other, and part of him had been very aware of this fact through the whole conversation, but this move took him completely by surprise. It felt so good, having her lithe body pressed to his arm, and feeling her silky hair slide against the skin of his neck. Before he had time to think it through properly, he reached out, took her hand, and twined their fingers together.

Instant relief. He'd been craving the touch of her skin for so many weeks that now it felt as if his whole body sighed, unwound, and finally settled down. Niki's fingers closed on his immediately, too, and they sat like that for a few minutes, quiet and blissful.

"Green curry for lunch?" he asked at last just to reestablish some link with reality.

"Why not," Niki said brightly, and their hands disconnected as they stood up and picked their hoodies from the ground.

But when they were walking back along the river, Kehuan couldn't resist grabbing her hand again, and didn't let go of it for the entire twenty minutes it took them to get to the Thai place, and even then, as they were sitting at the table outside and waiting for the food, he kept playing with her slim fingers and stroking them with his thumb.

He began to think maybe he'd been too strict with himself after all. Niki seemed really happy to hold hands with him, and a little bit of skin contact wouldn't hurt anyone.

How could it when it felt so wonderful.

* * *

"What have you been doing all summer, girl?" Kamila asked Niki on the first day of school. "You didn't even call."

"I did, though" Niki denied. "You were busy, remember?"

"Yeah, I was," Kamila winced. "I hope your holidays were better than mine."

"Did you work?" Niki often wandered about her friend's family life. Kamila was very vague about it.

"Something like that," Kamila answered. "I was taking care of my sister. Were you taking good care of your brother?"

Niki felt her cheeks flame up, and Kamila chuckled gleefully.

"It's so much fun watching the two of you, you know," she said. "But heads-up, I've already heard some gossip. Apparently, people kept seeing you in different places together, and I'm curious what sordid deeds you were performing in public to scandalize the audience so much—"

"We weren't doing anything out of the ordinary," Niki said vehemently. "Have they got nothing better to do with their time?"

"Obviously not," Kamila answered. "Haven't you noticed yet? Most people lead such a boring, grey life. You're their escapist drama in daily episodes."

Right at this moment Yeona and Rima appeared in the doorway, and all the girls in the classroom reacted by adjusting their clothes or hair, and straightening up or changing their pose a little, as if some invisible camera got suddenly switched on, and they all wanted to be recorded looking their best.

Niki snickered.

"As you see, you don't need to worry too much," Kamila told her ironically, raising her hand in response to the twins' greeting smiles. "Fortunately, there are other entertainment channels available, live streaming."

* * *

Taejin hadn't seen Niki for almost six weeks. After the seaside trip in July, his father had taken the whole family to Korea for the rest of the summer.

Mother had been really upset with the perspective of another two years away from home, and they all went without a peep of complaint, to pacify her a little.

But now he was back, and before the classes at the university started again in October, he still had some free time he'd love to spend with Niki if he only could find a way to do it without setting his cousin off.

Lately, each time he dropped in at their place the atmosphere grew kind of intense, now that Sori was gone and there were just the three of them. Taejin had stopped pretending he was coming just to see Kehuan, and Kehuan had stopped pretending he was glad to see him there. It was really a pain because alienating him wasn't Taejin's intention at all. The guy was still family, and Niki's brother, and his best friend.

Luckily, the twins popped round regularly as well, usually in the company of that pretty redhead they seemed to be close friends with, and sometimes with Jason as well. Things got much lighter then. With them around, each meeting inevitably transformed into an impromptus small party, something unimaginable in their own house. But there was nobody who'd care to put a ban on partying at the Chens' place, and if it hadn't yet turned into a major revelry hub, it was only because Kehuan was such a misanthrope.

Taejin sometimes wondered about the sense of keeping such a big apartment when there were just Anna, Niki, and Kehuan in it most of the time. But apparently, Kehuan's father liked to have his space when he was in Warsaw, and he certainly didn't hurt for money. The whole family configuration of the Chens had always been a little bit of a puzzle, but so many pieces of it seemed thorny and untouchable that Taejin had long ago decided to leave it alone.

Kehuan's mother. Niki's mother. The circumstances of that accident when Niki was young. Her father's permanent absence. The strange relationship between Chen Liang and his wife.

Anna herself was quite a mystery to Taejin, too, this mother staying on the margins of the family life, and paying no attention to her children. Though he guessed it wasn't so strange since neither Niki nor Kehuan was really her own.

It was a whole archipelago of sore spots.

But at least all these musings finally gave him an idea.

* * *

Niki noticed Taejin as soon as she went out of the school gate. It was hard not too: he was rather conspicuous, not to mention well-known at the school, and his presence created a small eddy in the flow of students, as some people stopped to say hello while others slowed down at the sight of him and then turned round to take a second look.

"Are you checking up on the twins?" she asked him, grinning. "No worries, they don't play hooky these days. Kamila keeps them under control."

Taejin laughed at that and came closer. "I was waiting for you, actually," he said.

"For me? Why?" Niki asked, curious.

"Can't I come and walk you home without any reason?" Taejin said with his trademark charming smile.

Niki wasn't sure it was such a great idea. Kehuan seemed to dislike it when she spent too much time in the company of Taejin, and she didn't want to upset him, even if it was a bit unreasonable in her opinion, since he was best friends with the guy himself. But Taejin had always been the big brother of their extended family, who did his best to take care of all of them, and it would be very rude to tell him to get lost, so she stayed quiet, and they started walking in the direction of home.

"Isn't it your birthday soon?" he asked after a moment.

"Yes," Niki answered, surprised again. "How did you know?"

Taejin rolled his eyes. "My mobile told me," he said. "People usually know the birthdays of their close friends."

He was probably right.

"So I was thinking, would you like to celebrate it properly this year?" Taejin went on. "Sixteen is a milestone."

"Milestone how?" she asked. "There's nothing special about sixteen."

"It has tones of cultural connotations."

"Maybe," she said dubiously. "I always get some birthday presents, but it's not what you mean, right?"

"No," he said, grinning. "I mean a party."

Niki considered the idea, frowning a little.

"Don't tell me you've never had a birthday party before?" asked Taejin. "Even as a child?"

"I did, once, but it was ages ago, when mum was still alive." A sudden thought struck her, and she added, "You know what, it is a milestone of sorts. My mum had me at sixteen."

"Seriously?!" Taejin was completely thrown. "But your father isn't that young, is he? How did they meet?"

"Through Kehuan, of course," she answered, shrugging.

Taejin stopped cold. He turned to her, his eyes suddenly really wide. "Are you saying Chen Xiao isn't your real father?" He sounded as if he'd just discovered a brand-new continent.

"Of course not." Niki surveyed him curiously. "You didn't know?"

"You were adopted?"

"Ah, it's a bit..." she hesitated and wondered if she'd perhaps said too much. "You can keep a secret, right?"

"Sure."

"Well, he didn't exactly adopt me. He just said I was his daughter."

"And someone believed it, just like that? And accepted, officially?!"

"My mum confirmed it, and Chen Liang."

"They all lied?!" Taejin looked a little dazed. "But what about your real father?"

"I don't know, and I don't care," Niki told him truthfully.

Taejin was silent for a long moment after that.

"It's so weird," he said at last. "As if I haven't known you at all."

"I'm myself," Niki told him coolly. "Whoever my father is."

What seemed weird to her was that she even had to state such a basic truth. But Taejin came from a culture where blood ties carried different weight, she reminded herself, and it was his right to see matters in a different light.

It was a good thing though she'd never had to explain things like that to Kehuan.

* * *

Taejin beat himself for days over his stupid first reaction.

She'd been absolutely right, of course. Niki was herself, and he didn't care if Chen Xiao was or wasn't her biological dad; the guy took her in, so she was his daughter now, end of story. He could tell she'd been a little miffed with his rash words, and worse, a little hurt, too. But they were out already, and all he could do now was try to be more thoughtful and sensitive in the future.

He shared the birthday celebration plans with his brothers, who were immediately on board, as could be expected, and called Sori as well. But Niki's birthday coincided with the beginning of the academic year, and Sori said she wouldn't be able to come. And then he braced himself, and went to talk to Kehuan—he'd figured the sooner he got over this hurdle, the better. But contrary to his sinister predictions, his cousin approved the project as soon as he'd heard that Niki liked the idea.

Two weeks before the big day the organizational committee gathered in his room.

Kamila offered to invite the guests—she knew whom to filter out, she declared, and the twins were going to handle the music and karaoke equipment, and the lights.

"Oldies for karaoke?" Taeyeon suggested, and everybody chuckled. Niki's quirky love for old songs was a regular topic of jokes.

"What about food?" asked Taejin.

"I'll take care of that," Kehuan said.

"Don't tell me you cook?" Kamila asked, raising her eyebrows in patent disbelief.

"I cook," Kehuan replied, deadpan. "But I'm not going to cook for twenty people. I'll order something she likes."

"Awesome," said Kamila, shaking her head in amazement. "You're full of surprises, brother."

They were talking in English, and the word didn't carry any special meaning in this language, but to Taejin it still sounded a little odd. Kehuan was a master of keeping people at a distance, and the fact that the insolent girl wasn't cowed by him in the slightest was quite an achievement, especially if one remembered their rocky beginnings.

The twins and Jason had been muttering among themselves for a while, and now Jason spoke aloud, "What about booze?"

Kehuan immediately lost all resemblance to a human being and looked ready to bite someone. "No," he said curtly.

"Oh come on, brother" Taeyeon implored. "Don't be such a killjoy."

"We'll keep it low-key," Taerim offered. "Just beer, and maybe some punch."

"You're still underage, you two monkeys," Taejin reminded them, resigned, though he had no idea why he bothered. As if the twins had ever paid attention to such insignificant details. But it was him who'd hear from their mother on their behalf, as usual.

Kamila snickered, while Kehuan meditated for a moment.

"All right," he said finally. "But I'll kick out anybody who gets drunk. No kidding."

"All right," Taeyeon repeated after him, nodding enthusiastically.

"And if I see anybody press Niki into drinking—"

"You won't," Kamila promised. "I'll see to it."

"But what if she wants to have a drink of her own accord?" asked Jason.

"Then I'll have a drink with her," Kehuan answered with a lopsided smile, astonishing everybody. "It's her party, isn't it?"

* * *

On the day of Niki's sixteenth birthday, before the party, Kehuan gave her his present.

Niki had been sitting in the beanbag in his room, contemplating the pair of inline skates which had just arrived by international courier service.

Kehuan was truly impressed with the way Chen Xiao was always able to guess what to get her to make her happy. For someone living on the other side of the globe, he was admirably conscious of his adoptive daughter's interests.

Kehuan sat next to Niki in the beanbag, took her hand, and entwined his fingers with hers with the same feeling of immediate relief he felt each time their skin touched.

"Satisfied with the present?" he asked, though he could tell she was.

"Absolutely," she answered, smiling at him. "Going to try them out tomorrow, first thing in the morning."

He nodded and then noticed a CD in her lap. "What's that?"

"Sori sent me a collection of Korean love songs," Niki said. "From different movies, I think."

Kehuan nodded again, a little amused. Yoon Sori often gave people musical presents, but her choices were sometimes a little baffling.

"I've got something for you, too," he said, opening his other hand.

Niki leaned closer to take a better look at the thin silver bracelet lying in his palm, and the two charms attached to it. One was a miniature painting palette, with tiny gemstones in different colors pretending to be paints, and the other a snowflake.

"It's fabulous," she said, beaming, and Kehuan's heart swelled in his chest.

"Left or right?" he asked.

"Left," she said and stuck out her left arm.

Since Kehuan was sitting on the right side, he had to turn a little to clasp the bracelet around her wrist, and the move put their heads close together.

"Thank you," said Niki, and kissed him on the cheek.

It was just a short moment when her lips touched his skin, but Kehuan's breath caught in his throat, and then his head turned of its own volition, and their lips met.

They both froze for a moment, and he felt his heart thump, but Niki's lips were so wonderfully warm and soft that he couldn't keep himself from pressing his own mouth harder on them. He'd never kissed anybody before, but he'd seen it done many times, of course, and it wasn't rocket science anyway. He tilted his head slightly to one side and moved his lips carefully against hers, and Niki responded by closing her eyes and drawing closer to him, sending a bolt of heat through his entire body. He withdrew a little, put his hands on both sides of her face, and breathed her in, smoothing the silky hair under his fingers, and stroking the skin over her cheekbones with his thumbs. And then he closed his eyes as well and kissed her again.

And they were still kissing when the doorbell rang ten minutes later.

* * *

Anna was sitting on the dark stairs, watching the party in the living room below. The room was lit rather symbolically, too, and nobody seemed to have noticed her so far.

The previous day, Veronica had climbed to the upper level and knocked at her door to inform her about the party, and to apologize in advance for the noise. Anna had been in bed, watching a movie on her flatscreen, and felt genuinely baffled the girl made the effort. They usually treated her as if she didn't live at this place anymore, which was just as well. She didn't long for any extended contacts with them, either. But when she'd heard earlier from her room all those young voices talking and laughing downstairs, and the music, she couldn't resist taking a peek, and had been sitting on the stairs since then.

It was such a nice party, with good food and good music, and boys and girls mingling and laughing, and dancing, some of them a little tipsy, but nobody drunk. Now that it was well after midnight, they were all sitting and lying around on the sofas and the carpet, singing karaoke. Some could sing quite well—she guessed they were Veronica's friends from the music club at school. But even those who weren't good seemed to have fun, and the others backed them up, creating makeshift choirs and adding extra melody lines. The choice of songs surprised her: rock and pop pieces from the times when she'd been a child, and some even older. Who'd think they'd enjoy this kind of music?

Kehuan sat on the couch with Veronica next to him, his arm thrown behind her back. Thick as thieves, as always, those two. The previous song had just ended, and he took the mic now. Anna knew he could sing well enough, too, as she'd heard them both many times in the kitchen, but apparently, the fact wasn't a general knowledge among their friends because people were cheering and clapping, as if they hadn't expected him to participate. The music started playing again, and this time it was Cohen's 'Hallelujah'. A moment later the others sang the chorus together with him, the melody just as haunted and heartbreaking as ever. The oldest Soeng boy, sitting on the floor next to Veronica, turned his head and looked up at her with a fond smile, and Anna felt a stab. Everybody always seemed to dote on that girl.

They all looked so young, attractive, and happy, so alive and full of hope, and what about herself? Was the world done with her already? She felt so bitter and jealous.

When she talked to Renata on the phone—which happened very infrequently—her sister always brushed aside her suffering, pointing out that Anna had nothing to complain about: she received plenty of money every month, both from Chen Liang and Chen Xiao, didn't have to work at all, and could still live comfortably in the luxurious apartment. Her life was so easy, Renata said, and maybe it was even true, but so what? Each day was so lonely and hopeless she sometimes thought she wouldn't be able to take it anymore.

How had it come to this? When had she become this used-up, desolate old woman, killing her time with drama channels and run-of-the-mill romance books? Where had her youth gone, and aspirations, and dreams?

She took a swig of wine from the bottle she was cradling to her chest, and as the music played on, and all the kids sang the chorus once again, she felt two fat tears roll down her cheeks.

10

Too Far

Taejin had an odd feeling since that birthday party. Something wasn't right, but he had a problem with putting it into words because they'd sound just too bizarre and outlandish. Different scenes from that evening kept playing in a loop in his head, and he couldn't properly concentrate on anything else.

Kehuan had danced with Niki. Nothing so strange about it, right? And yet. Taejin had never seen his cousin dance with a girl before, not once. Besides, they shouldn't have danced like that, it just didn't look right.

Later in the kitchen, when they were preparing some snacks, Kehuan needed something from the cupboard Niki was standing next to. He'd stepped close to her and put his hand on her lower back, and the sight of this casual, intimate touch froze Taejin in place.

The living room, the kitchen, and the hall at the Chens' made one big open space, and at a certain moment, he noticed the two of them standing in the dim hall and talking. Niki was leaning against the wall with her head tilted back because Kehuan was so much taller, and he was bending towards her, which looked as if they were just about to kiss, and the disturbing image was burned under Taejin's eyelids.

Then they all settled around the living room to sing karaoke. He wanted to sit with Niki, but Kehuan caught her hand and pulled her next to him on the sofa, throwing his arm behind her back. Taejin would think nothing of this gesture if not for all those things earlier. There were just too many details not adding up together, or rather adding up in a very peculiar way.

He couldn't believe it and didn't want to believe it. What nonsense.

And then the loop would start playing again.

* * *

Chen Liang came to Warsaw for several weeks at the beginning of November, and his arrival annoyed Kehuan just as much as it made him glad.

His father still cultivated the habit of working in the office all day, even if there was no real need for that anymore, but it wasn't so important, since Niki spent her days at school, and Kehuan also had his classes at the university.

It was the evenings where the enticement and the danger lurked together, and Chen Liang spent his leisure time at the end of the day in the living room, reading or watching films, or surfing some news pages on his laptop. He'd long ago adopted the second room upstairs for his bedroom, but it was rather small, so he preferred to stay downstairs. His presence, however unobtrusive, still served as a deterrent. Kehuan was much more conscious of his father than of Anna, and it helped him keep some distance from Niki, which was good, even if it aggravated him to no end at the same time.

He was aware that the situation between them was getting a little out of hand. Since that first kiss on the day of her birthday he just hadn't been able to stay away from her. Niki was like a powerful magnet, and it didn't matter in which direction he tried to move, he somehow always ended up close to her, and closer each time. They kissed on every occasion, and the atmosphere around those kisses quickly escalated from a tentative, innocent experiment to something much more heated and carnal, though still experimental at its core, as they were both learning their bodies and their reactions.

The first time his hand had wandered under her clothes had been a coincidence, or so he told himself; she'd been wearing jeans and a loose, short T-shirt that day, and when he put his arm around her waist during the kiss, his palm accidentally touched the skin of her back. They both went rigid for a moment, but Niki's skin around her slender waist was so smooth he just had to stroke it, and his other hand wandered there as well just a moment later, and it was only a natural progression that Niki also put her hands under his T-shirt, initiating a new level of excitement, and taking that kiss to a new category of pleasure.

That was all that happened at the time, but the damage was done. Their hands had learned the touch of each other's skin and grew bolder, and next time there was no waiting for any accident, no hesitation, and no keeping them in one place, either.

These experiments in passion were just as wonderful as they were risky, and Kehuan, who normally had willpower enough for several people, couldn't force himself to put a stop to them, or even slow the progress down in any way.

He tried talking about it to Niki on a few occasions, and it went a similar way each time.

"We can't go any further," he told her once. "Seriously."

"Okay," Niki agreed, looking at him earnestly with her gorgeous eyes.

"I'd love to, but it wouldn't be right." He didn't want her to misunderstand. "You are so young, Niki."

"I know," she said, smiling at him sweetly, and he involuntarily took a step forward. "We can do it all later, right?" she said, and Kehuan's blood sang in his veins.

"Everything you want," he promised, while his brain obligingly started presenting assorted things she might want, hopefully. He inhaled, reached out, and pulled her closer.

"Good," she whispered in his ear, sending a shiver down his spine.

"So let's try to slow down, all right?" he implored, even as his lips were on her collarbone already, and his hands started roaming over her lovely body.

"Yes," she whispered, kissing him gently under the corner of his jaw, and he was gone.

So Chen Liang's visit really came just in time. And yet, while Kehuan was thinking with growing trepidation about the day his father would leave again, he couldn't wait for it as well.

He was so starved for her.

* * *

On the last weekend of his stay in Warsaw Chen Liang decided to talk to Anna.

They'd had some exchanges before, of course, but these were all just small talk. He had something more serious to say to her, and he'd waited with it until the very last moment because he felt it might spoil the atmosphere between them, already stuffy enough.

"Anna," he said as soon as he made sure Kehuan and Niki were out of the apartment. "I noticed you've been drinking quite a lot recently."

Anna gave him a look which was an interesting combination of anger, guilt, and defiance.

"So what?" she answered. "It's not your problem anymore, is it?"

"No, certainly not," Chen Liang answered politely. "I respect your right to waste your time and money in whatever manner you choose. I was just wondering if Chen Xiao would be as understanding if he realized the situation."

Chen Xiao paid Anna substantial money every month for looking after Niki. He knew that his girl didn't really require that much attention; she was a very self-dependent teenager, just as Kehuan before. But it was still reasonable to have some adult in place in case she needed help, and Anna was the most convenient option, and adequate enough. But not if she soaked her days in alcohol.

"I don't really drink that much," she said now, a little cowed by his warning. "Not when Veronica is around, anyway."

"I'm not sure I can agree," he answered. He had eyes, and nose, and first-hand experience in these matters. "But it isn't my intention to criticize you."

"What's your intention, then?" she asked. "Because I doubt you've started this conversation out of your concern for my well-being."

Chen Liang squelched his irritation. Whatever he said, it probably wouldn't mend anything between them, so better stick to practicalities.

"I wanted to ask if maybe you'd be interested in getting a job," he said.

"Why?" she asked ironically. "Are you going to stop paying the alimony?"

"Of course not," he answered shortly. "But it would be an occasion for you to go out and have some contact with other people. You might feel better."

"What a good Samaritan you are," Anna said acerbically. "But pray tell, who's going to employ a forty-something woman whose last working experience is from eleven years ago?"

"If you're interested, I can help with that," he offered, ignoring her tone. "I have good relationships with the owner of this job agency we've been using recently."

Anna was quiet for a moment. "I'll think about it," she said at last, in a slightly more agreeable tone.

Chen Liang nodded. "Let me know your expectations," he said.

"So I can still have some expectations," she said bitterly. "Good to know."

"You can," he answered, allowing himself for some nastiness, too, "as long as they are within a reasonable scope."

He felt a little bad for her because of everything that happened between them, but honestly speaking, if he was trying to help now, it was mainly because of Chen Xiao and the children. If she accepted the help, all right, but he wasn't going to take much more of her venom. He had no patience left for it.

* * *

At the beginning of January, Taejin was eating lunch in a small eatery close to the technical university campus, revising for the test he had in the afternoon, when he suddenly heard his name spoken aloud.

There was a small gaggle of female students in the booth behind him, chattering and giggling noisily, but they'd been talking in Polish before, which made ignoring them quite easy. He'd had lessons on the local language for ten years, but never developed any enthusiasm for it, or reached any decent level of fluency, and had to really concentrate to grasp what a person speaking Polish was saying, and even then, it was usually half guesswork. But a moment ago two new girls had joined the group, and they all switched language. Either the newcomers were foreigners, or they thought people wouldn't understand them if they gossiped in English. Concentrating on his notes became harder then, and now that one of the girls said his name, he gave up and started to listen.

"Yes, I know him," announced one of the girls in a very confident voice. "But I like that friend of him better."

"Which one?"

"That other Korean guy. Kehuan Chen."

There was a small chorus of 'ahs' and 'ohs'. Apparently, the other girls knew Kehuan, too.

"I don't think he's Korean," noticed a quieter voice.

"Who cares? The important thing is, he's hot."

"I don't know," said a different voice dubiously. "He never smiles. Like never. Doesn't talk to anybody, too. It's so weird."

"I know one girl from the international school," said yet another voice. "She once told me he's always been like that. Good-looking, but like an alien. She said his sister was the same, a total weirdo."

Taejin didn't mind them trashing Kehuan, it was actually kind of funny, but he got immediately annoyed at the mention of Niki. Stupid busybodies.

"I think he's got a girlfriend, though," said the quieter voice. "I saw them in the park once in the autumn. She was rollerblading around this small square, and he was watching her. And he was smiling, definitely. They kissed later."

"Damn," said the first girl with displeasure. "Was she pretty?"

"Very," replied the second one. "Lovely blue eyes."

Taejin felt ill all of a sudden. He gathered his stuff with trembling hands and put it hastily into his bag, and then snatched his jacket and strode out of the place, carefully avoiding looking in their direction. He didn't want to hear anything else.

* * *

Kehuan returned home in the afternoon and went straight to Niki's room.

She was standing next to the big table, dressed in her paint-splashed working T-shirt, with her hair caught up in a high ponytail and the calligraphy brush in her right hand.

He came closer and peeked over her shoulder at the big sheet of paper. It was a pencil draft of some leaves and flowers, and a big peacock butterfly. She'd just finished writing the Chinese character in the bottom right corner, and the black ink was still wet and glistening in the light of the large floor lamp illuminating the table.

"Another poster?" he asked, putting his arms around her from behind. He kissed her ear and breathed in her scent.

"Uh-huh," she confirmed. "Mrs. Krawczyk called yesterday. Wanted some insects this time."

She glanced at him over her shoulder and made a funny face, and he chuckled.

"Have you had dinner?" he asked, tightening his arms and watching her delicate profile.

"Not yet," said Niki absent-mindedly, eyeing the draft of the poster with a frown and probably considering where to apply the next strokes of ink.

She often got this way while working, and Kehuan didn't mind, generally, but sometimes he felt the need to make sure she noticed him properly. So he took the brush out of her fingers and put it carefully on the blotter, and pushed the sheet of paper away so it wouldn't get damaged. Then he spun her around, put his hands on her waist, and lifted her up on the table.

"What are you doing?" she laughed, propping her outstretched arms on his shoulders.

Kehuan stepped closer, put his hands on both sides of her face, and kissed her. Niki lowered her arms and caught his shirt on both sides to pull him closer, but since she was sitting on the table, his hipbones hit her knees. They both looked down, and then she slowly and deliberately drew her legs apart.

Kehuan's entire body suddenly went tense and hot, and weak, as if she poured over him some scalding hot, intoxicating liquid.

He made the last little step forward without conscious thought, and their bodies touched in the sweetest way. He was afraid to move. He was getting hard rapidly, and heard Niki's quiet intake of breath. His hands were pulling her body closer to his, though he didn't remember shifting them, and he couldn't keep still any longer, he had to move.

They both made a sound at the same time, a quiet exclamation of wonder and delight, and he moved again, pushing harder into her, while his mouth found hers and started moving in concert with his body.

Some small voice in the back of his head was whispering urgently that it was dangerous what they were doing, so dangerous, better stop when you still can, but it was absolutely impossible to stop, with that sweet feeling radiating from the place their bodies were connected, and with Niki gasping and pushing her hips against his, her lips half opened now, her eyes shut, her cheeks flushed, the most beautiful thing he'd ever seen. And then those eyes opened suddenly, enormous and amazed, and the next gasp turned into a different sound, urgent and demanding, and Kehuan's felt himself harden and swell even more. His body tightened like a string, and as he pushed against her once more, she said in a high, clear voice, full of wonder, "Kehuan...", and he exploded.

And as she swayed and shivered in his arms, and he was kissing her jaw, her hot blushing cheek, her eyelid, and her delicate temple, he couldn't make himself regret it, not even one bit.

* * *

Niki left the ice rink tent with the skates hung over her shoulder. It was already dark outside.

She went ice skating almost every day now. This semester Kehuan had his classes until late every day, and couldn't pick her up, so if the twins or Kamila didn't come to skate with her, she'd go home on her own. But this time a tall figure of a young man moved in her direction as soon as she was out of the tent, and before she could get alarmed, he went into the splash of light near the entrance.

"Hello, big brother," she welcomed him in Korean, smiling. "Are you here to ice-skate? Or have you come to be my escort again?"

Taejin smiled, too, but Niki could tell he wasn't in an upbeat mood.

"I'll walk you home," he said. "Want me to carry the skates?"

"They aren't heavy," she answered, and they started walking. "What's up?"

Taejin stayed quiet for a long moment, and then suddenly stopped, and turned to face her.

"Niki," he said, and there was a strange note to his voice, earnest and pleading. "Would you like to go out with me?"

"To go out where?" she asked, confused.

"To go out on a date," he clarified.

Niki just gaped at him, dumbfounded.

"You are joking, right?" she guessed finally and smiled, a little entertained by the idea. "Gosh, it'd be really weird. Almost as much as dating one of the twins... Ah, no, not even going there."

"I'm not joking," he answered seriously. "I know there's the age gap between us..."

"The age gap doesn't matter," Niki said, feeling very self-conscious. "But you must know that Kehuan and I—"

"Niki," Taejin said hastily, "Please think about it."

* * *

She was looking at him with so much confusion and dismay that he could tell without a doubt she'd never even considered the possibility.

After that overheard conversation one week earlier, he kept thinking about what he should do. He'd been really angry, but not at her. It was

Kehuan who should have known better. They were family, for goodness' sake, even if there were no blood ties between them. But she was only sixteen, and even now, when she was staring at him so obviously groping for some polite words of rejection, he just felt sorry and concerned. Was she very upset?

That week's worth of meditations gave him a deeper insight into his own feelings, and he'd been surprised to discover how much he didn't want her to feel hurt, or to get angry at him. It turned out he liked her even more than he'd thought. But it was just one more reason to disentangle her from this mess, even if it would cost him.

"I know what you're thinking," he said in the end when she kept quiet. They started walking again. "But you can't date Kehuan, Niki."

"Why not?"

"He's your brother."

"He isn't, though," she said, glancing at him curiously.

"All right, not a brother," Taejin conceded. "Cousin. But Sori is my cousin as well, and it's just as good as being siblings."

"I don't agree it's just as good. But we aren't even cousins," Niki said, sounding as if she was trying to explain something very simple to a retarded child.

"Even if you've been adopted, you are a member of the family now," he said patiently. "You are cousins."

"Taejin," she said with a strange note in her voice, "our families aren't related in any way."

"His father and your father—"

"Are friends," said Niki very calmly and very firmly. "That's all."

Taejin stopped and stared at her, feeling as if the ground was suddenly sinking under his feet.

"But the family name..."

"Chen? It's like Kim in Korea. The most popular surname in the country." She smiled a little. "Kehuan told me once he had three other Chens in his class when he was going to school in Taipei, none of them related to the others."

Taejin gulped. "But why..."

"Why what?"

"Why do you live with them, if that's the case?"

"Where should I live? I have nobody else in Warsaw," Niki answered. "Chen Xiao's in Canada."

"You could live in Canada with him," Taejin said, though it wasn't what he wanted to suggest at all.

"But Kehuan is here," she answered simply, breaking his heart.

* * *

Kehuan didn't understand how he could've ever thought hormones and pheromones and all that stuff was a bad thing. But of course, it had been before Niki entered this sphere of his life and brought light into it. It had all become so fascinating then, a whole new world for the two of them to discover together. They couldn't cross certain lines, and it chafed a little, but even within those limits sex with Niki was a fantastic adventure.

He loved exploring different ways of bringing her pleasure, and it was usually enough to bring him pleasure, too, even if Niki was quite enthusiastic with her own experiments. Clothes were an impediment they more and more often disposed of, and they got bolder and more curious every day. Life was so beautiful.

At the beginning of February, he had the midterm exams at the university, though, and needed to concentrate a little on them, even if they weren't particularly hard. Fortunately, Niki had the two-week-long winter break at school at the same time, and she'd already received an invitation to Finland from the host family she'd stayed with the previous year. Chen Xiao approved the trip, as could be expected, and both Kehuan and Niki agreed she should go. She was eager to meet those people again, and in the meantime, he'd have the time to focus on his exams. Win-win.

But as soon as she left, he started missing her. And not just missing her like the previous year, when she'd been away for several months. Now his body was missing her, too, and it was driving him nuts. Three days of her absence, and he was climbing walls. He wanted her back, like right now.

Jason Sullivan called at the weekend and invited him to a bar. Kehuan's old buddy from the music club had started college this year, and he'd just finished his first midterm exam session. Now he required some company to celebrate it.

Kehuan went, mainly to kill some time. He drank more beer than normally and talked a little to Yoon Sori, who came to Warsaw for a short visit, and whom he hadn't seen since the previous summer. Then he also got introduced to several people from Jason's faculty of architecture, but they all seemed rather dull to him, and after an hour he was as bored as always at such events.

So he went out of the bar, and though he couldn't remember later how it'd happened exactly, he ended up roaming around the whole neighborhood near the international school and checking all the places where Niki used to play as a child and hang out later, just in case she was hiding somewhere there and avoiding him, and not practicing cross-country skiing in the middle of the snow-covered taiga some thousand kilometers to the north from Warsaw.

Jason didn't want to leave him, and tagged along all night, maybe because he had an exceptionally strong herding instinct, or maybe because he thought wasted Kehuan was hilarious. They returned together to his student apartment early in the morning, half-frozen, and on the next day, apart from the obligatory hangover, both of them were plagued with fever, running nose and sore throat.

Niki returned a few days later, just in time for Kehuan's twentieth birthday. They went to their favorite Thai place for a meal, and then she took him clothes shopping. She wanted to buy him a nice new shirt as a birthday present, she said, and it would be no fun if he didn't try it on.

They visited several stores, and it turned out kissing in a changing room with your shirt off, while other people were walking and talking behind the thin door, was great fun indeed; one needed only to make sure there weren't any CCTV cameras close by. Kehuan wouldn't have anybody watch Niki in such circumstances.

* * *

A few days after Kehuan's birthday Niki tiptoed into his room in the middle of the night and sat in the beanbag, as she often did when she couldn't sleep. She was always careful to keep quiet, even though she knew he didn't mind.

The room was dark, but not completely because of the giant window and all the lights outside. Niki had brought her sketchpad and had just started drawing the hundredth version of the same city landscape when she heard a quiet sound.

She looked back and saw Kehuan, watching her with half-closed eyes from his bed. She smiled at him apologetically.

"Did I wake you up?" she whispered. "Sorry."

"Is it really you?" he whispered back, opening his eyes wider. "I thought I was still dreaming."

"Go to sleep," she told him, still smiling, and stood up from the beanbag. "I'll go back to my room."

"Niki," he whispered. "Come here."

Niki came closer to his bed and sat on its edge.

"What is it?" she asked.

Kehuan smoothed his hand down her forearm. "You are cold," he said.

"It's all right," she said, but he pulled at her hand, and drew her into his embrace, and then put the blanket over both of them.

He was so hot. She laughed quietly at the thought because it was absolutely true in both meanings of the word. Kehuan slept in boxer shorts and an old T-shirt, but these landed in a heap next to the bed about three seconds after she entered it, together with another of his old T-shirts which she used as her nightgown, and Niki could now touch his naked body, and see some of it, too. He was beautiful, all long, lean muscles covered with smooth skin a tone or two darker than her own.

His hands were moving now, too. Whenever Kehuan touched her, it was as if some magic light was traveling over her body, illuminating its parts and fragments, and it seemed to her they only truly came into existence when she felt his hands on them. It was a very strange and wonderful feeling, and she breathed deeply when one of his hot hands moved down her side now, stroked her waist, and continued down again, over her hip and thigh, while his equally hot mouth covered her breast. She couldn't help making a quiet sound.

"Niki…" he whispered, and it sounded like a question, breathless and pained.

"Yes," she whispered back because it was the only answer that ever came to her mind when they were together like that. Yes to everything.

His hand was between her legs now, and Niki felt it beginning already, the waiting, the wanting, the heat, the weakness, the pleasure. Kehuan moved over her, and she could feel his manhood pressing hard against her hip. It wasn't in the right place, and she shifted a little, to move it closer to where it belonged.

Kehuan froze.

"Niki," he groaned. "Please…"

So she stopped moving, waiting for him to make up his mind.

And he did. A moment later she felt him press against her entrance, and she bent her knees and drew her legs further apart.

"Yes," she whispered again, and he pushed slowly into her.

It was such a peculiar feeling, pain and pressure, and heat, and excitement, all mixed together. The pain prevailed, and she must have made some sound of distress because he froze again.

"Are you all right?" he whispered, smoothing his hand down her side once more, and kissing the corner of her lips. She could feel his body trembling and spasming over her.

"Yes," she whispered back after a moment, for the third time. The pain was subsiding gradually now, and she needed to move her hips, just a little; her body was whispering to her, too, telling her it would get better then.

So she did move a little, and then Kehuan moved, too, and it really did get better after that.

So, so much better. The absolute best.

* * *

Kehuan couldn't believe it'd happened. But it had, undeniably, and just like before, he couldn't really bring himself to regret it. They hadn't done anything illegal, after all, and it had been glorious.

There were possible consequences, though, and he was worried about Niki now. What if she got pregnant? She was so young.

He remembered Alina, and wanted to hit his head against the wall, multiple times. What an idiot he was. As if he couldn't have predicted it and thought about protection. But now they could only wait, and if she did get pregnant, they'd deal with it together, like with everything else. But Niki didn't seem worried, and after a few days informed him cheerfully it was all right; they dodged the bullet.

Kehuan did some long-overdue thinking then.

He obviously had no willpower at all when she was concerned, and pretending it wouldn't happen again didn't make any sense. But it really was a little too early for Niki, even if she didn't seem to think so herself.

He remembered Jason and his student apartment and gave him a call the same afternoon.

"Have you got some room over there for me?" he asked without preamble.

"Why?" Jason asked with astonishment. "Did you get bored with too much space and luxury?"

"Something like that," Kehuan answered. "It's just for a week or two."

"Why, come and enjoy squeezing with me in my dinky room, then."

Kehuan planned to find some more permanent solution during the time he stayed with Jason. He explained it all to Niki.

"We really can't keep having sex like that, Niki. You are too young," he told her.

"I don't think so," she answered, sounding a little sulky. "But if that's what you want, go ahead."

The problem was, it wasn't what he wanted at all, and her displeasure and the untroubled attitude didn't help his resolve. Still, he packed some of his clothes and his laptop and moved out to Jason's place.

He still came home every day to see her, though. It was impossible not to.

* * *

After that conversation with Niki Taejin felt so crestfallen and wronged that he decided to confront Kehuan in the end, even if it wasn't really going to change anything. But he wanted to know at least why he'd been treated like a fool for so many years.

They met at the end of February, in the big park near the Chens' place, by the frozen pond. It'd snowed heavily at night, and the big lawn behind them had turned into a giant field of virgin snow, sparkling in the sharp winter sun, while the branches of the trees surrounding the pond seemed close to buckling under the thick white cushions. As they talked, puffs of vapor went out of their mouths, as if they were two angry dragons having an argument.

"Why have you never told me?" Taejin asked. "About Niki?"

"What haven't I told you about Niki?" Kehuan asked in turn.

"That she's not your family," Taejin's voice vibrated dangerously.

"I told you many times," Kehuan answered, looking at him steadily. "You never listened."

"I didn't understand what you meant," Taejin said angrily. "I was in love with her, and you knew it."

Kehuan was silent for a moment.

"I had some suspicions," he finally admitted. "But you never said anything, neither to her nor to me. Why would I start this conversation?"

"I just waited for the right time," Taejin said bitterly. "But you were always so angry when I even mentioned her..." he suddenly laughed at his own words. Ah, the irony.

"Niki's mine," Kehuan told him flatly, "to have and to hold."

Taejin gaped at him.

"But even if she wasn't, I'd never allow you to date her," Kehuan went on, surprising him completely.

"Why?!"

"Why? Because you don't even speak her language properly," his cousin told him. "You've never put any real effort into learning it, for all these years you've known her."

Taejin realized Kehuan was talking about Polish. He often forgot it was Niki's native tongue; she spoke it so rarely in his presence.

"So what?" he said dismissively. "We can talk in English, and besides, she speaks Korean."

"Of course. Korean. Whoever wants to be your friend, needs to learn your language, not the other way round," Kehuan's commented, his voice dripping irony.

"That's it? The language?!"

"No. Your mother hates her," Kehuan continued. "And I wouldn't allow her to be mistreated."

"My mother doesn't hate her—"

"She thinks Niki's trash. Why do you think she never comes to hang out with the twins at your place? Why is it always our place?"

"That's Rima and Yeona's fault. You know they've been putting blame on her for everything for years..."

"And have you ever put things straight?" asked Kehuan. "When did you say it's your precious younger brothers who were at fault, not Niki?"

Taejin stayed quiet for a moment.

"Niki's never complained about my mother treating her badly," he said defensively at last.

"Of course not. She's twisted this way. Mothers are sacred cows to her. She even tries to be nice to that stupid Anna, who's been mean to her so many times, because Anna's some kind of a mother figure in our house."

"I wouldn't let my mother—"

Kehuan snorted. "Please. It's your mother who wouldn't let you," he said. "She wouldn't let you be with Niki, to begin with. And you'd do whatever she said, as always."

"I'm not that spineless."

"You do everything other people want you to, starting with your family," Kehuan told him contemptuously. "You wanted to study biology, but you are in power engineering because that's what your father chose for you. If your parents tell you to move back to Korea, you'll just pack and go, and leave everything and everybody behind, Niki included. Your younger brothers manipulate you however they want. If your buddies want you to drink, you drink, if somebody gives you weed, you'll smoke it. You sleep with every girl that smiles at you."

Taejin felt angrier and more humiliated with every word Kehuan said, and that last accusation touched a raw nerve.

"That's not true," he said heatedly. "It happened only a few times. Just because you're such a bloody monk, who's never..."

Kehuan's expression changed, just a tiny bit, but Taejin stopped cold.

"You have," he realized, bewildered. "When? With whom?"

Kehuan didn't answer, and his long black eyes became more inscrutable than ever.

Taejin's heart started beating heavily as if it knew already something he didn't yet, and then it finally struck him.

"You didn't," he said incredulously, utterly appalled.

Kehuan kept silent.

Taejin was almost choking on his outrage and fury. "Tell me you didn't."

"Why?"

"She's sixteen, you jerk! You went too far."

"Not too far," Kehuan said, looking a little troubled. "Perhaps too fast. We'd get to this point anyway, sooner or later."

Taejin stared at him, feeling as if they were complete strangers.

"That's it," he spat in the end. "We're done, you and I."

"As you wish," Kehuan answered dispassionately.

"We're done," Taejin repeated bleakly. And his heart broke the second time.

* * *

"I've never seen anybody sleep here apart from Niki," noticed Kamila, looking at Taerim lying with his eyes closed on a secluded bench on the outskirts of the school grounds. "Is it contagious?"

The day was quite warm. The last remains of snow had melted away during the previous week.

"Cease bullying us, woman," answered tiredly Taeyeon, who was sitting on the bench next to his brother. "We had a weekend from hell."

Taerim, who apparently hadn't been sleeping, rose to a sitting position as well, making room on the bench for Kamila and Niki.

"What happened?" Niki asked.

"First our aunt declared she's going to stay here permanently and to apply for Polish citizenship," said Taeyeon. "Together with Sori."

"Holy cow," Kamila muttered, amazed. "Just like that?!"

"I'm positive she's been thinking about it for a long time," Taeyeon answered. "But our mother went into a frenzy. They had a showdown of all showdowns, and then aunt said she was moving out to her own apartment. She'd had it all arranged already, and only needed to move her stuff."

"Approached the battle fully prepared," Taerim added. "I approved. Mum would torture her for weeks otherwise."

"Where is she going to live now?" asked Niki in a small voice.

"On the other side of the Vistula, near the old town main square," Taerim answered. "She's renting a small flat close to her tourist office."

Kamila noticed that Niki looked saddened by the news, but didn't say anything else.

"We had to help her move. It was hours of carrying boxes and stuff," said Taeyeon pitifully. "I'm still sore all over."

Kamila was sure the claim was all sham. The twins still trained gymnastics three times a week, so a little bit of physical labor during the weekend had no chance to hurt them.

"So we missed the beginning of the second fracas," Taerim went on with the story. "But it had something to do with you, Nik."

"With me?!" Niki looked caught off-guard. "Why?!"

"No idea, but our big brother went into a giant fight with both our parents." Taerim shook his head in awe. "Unbelievable."

"Yeah, I had no idea he had it in him," Taeyeon added contemplatively.

"He said he didn't want to study power engineering anymore and would quit the technical university. Father gave him the ultimatum then: either he goes on with the studies or returns to Korea, and Taejin said if things are like that, he's going back to Korea."

"What?!" Niki looked really unnerved now, and a little frightened. "But why??"

Taerim just shrugged. "Who knows?" he said. "But that stupid blockhead's going to get drafted as soon as he sets foot in the country."

"You don't know that for sure," Taeyeon said in a mitigating tone.

"Drafted? You mean conscripted, to the army?" Kamila checked.

"Yep. For two years," Taerim confirmed.

"And you are officially banned from our house, Nik," Taeyeon told her, smirking.

"Forget the house, we are forbidden to hang out with you," Taerim added, sounding just as wryly amused as his brother. "We are breaking the law right now."

Kamila looked at Niki. Her girl looked rather pale at this moment.

"What on earth happened?" Kamila asked her, bewildered.

"I don't know," Niki answered. "I think I need to talk to Kehuan."

* * *

When Kehuan returned home, he found Niki standing in front of the middle window in her bedroom. At the sound of his steps, she turned around and looked him squarely in the face.

"What's the matter?" he asked, slightly alarmed with her expression.

"Do you know what happened with Soeng Taejin?" she asked in turn, pale and upset.

"What happened?" He hadn't heard a peep from his cousin since their stormy discussion two weeks earlier.

"He apparently had a big argument with his parents, and decided to quit his studies and return to South Korea all of a sudden," Niki said, watching him carefully. "Where he might get conscripted on the spot, by the way."

Kehuan felt the situation was somewhat dicey right now. She obviously suspected he'd had something to do with Taejin's sudden rebellion and this rampant streak of rash decisions, and she probably wasn't much off the mark, though provoking his cousin in such a way certainly hadn't been his intention.

But he felt a little annoyed, too, with her being so concerned about another guy.

"Taejin's an adult," he told the cat dismissively. "Maybe he's decided to start living as one, for a change."

"Aren't you worried about him at all?" Niki asked, even more upset. "He's your best friend, and family, isn't he?"

Kehuan considered. Yeah, he was the tiniest bit worried, but he also thought it might yet turn into the best thing Taejin had ever done.

Maybe not the conscription, though. What a waste of time.

"So what do you want me to do?" he asked, coming closer to Niki and putting his arms around her waist.

"Talk to him?" she suggested.

"He won't listen to anything I say now," Kehuan told her with great conviction. "Believe me. It'll have to be someone else this time."

"So you did have something to do with it," she noted irritably. "I knew it."

"Niki," he told her tenderly, "it isn't always possible to keep everybody happy."

She sighed heavily and admitted, "I know."

"I'll think what to do about Taejin," Kehuan promised. "But can you now stop fretting, please? It's getting on my nerves."

"You are impossible," Niki told him, resigned.

"I know," he said. "Let's go make dinner."

They made dinner, and talked some more about Taejin, and also about Kim Hana and Yoon Sori. After that, they changed the topic to Niki's tentative plans to go to college in Canada, and then suddenly it turned out it was late.

"Maybe I'll stay here tonight," Kehuan offered hesitatingly. "I'm beat."

"All right," said Niki.

Just as he was about to go to sleep in his room, Kehuan thought it'd be nice to say goodnight to her, so he knocked at the door of her bedroom and went inside. Niki was already in bed.

He told her goodnight, but then he really needed to kiss her, just once. He somehow ended up in the bed, and things got heated about thirty seconds after that.

"Niki," he whispered desperately. "I'd better go..."

"Don't go," she whispered back, and he could feel her smile against his lips, even if he couldn't see it in the dark. "I have rubbers."

Kehuan had them too, but it was the hottest come-hither line he'd ever heard, and absolutely irresistible.

* * *

Anna had recently started to enjoy her life again, at least a little.

At the beginning of the year, she'd begun working part-time in a big real estate agency in the city center. She didn't earn any big money, but it wasn't that important, since she was receiving decent alimony every month from Chen Liang, anyway, and a generous additional sum from Chen Xiao. The job was ordinary office work, some administrative and secretarial stuff, nothing really complicated or challenging. But after the first two months she had to admit grudgingly that her ex-husband had been right: going out of the apartment every day, having to put on decent clothes and makeup, and meeting other people regularly made her feel human again, even if her life still wasn't a matter of dreams. But she didn't drink so much wine in the evenings now and went shopping for new clothes several times. After that, she started thinking about changing her hair color and signing up for some classes in a fitness club to get into better shape. She hated the sight of her present self in the changing room mirrors.

Anna's closest coworker, occupying the desk next to hers, was a thirty-year-old attractive woman with long blond hair and brown eyes, named Sabina. She was very talkative and sociable, and Anna soon got virtually acquainted with the whole crowd of her closer and further friends. Sabina loved to gossip about them all the time, and she kept inviting Anna to various social gatherings. Anna had initially declined all the invitations, but she agreed to go together to a pub at last, and they spent a very pleasant evening. It turned out her life wasn't over yet. There were still people who laughed at her jokes, and were interested in her opinions, and enjoyed spending time with her.

Anna woke up the next day a little hungover, but full of optimism and energy. She went down to the kitchen to drink some coffee before leaving for the office, but she stopped in the hall at the sight of Veronica's school backpack laying on the floor next to the clothes rack.

It was strange. Veronica didn't normally leave it there, and besides... Anna checked her mobile and frowned. The bag and its owner should have been at school since half an hour ago. She crossed the hall, opened the door to the girl's room, made two steps inside, and stopped dead in her tracks.

Kehuan and Veronica were both in the bed, fast asleep, and as much as Anna could tell, naked.

He was lying on his back, with his long arms wrapped around the girl sleeping with her head on his chest. Veronica's long dark hair was spread all over them, and Anna couldn't see much of her face, but she could see Kehuan's, tranquil and gentle, and she breathed in wonder. They looked so young and beautiful, and blissful, a couple of fairy tale lovers.

The thought woke her up. She was supposed to keep an eye on the girl, that's what Chen Xiao paid her for and why she was still able to live in the apartment after her divorce from Chen Liang.

How long had it been going on?

Anna looked at them again and shook her head disapprovingly, annoyed and a little nervous. What should she do now? Call Chen Liang? But she wasn't so eager to listen to his polite barbs, and besides, Kehuan wasn't the problem here. He was twenty, after all.

So she went out of the room, closed the door behind her, took a deep breath, and dialed the number of Chen Xiao in Vancouver.

11

Time and Space

Kehuan shelved for now the problem of his inconsistency with Niki, since his frame of mind after that second night wasn't exactly right for finding a way to prevent him from sleeping with her again; rather the opposite. But he gave some thought to the other issue he promised to consider, and in the end, he decided to call Yoon Sori.

"Sori," he said after they'd greeted each other. "Have you heard about Taejin?"

"Yes," Sori answered. "The twins told me. They're very worried about him."

There was a first for everything, apparently.

"Could you talk some sense into him?" Kehuan asked. "Or maybe ask your mum to do it?"

"We can try," Sori answered. "But his decision and ours coincided in a rather bad way. I'm not sure he'll want to even speak with any of us now."

Right. Kehuan recalled what Niki told him about Kim Hana and Yoon Sori's plans to change their citizenship.

"Why are you doing it?" he asked with interest.

"It's been the plan from the beginning, to move to Europe for good," Sori said. "The only question was if we were going to stay in Poland, or move somewhere else. But we've lived here for so long already, and learned the language, and have friends..."

"Anyway, if you get Polish passports, you'll be able to live anywhere in Europe," Kehuan noticed.

"True," Sori agreed. "It's all going to take some time, though. But I'll tell you, I'm glad we have the disclosure out of the way. It's just a pity it happened at the same time as this matter with Taejin."

"Let me know if you manage to talk to him," Kehuan said and finished the conversation before she asked if he knew what had brought it on.

* * *

Kim Hana met with her nephew two days later, and she learned that Taejin wasn't really upset with her and Sori about their decision, but was also quite determined to stick to his own.

"I've already withdrawn my papers from the technical university," he told her. "It's done."

"Would you prefer to study something else?" Kim Hana asked, concerned.

"Yes, but I don't know when it'll be possible," he answered grimly. "I know it's quite likely I'll get drafted after I return to Korea. Everybody keeps reminding me about that."

"Taejin," she said carefully, "do you want to go to the army? Because I don't think you'll be the best match over there."

"Why?" he asked with irony. "Is something wrong with me?"

"Nothing's wrong," she assured him. "But you've grown up in Europe, and I'm not sure you realize how much of a culture difference it makes. You may not be accepted there so easily, and you'll probably have a problem with accepting some things, too."

"You suggest I'm not as Korean as I think," he interpreted, not incorrectly.

"Perhaps," Kim Hana agreed. "I don't want to argue with your choices. If you really want to go back, you can do it anytime. But I think you should give yourself some time to cool down and to think things through."

"And what am I supposed to do with myself in the meantime?" he asked angrily. "I'm not going to stay at my parents' place, even if father allowed it."

Kim Hana stayed quiet for a moment.

"Can I ask what really happened?" she asked in the end, trying to sound as neutral as possible. "Why are you suddenly so at odds with your parents? You never had any problems in the past."

"Because I always did whatever they told me to," he replied bitterly.

"You've been raised this way," she said. "And so were they."

"And so were you, and my brothers," he noticed. "And yet you are capable of putting your foot down, and those two monkeys have always been doing whatever they wanted."

"Everybody's different," said Kim Hana. "I was the family rebel of our generation, and the twins are very strong-headed. But I always had the impression that you were rather content with the status quo."

"Maybe I was, but now I want to start living on my own account."

"But why can't you try living on your own account here? Leaving Europe will be easy, but coming back may turn out very difficult."

"And what am I supposed to live on?" Taejin asked. "Where will I stay? It all sounds good until you start thinking about money."

Ah yes, Kim Hana thought, wasn't it always the case. And for her nephew, it was, in all probability, the first instance in his life when he had to worry about such basic, practical problems.

"You'll simply have to work," she told him calmly, and then meditated for a moment, weighing her options. Finally, she made a decision. "You can live with me for a couple of weeks, and I can lend you some money for the start. I'll help you with finding a job, too. Then it's all up to you."

There was a lengthy silence while Taejin considered her offer.

"All right," he said at last, looking and sounding a bit lighter. "I'll try. Thank you, aunt."

Kim Hana could take him in for some time, and put him in that minuscule room in her small apartment she kept for Sori, but she didn't really have any money to spare, or any connections to find him a job. But she knew someone who had both, and for the first time in the history of their acquaintance, she decided to ask Chen Liang for help.

After all, wasn't it what friends were for?

* * *

Kehuan had no idea what to do now since it'd become clear that moving out of the apartment didn't solve anything.

The last two nights he'd slept at Jason's place again, but so what? The magnet called Niki was working all the time, bending the trajectory of his thoughts as surely as his movements. He knew it was just a matter of time until he'd end up in her bed again, no matter how much he promised himself he wouldn't, and the sooner the better... no, wrong, wrong! The only thing which would stop him for certain was Niki herself saying no, but mercifully... ah, no, unfortunately, Niki always said yes, and wasn't he one lucky guy... Damn, wrong direction again.

It was really hard to keep thinking the right way because however troubled and irresolute about that whole matter Kehuan felt, he was also totally euphoric about that second night, and Niki seemed really happy, too.

On the third day in the afternoon, he came to the apartment, carrying two bags of groceries he'd bought on the way from his classes.

"Niki!" he called aloud from the hall, looking in the direction of her bedroom. "Come take the food from me!"

He heard some sound behind him then and turned around. And there, a few steps away, in the living room, was Chen Xiao in his wheelchair, looking uncharacteristically somber.

They eyed each other for a long moment, and neither of them spoke, and as the seconds trickled by, Kehuan felt more and more as if the whole problem was slipping out of his hands, just as the grocery bags had. He could do nothing to solve it anymore; things started untangling and simplifying on their own, in a rather frightening manner.

He and Chen Xiao had known each other for such a long time. They liked and trusted each other, too, and in the last years, as Kehuan gradually turned from a teenager to an adult, their relationship began to evolve from that of the guru and his apprentice to that of two friends and workmates. They'd always understood each other quite well and didn't need many words to communicate. As he was looking now at Chen Xiao's solemn, concerned face, and Chen Xiao was looking at whatever expression Kehuan's own face was wearing, a lot of the necessary information exchange was already out of the way before any of them even opened their mouth.

"It can't go on, Kehuan," said Chen Xiao at last. "I can't allow that."

Kehuan had a feeling as if he got submerged in freezing water. Here was someone else who could say no to everything, just as effectively as Niki.

"What do you mean?" he asked, readying himself for battle.

"She's too young for that," Chen Xiao said calmly. "And I guess you are too old to keep things platonic."

"If you suggest I pressured her..."

"I know you wouldn't do that," Chen Xiao assured him. "But it doesn't mean you haven't influenced her in any way."

"What?!"

"Think about it," Chen Xiao said. "You've been living together since she was six years old. Niki thinks you hung the moon. If you suddenly decide you want her, of course she'll agree. But is it really her own decision?"

"There's nothing sudden about it," Kehuan answered testily. "I've always known I'd want her. And I think she's always known it, too."

"All the more," said Chen Xiao. "She had no chance to refuse. She's been in your shadow for too long."

In his shadow. Kehuan had never thought about it that way. Was it true?

"So what do you suggest?" he asked, dreading the answer.

"You have to step back," said Chen Xiao sternly, but seeing Kehuan's violent reaction, he added quickly, "Not forever. You know I have absolutely nothing against it if you're what she really wants. But you need to give her time and space to grow up on her own, and to start thinking and choosing for herself."

"How much space? And time?" Kehuan growled.

"I think you need to separate completely for the time being. I'm not sure about the time. Until she comes of age?"

Kehuan gaped at him in growing horror. "You must be joking," he said, feeling and sounding as if something was stuck in his throat.

"Can you swear you won't have sex again until then if I let you stay with her?"

Silence.

"I thought so," said Chen Xiao.

If it were anybody else, Kehuan would fight tooth and nail. If it were Anna, he'd deal with her at once, and if it were his father, he'd try to reason with him, and to convince him, and if it didn't work, he'd simply disobey. He thought that even if Alina were still alive and tried to separate him from Niki, he'd fight with her as well. But Chen Xiao was the one person Kehuan couldn't fight because he'd never forgotten that this was the man who'd saved five-year-old Niki from the streets, and had given her his name with everything that came with it, like comfortable life, and good education, and financial security. And he'd also kept his end of the deal for all those years, even when it turned out he wouldn't be able to have his adoptive daughter around, and there'd be no chance for him to experience all the joy and satisfaction that could come from raising a child. Chen Xiao had never once complained about the situation, and always strove to arrange things in a way that would be best for Niki, and since Kehuan had no doubt it was the case this time as well, it gave him no room to fight at all.

"So what do you want me to do?" he asked again and didn't recognize his own voice.

"Come with me to Vancouver," said Chen Xiao. "It's the simplest solution."

"What about college?" asked Kehuan, though he couldn't care less about college at the moment.

"You can take a gap year, and then return here, or transfer to a university in Canada," Chen Xiao answered, and Kehuan could tell he had it all figured out already. "In the meantime, you can work with me."

Kehuan's mind was seizing up in terror and pain as he was desperately looking for some escape route.

"If you think you can't do that, I'll take Niki with me instead," Chen Xiao added, observing him closely.

"No," Kehuan said at once, grimly appreciating the tactical maneuver of his opponent. "Leave her be. She's got the school here, and friends, and her entire life."

"I'm glad you see it this way," Chen Xiao said mildly. "I know you care about her."

"Where is she now?" asked Kehuan.

"Anna said she went ice-skating with the Soeng twins and some other friend," Chen Xiao answered. "She should be back soon."

"Can I talk to her?" Kehuan asked, feeling as if his entrails were folding up on themselves, making him nauseated.

"Better not," said Chen Xiao. "I'll explain it to her. Go pack your things."

"Now?"

"Yes."

* * *

Niki returned home at six. She thought Kehuan would be there already since he'd said on the previous day it was high time for some kitchen experiments again. But the only person she saw at the apartment was Chen Xiao. Surprise.

"When did you come?" she asked after giving him a welcome hug.

"Today in the morning," he answered. "I had some business here, and wanted to see you, of course."

"Are you staying at the hotel?" Niki asked, feeling a little uneasy, as always in his presence. It was really strange and sad how this involuntary reaction lingered over the years, making her feel at once apprehensive and guilty every time she saw him, and relieved and guilty every time he went away.

"Yes," Chen Xiao answered. "But I thought we could have dinner together."

"Cool," Niki answered. "But I haven't got anything ready. We were going to cook something new with Kehuan today. It's strange he's not here yet."

"We can order some takeout," Chen Xiao offered with a smile. "I'm pretty hungry already, and I bet so are you, after all this skating."

"All right," Niki agreed. "What do you feel like having?"

"Choose whatever you like," he told her. "You know I'm not picky."

Niki ordered the food and then sat at the table in the living room while Chen Xiao parked his wheelchair next to it.

"How are things at school?" he asked.

"Very well," Niki answered, pleased with herself. She was really doing well now, especially since she'd started studying together with Kamila, who was an excellent tutor.

"Have you thought about applying to Vancouver?" he asked.

There was still almost a year for this decision, but Niki didn't mind discussing different options in advance, all the more so because she wanted to give Kehuan enough time to organize his matters as well.

"Yes," she said. "I think I'll try. But I'll apply here, too, just in case."

"Excellent," said Chen Xiao. "Best to keep your options open."

Their takeout arrived half an hour later.

They ate and then talked some more while Niki cleaned the kitchen and made coffee for him. Chen Xiao was waiting for the right moment to tell her the news, and he was already bracing himself for her reaction.

"Niki, I need to tell you something about Kehuan," he said at last when she was done with the chores.

"What about him?" she asked, eyeing him warily.

"He came over earlier," said Chen Xiao. "I sent him away."

"Why?!" she exclaimed, surprised and indignant. "He lives here!"

"Not anymore," Chen Xiao told her. "As I said, I sent him away."

"Away where?"

"To Vancouver."

Niki froze. "You sent him away to Vancouver," she repeated slowly after a moment. "Why?!"

"You know why," he said and watched with concern as her face suddenly flushed with crimson. "Niki, you are too young for that. And too young for him, at least for now."

"When is he leaving?" she asked, looking ready to run out of the apartment at once.

"He already left," Chen Xiao said. It wasn't true, but he thought a clean break was the best thing in this situation, and he didn't want her to go looking for the boy. It'd only make it more difficult for both of them.

"You shouldn't have done it," Niki said in a low voice. She looked angry now, and Chen Xiao thought he'd never seen her truly angry before, and certainly not with him.

He groped for the right words, and finally decided to simply tell her the same truth he gave Kehuan earlier.

"Niki, you need some time away from him," he said plainly. "You've lived so long with Kehuan you may not realize that, but I can see it very clearly. You need time and space to grow up on your own. I know it may seem hard—"

"You know nothing," said Niki, still in that low, angry voice. "Nothing at all."

"I'm sorry, honey."

"You shouldn't have done that," she repeated and marched out of the kitchen.

So. That went well.

* * *

Niki decided to call Kehuan the very next day, but then realized it wasn't going to work. He wouldn't be using his Polish phone number in Canada. Every time one of them went there during holidays, they'd bought a local prepaid SIM card for the duration of the stay. These numbers were only temporary, though, and different each time, so she had to wait until he texted her and let her know his new contact details. Right now she could try to catch him on Skype instead.

She logged in early in the morning, which meant late in the evening in Vancouver, but he was offline. She tried again the next day, this time in the afternoon, but without success again. In the end, she decided to wait until he reached out to her.

Because he would, of course. Kehuan wouldn't let anybody chase him away from her side so easily.

* * *

Chen Xiao gave Kehuan three days to deal with the matters at the technical university.

It turned out he didn't have to take a gap year after all, at least not yet. Since he'd been a model student so far, they advised him in the faculty office to apply for a break period instead. He still could get the credits and complete the year if he passed the final exams at the end of the year. He'd just have to study for them on his own and to take some additional tests, but he didn't expect it would cause him any problems, and besides, he didn't really care.

He was wondering what Chen Xiao had told Niki. He'd expected her to call him and ask some questions, but she hadn't. Was she angry at him? Disappointed? Unhappy? He'd promised he would give her space, and Chen Xiao insisted it also meant not calling on his own, but Kehuan was leaving the next day, and he wondered if they were really going to part like that, without a word. He seriously considered sneaking to the school to see her, just for a moment, but it would be a breach of trust. Chen Xiao had left already, and Kehuan had given his word he wouldn't try to meet with Niki in his absence.

He didn't know what to think anymore. In the past, he'd always been very confident in Niki and himself. If someone had asked (though no one ever had), he would've said they'd been fated to meet and to be together. He couldn't imagine his life going a different way, and he'd always been certain Niki felt the same.

But Chen Xiao's words rattled him more than he'd thought at the beginning, and Kehuan kept turning them over in his head. Was it possible he'd been really influencing her decisions all this time? Was it possible she would've chosen something else for herself if that hadn't been the case? Was it possible it was all him?

And then the next day came, and there was nothing else to do but board the plane and fly away, leaving his soul behind.

* * *

Kehuan was online finally, and he answered as soon as Niki called him.

"Hi," she said. "I was worried already. Didn't you switch on your laptop at all last week?"

"I did," Kehuan answered, sounding a little baffled, but also sad. "But not much. I was busy."

"Are you all right?" she asked anxiously.

"No," he said. "Niki, I'm so sorry."

"What are you sorry about? It's Chen Xiao's fault," she told him. "I'm sorry he banned you all the way to Canada because of me. When are you coming back?"

Kehuan stayed silent for a moment. "I don't know," he said at last.

"What do you mean? Don't you have classes at the university?" Niki asked, starting to feel a little uneasy. He sounded strange.

"No, I took a break period," he said. "I don't need to go to classes this semester."

Niki paused. What was he trying to say? He certainly couldn't mean what she thought.

"You aren't going to stay there until June, are you?" she asked after a moment, making it sound like a joke.

"I am," he said.

Neither of them said anything after that, and the silence got deeper with each passing second.

"Why?" Niki asked in the end, and she hated the sound of her voice at this moment. As if she was a five-year-old.

"Chen Xiao told me to give you space," Kehuan said in a wooden voice. "And I promised I would."

"He's wrong," Niki said passionately. "Don't listen to him."

"I don't know, Niki. I'm so scared he might be right, actually."

"Right about what? Us sleeping together?" she asked with disbelief.

"Yeah, about that, too. I'm sorry," he repeated, and Niki hated the word. "You really are too young..."

It hurt. Niki wasn't a delicate flower, and never had been, despite what many people thought about her, but this seriously hurt.

"Kehuan," she said quietly. "Please don't say that."

"It's my fault," Kehuan said. "Niki, he said we need a break. I think maybe he's right."

A break until June. Niki wondered how she'd live through these three months. But then she remembered her trip to Lahti the previous year. It had been even longer, and Kehuan hadn't said a word of protest.

"All right," she said, making an effort to sound cheerful. "I guess you need to pay me back for Finland."

"What? No, that's not it at all," Kehuan said. "It's just what Chen Xiao said. You need space to grow up on your own."

"I'll do my best," said Niki, and disconnected. She was afraid she'd burst into tears otherwise.

She suddenly recalled the conversation they'd had with Kamila once. Kehuan's all grown up, she'd said back then. And me...

And she was still the same, apparently. The same silly little Niki, who'd thought for a moment she was finally a match for him.

* * *

Anna was a little concerned about Veronica, who had changed almost overnight, and for the last two weeks had been moping around the house without any purpose. Anna understood mood swings, and kept giving the girl different chores to keep her occupied, and made quite a lot of effort to talk to her, too. But even as she worried about Veronica, she felt exasperated with her, too. In her opinion, the girl had been coddled for much too long by all Chens, and it really was time for her to stop behaving like a spoiled brat.

"Cut the martyr act," she finally told her one day. "Are you starving? Are you homeless? Is anyone beating you? There are people with real problems out there. Stop behaving as if someone did you some terrible harm."

Veronica looked at her with the eyes of a wounded animal, and Anna felt even more impatient. This girl, seriously. No spine at all.

"You are so childish," she said scornfully. "Get a grip already."

It probably wasn't the best tone to use at the moment, but Veronica had always had a real talent to irritate her.

"Am I really so childish?" she asked now, sounding sad.

"Of course you are," Anna answered. "Look at what you do with your time. Rollerblading for hours, and making pictures out of feathers? Is it adult behavior?"

"Many adult people make a living out of art," Veronica answered defensively. "Or at least make art as a hobby."

Anna just scoffed. Didn't someone have a high opinion about themselves. That's what came out of all the members of the family fawning over the girl for years: spoiled, conceited, and whiny. What a charming mélange.

"You've got your final exams next year," she told her dryly. "You'd better put your time into studying if you plan to go to college and want to get accepted anywhere at all."

If not for having to deal with mopey Veronica, Anna's life could be considered quite good right now. The work was maybe a bit dull, but it was only a few hours a day anyway, so she didn't mind. More importantly, she finally had a private life worth mentioning.

She was meeting regularly with Sabina and her crowd, and it was slowly becoming her own crowd, too. She'd also started going to the gym regularly, and the results were already visible. Looking at herself in the mirror wasn't such a stressful experience anymore, and she really enjoyed shopping now, when clothes looked good on her again.

Maybe she should take Veronica on a shopping trip at the weekend. It could improve her mood somewhat.

Of course, she knew the main reason behind all the drama was Kehuan, or rather no Kehuan. But the girls could only blame herself. Chen Xiao had reacted exactly as a parent should.

"Thank you, Anna," he'd told her before leaving, in a significantly friendlier tone than he'd used with her in the past.

"It's nothing," Anna answered, feeling good. "It was my duty."

"I didn't tell Veronica about your call," he added thoughtfully. "It's better if she doesn't know you summoned me. She could feel resentful, and I want her to be comfortable here, and to have someone to lean on."

"Of course," Anna answered, though she felt like rolling her eyes.

With Chen Xiao, everything was always about his precious daughter and her precious feelings, as if the rest of the world didn't matter at all.

* * *

Kehuan was living in limbo. Nothing ever really happened, and even if he tried to use this time out in the most productive way, his life felt like an endless chain of days that were all exactly the same, with no color and no meaning.

He worked all days, and there were times when he wouldn't even go home to sleep. He just dropped by Chen Xiao's house for a moment during the day to shower and change clothes, and then returned to the office again, and if he was too tired to go on, he slept on the couch in the corner of the room. It happened sporadically with other programmers as well, when they had some project going on and were under the pressure of time, but Kehuan was doing it for a different reason. He'd never been a workaholic, unlike his father, nor did he wish to become one, but work was the only area of his life where he could function without thinking about Niki nonstop. He was killing time.

He remembered how he'd missed her the previous year when she went to Finland for several months. It had been bad then, but not like now. Things had been still the old way between them, and besides, at least they talked regularly and laughed together at different silly things. Now it was different. Chen Xiao had told him to leave her alone, and Kehuan was trying to do just that, but it felt like slowly suffocating.

She didn't try to contact him again, and he didn't know if he felt more frustrated or relieved because of that. He wanted to see her on the screen at least, and to hear her voice, and to know about her life back there, but he'd felt unspeakably wretched after that one conversation they'd had, and could tell she'd been really down, too. Maybe it was better for both of them to skip communicating altogether for now. But was it really? He couldn't decide.

He missed her so much he really couldn't breathe sometimes.

He missed looking at her while she was painting or doing the ink calligraphy, leaning over her big table, completely engulfed in her work, with brow puckered in concentration.

He missed her voice, humming and then suddenly bursting into a song while they were cooking together.

He often imagined walking with her. He'd be on her left side and half a step behind, watching her profile as she gazed around, forever the wanderer taking the world in with curious eyes, and she'd turn to him from time to time with that special little smile she gave nobody else.

His body missed her, too, and there was no getting over it, whatever surrogate means he could use. He couldn't even count all those nights he lay in his bed or on that bloody coach, imagining looking into her eyes up close, and watching the little beams of dark blue and gold floating in the translucent space, silky hair sliding against his skin, his hands moving along her slim body under a loose shirt, and then taking this shirt off, and slipping the leggings down her hips and legs, and everything that went after that. It was hard to believe how such sweet, alluring visions could turn into torture over time, when they haunted him night after night.

So how do you go on, knowing it would be months and months before you'd be able to breathe properly and feel the sun on your skin, and really live again?

He submerged himself in the land of math, algorithms, and codes. It was something abstract and engaging at once, and when he solved some theoretical problems, or searched for solutions to the more practical ones, and wrote the code, and then tested his work, he'd get occupied enough that he wouldn't count minutes at least, even if he still counted hours.

* * *

Niki pondered Anna's words for a long time, but she didn't think she could agree with them. Spending time on art wasn't childish, and neither was doing sports. These were things the old and the young could equally enjoy and appreciate.

But she started to think maybe in the past she talked too much about this stuff to Kehuan. His interests lay in serious things, like mathematics and computer science, and he must've been utterly bored with her constant prattling about this and that material or new topic for her work, or painting techniques, and the stories about some skating moves she'd like to master.

She suddenly cringed, remembering how she used to tell him in detail about that silly comic when she was in Lahti last year and they met every day on Skype. He'd always listened so patiently. She guessed she really was a child.

She finally started calling him again, every week or so, but their conversations were stilted. It was always Niki who called, and she didn't want to be a nuisance, but she had no idea what to talk to him about to sound grown-up, so most often she just asked him about his day and his life in Canada. But Kehuan usually seemed pretty subdued and answered in monosyllables, and with time they talked less and less.

She felt really depressed about it but consoled herself it was only till June. She'd put a real effort into becoming a more mature person in the meantime, and then he'd come back, and everything would be all right again. It had to; they were Kehuan and Niki, after all.

* * *

"Eat something, girl," said Kamila and couldn't believe she was doing this.

Here was her newest hobby: sitting in the school canteen and trying to stuff some food into Veronica Chen. Life could be really ironic.

But she was getting worried. Niki was thinner each day, and it didn't even look attractive anymore. Kamila had tried talking to the twins about it, but they were just as helpless as herself.

"It's been always like that with her," Taerim told her. "We've all tried to fatten her up for years, but it's no use."

"But she was better already," Kamila countered. "She ate quite well in Finland, remember? She regressed."

"That's because of Kehuan, that jerk," said Taeyeon crossly. "I don't know what he thinks he's doing."

"Do you know why he left?" Kamila asked. She couldn't get a word out of Niki on the subject.

"No idea," said Taeyeon. "But I know he's in Canada, working with Niki's dad."

"Don't they know, both of them, how miserable she is?" Kamila asked disbelievingly. She didn't really know Niki's father, but she'd expected better than that from Kehuan Chen, seriously.

The twins had no answers for her.

Kamila suspected things were more complicated than they seemed on the surface, though. A few days earlier two girls from the last grade approached Niki during recess and did their best to give her a hard time.

"Where's your brother, Veronica? We haven't seen him lately," asked the first one, a heavy brunette called Alicia. "Ah, sorry, not brother. Boyfriend, I mean."

"Did you break up?" asked the second one, a very fair blonde with white eyebrows and eyelashes. "Do you have separate bedrooms now? Again?"

"He doesn't even come to pick you from school anymore," said Alicia again, faking sympathy. "Are you sure you can find your way home without him?"

"Shut up," said Kamila impatiently. "Don't you have anything to do? Go run around a little, lose some weight." She was actually planning to do that herself later.

The girl's face flushed with anger. "Nobody's talking to you, red," she said scathingly.

"It must be tough to live in one place with your ex-boyfriend," added the blonde musingly. "What if he brings a new girl home? Will you cry in front of his bedroom door?"

"She'll just pretend again to be his sister," Alicia sneered, glancing at

Kamila defiantly. "Until he needs an easy lay again."

Just then her face suddenly changed and assumed a much nicer expression.

"Speaking of easy lay," said a smooth baritone behind Kamila. "Don't we know each other?"

The girl flushed again, embarrassed and uncertain now, while her blonde friend looked at her in outrage.

"Scram, both of you," said Taerim curtly.

Kamila had to admit the twins had many useful functions, but at the moment she was concerned about Niki, who was sitting on the bench with her head hung down.

"I guess I was pretty easy," she said at last, and Taerim cursed under his breath, sat next to her, and put his arm around her shoulders.

"Stop talking rubbish," he told her gruffly. "Come have lunch. Taeyeon's keeping a place for us in the line."

* * *

Niki thought about the matter of being easy, and in the end, she decided it didn't make much sense. She'd wanted to be with Kehuan, so why would she be difficult about it?

But it still bothered her, the girl's contemptuous tone, the veiled suggestion that she'd got dumped because of that, even the way Taerim used the same word as a weapon against her tormentor.

She really wanted to ask Kehuan about it. After all, his opinion was the only one that really mattered. But she didn't.

She got cold feet at the last moment. Because what if he said it all had been a mistake, or that she should've been more guarded and less enthusiastic, or that it was her fault they'd got separated? There were countless ways this conversation could go to hurt her, and damage them beyond repair, and Niki was simply too scared to risk it.

There were already so many fissures in that certainty in her which used to be a solid rock before.

* * *

Chris Morton didn't like to listen to gossip, and he especially didn't like to listen to gossip about Veronica Chen. It was his last year at the international school, and he wasn't sure if they'd ever meet again after it, but she still occupied a special place in his heart, even if he'd abandoned all hopes long ago.

It had been quite a shock when the guy Chris had been always so wary of as her older brother had suddenly transformed into her boyfriend half a year ago. They'd been the talk of the whole school for some time. He remembered his own dismay and the healthy surge of self-derision that came after that.

One thing could be said for sure about this place: it had cut him down to size properly.

Let's take that one time when he'd finally got to play together with all those musicians he had coveted so much for his band, including Mauricio de Silva and Ridhaan Khatri. They were preparing another charity concert, with covers of famous rock songs. He'd been ecstatic about the whole thing right until the rehearsals began because then he discovered this dream band wasn't his band at all. All the musicians in the group were much better and more talented than himself (maybe except Jason), and he quickly learned that playing with them had its price. They had their own opinions and ideas about how to do things, and those opinions and ideas were usually much better than his own, and in the end, the whole enterprise turned for him into yet another very educational exercise in humility.

Funny thing, he was the president of the music club now. He enjoyed the job, even if it was only for one year, but the club wasn't the same without Mauricio. Chris admitted openly now he couldn't hold a candle to the guy.

They had one more event to organize this year, planned for Children's Day. The last one before he finished school. It overlapped with his final exams, and his parents kept asking if it was really necessary to waste his time on arranging concerts right now, but he wanted to do it right. They had the program ready, and the band organized, and the rehearsals going on, and he had just one more wish. To get Veronica Chen to sing again. Half of the previous year she'd been in Finland, and this year she didn't return to the club at all. Chris suspected it was because Mauricio was no longer there.

The concert was in a few weeks now, and he was almost sure she'd refuse if he asked her to participate, but what was there to lose for him? His self-esteem? In tatters already when it came to her. So he decided to give it a try and found her outside during the long recess.

She was with Kamila and the Soeng twins, of course. It would be too much optimism to hope he'd get her alone, especially now, when people were dishing her again because of Chen.

"Veronica," he said. "Have you heard about the concert we are doing with the club?"

She looked at him with her wonderful eyes, and he felt the usual pang. His elfin princess, lovely, remote, and completely unattainable.

"I've heard," she said. "But you know I'm not in the club now."

"Would you agree to sing just one song?" he asked. Nothing ventured, nothing gained, even if the twins were smirking mockingly. "It's for charity."

"Isn't it always for charity?" asked Kamila.

Chris didn't hate her anymore, but he wasn't a fan of her either. Though he guessed she was doing a decent job walling Veronica off from the most vicious gossip.

"It's for orphans this time, and for abandoned and neglected children," he said, and Veronica suddenly straightened up and regarded him with new interest.

"Is it really?" she said. "Maybe I'll sing that one song, after all."

Kamila and the twins first gaped at her, and then exchanged a look over her head.

"Yes, why not," said Kamila. "I can do the background vocal, as always."

"You can sing another song instead if you wish," Chris offered. No sacrifice here; she had a nice voice, too, and could sing well.

"And we'll do the background," concluded one of the twins, though Chris had no idea which one. "It's a date."

* * *

Soeng Taejin came to Warsaw for just one day and went to the concert at the school.

He'd been living in Cracow with Sori for the last two months, in a student apartment they shared with two more young people, and working in a small company dealing in ingredients for Asian cuisine. He was going to apply to university again in a few weeks, in Cracow this time because he had to keep the job at least part-time. And since he'd discovered that university courses in Polish were much cheaper than those in English, he'd been also putting a lot of effort into practicing the language, cursing himself for all the time he'd lost in the past.

Taejin often thought about himself from not so long ago with very mixed feelings. There was some envy because that guy he used to be had had everything so easy. And pity because he hadn't had a clue about so many things. Anger, because he'd completely bungled a few really important things. Amusement, because he'd been so sure of his opinions and beliefs. Two months out in the real world, and he was a different person. If better, it was yet to be seen.

But some things stayed the same.

He missed his parents. He missed Kehuan. He wanted to make peace with all of them, but he was still feeling too raw about everything that had happened. He missed Niki, too, and since she was the one person in this whole mess he'd somehow managed not to alienate, when the twins told him she was going to sing at the concert, he decided to come to Warsaw.

It was an open-air concert on the school grounds, and it had a theme, obviously: all songs were about missing home or going home, or homelessness. Niki sang just one piece, but it felt so good to listen to her again. Taejin was the weakest link in their family when it came to music, but even he could appreciate her voice.

Oh, this girl.

He was still in love with her. It didn't go away so easily, as it turned out. After that fight with Kehuan in February, he thought he was done with

Niki, and with his treacherous cousin as well, but it simply wasn't true.

The concert was finished after forty minutes, and Taejin went to find his brothers and their adopted triplet. They were with Kamila, and they all talked together for a few minutes. Then the twins disappeared, taking the redhead with them, and left Taejin alone with Niki.

"So are you all right?" she asked, smiling at him. She looked too thin, and Taejin wondered why.

"I know you talk to Sori and hear all the news about me regularly," he answered, smiling as well.

Niki laughed. "It's not the same when somebody else reports it," she said. "How's work?"

"It's work," he told her dryly. "It's all right, I guess."

"I hear you're going to enroll again and study biology this time," she said. "Good for you."

"Niki, let's have lunch," Taejin said. Old habits die hard. He was worried about her already. "I'm hungry."

"You aren't," she told him. "You just want to shove some food down my throat."

"Why aren't you eating again?"

She shrugged.

"When's Kehuan coming back?" Taejin couldn't believe it actually went out of his mouth.

"He's got his finals at the end of the month," said Niki, and he thought her reply was a bit incongruous with what he'd asked.

"Why did he even go to Canada?" Taejin asked. That was the million-dollar question nobody knew the answer to.

"To give me time and space," she said in a sing-song voice. "So I can properly grow up at last. Apparently, I'm still too young for him."

"I didn't think you were too young in Kehuan's opinion," Taejin blurted out before he managed to bite his tongue. "For anything."

"Me neither," Niki agreed, smiling wryly. "But there you are, big brother. We were both wrong."

* * *

Anna was getting really annoyed with her ward. Being brokenhearted was fine and dandy, Veronica was a teenager after all, and she probably needed her portion of drama to feel properly noticed, but the no eating nonsense was too much. Chen Xiao called Anna every two weeks to ask about his daughter, and she didn't feel comfortable giving him all these roundabout answers considering the girl's health.

"Veronica, I really have no time to stand over you to make sure you've eaten your breakfast," she said impatiently one morning. "I have work, you know."

"So go," said the girl irritably. "I'm fine."

"You're not fine," Anna told her. "Have you looked in the mirror lately? You need to eat more, I'm not joking."

"Let it be," Veronica answered. She seemed to be in a particularly bad mood this day. "There are enough people already prying into my eating habits."

"Yes, because everybody has to eternally take care of you. Do you think it's attractive? A near-adult girl requiring other people to feed her?"

"So I'm near-adult now," said Veronica ironically. "Wonderful news."

"In theory, yes. But look at how immature your behavior is," Anna said impatiently. She was going to be late for work, but maybe they needed to have this talk from the beginning to the end for once. "Can't you really take care of yourself? Do other people have to treat you as their duty, like Kehuan always did?"

"Kehuan didn't treat me as his duty," said Veronica, cut to the quick.

"Maybe not, but he had to look after you all the time," Anna said. Maybe it was a little bit of exaggeration, but she wanted the girl to wake up finally. "Can you imagine how tiring it is? I'm not surprised he left."

"He didn't leave because of that," said Veronica quietly. She looked close to tears now, and Anna felt a little bit of pity, but she wasn't finished yet.

"I'm sure he thought many times it'd be nice if you could deal with your problems yourself, without him always needing to watch over you," she said mercilessly. Sometimes a cold shower was the best thing. "And so do your friends."

* * *

Kehuan had the exams at the university in the last two weeks of June, and his flight to Warsaw was just a few days away when Chen Xiao received the message from the Taipei company that Chen Liang was in the hospital. They immediately contacted Chen Liang's assistant over there and found out it had been a minor heart attack.

Kehuan thought he should go to Taiwan at once, but after some additional exchange with the assistant they established there was no immediate danger, and in all probability no need for surgery either, and on the next day Kehuan could actually talk to his father, who told him to go to Warsaw and take the exams, for goodness' sake. So he went, with the plan to go to Taipei for a few weeks, or longer if it turned out necessary, as soon as he was done with the finals.

Chen Xiao gave him a special speech before letting him go.

"I know you miss Niki," he told him. "But you promised to stay away from her, so make good on it."

"How much longer?" Kehuan asked. He was so fed up with it. He was so fed up with his life without her, too.

"We agreed to at least a year," Chen Xiao answered in a steel voice.

"I didn't agree to anything," Kehuan told him bleakly. "You twisted my arm."

So he didn't call her for the whole two weeks, but she was so close now. Not somewhere on the other side of the globe, but right here, ten minutes away by metro. It was driving him crazy.

In the end, he went to just peek at her from a distance, and waited in the vicinity of the apartment block for two hours until she finally appeared, with rollerblades hung over her shoulder. She was wearing a T-shirt and denim shorts, her regular summer outfit, and even as Kehuan's heart lurched at her sight, he got suddenly distracted by the sharp angles of her elbows and the thinness of her legs.

Niki looked five years younger than he remembered. He couldn't see her face very well before she disappeared inside the building, but he was thrown out of balance. Was she ill? She hadn't said anything last time they'd talked, but three weeks had passed since then. Maybe she got sick later?

He called her, though it was against the rules. But he had to check.

"Niki," he said, and heard her intake of breath on the other end. "It's me."

"Are you back?" she asked, and the hope in her voice made his heart squeeze painfully.

"Not really," he replied quietly. "But how are you? Are you all right?"

"Aren't you in Warsaw?" she asked again, ignoring his inquiry.

"Yes, but I'm going to Taipei tomorrow," Kehuan said, feeling terrible. "Niki—"

"You are going to Taipei tomorrow," she repeated in a peculiar tone. "For how long?"

"I don't know," he answered truthfully. "My father is ill."

There was silence on the line now, and he felt uneasy.

"Niki?" he said. "Are you there?"

"Do you want to meet?" she asked at last. "While you're still here?"

"I can't," Kehuan answered and felt like hitting and smashing something, anything.

"So why have you called?" she asked, and her voice broke. "To say goodbye? Because you forgot to do it last time?"

"Niki, I'll be back," he said pleadingly. He wasn't supposed to say that, but screw it. "Just wait."

"Just wait," Niki parroted, and for once it didn't sound funny at all. "I'll try."

* * *

"So he went back home," said Kamila on the phone, her voice heavy with disbelief. "Just like that?"

Home. Niki hadn't thought about it this way before, but maybe that was the truth. Taiwan was Kehuan's country, after all, even if the memories he'd shared with her from the year he'd lived in Taipei seemed rather grim.

"Are you very busy?" she asked Kamila because the sense of utter loneliness was eating at her.

Her friend sighed. "I am," she said. "I really wish we could meet."

Niki knew Kamila always took care of her sister during holidays. They suspected with the twins the sister was ill somehow; she was only three years younger, so why would she require constant help otherwise?

"Isn't it hard to look after someone all the time?" Niki asked, remembering Anna's words.

"Sometimes it is. I wish I could just leave, and do whatever I want," Kamila answered tiredly. "I have to go. We'll talk in a few days again."

There was nobody else around. The twins had gone on vacations with their parents, after giving her an unexpected group hug.

"We can't ditch our folks right now. They're still in mourning for their perfect oldest son," said Taeyeon, and she knew he wasn't really joking.

"We'll call you," Taerim promised. "Three times. Or maybe even four."

Anna had gone away as well, with some new friend she'd met at work. She'd invited Niki to join her on the trip, but Niki really needed a break from Anna's brand of tough love, and her guardian didn't seem very crestfallen when she declined the offer. The apartment was completely empty, just her and nobody else, and the whole city felt like that, too.

So Niki went for a walk again. It was a habit as old as her oldest memories.

The big park, the streets, the garden square, the old residential area near the school, the small park near Kehuan's old apartment, the riverbanks, the bridge, the embankment on the other side of the Vistula, another bridge, the streets near the apartment again. It had been several hours until she got back.

Perhaps deep down she'd had this irrational hope she'd see him somewhere there, but it was wishful thinking, of course, because no amount of walking around Warsaw would let her meet Kehuan anymore. He'd returned home.

12

The Art of Survival

Kehuan arrived in Taipei in the morning, and directly from the airport went to visit his father.

During those two weeks he'd spent in Warsaw, Chen Liang had been transferred from the hospital to the cardiac rehabilitation center, where he was supposed to stay for some time. Then, if everything went well, he'd return home and go on with the rehab as an outpatient.

Kehuan was glad to find his father in good shape and mood, but he was a little taken aback by the information that Chen Liang had undergone angioplasty and stenting in the meantime, without letting him know.

"You had your exams," his father told him crisply, "and it really wasn't a big deal. The whole thing lasted half an hour."

Kehuan wasn't sure Chen Liang even needed him there. It seemed he'd been handling his health crisis quite well on his own. But he looked happy to see his son, and Kehuan supposed mental well-being was just as important as physical, and in any case, he didn't have any better place to be. The only destination he wanted to travel to was closed to him, so here or Vancouver, who cared? He could kill time anywhere.

Chen Liang had been living in the same apartment Chen Xiao used to occupy in the past. After he'd moved back to Canada after the accident, it had been transferred to the company and turned into corporate lodging, available for any member of the upper management staff who needed it at the moment. Over the last few years, as Chen Liang spent more and more time in Taipei again, he became its main resident.

Kehuan went to the apartment after the visit to the rehab center and unpacked his stuff in the spare bedroom. It felt strange to be there again. The place didn't even look much different from what he remembered, though it had undergone a few renovations over the years.

He was jet-lagged and exhausted after the long journey, and after all those tests and exams he'd had to take earlier in Warsaw, so he went to sleep, and dreamed about Niki. But it wasn't a good dream.

He was walking around, looking for her, and in the landscape of his dream the Warsaw places mixed with the Baltic beach they used to walk on during holidays, and the small mountain village they'd once started their hiking holidays from, and even the park with giant fir trees on Vancouver Island they'd visited together, and a few other completely random locations. He thought he saw Niki from a distance several times, but when he tried to catch up with her, she was already gone, and he got more and more agitated until he suddenly woke up with his heart hammering in his chest and an overwhelming sense of dread and loss.

It was the afternoon in Taipei, and the sun was shining. When he got up and looked out of the window, the city, so different from the one he got accustomed to over the years, looked very inviting. But his heart was still pounding, and he couldn't shake off the ominous feeling, and it cast a mournful shadow over everything he could see.

* * *

It turned out Warsaw wasn't a completely empty city, after all.

Niki spent a big chunk of each day rollerblading in the park, on that small square she'd once found. It was really just a patch of asphalt, but it was secluded and usually deserted, so she could exercise there without the risk of bumping into other people. And she was practicing spins on that day when she heard some whistles and catcalls.

"Hey baby, spin your ass once again," a male voice called, and others guffawed raucously in response. Niki rolled her eyes and turned around to check what new tribe of Neanderthals migrated over from heathen lands.

A group of five boys, or rather young men, stood on the edge of the square, observing her.

"Isn't it this chick that always hangs out with the Chinks?" one of them asked suddenly. He was holding a soccer ball under his elbow.

"Shut up," said another, with blonde hair, and she recognized him. It was that tall, burly young man Kehuan sometimes played basketball with. She didn't remember his name, but he was the one who'd once pulled her down from the wall, starting the brawl with Kehuan and Taejin.

Well, well. The infamous nazi boys. Or rather ex-nazi—at least some of them.

"Don't pay attention to that imbecile," said the blonde guy. "What's up? I haven't seen you for ages, and Kehuan as well."

Niki's chest constricted painfully, and she didn't answer.

"Hot for skating," noticed someone. It was, and Niki had been about to quit for the day when they appeared.

"We were just going to have something to drink," said one of the guys, giving her a seductive smile. "Want to join us?"

She wondered for a moment if he was the one who'd catcalled earlier, but it didn't really matter. She was hot and sweaty and had a beginning of a headache after too many hours in the blazing sun.

"Yes," she said. "Let's go."

That threw them for a loop, but Niki didn't wait until they recovered. She just picked up her tennis shoes and started skating along the park alley. The guys had to trot to keep up, which made her smirk. Move your ass, baby.

There was a small café at the entrance to the park, with a few plastic tables and chairs outside, under big yellow umbrellas. They put two tables together and bought some drinks and ice creams, and chips. The guys were a rambunctious crowd, and after a few minutes of listening to their crude banters and dirty jokes Niki felt disgusted and entertained at once.

"What's your name, baby?" asked the guy with spiky brown hair, the master of seductive smiles. "I'm Patryk."

"Niki," she said automatically, surprising herself.

She'd been introducing herself as Veronica for years, but the question had caught her off guard, and she said what first popped in her head. So she was still just Niki deep down. Good to know.

"Want me to walk you home, Niki?" he asked, looking her deep in the eyes.

"Chill, man," said the blonde guy. Marcin, as she'd heard someone call him a moment earlier. "Unless you've got too many teeth. Because her boy sure can knock some out for you."

Niki's chest constricted again.

"I'll go," she said, getting up. She'd already changed earlier to the tennis shoes, so now she just collected her wrist guards from the table, and hung the rollerblades over her shoulder. "See you around."

Two days later they came to the little square again and watched her skate for twenty minutes, exchanging boisterous comments and shouting words of encouragement, and making her laugh and roll her eyes simultaneously. The guys were going to play soccer next, and Niki decided on a whim to join them. She wasn't any star at soccer but could play passably well, as it had been the main team sport at the school for the whole primary. They all went for pizza after that, and she managed to squeeze in an entire slice, a real success.

On the way home, Niki mused it was nice to have some company again, and the thought sparked a sudden idea in her head. As soon as she entered the apartment, she dropped her rollerblades in the middle of the hall—there was no one to trip over them anyway—and went straight to her room to start drawing.

She was in a mood for a new comic. It was going to be a story for children this time, and she had a feeling it would be great.

* * *

Niki didn't call anymore, and it bothered Kehuan a lot.

Earlier, the calls hadn't been frequent, and the conversations between them awkward and stiff. Kehuan had the impression she was trying to choose a subject carefully each time, which wasn't like her at all, and he was so depressed he had no idea what to say to her either. But he hadn't realized how much those short, stifled conversations comforted him until they stopped. Now he had no link to her at all. He'd promised Chen Xiao he'd refrain from calling on his own, but this promise was getting harder and harder to keep. He recalled the long talks they used to have on Skype during her stay in Finland and felt even more dejected.

But it reminded him of that comic of hers, so he opened the webtoon page to look at it again. And surprise, surprise, there was an invitation to a new story, and when he followed the link, he had to smile, despite everything.

Niki was drawing a comic for children, in her beautiful ink-and-pastel style, and the main character was a little cat, roaming around and having adventures while meeting different other animals.

In the first episode the cat was lonely and bored, but then it met a big wolf and they became friends, and Kehuan's throat clogged up completely when he saw the last illustration, where the cat and the wolf were sitting side by side under a big tree and watching the sunset.

In the second episode it was raining, and the little cat was all wet and cold. The wolf was looking for some shelter for its friend, and he found a cave, but it was already inhabited by a big shaggy bear, who was very grumpy and unwilling to share its lodgings with other animals. But the episode ended with the bear grudgingly taking the little cat in, and the wolf watching them from the entrance of the cave with a satisfied expression on its animal face.

Kehuan felt so completely sucker-punched.

It wasn't Niki's real story, of course, and yet it was her story; he suspected the bear wouldn't have been portraited as so bad-tempered and narrow-minded if she wasn't so annoyed with Chen Xiao at the moment, and this observation made him chuckle in amusement, for the first time in several months.

He quickly returned to the main page to check for more parts. There was only one left, about a very graceful black swan whom the little cat observed with envy. It was a very funny episode because the cat kept trying to copy the swan's moves while staying on dry land, and the pictures were hilarious. The wolf was only present in the background this time, observing the two other animals and giving a very strong vibe of standing guard over them.

He wanted to call her at once. He wanted to board a plane, go to Warsaw, and hug her. He wanted to stand guard over her again, but here he was, in Taipei, needlessly, meaninglessly, hopelessly killing time. Did it make any sense? Kehuan couldn't remember anymore why he was even doing it.

But then he recalled that his father was ill and that he'd given his word to Chen Xiao, so he clenched his teeth and stayed where he was, heartsick, desolate, and angry.

* * *

Niki played soccer with the guys several more times, and they ribbed her a lot about her poor skills with the ball, but she didn't mind. She'd always liked physical activities, and playing a team game required concentration, which at least took her mind off all those things she didn't really want to think about anymore, like her general immaturity, and childish interests, and lack of self-dependence, and impulsive approach to sex; all these inadequacies everybody had been pointing out to her lately.

After that, they usually invited her to eat some fast food together, and it was strange, but her throat wasn't constricting so bad when she was listening to their silly joshing. She could eat more than usual, and fast food was certainly better than nothing.

Once, when she was returning in the evening from yet another long ramble, she noticed Marcin and Patryk sitting in a large group of young people outside some pub or club. There were girls with them this time, too, all dressed in fitted, sexy clothes. Niki raised her hand in a greeting, and they called out to her, but she didn't join them. The girls were giving her the stink eye, and she didn't think she'd be a good fit in that company.

Besides, she had her comic to draw.

She'd created a special website for it. Kehuan had once shown her an easy drag-and-drop program for creating websites, so it hadn't been that difficult, just a little time-consuming. But Niki had time aplenty these days, and when the website was established, it took just a few minutes to upload a new episode.

She'd also created a forum for her new story, and posted there a joking invitation for everybody under the age of twelve to send their comments. There were already a few, though one was from a parent. But they were all positive and gave her a boost to go on with it. If she was childish, she'd be childish all the way, she thought rebelliously.

It all kept her occupied and gave her something to look forward to each day, but she still felt very lonely. Some voids are impossible to fill, no matter what you do.

* * *

Niki was wondering what was happening with Anna. Not that she missed her that much—to tell the truth, she might not even notice that her guardian had been away for a little bit too long if not for the owner of the apartment, who appeared on its doorstep at the beginning of August, looking very displeased.

"Are your parents at home?" he asked, and Niki was seriously tempted to snort in his face.

"Not right now," she answered prudently instead. "Is there a problem?"

"I received a payment reminder from the energy company," he said. "And from the gas company. The last bills haven't been paid."

"Oh," said Niki, thinking hard. "I'll tell them to pay everything when they return. Can you leave me the reminder notes?"

He watched her for a moment dubiously. "Are you sure you won't forget, child?" he asked in the end.

"Of course not," Niki assured him. "It'll be done today."

It turned out easier said than done, though, as the sums on the bills weren't small.

Niki had a personal bank account, and she was getting royalties in monthly payments from Mrs. Krawczyk, the owner of the online store, for all the posters of her design that got sold, though it wasn't any big money. She also earned a little from that Finnish comic story, and besides, Chen Xiao transferred her a generous allowance every month, for clothes and art supplies and such stuff. But Niki had been paying for many other things from these funds, including food when the fridge was empty, and she didn't have much money left right now since she'd been living on her own for a month already.

Niki really didn't want to ask anybody for help—after all, she was supposed to grow up and become more independent without bothering other people all the time. But in the end, she had no choice but to call Chen Xiao.

"Niki," he said, surprised and happy. She hadn't called him on her own initiative since their argument in March. "How are you?"

"I'm sure you receive regular reports from Anna," Niki replied and held her breath, waiting for his reaction.

"Yes, but it's not the same," he told her warmly. "I hope you're having a nice holiday, honey."

"Very," Niki answered dryly, feeling absurd. "But I have some additional expenses because of that. Could you send me some extra money?"

Chen Xiao stayed quiet for a moment. Niki thought he must've realized she called to ask him for dough, and she felt bad.

"Of course," he said at last and chuckled. "Teenagers and holidays. How could I not think about it?"

"Thank you." Now she felt even worse. "Have you been well?"

"Yes," Chen Xiao answered. "But I'd appreciate it if you sent me some holiday photos in return."

Niki decided to test the waters some more. "What kind of pictures would you like?"

"I don't know. Doesn't matter. From the beach, perhaps?"

Right. That might be a bit problematic. Though Niki supposed she had in her phone some pictures from previous years she could utilize.

They said goodbye and disconnected.

A few hours later she had a nice sum on her bank account and could pay the bills. But now she started to worry a little. Where the hell was Anna?

* * *

Anna went on holiday and met the love of her life.

It was hard to believe since she was forty-five, but it really felt as if she'd never been in love before. Sure, she'd had feelings for Chen Liang at the beginning of their marriage, but they turned out to be one-sided, and look how it all ended. Not the stuff for a romance book.

But now it was a different story. The man she'd met this summer was of a completely different sort, gentle and affectionate, and Anna finally felt like a real woman, cherished and doted on. And in her heart of hearts, she thought, who knew? Maybe it wasn't too late to start a family as well. Dominik had said several times he liked children and wanted to have them in the future, just not yet.

He was younger than Anna by fourteen years. Some people might scoff at the idea of love between them for this reason, but that was just their own prejudice and insecurity speaking, nothing else. Dominik told her many times how he appreciated maturity and wisdom, and besides, Anna looked ten years younger than she was. He stated that many times as well.

It was a pity some people couldn't stomach others' happiness, though. Two weeks after meeting Dominik Anna had a falling out with Sabina because of him, which was ridiculous, since they'd originally met through the younger woman. They'd bumped into him on the promenade by the sea, and Sabina introduced him as a brother of a classmate from high school. But later she got all petty and judgmental.

"Anna, please don't get angry with me for saying this," she said one day, sounding a little hesitant. "Dominik's an attractive guy, and very entertaining, but you should be careful with him."

"Why?" Anna asked, already miffed on his account.

"He's a bum, honestly speaking," answered Sabina. "I've known him forever, and he's never had a permanent job."

"He told me all about it," Anna told her, feeling superior. "If you need to know, he had really bad luck with his bosses in the past. But he started working in this transport company last month, and he's certain this time it'll work out."

"And they'd given him two weeks of vacation after one month of work," said Sabina sarcastically. "Does this story add up in your opinion?"

"He charmed the lady in HR," Anna answered, smiling. It was the funniest anecdote she'd heard lately.

"That's another thing," Sabina said. "He's got a very colorful history with women."

"It's understandable," Anna answered indulgently. "He's gorgeous."

"Yes, and he knows it," Sabina said pointedly. "And let me tell you, all his girlfriends in the past were quite wealthy. He's not interested in females without money."

Anna eyed her suspiciously. It sounded as if someone was jealous. Was it perhaps a case of sour grapes?

"Thank you for your concern, but I think I can judge for myself a person's character," she told Sabina haughtily.

Their relations cooled a lot after that. Anna felt disappointed about it, and a little perturbed, and called her sister for consultation, even though they hadn't talked for a long time. But it was a mistake. She'd forgotten that all Renata ever did was criticize her and all her choices, and gloat over everything that went wrong in Anna's life. This time her sister went so far as to bring up their late mother and her pitiful marital life and to suggest that Anna was about to enter the same path. Anna felt so angry and frustrated with this conversation that when it ended, she shrieked and threw the phone, and swore not to call her sister ever again.

Their holiday ended two days later, and Sabina went back to Warsaw after that, but Anna didn't. Dominik suggested the two of them should stay a little longer and perhaps visit Danzig together since it was a city made for lovers. Anna was charmed, and she called the company to get an extra leave of absence. They spent together two unforgettable weeks, romantic and passionate at once, and after that, she knew they were meant to be, whatever other people said.

But she had to return in the end, to check on that troublesome girl. Chen Xiao kept calling her for updates every other week, and even if Anna was certain Veronica was fine, it was better to go back and confirm it, just in case.

Dominik was going with her, of course; parting was out of the question. He'd lived in Łódź, and he had to quit that new job to accompany her, but she was sure he'd find something better in Warsaw anyway. And when he asked if she could help him find a place to live, Anna simply invited him to the apartment. It was certainly big enough, and it was just Veronica and herself in it now.

"But I must warn you, I have a ward," she told him, wincing. "She's a real brat, but her father is disabled, so I've been taking care of her for years."

"You're an angel, Anna," he answered with reverence. "I knew it from day one."

* * *

Niki hated him on the spot.

He was so slimy. Good-looking perhaps, but there was something about this guy that made her pat her pockets to check if she still had her phone. And he kept leering at her with those pushy eyes, girly and long-lashed, and Niki felt like taking a shower after five minutes in his company.

Where Anna had found this specimen was a true mystery, but it didn't matter that much. More problematic was the fact that she installed him in the apartment. He slept with her upstairs, but Niki still had to deal with his presence during the day because he quickly developed a true fondness for their living room, which unfortunately formed one big space with the kitchen, and it was impossible to avoid him completely if she wanted to eat. The only solution she could think of was to keep to her own room as much as possible and to use the kitchen when he was out or upstairs, but it meant cooking and eating at completely random and sometimes bizarre hours.

Because of him, the whole apartment felt dirty and strangely unsafe. She could see clearly there was no point talking to Anna, though. She was completely smitten with the guy, and besides, she'd never listen to Niki's opinion.

Despite that, life became a little better in these last weeks of the summer. Taeyeon and Taerim returned from holidays, and Niki had her regular company at last. Even so, she still played soccer from time to time with Marcin and his boys. Now the twins joined them as well, and they were very diverted by her new buddies. They also came round to the apartment several times, and on one occasion met its new inhabitant.

Niki loved the twins to bits. One look at the guy, second between them, third at her, and all was said without a word. They weren't spiritual triplets for nothing.

She kept drawing her comic story, and it even started bringing her some minuscule additional income, now that she made it partially paid. She was very fond of it and had so many ideas for new episodes, but at the beginning of September the school year started, as was its pesky habit, and it was her final year.

Niki was determined to study hard and do well at the exams. She still planned to apply to the university in Vancouver, and she was hoping Kehuan would stick to his word and go with her if she got accepted, though her belief in things he'd said in the past had been sapped by this time more than she wanted to admit to herself.

She didn't want to give up on Kehuan, but she couldn't understand why he was behaving this way with her. Niki preferred to believe he had his reasons, better than what he'd told her because those were just some weak excuses. But she had no idea what to think anymore, and so she simply stopped thinking about it at all. She'd been hurt so much already she couldn't and wouldn't take more of it.

* * *

Kehuan opened Niki's website to check it for a new episode. This was the only thing keeping him afloat these days: children's comic story. His art of survival.

He couldn't sleep well anymore because his nights were plagued with nightmares. His subconscious was obviously trying to tell him something, and he wanted very much to tell it back it was enough, he'd got the message already: go to Warsaw, get back with Niki, and stay with her forever and ever. But he still couldn't follow this excellent advice, and the dreams, and then the lack of sleep started to take a toll both on his physical and mental condition.

Kehuan's default reaction to stress had always been anger, and he was angry all the time now. He was furious at himself because it was his own fault it had come to this, and at Chen Xiao for creating this cage he was sitting in, and even at his father for being ill, though that was completely unfair, of course.

He found a martial arts club nearby and started training regularly again, just to find some outlet for this ever-present anger, and it helped a little, as it always had, but he was so miserable that apart from everyday short exchanges with his father he stopped talking to people completely.

He was doing coding for the Taipei company now, and they all looked at him in the office like at some dangerous beast because all he ever did when people tried to chat with him was growl. They bore with it because he was Chen Liang's son, and also because Kehuan was a very good programmer, and they were always in dire need of one more good programmer there, but he could tell they all thought he was unhinged.

He looked at the screen now, and yes, there was a new episode, and Kehuan first watched the free shorter version, and then paid with an SMS for the extended one, and opened it using the code. His clever girl.

Many of those stories seemed completely fictional to him, though they might simply be about people he didn't recognize. It was very probable, actually. But the others...

The episode with the tiger who rescued the little cat from drowning and taught it to swim had been a real blow to the chest, especially when Kehuan looked closer and discovered that the big cat and the small were drawn to have a similar pattern of fur, only with different coloring. He wondered if Taejin was following the story as well, and what he thought of it.

The two monkeys who climbed trees with the little cat and played jokes on it made him smile again, as well as the sneaky chameleon who persuaded the cat to play hide-and-seek with it. Was it supposed to be Mauricio?

Today's episode was about a cute and crafty fox, who kept stealing food from the little cat until it got caught, and then they made friends and went and stole some food together from the two monkeys.

Oh, Niki, you little devil. Kehuan laughed quietly and then put his hands over his face, and felt appalled to discover tears under his fingers.

Yeah, what they said. Unhinged.

* * *

Dominik Rapacki had a rule to always take what life offered.

This world was a nasty place, especially for someone born in a family without clout or dough, and he'd struggled to maintain an acceptable standard of living since he'd finished school. It wasn't easy to find a job that would bring decent money. All such positions were reserved for privileged assholes with degrees and connections, and he had none. He had to take the scraps he was given. Most of it was totally beneath his smarts, just as the deadheads he had to work with, and so it never lasted long—he was fed up with everything pretty soon each time.

But there was one area of life where he could truly shine and properly utilize both his wits and appearance: women. He'd discovered it long ago. He'd been still in high school when an elegant older lady approached him in a shopping mall and offered him a nice round sum for spending some time with her. He'd been a sex-crazed teenager back then, so it was a win-win situation: he got physical and monetary gratification at one go. They kept meeting for a few years, but Dominik saw no reason to stick to one woman even then. If one had a talent for something, one should make use of it, that's what he said.

Later, he had many other profitable relationships, though each of them ended after some time. Occasionally the woman decided she wanted something else, but more often he got bored or decided the takings weren't so great, and he ended things to look around for something new.

This time it seemed he hit the jackpot. Anna was so hooked on him he could get her to do anything he wanted; it was child's play. He only had to bed her regularly, listen patiently to the sob stories about her neglectful ex-husband and patronizing sister, and tell her every day she was beautiful, plus throw in some romantic claptrap, and he had her in the palm of his hand. Sex with her was no hardship; she was a little old, but attractive enough, and look what he got from it. The apartment itself was worth it. He'd never lived so well, at least not for longer than a day or two, and he already itched to invite over some of his buddies. He wanted to see their ugly mugs when they took in this place. Besides, his new lady had dough galore, and she didn't skimp. As he got it, the money came from two different guys, and he approved. Why not milk two cows if you had a chance.

And there was an extra bonus, too.

From the first moment Dominik saw that pretty little doll, he'd known he'd have her. She was playing hard to get for now, but they were living together in this place, and there'd be many occasions to make friends. It was just a matter of time, and he wasn't going anywhere in a hurry.

* * *

Kehuan called Niki on her seventeenth birthday. He couldn't just skip it, Chen Xiao and his rules be damned. But it only made him more depressed in the end.

"Hello," she answered the phone in Polish, and he realized she didn't even know his current number in Taipei, and had no idea it was him.

"Niki," he said. "It's me."

"Kehuan," she said, and the hope in her voice sounded much more tentative and guarded this time. "Are you back?"

"No, I'm still in Taiwan," he said. "I just wanted to hear you, and to wish you happy birthday."

Niki was quiet for a moment. "Thank you," she said at last in a different tone. "How's your father?"

"Much better," Kehuan answered. "He's already at home, doing the rehab. Wants to get back to work next week."

"The doctors are okay with it?"

"Yes, if he takes it easy."

"That's good. Are you going to stay there?"

"For now."

There was another moment of silence. "Give my best wishes to your father," she said finally.

"I will," Kehuan promised, unnerved by her polite tone and the official tenor of the whole conversation. "Niki—"

"But please don't call me again unless you decide to return," Niki said firmly.

And she hung up on him.

* * *

Chen Liang was taking it easy.

He did rehab, went on strolls, read books and listened to music, and had a lot of time to think. And as it often happened with people in similar circumstances, he reflected a lot about his life. He thought about Lee Soojin, and his son, and about different things he'd done and hadn't done, and also about other people who were important to him, like Niki and Chen Xiao.

Every time Kehuan came to check up on him, it was hard to miss how downcast and heartsick he looked, and in the end, Chen Liang decided to talk to his son.

"Why are you here?" he asked.

Kehuan looked at him, confused. "I came to visit you?..."

"Why are you in Taipei?" Chen Liang specified.

"Because you got ill."

"I'm much better now. You can return to Warsaw."

"I can't," his son answered, and there was a whole sea of longing in his eyes.

"Why not?"

"Chen Xiao asked me to stay away for the time being," said Kehuan.

"Why?"

There was a moment of loaded silence, and Chen Liang wondered if his son would even answer the question.

"We slept together with Niki," Kehuan said at last and looked him in the eyes, obviously waiting for a reprimand.

"I thought something like that might've happened," Chen Liang said dryly. "You could've waited with it a little longer, but I think it wasn't against her will, was it?"

"Of course not," Kehuan answered, horrified. "I'd never..."

"Of course you would never," Chen Liang agreed. "You've always done everything you could to make her happy."

"But Chen Xiao thinks I should leave her alone for now," Kehuan said bleakly. "What can I do?"

"I may be wrong, of course," Chen Liang said, "but I think Niki wants you there."

"Yes," Kehuan admitted.

"Since when have you started to listen to what other people tell you to do? In the past, you only ever did what you thought was right. Or what Niki wanted."

Kehuan watched him intently. "Are you saying I should ignore Chen Xiao?" he asked, sounding hopeful.

"I'm not sure," Chen Liang said. "But think carefully about what you're doing. Some things are hard to undo later."

* * *

It was Friday evening, and Niki was reading in her bedroom when she heard some sound behind the wall. She ignored it at first, but then she realized it had come from Kehuan's room, where there was no reason for any sounds these days.

She put away the book, went out of her room, and stood at the open door of Kehuan's room. Just as she'd suspected.

"What are you doing here?" she asked angrily. "It's not your place."

"I've heard there's a nice view from the window in this room," Dominik answered with an insolent smile, while his eyes moved blatantly all over her body.

Ugh.

"If you saw it already, please leave the room," Niki told him. "There's nothing interesting in here."

"I wouldn't say that," Dominik crooned, moving slowly in her direction. "You are sure very interesting, sweetie."

Niki felt uneasy. "Where's Anna?" she asked, stepping back.

"Asleep in our bedroom," Dominik answered with a creepy smile, and before Niki had time to feel indignant at the pronoun, he added, "Too much wine, I'm afraid."

This was the moment when Niki really grasped the situation. That undefined impression that the apartment wasn't safe anymore became suddenly very defined, and she felt the blood drain from her face.

But showing fear right now wouldn't help things much.

"Get out of here," she said firmly, clenching her fists. "This part is out of bounds for you."

"Says who?" he scoffed and moved even closer. "Don't be so uptight. I came to spend some time with you, sugar. Aren't you lonely?"

Niki was really afraid now. She tried to take a step back again, but the sleazebag had obviously predicted it because he suddenly stepped to the side and pushed her with his entire body into the corridor wall.

Niki had never been interested in learning martial arts, and she regretted it from the bottom of her heart at this moment. She was very agile, though, and managed to duck under his shoulder at the last moment, and slip out from between his torso and the wall.

She jumped back a few steps towards the main hall.

"Stop it," she said furiously, and decided to make herself clear, just in case he was confused somehow. "I don't want you. Get away from me."

He just laughed, and Niki knew then there was no misunderstanding, and no chance to avoid him unless she escaped or managed to hurt him somehow. And since she had no idea how to hurt a person and wasn't sure she could do it, she turned around and made a dash out of the apartment into the outside hall.

What now?

"Come back here," Dominik called after her, annoyed, and walked out as well. "Where will you go at this hour? I'm not going to hurt you."

Yeah, right. Niki took a few steps backward, watching him closely, and when he started moving in her direction again, she spun in place and ran down the stairs.

* * *

Chris Morton was on the bus, returning home from a meeting with a few friends, when he noticed her on the bridge. She was walking in the same direction the bus was moving, and he couldn't see her face at first, but he was almost sure it was Veronica; he'd watched her from behind often enough in the past. He rotated in his seat by the window as the bus passed her, and it was really Veronica Chen, on the bridge at midnight, without a jacket, and without shoes.

Chris jumped out of the bus at the nearest stop and sprinted back, afraid he might miss her if she'd left the bridge already and turned into some side street. But he found her without a problem.

"Veronica...Where...are you going?" he panted out. "Why...aren't you... wearing shoes?"

She was hugging her body with both arms, so Chris took off his jacket and put it over her shoulders.

"Has something happened?" he asked, gazing into her face. She looked tired and scared.

"Could you walk me home?" she asked hesitantly, and Chris thought it was certainly a first between them.

"Sure," he answered. "But can you even walk like that? Won't you hurt your feet?"

"I'll manage," she said. "The socks are thick."

It wasn't very far from this point to the apartment block where she lived, but he kept glancing worriedly at her feet all the way. He should've offered to give her a piggyback ride. Thank goodness the nights weren't very cold yet.

They entered the hall and stopped in front of the elevator, and she turned around hesitantly.

"Could you ride upstairs with me?" she asked again, and Chris was certain now that his first impression had been right: she was frightened.

"Let's go," he said concisely.

She lived on the last floor, and there was only one sturdy door with a digital lock on this level. Veronica typed in the code and opened the door, but she didn't go inside. She just stood there, as if she wasn't sure it was a good idea to enter the apartment.

"Want me to come in with you?" Chris asked since he could see the pattern already.

"Please," she said.

He went in first and looked around. The place was dim, but he could see opposite the entrance the stairs leading up to another level, and the big open space on the right was probably the living room.

Veronica went in behind him, but she didn't switch on the light. She just tugged on his sleeve and turned to the left, and Chris followed her.

There were three doors at this end of the hall, and she checked inside each of them before she looked at him again, uncertain. She'd switched on the light in one room, and he could see her face clearly now.

"Do you have to go home at once?" she asked, regarding him carefully with her gorgeous eyes, and though Chris understood perfectly well it wasn't that kind of invitation he wished for, it still made his heart jump.

"No," he said quietly. "I can stay."

"You can sleep in Kehuan's room if you don't mind," she offered.

Later at night, Chris stood in front of the enormous floor-to-ceiling window, gazing at the dark sky and the city lights. He couldn't sleep.

Kehuan Chen's bedroom. It was so absurd. Who'd have thought he'd end up here one day, or rather one night.

The room wasn't really dark because of the big window, and Chris walked around without switching on the light. He stopped in front of the wide bookcase and looked at the spines. Chinese. English. Some Polish books, too. Another language with yet another system of characters. Korean perhaps?

The place was quite austere, with no stuff lying loose around. He stopped in front of the piano to contemplate the two big posters hanging over it side by side. He remembered them from the school exhibition a few years earlier.

There were two more pieces of art Chris could bet were Veronica's work as well: a lovely relief with snowflakes, and a breathtaking wooden structure reminding an ocean wave.

What a place.

Chris would give a lot for this room to belong to him, together with everything it represented, but it didn't of course, and the important question was, where the hell its owner was roaming while Veronica Chen was afraid to set foot in her own house.

* * *

The next morning she offered him breakfast, and then they left the apartment together, Veronica with rollerblades hung over one shoulder.

"Thank you, Chris," she said, and his heart flipped in his chest again at the sound of his name. Another first.

"No problem," he answered, and they parted ways, just like that.

But Chris wasn't going to leave it just like that, and after returning home and thinking a little he texted Jason, who send him contact details to one of the Soeng twins.

They met the same day in the afternoon in a pub not far from the international school. Chris was a little taken aback when he saw Kamila enter the place as well, but he summarized the whole incident for them, together with his speculations. Kamila seemed surprised, but the twins weren't really.

"That pig," said one of them heavily. Chris still wasn't able to tell them apart. "What do we do now?"

"Who are we talking about?" asked Kamila, echoing Chris's thoughts.

"Anna's lover boy," the other Soeng spat in answer. "He moved in in August."

"Niki didn't say a word," Kamila observed, looking stunned. "Why?!"

"That's not the point," Chris said impatiently. "You need to inform someone."

"Whom?" asked Soeng number one. "There's no one here but Anna right now."

"She's Niki's guardian," Kamila explained. "A real piece of work."

"So where's Chen?" Chris asked, and all three of them winced at once.

"In Taiwan," Kamila answered, sounding cross.

"Doesn't Veronica have any other family?" he inquired again, realizing how little he really knew about her.

"Father," answered Soeng number two. "In Canada."

"Unbelievable," said Chris. "Are they taking part in some kind of family challenge?"

"We have no contact with him, anyway," said the twin, dismissing the comment. "Neither with Kehuan at the moment. And besides, it looks like Niki doesn't want to talk about it with any of them. We have to come up with something else."

"Someone needs to sleep there," said Kamila. "So she's not alone."

"Could you perhaps?" asked Chris.

"Oh, that's brilliant, Moron," said Soeng number one scathingly. "Throw in foxy in the bargain, so the guy has more options."

"It's not such a bad idea, actually," said Kamila, waving down the irritated twin. "I don't think he'll do anything when there's a witness, even if it's another girl. But I can't stay there every night. My mum would have a fit."

"Our mother would have a fit if she knew we even talk to Nik," said Soeng number two ironically. "But I suppose we can try sneaking out in turns."

"I'll ask Jason, too," said Chris.

"We need to make a roster," said Soeng number one.

"God, what a mess," said Kamila irritably. "I wish Chen would see the light already, and come back."

* * *

Dominik was goaded beyond belief. That little slut dared to actually bring another man for the night while he was there. Oh, she was going to regret it.

Before, it had been just a little bit of sport, and he'd let her go after sleeping with her once or twice. Or maybe not, on the other hand. She was really cute, and he had a feeling she'd be great in the sack.

But anyway, now it became a challenge. If she was trying to mess with him, he'd show her who was the boss here now.

* * *

Two weeks later Anna marched into Niki's room, fuming.

"You can't have boys here for the night, Veronica," she said crossly. "Even if you think you're an adult, which you're not, it isn't proper behavior."

"They're just friends," Niki answered, watching her warily. Anna seemed to get more and more annoyed with her recently. "We aren't doing anything."

"Oh really," Anna scoffed. "As if I'd believe it. Don't think I can't see you making eyes at Dominik, too. I've never thought you'd become such a slut, just because Kehuan dumped you."

Niki gaped at her, speechless. She needed a moment to gather her thoughts.

"You must be joking," she said at last, very angry. "It's that sleazebag—"

Anna hit her without a warning, an open palm hard slap to the face, and

Niki swayed on her feet and pressed her hand to the cheek.

"Don't you dare," Anna warned furiously. "You are grounded, and don't even think about bringing someone for the night again."

* * *

"Call Kehuan, Niki," said Kamila, feeling helpless. "Please."

"His father is ill over there," Niki answered stubbornly. "And besides, I don't want him to run here in some rescue mission. If he doesn't want to come just for me, I don't want him to come at all."

"So call your father," Kamila insisted. "It's getting out of hand. What will you do if that pig tries something again?"

"I've asked the twins to help me install a lock on my bedroom door," Niki said. "And on Kehuan's, too."

"Why on his?" asked Kamila, baffled.

"I don't want the sleazebag to go in there again," Niki said with revulsion. "He's making everything dirty."

Kamila wasn't sure it would be enough, but she didn't say another word.

She had no idea why Niki was so adamant in trying to solve that whole mess on her own when it was obvious she was out of her depth there. And her girl didn't look so good, too. After the holidays she seemed to have gained some weight, but now she was gagging on food again. Kamila suspected it was all somehow connected to Chen, and she had a few things to say to him when he finally returned.

If he returned.

* * *

Chen Liang was getting more and more concerned about Kehuan, but when he started to really think about the whole situation, he felt uneasy about its other aspects, too, and in the end, he decided to call Chen Xiao.

They talked a little bit about his health and business matters, and then he got to the point.

"You exiled my son from Warsaw," he said. "I think it's not right."

"Do you know why I did it?" Chen Xiao asked.

"I guess because Kehuan and Niki slept together," Chen Liang answered bluntly. No point in beating around the bush between the two of them.

"So you do know."

"Kehuan didn't do anything illegal," Chen Liang noted.

"I know that. But it was still wrong," Chen Xiao said very firmly.

"Ah, wrong and right," Chen Liang mused. "You can tell them apart for sure, I see."

"Alina had been the same age as Niki…"

"Yes, Alina. I thought it might have something to do with her."

"It ruined her life," said Chen Xiao with the same old grief which had always been in his voice when he spoke about Niki's late mother.

"I don't know about that," Chen Liang answered calmly. "She met some guy at sixteen, and got pregnant, and had the child, and it certainly made things very difficult for her. But I never heard her say she regretted it, not even once. Did you?"

"No," Chen Xiao admitted, "But still…"

"Even if it had been a mistake, Alina got over it," Chen Liang told him. "And Niki isn't Alina, I should say."

"But she's so young," said Chen Xiao, sounding a little less confident.

"Being young doesn't always mean you don't know what you are doing. And being older doesn't automatically prevent you from making mistakes," said Chen Liang, and thought ironically, look at me, one little heart attack, and what a philosopher I've become.

"Look at me," he spoke again, echoing his thoughts. "I made my worst mistakes as an adult man, and not even a young adult at that."

"Do you suggest I should let Kehuan be with her, just like that?"

"You threw away my son, who's always protected Niki and kept her as happy as possible, and instead left her with Anna, who you have to pay to look after your girl. Does it make sense to you?" asked Chen Liang a little impatiently.

"You think Anna can't take care of her?"

"Oh, she can," Chen Liang said dryly. "In the best fairy tale step-mother style."

"Don't exaggerate. I know she can be a little harsh, but she cares about Niki."

"I can see how you might think that. Anna's always made a lot of effort to look good in your eyes, and it wasn't so hard, seeing how you only visited for short periods of time. But I watched her with the children for years, and believe me, leaving Niki alone with her isn't the best idea."

Chen Xiao was silent now, digesting his words, and Chen Liang decided to finish the whole conversation and give the guy some time.

"Please reconsider your decision," he said by way of goodbye. "Before we all come to regret it."

* * *

Niki cut her hair short again. She remembered many people lamenting over it back when Kehuan had to shear it off in middle school, and she thought maybe it would help the situation if she simply became ugly.

"That's not a solution," said Kamila, exasperated. "It's not your fault, or your hair's fault, that he's a scumbag. And it won't work, girl. You're still nowhere near ugly enough."

Unfortunately, Kamila proved right. The change in Niki's appearance didn't seem to work on Dominik. He was getting pushy again, and when Niki was at home, she was practically a prisoner in her own room. She spent as much time as she could out, though it was November already, and the weather wasn't very encouraging.

One day after lessons she met Marcin near the school, and the sight of him triggered an old memory, which in turn gave her an idea. If she took a leaf out of Kehuan's book and managed to record the sleazebag, maybe she could change Anna's opinion of him after all, and convince her to throw him out. Niki wasn't pinning her hopes on it, but it was certainly worth a try.

But while she succeeded with the recording, no opportunity presented itself to talk sense into Anna because Anna was drinking again, and every time they met, she was either tipsy and spouting idiotic accusations in Niki's direction, or hungover and really crabby. Niki thought she'd even stopped going to work lately.

At the end of the month, the owner of the apartment popped up once more, really annoyed this time, since the bills hadn't been paid again. Anna was out of commission, so he had to talk to Niki this time as well.

"Tell your parents if it goes on like that, I'll dissolve the lease contract," he declared belligerently, and she thought with a sudden surge of black humor that maybe this would be the solution to her problems.

The next day in the morning Niki listened through the door to the sounds in the kitchen, and when she heard Anna's voice, she unlocked the door of her bedroom and went out.

"Anna," she told her guardian. "You have to pay the energy and gas bills."

"I don't have the cash right now," Anna grumbled in answer. She looked terrible, with puffed-up eyes and blotchy skin.

Niki noticed Dominik examine his lover with narrowed eyes.

"Maybe you could pay the bills this time," Anna spoke again sulkily, looking at Niki. "You get quite a big allowance, don't you? You could finally make some contribution to the household."

"I've already done it once," Niki answered. "I don't have so much money."

"You can always call your father and ask for more," Dominik cut in with a smirk. "I've heard he adores you. He sure won't refuse."

"If I call him, we'll have a longer talk," Niki warned and watched with satisfaction as the smile wavered on his slimy face.

Anna looked a little alarmed, too.

"Forget the bills," she said sourly. "I'll pay them next month."

* * *

Anna wasn't going to let Veronica ruin her new life with some childish complaints, and she didn't think Chen Xiao coming to Warsaw right now was the best idea—he might have some reservations about the present arrangement. It was better if she and Dominik got married first. Then Chen Xiao would certainly have no objections to her husband living in the apartment with her.

"I think I need to take away her phone," she said to Dominik in their bedroom that afternoon, chewing nervously on her lower lip. "She's such a drama queen. Who knows what tales she'll come up with when she talks to her daddy next time."

"Do it," Dominik agreed. "Teenagers spend too much time on their phones anyway. You'll be doing her a service."

"You're right," she said gratefully. "She needs to concentrate on her schoolwork right now. I should've thought about it earlier."

Dominik moved closer and kissed her.

"You have too much on your shoulders," he murmured and started to unbutton her shirt. "And that girl really can be a nuisance."

"Exactly," Anna agreed a little breathlessly. He had this effect on her. "And I know she's been behaving inappropriately towards you ..."

"Don't worry about it, darling," he reassured her with a charming smile. "I can handle it."

* * *

Kamila was gaping at Niki's swollen cheek and split lip corner, and didn't know what to say.

"And did they really take it away?" asked pale Chris.

"Yep. But don't worry, I'm going to steal it back," Niki answered with a determined look on her face. "As soon as I have a chance."

"Niki, be careful," Kamila warned. "He can do you serious harm, and it looks like Anna won't lift a finger in your defense."

Niki laughed mirthlessly.

"That's a given," she said and pointed to her lip. "It's her own job. But I really have to retrieve it."

The twins stayed silent, and it wasn't until Niki left that any of them spoke.

"I take it back. We need to contact Kehuan and Chen Xiao somehow," said Taerim grimly. "I don't know what to do anymore. Can't believe I'm saying that, but I wish big brother was here."

There was a moment of silence.

"I know how we can reach them," Taeyeon said suddenly. "We need to call aunt."

"Whose aunt?" asked Chris, just as disoriented as Kamila.

"Our aunt, Kim Hana," said Taerim, and patted his twin on the shoulder. "Good thinking, bro. Let's do it."

* * *

Chen Liang was reading when Kehuan entered the living room. At the sight of his son he took off his glasses and put them on the table, together with the book.

"Why are you still here?" he asked.

"What do you mean?" Kehuan asked back, looking and sounding tense and ready to blow up at any moment, as had been his norm lately.

"You don't want to be here," Chen Liang told him. "Go back to Warsaw already."

Kehuan just glared at him.

"Oh come on," Chen Liang said. "I know I've never understood you very well, but this I could always see very clearly. You want to be where Niki is."

"Of course, but it's not that simple," his son answered crossly. "Chen Xiao—"

"Kehuan," Chen Liang said contemplatively. "Do you remember your mum?"

Kehuan gave him a surprised look. "Yes," he answered, "Though not very well."

"I guess. You were very young when she got ill," Chen Liang said, feeling the pang of loss and sorrow even now, after so many years. "I loved her very much."

Kehuan gaped at him, obviously perplexed by this sudden heart-to-heart.

Chen Liang smiled sadly.

"I only had a few years with Lee Soojin," he went on. "But I used them the best I could, and have no regrets."

Kehuan looked as if he'd stopped breathing altogether.

"I'm well enough, you don't have to worry about me," Chen Liang told him. "And I know Chen Xiao means well, but it doesn't mean he's necessarily right. Stop wasting your time here, go and use it better. It's as they say: you never know how much of it you'll have."

* * *

Kehuan went to his room, opened his laptop, and booked the flight to Warsaw. Then he started packing his suitcase with hands shaking with impatience. Suddenly he remembered their last conversation with Niki. He took out his phone and dialed her number, but the call went directly to the voice mail.

"Niki, I'm coming back," he said anyway, hoping she'd hear it later. "I'll be there on the day after tomorrow. I'm coming back."

He disconnected and thought for a moment, and then decided to call Chen Xiao as well, to inform him about his decision.

"Kehuan," Chan Xiao said, answering the phone after the first ring. "I was just going to call you."

"I'm going back to Warsaw," Kehuan told him without preamble.

"Good," answered Chen Xiao. "Me too. How fast can you get there?"

That wasn't what Kehuan had expected to hear, and somehow it didn't sound right.

"Why are you going as well?" he asked carefully.

"Do you expect me to stay here and do nothing?!" Chen Xiao exclaimed.

"About what?"

"Hasn't she told you?"

"About what??" repeated Kehuan, utterly confused. "I haven't talked to Niki since her birthday—"

"Not Niki," Chen Xiao interrupted impatiently. "Kim Hana. She called you as well, didn't she?"

Kehuan felt cold all of a sudden.

"Why would she call me?" he asked.

"Something's wrong over there," Chen Xiao answered, sounding worried and unnerved. "Apparently, some strange man has been staying in the apartment..."

Kehuan was hearing some swooshing sounds in his ears now and couldn't understand the rest of Chen Xiao's words very well.

"I have to go," he said and ended the call.

Half an hour later he was on the way to the airport. He was going to try to change his reservation to some earlier flight, but even if it wasn't possible, he couldn't bear to spend another night at this place.

* * *

Niki heard the main door slam shut, and she tiptoed out of her room.

It was a rare occasion when Anna and Dominik got up so early in the morning, but she clearly heard their voices in the hall a moment ago, and it looked like this was her chance to get her phone back at last, even if she would be late to school.

She climbed the stairs to the upper level, thinking that in all the years they'd been living in the apartment, she'd done that maybe ten times. The last occasion had been her wonderful birthday party more than a year earlier. But it wasn't the moment now to think about it and get all mushy. Who knew how long Anna and the sleazebag would be out.

Niki entered Anna's bedroom, looked around, and made a face. What a pigsty. And the smell, ugh. She started checking quickly all the places where one could hide a phone, the chest of drawers, the closet, the vanity table. Nothing. Then she noticed the half-unpacked suitcase under the window. She kneeled beside it and started quickly combing through the men's clothes inside, and there was her phone.

"Well, well, well," said gleefully the loathsome voice behind her back. "Look who decided to crawl out of her shell."

Niki spun round, rising quickly to her feet, and came face to face with Dominik.

"I knew you'd end up here sooner or later, little witch," he purred, closing in on her.

Suddenly, he leaped forward and pushed her with both hands, and Niki lost balance. She landed on her back on the messy bed, and the breath whooshed out of her lungs. For a moment she was disoriented, but then the adrenaline kicked in and she rolled to the side as fast as she could, before he had time to pin her down. She jumped to her feet on the other side of the bed, in the narrow space separating it from the wall.

"You sure know how to tease a man, sweetie," he laughed, jumping over the bed after her.

Niki was cornered now, and she could feel her knees tremble. Dominik grabbed her shoulders and slammed her against the wall, pushing his body against hers, and she took a desperate swing with her right arm, her hand still clenched on the phone, aiming for the side of his head. He noticed the movement at the last moment and turned in its direction, and the phone hit him in the face.

Dominik howled in pain. He let go of her, clutching at his eye, and Niki scrambled out of the narrow space, pushing him aside. She jumped out of the room, with bloody Dominik on her heels, and there was Anna, standing at the top of the stairs and gaping at the scene in front of her with bulging eyes. Suddenly, her face contorted.

"You bitch, what have you done!" she screeched.

Niki lurched towards the stairs, trying to bypass her, but at that exact moment, Anna took a swipe and delivered another unchecked, open hand blow to Niki's face. She was evidently developing a taste for them.

Only this last slap had more serious consequences than the previous ones because Niki, being the lightweight that she was, lost balance and tumbled sideways down the short flight of stairs, her feet tripping and sliding against the smooth rounded edges of the wooden steps. She flew towards the wall at the back of the landing and automatically threw out her hand to cushion the contact.

But at the very last moment the old, well-ingrained reflex resurfaced, not the hand! And Niki pressed her right arm to her torso, twisting in the air, and hit the wall with her shoulder instead, and then with the side of her head.

She still managed to feel surprised by how loud a crack someone's skull could make when it hit a hard barrier, and then everything went dark.

13

All the King's Horses

Kehuan couldn't remember any flight in his life to last so long, and the two hours he had to spend at the airport in Amsterdam waiting for his connection to Warsaw turned out even worse.

He sat in front of the gate and changed the SIM card in his phone, and then called Niki from his Polish number. The call again went straight to voice mail. He was starting to feel really edgy about it. Why would she keep her phone switched off all the time? But then he realized it was Thursday, eight-thirty in the morning, and Niki had to be at school.

A minute later his phone rang, and he answered it without even checking the caller, but it was just his voice mail.

The first message was quite old, back from August, and surprisingly, it was recorded by Marcin Kasperczyk. Kehuan had his number on his contact list, but he didn't remember ever talking to the guy on the phone before.

"Hi Kehuan," his ex-stalker and ex-basketball buddy said. "I just wanted to tell you that we've met Niki several times lately. She's rad, man. But she looks, um, I don't know...unwell. I heard you're away, so I just wanted to let you know. So, um, that's all."

The second message was from October, from a number he didn't recognize.

"This is Chris Morton," a male voice said stiffly. "I got this number from

Jason Sullivan. I'm not sure if you're aware that something bad is happening in Veronica's home. We are trying to help, but I think you should come back."

The next one was from another unidentified number, from a few weeks ago.

"You jerk," said a cross female voice. "If you don't come back right now, I don't know what I'll do to you when I see you. I know your father's ill, but you really need to return. Ah, it's Kamila."

The last message was from Soeng Taeyeon, and it was from Tuesday.

"Where are you, man?!" he said, sounding agitated. "Didn't you get the message? Come back already, we don't know what to do. It's about Niki... I don't know where to start. Kehuan, seriously. Come here asap."

That was all.

Kehuan stared at the phone while his heart was gathering momentum to jump out of his chest.

After that conversation with Chen Xiao two days earlier he'd freaked out at first, but later, when he was sitting at the airport in Taipei and analyzing the situation, he came to the conclusion that nothing really bad could have happened because he'd have been the first person Niki would've called in an emergency. Right? Of course right.

But now, when he dialed the number to the voice mail and listened once again to all the recorded messages, he got this dreadful feeling that he'd been completely wrong. Obviously, something bad had happened, and Niki hadn't contacted him at all.

Now he really couldn't bear sitting still and waiting for the plane. He started pacing around the terminal with the phone in his hand, trying to reach Niki, the twins, Kamila, and even Chris. None of them answered, and Kehuan once again remembered that it was a school day, and in all probability, they were all having classes at the very moment.

But he had a strong sense of foreboding now, and when he finally boarded the plane to Warsaw, it was to spend the worst two hours in the air he'd ever had.

All turbulence was just inside his head, and yet it was enough to make him feel terrified and sick, as if he were to plummet down to the ground at any moment and get smashed into million tiny pieces.

* * *

"Call her, Kamila," said Taeyeon nervously as soon as they were out of the classroom after the first lesson.

Kamila dialed Niki's number, but the call went directly to the voice mail.

"It's still switched off," she said. "They must've put it away somewhere."

"We need to go there and check in on her," Taerim said tensely. "I've got a bad feeling."

"Let's go," Kamila decided at once, and both twins gaped at her in astonishment.

"Wow," Taerim said weakly. "That's new."

"Wait a second," said Taeyeon, looking at the screen of his phone. "Kehuan called!"

"Call him back, now," Kamila said. She noticed she had a notification about two unanswered calls as well. Did it mean Chen was coming back? Finally?

"Voice mail," said Taeyeon, frustrated. "Okay, let's go. Kehuan can wait."

But the apartment seemed empty. Nobody answered on the intercom, so they sneaked into the building after a young woman busy with maneuvering a pushchair with a toddler. They rode up to the last floor and listened at the door, but could hear no sound inside.

Right then, Taerim's phone rang.

"It's Jason," he said and answered the call. "Yo, man. What's up? Speak fast, I'm busy."

Kamila was standing close enough to hear Jason's answer.

"Listen, man, Marcin called me," he said. "That Polish guy we sometimes—"

"Yeah, I know," Taerim interrupted. "What's with him?"

"He called about Niki," Jason said, sounding uneasy. "Is she with you perhaps?"

Taerim straightened up. "We are looking for her right now," he answered. "What did he say?"

"Well, his buddy had seen her this morning, and he'd said, I'm quoting, 'she was worse for wear'," Jason reported.

"What?!"

"The guy apparently noticed her on a crosswalk while he was driving a car. According to him, she wasn't walking straight."

"Damn."

"What's going on?" asked Jason.

"No idea," Taerim told him somberly. "But we need to find her, and pronto. Niki doesn't drink. If she couldn't walk straight, there must've been another reason for that."

* * *

Kehuan's plane landed in Warsaw at eleven, and he switched on the phone as soon as the wheels touched the tartan. He'd had three new calls in the meantime.

"Taeyeon," he said without preamble as soon as the younger Soeng picked up. "I'm here."

"You're in Warsaw?!" asked Taeyeon after a moment of stunned silence. "Right on time, man. Something happened. Niki disappeared."

Kehuan felt a shiver travel down his spine at the familiar sound of the words, but he told himself to keep cool. Panicking never solved anything.

"Our place?" he asked.

"Nobody's there," Taeyeon answered. "Though maybe you should check it. We had no way to get in."

"I'll call you when I'm there," Kehuan told him succinctly. "Stay in touch."

He decided to ditch his luggage, but the formalities at the airport still took some time, and it was almost an hour and a half later when he finally punched in the opening code and entered the apartment.

"Niki!" he called, but there was no answer.

The door at the left end of the hall, leading to her room, was wide open.

He walked inside and breathed deeply, looking around. Ah, this smell. Paint and ink, and wood, and Niki. The most wonderful smell in the world.

But she wasn't there, and Kehuan went out to check his own room next, only to discover that he couldn't. The door was locked up.

* * *

Anna got a little scared when the brat tripped over her own feet and fell down the stairs, flailing her arms, and then crashed into the wall. But that flight of stairs really wasn't long, just a few steps between the top corridor and the landing, so she was certain it was pure theatrics when Veronica slid down the wall to lie unmoving on the floor, with her eyes closed. Still, Anna decided to walk down and check on her. But right then Dominik swore violently behind her, and when she turned around and took in his bloody face, all thoughts about the girl flew out of her head at once.

She was terrified his eye could be damaged, but when she rinsed his face with cold water in the bathroom, it turned out it wasn't the case, thank God. But the eyebrow ridge was split open, and it bled copiously. A big bruise had already formed around the eye, and the whole area was rapidly swelling up.

"We need to get you to hospital," said Anna anxiously. "It won't heal properly otherwise. It probably needs to get stitched."

"I'll kill that little bitch," Dominik declared furiously, examining his black eye in the mirror.

Anna twitched and ran out of the bathroom, but when she looked at the landing, it was empty. Of course, she thought contemptuously, feeling relief at the same time. Exactly as she'd suspected, the whole accident had been a sham, and when Veronica realized nobody was going to pay attention to her antics, she got up and left. She probably simply went to school.

Anna returned to the bathroom.

"We'll deal with her later," she promised Dominik. "Let's go and have it treated first."

* * *

"Why did she even hit you?" she asked after they'd left the emergency room at the hospital. It had taken a small eternity because there'd been already several other people waiting in a queue.

Anna wasn't going to let the girl off so easily this time, but she felt a little uneasy about this sudden transformation of her infuriating but harmless ward into a thug. Veronica was a troublemaker, but she'd never shown any violent tendencies before.

"She sneaked up to our room to find the phone, but when she saw I was there and would take it back, she went berserk," Dominik reported, sounding very upset. "Thank heavens you returned in time because I really had no idea what to do. I didn't want to harm her, but she was so aggressive..."

Anna shook her head, disgusted. Veronica obviously thought she'd get away with anything. It was high time to set her straight.

"But why did you return?" asked Dominik. "I thought you were going to your office."

Indeed, this morning Anna had decided to check if her job was still there. She'd been a little short on money lately, and this additional income, however pitiful, would come in handy.

"I forgot my wallet," she said. She couldn't remember when and why she'd taken it out of her purse. "I realized it at the newsagents."

Dominik didn't comment. Instead, he put his arm around Anna's shoulders.

"Thank you for taking care of me," he whispered in her ear. "You're wonderful."

Anna's heart melted.

"But do you remember the guys are coming over today?" he asked after a moment. "Let's have lunch now, and go shopping." He winked at her with a playful grin. "I could do with a new shirt."

Anna hesitated.

All her credit cards were maxed out for the month already, and she didn't have much left on her account either. But when he smiled at her like that, she knew she'd do anything for him, and what was money anyway? Just the means to make someone you loved happy.

* * *

Kehuan met with the twins and Kamila near the school, and he was surprised to see Jason and Morton as well. But it wasn't the time to ask questions.

"We've already checked a few places," Kamila reported and specified the locations. "Any other ideas?"

Kehuan and the twins recited the long list of Niki's favorite hangouts, and they decided to split up to check them all in the shortest possible time, so they wouldn't miss her if she moved.

"Maybe someone should go to the apartment as well, and wait there," Kehuan noticed. "In case she returns home."

But Morton contradicted him at once. "That's doubtful," he said with great conviction. "Veronica avoids staying there as much as she can. I bet she'll be walking around till late again."

Kehuan stared at him, amazed by how well the boy knew Niki's habits, and also by how at ease around him he seemed now. But it was all unimportant compared to the true meaning of Morton's words.

What could scare Niki at home so much? The possible answers made him sick. But this also had to wait.

"Let's go," he said, and they scattered.

An hour later all the sites had been checked, and Niki was still MIA.

"What now?" Kamila asked on the phone, sounding tense and upset.

Kehuan thought hard. He remembered that summer years ago when Niki kept looking for Alina in all the places where her mother used to work. She had no reasons to do it now, but if she wasn't thinking straight, maybe?...

So he once again gave Kamila a handful of locations to check, and heard the twins' voices in the background, confirming that they knew where to go. And then he ran to that old decrepit tenement house, wondering if he'd have to check for her in this godforsaken place forever.

But Niki wasn't there, nor anywhere else, and when Kehuan finished talking to Kamila, walked down the creaking stairs, and stepped out of the gate to the street outside, he suddenly felt really frightened, because now he was completely out of ideas.

* * *

Niki opened her eyes and looked at the smooth cement wall she was leaning against. It had an irregular pattern on it, gray on gray, and she slid a finger along one line. She felt so groggy. Where was this place?

The morning events were clear in her head up to the moment she fell down the stairs. After that everything became a mishmash interspersed with blanks. She'd obviously got dressed and gone out, but she must've been seriously befuddled to put on her light jacket and sneakers instead of the warm winter outfit. She got so cold later. It was December already, and the temperature outside hovered around the freezing point. That was probably why she ended up sitting on the stairs inside some building, though she didn't remember getting here.

She'd been walking around, feeling cold and nauseated, and even vomited twice. But everything seemed so funny at the same time, especially the memory of the creep's bloody face. She'd hit him with the phone. Wasn't it marvelous?

At one point, when she was crossing a street on the green light, her legs somehow took her diagonally instead of straight ahead, and when she bumped into a car waiting in front of the crosswalk and raised her hand to the driver in an apologetic gesture, she saw it was Patryk.

Or was it? Maybe she'd just imagined it.

She felt a little bit of queasiness even now, though her stomach was completely empty. Everything was fuzzy, and her thoughts kept skittering in all directions. She closed her eyes and dozed off for a moment, but approaching footfalls woke her up, and she rose hastily and climbed up the stairs to the next floor. And that was when she recognized the place and snorted at herself in sudden mirth. Oh Niki, you incurable optimist.

That probably meant there was still hope in her. But was it a good thing or a bad thing? She couldn't tell right now and didn't have the energy to think about it. Her shoulder hurt after its encounter with the wall, as did her face after Anna's blow. The headache was the worst, and she was still cold, and very tired. So she sat down in the middle of another flight of stairs, put her head against the gray wall, and slept.

* * *

"I think we need to call the emergency units in all hospitals around," said Kamila, and her voice wavered. "And if it doesn't work, the police,".

Kehuan nodded, turning another disturbing option over in his mind.

"Could it be that Anna and that guy have taken her away somewhere?" he asked, clenching his fists. Imagining the reasons why they might want to do such a thing was freaking him out, but he had to think logically and consider all possibilities.

"Probably not," said Jason. "We heard in the morning from Marcin Kasperczyk, and he said one of his boys had seen her earlier on the street. That's how we knew she was somewhere ar—"

"Where was it?" asked Kehuan abruptly.

"He didn't say."

"Ask him now."

Marcin picked up the phone, but he didn't know the answer to the question. He said he'd talk to his friend, and it was another ten eternal minutes until he called them back.

"He says near the little park with the swings, where he first met you, and later Niki," Jason relayed, holding the phone to his ear. "He says you'll know the place."

"Yes," Kehuan said, feeling very strange. "Tell him thanks."

They all looked at him hopefully, and he prayed he was right when he told them, "I know where she is. Let's go."

And he ran.

* * *

Niki heard the sound of multiple footsteps coming closer, and several voices talking in agitation, so she stood up and tried to move again. But she got dizzy and had to sit back at once or she'd tumble down the stairs, and she'd really had enough of that for one day, thank you very much.

She closed her eyes again, but then the footsteps were right there. They stopped, and she heard rustling as someone moved even closer. Niki could hear their breathing now, right in front of her, so she made an effort and opened her eyes.

It was Kehuan. Who else?

"Hi," she said, smiling at him. Had she spoken in Polish?

Kehuan's eyes were moving all over her face, aghast.

"Niki, what happened?" he asked quietly, taking her hand. He was speaking in Polish, too. "Why are you sitting here?"

What a strange question.

"I've been waiting for you," she answered. But then she remembered something else, and said with a frown, "Can we stay here? The new apartment's all dirty."

"Let me see her," said Kamila's voice, and then she was in front of Niki, watching her closely. "How are you feeling, girl?"

"Dizzy," Niki answered. "Can't stand up."

"Did you hit your head perhaps?" asked Kamila, looking her deep in the eyes in a somewhat technical manner.

"I did," Niki agreed and giggled. "But I hit him, too. With my phone."

She showed them the phone in her hand. The screen was cracked.

"Do you think it still works?" she asked them worriedly. "I've got something important there."

"I think she's concussed," Kamila said somberly. "We need to call the ambulance."

"Wait," someone else spoke behind Kamila, in English this time. "Marcin said he'd be here in a moment with his friend, and they've got a car."

"I hit him with my phone," Niki repeated to herself and giggled again.

Wasn't it funny?

"Why?" asked Kehuan, sliding his careful hand over her head as if he was looking for something.

Niki sobered up and pursed her lips.

"Did he try something again?" asked Kamila.

"Yes," Niki admitted with revulsion. "But I hit him with my phone. He was bleeding like a pig!"

Kehuan's hand stopped at the right side of her head. His fingers were moving even more carefully now as he turned her head to the side.

"That's because he is a pig. But did he strike you, too?" Kamila asked again.

"Nah, it was Anna," Niki replied. "You know how she likes those drama slaps to the face, right?"

"Yes," Kamila agreed. Kehuan twitched and gaped at Niki with dismay.

"She knocked me down the stairs," Niki explained. She was feeling oddly chatty. "But I think it was by accident. I was going to play it to her, but never got a chance."

"To play what?" asked one of the twins. She was almost sure it was Taeyeon. "Give me the phone, Nik." And he extricated it from her fingers.

Oh well. She guessed somebody else would have to play the recordings to Anna now.

"Niki, I'm going to move you," Kehuan warned. "We have to go."

"No," she answered stubbornly. "We can live here again."

"We'll live wherever you want," he promised grimly. "But right now we need to go to the hospital."

* * *

He hadn't recognized her at first. She was sitting on these stairs in his old apartment block, with her eyes closed, and he thought for a moment it was some abused child.

Dark hair stuck out from her head messily, short again, and she was so skinny he'd been afraid to squeeze her hand. The left side of her face was slightly swollen, and she had a big red mark on the cheek and a split lip corner, which looked as if it had half-healed already and then got split back again. Which was probably exactly what had happened.

The right side was much worse. She had a giant bump underneath the hair, and her face looked black and blue from the profile. He was surprised she could even open the eye, but he guessed it was because the bruise and the swelling were all on the side. She must have hit her head sideways against something hard, and Kehuan thought it was a miracle she hadn't shattered her jaw or cheekbone in the process. Though it remained to be seen if there was no more internal damage, invisible on the outside.

He gathered her up carefully, and carried her down the stairs, wondering bleakly how much she could weigh; she felt like a feather. Niki had closed her eyes again, and he wasn't sure if it was all right to let her sleep, or if he should try to keep her awake.

"Why did you cut your hair again?" he asked quietly. He remembered that she'd always preferred it long.

"Needed to be ugly," she mumbled after a moment, without opening her eyes.

Kehuan was so furious now that he stopped speaking altogether. He let Kamila take the lead, and she was talking to the driver at the moment. It was some other guy, not Marcin, but Kehuan didn't care. He just got in the backseat of the car, cradling Niki to his chest, and started planning bloody murder.

* * *

The small crowd in the hospital swelled with every passing hour.

Kehuan, Kamila, and Niki reached the emergency room at about three o'clock, and Jason and Chris, who had taken the bus, joined them some forty minutes later, followed closely by Taerim and Taeyeon. Unexpectedly, the twins had Yoon Sori and Soeng Taejin with them, too. Kehuan supposed they must've called their brother and cousin much earlier, probably still in the morning, but he didn't ask. He was in silent mode.

It was already getting dark outside when Niki was taken for tomography, and soon after that, Kim Hana arrived with Chen Xiao, bringing him straight from the airport.

The examination was over now, and Chen Xiao was talking to the doctor. Kehuan sat by Niki's bed in the hospital room, alone. She seemed asleep again, and the room was quiet, so he could hear the hum of all the hushed voices outside.

Suddenly the door opened and Soeng Taejin stepped inside. He stood over the bed for a moment, watching sleeping Niki with a stony face, and then fetched a chair from under the wall and sat next to Kehuan.

"I don't know whom I should hurt now," he said evenly. "There are just too many candidates. That scum. Your stepmother. You. Myself. Who do I start with?"

Kehuan stayed silent, watching his hands.

"What did you say before?" Taejin continued, and his voice gradually lost the impassive quality, heating up. "That you'd never let anybody mistreat her?" He laughed sarcastically. "That if I was ordered, I'd just pack and go away, and leave her behind?"

The words were taken out of context, but even so, Kehuan felt each of them like a physical blow.

"But I'm no better," Taejin added unexpectedly in a quieter voice. "I saw her in June, and she was so miserable, and looked so sickly. But I just thought, not my problem anymore. Even if it pains me, I can do nothing about it anyway. And then I went back to Cracow, and didn't speak to her again even once, because I was so very busy. What a fantastic big brother I've turned out to be."

Kehuan looked at him now. Taejin was sitting in a pose mirroring his own, with his head hanging low, elbows propped on knees, and fingers of both hands twined tightly together.

The door opened, and Yoon Sori put her head in it.

"Chen Xiao wants to talk to both of you," she whispered, looking just as upset as her cousin. "Kamila and I will stay with her now."

Kehuan and Taejin went out. Chen Xiao was conferring with the twins down the corridor, but as soon as he saw them, he wheeled over and relayed the health bulletin.

"The tomography didn't show any broken bones or internal bleeding," he said. "But they still want to keep her here for a few days, for observation."

Kehuan nodded and breathed easier.

"I've chatted a little with Taeyeon and Taerim here," Chen Xiao continued, and suddenly he sounded very calm and dangerous. "And I think it's time we paid a visit to the apartment."

"Yes," said Kehuan and Taejin at the same time.

"We are going, too," declared Taerim, his pretty face untypically grim.

Chen Xiao frowned.

"Niki's our sis," the other twin reminded him fervently.

"Let them go," said Taejin, surprising Kehuan again.

"All right," Chen Xiao surrendered. "But you two stay back, understood?"

"Sure," Taerim agreed with alacrity. "We'll just do the backing vocals, as always."

* * *

Anna was glad she'd bought that new designer shirt for Dominik. The guests arrived around five, and it was such a pleasure to watch her man preen and show off his new life. She could tell Dominik's new image made a proper impression, even if his friends ribbed him a little about the black eye, and they were duly awed by the surroundings, too. When they all sat down to eat, the guys made a toast with wine, saluting Dominik's luck as well as his great taste in women.

Around seven the lock in the door to the apartment chimed, signaling that someone just entered the opening code.

"Veronica's finally back," Anna said to Dominik in a low voice, breathing a sigh of relief. She'd been feeling a little uneasy all day about the morning incident, even if it had been entirely the girl's fault.

"Tell her to come here," he ordered, grinning, and made an inviting gesture with his arm. He was having a great time with his pals. They'd switched from wine to vodka some time earlier, and he'd already had a few cups. "Guys, I'll show you a really sweet piece of ass."

Anna twinged in surprise and threw him an offended look, but Dominik's buddies shouted their approval, roaring with laughter. But it wasn't Veronica who came through the door.

Anna gasped and jumped to her feet as Chen Xiao rolled in his wheelchair. All the Soeng boys walked in next, with Kehuan bringing up the rear, and when her stepson turned his head to pin her down with baleful black eyes, his face completely devoid of any expression, Anna felt suddenly sick. Her knees quivered, and she had to sit down again.

"Good evening, Anna," Chen Xiao said politely, moving on into the living room. "It's been a while. I can see you're enjoying yourself."

Dominik and his friends fell silent, watching the newcomers in confusion.

The Soengs scattered around the living room, looking bored, but Kehuan prowled up closer. He stopped next to Chen Xiao, quiet and still, and fixed Anna and the guys with slitted eyes, a wild beast waiting for the right time to pounce.

Anna furtively wiped her sweaty palms against her skirt.

"Who's the cripple?" Dominik sneered behind her back. "Is it Veronica's daddy? You never said he was a Chink."

His friends guffawed.

"Be quiet," she whispered. Her heart was racing.

"Where's my daughter?" asked Chen Xiao mildly.

"She hasn't returned from school yet," Anna answered, and smiled at him with trembling lips.

"Niki wasn't at school today," informed one of the Soeng twins, and she remembered belatedly that they were in the same class as Veronica.

"She probably skipped lessons again," she offered, laughing nervously. "You know how she likes to wander around..."

Her eyes kept skittering toward Kehuan, the silent menace.

"Indeed," Chen Xiao agreed. "Just like during holidays, when she's always out somewhere, strolling on the beach. But I think you should give her a call, tell her I'm here."

"Ah, I think she left her phone behind today," Anna said.

"Did she now," mused Chen Xiao.

Where was the phone? Was it still upstairs? The battery had to be dead, it'd been several days already. Or has Veronica taken it with her?

"What's going on?" asked one of Dominik's guests curiously. "Who are these guys?"

"That's the looser with the dough," Dominik informed him with a smirk, and Kehuan's eyes shifted to him.

Anna gulped. Dominik had obviously assumed none of the Asians in the room spoke Polish, and she had no way to tip him off now that he was wrong.

Taejin Soeng, who'd just walked up closer, took out his phone and dialed a number, and a moment later a ring sounded somewhere in the room. One of his younger brothers made a show of looking around and picked the phone from a bookshelf. Anna had no idea how it ended up there.

"Found it," said the boy with an angelic smile on his pretty face.

"The screen is cracked," noticed his twin, looking over his shoulder. "How come?"

"Veronica isn't very careful with it," Anna croaked, as the alarm started blaring in her head.

"True," Chen Xiao agreed. "She'll use it to hit anything that comes too close."

She had to force herself not to glance at Dominik, but it turned out to be an unnecessary effort.

"Are you this guy who doesn't understand the word 'no'?" asked Chen Xiao with interest, moving his attention to her lover.

Dominik glanced at Anna questioningly. She realized that he hadn't understood much from the previous conversation, but before she had time to react, the oldest Soeng repeated Chen Xiao's words in Polish. Dominik just laughed derisively in answer, and Anna felt like doing the same, despite all her nervousness.

"What do you mean?" she asked haughtily. "If you are suggesting something—" Suddenly, his earlier comment about the girl popped up in her mind, and she stopped in mid-sentence.

None of them answered. Instead, Veronica suddenly spoke, and it took Anna a few seconds to realize that her voice was coming from the phone in the twin's hand.

"Step back," the girl said angrily. "I told you many times I don't want you."

"Oh come on, sugar," Dominik's voice cajoled in his most seductive bedroom tone, and Anna whipped around to look at him in dismay. "I know you don't mean it."

"But I do," Veronica insisted, and there was a sound of some scuffle. "Stop it!"

"You're such a tease," murmured Dominik in the recording, while his real-time version observed Anna with narrowed eyes. "You can't run away forever—"

The recording ended at that, but there was another one.

"—with Anna?" Veronica asked in a sharp tone.

"Forget Anna, she's just a money bag," Dominik answered scornfully, and Anna's jaw hung open. "But you're such a pretty little thing. We could have a lot of fun together—"

"Get lost!" Veronica cried, and there was a sound of something tearing, and then running steps and jagged breathing, and a door slamming shut.

"I guess we are suggesting something," said Taejin Soeng with a very unpleasant smile.

Anna stared at her lover, utterly mortified. His friends exchanged furtive glances, looking a bit uncomfortable, but Dominik just seemed annoyed.

"I didn't start any of it, it was all h—" he began defiantly, but had no chance to finish.

Silent Kehuan made one unhurried step forward, and then he suddenly became a blur.

* * *

"Don't kill him," said Chen Xiao dispassionately. "We don't need the problem with carrion disposal."

Dominik coughed a few times and spit out three of his front teeth, and then a molar. A roundhouse kick to the mouth could do quite a lot of damage.

He was lying on the floor, wheezing and clutching at his left side with both hands. His broken nose was swelling rapidly, just as the area around his right eye. Since Niki had already smashed earlier the left eye, Chen Xiao supposed Kehuan was striving to maintain some symmetry there. Probably in that spirit he now added one more solid kick to the worm's right side.

Chen Xiao approved. Symmetry was an important thing.

Anna made another muffled sound, pressing a hand to her mouth, but she didn't try to get between Kehuan and her lover, ever the conformist.

There was nobody else to stop the thrashing now. The two other guys who'd sat there earlier had shown some inclination to intervene at first, but Soeng Taejin had been simply delighted to persuade them otherwise, and they'd both left the apartment in a great hurry.

Chen Xiao kept observing Anna. The guy was vermin, not even worth a second thought, but she was a different story. He'd thought earlier it was unbelievable he'd let her fool him for such a long time, but now he could see how it'd worked. Anna was a very proficient deceiver because she believed each of her own lies as soon as they flew out of her mouth, and lived in the world of illusions. She was a master of lying to herself, and that made her so good at lying to other people.

"Anna," Chen Xiao asked her now conversationally. "Have you ever been slapped in the face?"

"No," Anna answered in a quivering voice. "You wouldn't dare..."

Soeng Taejin, who'd been standing in a relaxed pose with his arms folded over his chest, observing Kehuan massacre the vermin, turned to her in a fluent move and slapped her casually across one cheek, splitting her lip.

Anna cried out and slumped to the floor.

"Does it hurt?" asked Chen Xiao mildly. "I suppose it might."

"I've looked after that brat for you for years!" she wailed, cradling her cheek and spilling angry tears. "Nobody else cared, only me! Is this how you pay me back?"

And she believed it, too.

"I think I've paid you back rather enough already," Chen Xiao reminded her. "And your care was so tender that my daughter's in the hospital right now."

Anna just glared at him, sobbing loudly.

He looked at the twins. "Go pack some things for Niki," he said, and they hurried to her bedroom.

"You're fired," Chen Xiao told Anna. "You've got time till the end of the month to move out of here."

"What?! But it's my home, too," she protested, suddenly scared. "You can't just kick me out."

"We are vacating the apartment," Chen Xiao informed her. "But if you are so attached to it, I guess you can sign a new lease contract with the owner."

Anna gaped at him in horror. "How would I pay for it?" she whispered.

"I have no idea," Chen Xiao answered indifferently. He was done with her.

He was sure she'd get her dues pretty soon. She was still receiving the alimony from Chen Liang, so she'd be able to pay for some cheap place, and he had a hunch the vermin would stick to her until he found some new patsy, which could be problematic after all the remodeling Kehuan had applied to his face.

And Chen Xiao could bet it was enough to leave those two alone, together, with no access to easy money, and they'd make each other's life hell in no time at all, without anybody's intervention.

* * *

Before they left, Kehuan went to take some stuff from his bedroom, since his suitcase was still at the airport, rotating endlessly on a luggage carousel or maybe stowed away in some storeroom by now. It was a good thing he'd left some of his clothes behind when he'd departed in March.

He opened his room with the key Kamila had found for him in Niki's backpack and went inside, switching on the light. He looked around, already annoyed with the prospect of having to pack and move all the books and other stuff. Honestly speaking, the only things he really cared for and wanted to retrieve were the piano and Niki's works.

The place looked exactly the same as always, except for the folded blanket on the bed. Kehuan frowned.

"Did someone sleep in my room?" he asked Taeyeon, who'd just stopped outside the door, watching him.

"I did," answered the twin with an unreadable expression on his face. "And Rima. And Chris. And Jason. Several times, until we all got banned."

Kehuan felt something tear in his chest for the hundredth time this day.

"Is that why there's a lock on my door as well?" he asked after a moment.

"No," Taeyeon answered with a smirk. "It's because you are so very precious, and Niki didn't want the swine to sully your perfect place. Satisfied?"

* * *

Kehuan thought about this exchange later, back in Niki's room in the hospital.

By the time he got there, he was swaying on his feet because he hadn't had any decent sleep for more than three days already. But he declined Chen Xiao's invitation to the hotel, and sleeping in the apartment was out of the question, not only because Anna and her rat were still there, but also because Niki had been right: it was filthy now, and nothing could be done to make it clean again.

That was what kept him awake, despite the exhaustion. The reflection that some things, once ruined, were truly irreparable, and the question of how much damage he'd really done to his relationship with Niki.

He'd left her alone with Anna, completely unprotected, for months. He must've been crazy.

Of course, he could argue it had been Chen Xiao's idea, his decision, and his fault. But it wasn't in Kehuan's style to shift the responsibility for his own mistakes on someone else. He'd agreed with Chen Xiao back them, albeit reluctantly, and left believing he was doing the right thing. He'd been so wrapped up in his emotional turmoil and guilt that it didn't occur to him that worse things could happen if he left Niki alone with her guardian from hell. And since worse things did happen, and Niki never called him for help, Kehuan could guess she was pretty mad at him.

She wasn't the only one, of course.

He'd met Jason and Chris Morton at the entrance to the hospital. They were just leaving, and Jason gave him a curt nod and passed him without a word. Morton hesitated for a moment.

"Get your shit together already," he said gravely in the end.

"I will," Kehuan promised. "Thanks for everything."

Kamila was also going home after staying in Niki's room all evening, and they exchanged a few words outside the door.

"You had things to say to me," he told her, remembering her recorded message. "Go ahead."

Kamila glowered at him for a moment. But he could tell she was wrung out by the events of the day, and just as exhausted as himself, and in the end, she just shrugged.

"Do I really need to?" she asked. It was a serious question despite her light tone.

"No," Kehuan answered.

So she nodded and left, and he went inside the room. He sat on the chair next to the bed and looked at Niki, thinking about everything that had happened.

She'd waited for him to come back.

He was well aware that her behavior and the words she'd spoken to him after they'd found her in his old apartment block were just a product of the concussion. He could easily imagine she'd have reacted to his arrival in a very different way had she been completely lucid. But he couldn't help hoping there was truth in her words all the same; it was her subconscious speaking, after all, and it told him she'd been waiting for him, despite everything. And she'd protected his room, too. She didn't want that place, which in so many ways belonged to both of them, and had such wonderful memories attached to it, to be defiled.

So he chose to believe Niki would forgive him in the end. Because if she didn't, well. How did it go? All the king's horses and all the king's men would not put Kehuan together again.

* * *

After the visit to Chens' apartment, Soeng Taejin went home with his brothers, wondering what reception awaited him there.

In the last few months, he'd been indeed very busy, studying and working at the same time, and he hadn't come to Warsaw for many months now, though at some point he'd started calling his mother regularly, and then his father as well. Their conversations were labored and very formal, but he could tell they also wanted to make up with him. Only it seemed they were expecting some profuse apologies, and Taejin wasn't sure he had it in him because he was convinced he'd been right back then, and they'd been wrong.

But it turned out it wasn't the day for reconciliation between him and his parents because Kim Hana came to their place as well, and brought up an entirely different topic.

"Why didn't you say anything before?" she reproached the twins. "This whole mess could've been solved much earlier if you only said a word to any of us."

"But is it all really true?" Kim Haneul spoke dubiously. "I just can't believe it. I've known Chen Liang's wife for years, we've met often enough at school on different occasions. She always seemed to be a very sensible person. Isn't it that girl telling some tall tales again?"

Taerim pointed to his mother with a flourish. "That's why we didn't say anything earlier," he said acerbically.

Kim Hana looked at her sister. "How can you doubt the word of your own sons?" she asked with astonishment.

"Easily," Kim Haneul answered dryly. "After all the lies I've heard from them over the years, and half of them concocted just so they could hang out with that girl. As if they really couldn't find a better company than this irresponsible brat."

Taejin looked at the twins pointedly. "Don't you have something to say to our mother?" he asked, and both his brothers looked away at the same time.

"Should I perhaps?" asked Taejin sarcastically. It was certainly long overdue. "Mother, I think you should know—"

"No," Taeyeon interrupted hastily. "I'll say it."

"Say what?" their aunt asked curiously.

"Mum," said Taeyeon. "Niki isn't like you think at all. When we were younger and skipped school all the time, it wasn't her fault."

"What are you saying?" Kim Haneul asked, mystified.

"We liked to play hooky, but we were afraid of you and father," Taeyeon confessed gloomily. "And Niki could get away with just about anything, so we always asked her to come with us, and later she'd take the blame for the whole thing."

"That's preposterous," Kim Haneul scoffed. "You need to think up a better story."

"But that's true, mum," Taerim decided to back up his twin. "It was exactly as Taeyeon said."

"I wasn't born yesterday, and I saw you with that girl for years," said Kim Haneul with great confidence. "She's been a terrible influence on both of you from the start."

The twins looked completely flabbergasted now, while their mother stayed unmoved. Kim Hana seemed wryly amused, and so was Taejin.

"Funny, isn't it?" he said to his brothers later with a little smirk. "What unpredictable consequences can come from sidestepping problems. Especially if you've been doing it for years."

"Go back to Cracow already, oh wise one," answered Taerim irritably.

"Don't worry, I'm leaving tomorrow," Taejin assured him. He had to, unfortunately. "And if it makes you feel any better, I've learned that lesson already as well."

* * *

The nurse woke Kehuan up in the morning, and after he returned from the bathroom, he sat next to Niki's bed and just watched her sleep.

She looked even worse after the night. The area around her left eye had swollen some more, and this side of her face was now in several different colors. He knew from Kamila's messages that Niki had been speaking coherently already last evening before he'd returned, and he had a feeling right now he was enjoying the last few minutes of calm weather before the storm. But even so, he could finally breathe after all those months of slowly suffocating. However angry at him she'd turned up to be, they were together again, and unless she decided to give him the boot, everything was much better already.

About seven, at the time she normally got up, Niki stirred awake. She looked around with one big bright eye and the other swollen up and nearly shut, and noticed Kehuan next to the bed.

"Why are you here?" she asked in a reserved tone, watching him warily.

"Niki..."

"Did you ride in on your white horse to save me again?"

What was the right answer to that? Screw it, he couldn't lie to her anyway.

"No," he admitted. "I decided to come back, and it somehow coincided with that mess."

He couldn't be sure, but she seemed to relax a little.

"Ah," she said dryly, "I guess I'm grown up enough now. Good to know."

Yep. Totally mad.

* * *

Chen Xiao had left Vancouver rather abruptly after that summon from Kim Hana, and after a few days in Warsaw, he had to go back to take care of different matters at home, though he planned to return for Christmas break again, to spend it with his daughter.

He talked to Kehuan and was quite impressed that in the three days since the accident the boy had already arranged a new place for himself and Niki. That small apartment the Chens used to occupy in the past had been sold a few years earlier, but Kehuan managed to find another rental in the neighboring block. He declared he didn't need any financial help, but Chen Xiao planned to pay for Niki's part, of course.

He didn't even try to talk Kehuan out of staying in Warsaw and living together with her again. He'd already lost the belief that keeping the boy away, even temporarily, was the best thing for Niki, and besides, he had a feeling Kehuan wouldn't listen to him now anyway.

Before his departure, he went to the hospital to talk to his daughter one more time. She looked much better, with the swelling down and the bruises slowly fading away, and he could tell she was feeling better as well, and itching to go out. So he decided to broach the subject finally.

"Why didn't you tell me?" he asked in a raw voice. Words couldn't describe how terrible he felt about that whole debacle with Anna and Dominik. "Was it because you were so very angry with me? But in that case, why didn't you call Kehuan? Didn't you know we'd both come and sort it out at once?"

There was a moment of silence.

"It was so foul," Niki answered at last, bending her lips with revulsion. "I didn't feel like talking about it to anybody."

"I understand," said Chen Xiao. "But still—"

"And besides," Niki went on, "wasn't it what you wanted me to do? To finally grow up on my own, without running to Kehuan with every stupid little problem?"

Chen Xiao stared at her in horror. "Niki," he said. "That's not what I meant at all."

"I guess it doesn't matter now," she said bitterly. "It didn't work anyway. You both had to come and rescue me again."

"That's what family is for, and friends," Chen Xiao said, bewildered with her strange notions. "To help you when you need it."

"Aren't you fed up with it, that you always have to save me? Isn't Kehuan, too?"

"Niki," Chen Xiao said slowly, searching for the right words. "People save each other in many different ways. When I was injured and crippled and didn't know if I ever would be able to move again... You saved me many times then. You talked to me and shared your life with me, and put some sense and purpose in my existence. And I know it wasn't easy for you."

Niki stared at him uncertainly with her beautiful eyes. "Did I really?" she asked in a very young voice.

"Believe me, you did," he assured her. "And as for Kehuan, you rescued him when you befriended him as a child, and if you ask me, you've been saving him from himself ever since. Kehuan's somewhat damaged on the fundamental level."

"So why did you order him to leave?" Niki asked crossly. "Don't you care for him at all?"

"Honey," he said, "I'm sorry. I only wanted the best for you..."

"Oh, I know that," she answered drily. "And of course you knew better than myself what was best for me."

"That's how parents often think," he told her quietly. "Mine were the same."

"And did you think they were right when they behaved this way?" Niki asked. "Or do you perhaps think that now?"

"No, and no," he answered, feeling wretched. "It seems I'm an old fool."

Niki stayed silent for a moment, but then she suddenly smiled, and then snorted, as if something funny suddenly occurred to her. The doctors had told Chen Xiao that she might suffer for some time from mood swings and headaches, and have problems with concentration and sleeping—as if she hadn't had enough of that already in the past. So he wasn't sure now if this sudden cheerfulness wasn't just a lingering effect of the concussion. But maybe not, judging by what she said next.

"Anyway, I did my best to deal with the problem on my own," she said, smiling impishly. "Made good use of my phone, didn't I?"

"You did," he agreed, smiling as well. "Both times."

14

The Obvious Things

By the time Niki left the hospital, Kehuan had managed to move all their belongings, with some help from Kamila and the twins.

During the entire time they spent packing, Anna and her rat didn't dare to stick their noses out of the upstairs room. It was a good thing. Kehuan didn't want to see any of them ever again, or he'd be forever tempted to hurt them some more.

A moving company transferred their stuff to the small apartment by the river, but he didn't have time to do any unpacking, and on the day he collected Niki from the hospital and brought her to the new place, all their things were still in carton boxes.

"The layout is identical with my old place," he told her. "Just in mirror image. If you want, you can take the room with the big window."

But Niki shook her head. "It's yours," she said simply. "Just put the beanbag there for me."

Each time they'd seen each other in the hospital in the previous days, she'd been polite and a little distant, which frustrated Kehuan just as much as it bothered him, and hearing that familiar phrase now made his heart suddenly expand. Maybe she wasn't that angry at him, after all.

Niki didn't want to skip any more days at school, and he had to finish the work he'd been doing for the Taipei office when he'd left Taiwan, so it took them another week to unpack completely and to settle down in the new living space.

The apartment didn't contain much furniture, which was good because it was really pocket-size, especially in comparison with the previous place. Niki didn't even take out her works from the boxes, apart from Alina's portrait, and at the weekend they had a short discussion about what to do with them.

"I'm sorry your bedroom's so small," Kehuan said. He thought maybe he should've looked longer for a bigger place, but he'd been in a hurry. "I guess you're going to miss your old room a little."

"It's perfect," Niki assured him. "Much better than staying there with that creep."

Kehuan didn't even want to comment on that. Thinking about Niki and the rat at the same time hurt his head.

"Are you still going to apply to Vancouver?" he asked. "Because in that case maybe it'd be best to simply ship all your stuff to Chen Xiao. We secured everything well, I think it can go as it is."

"Vancouver's still on," Niki told him. "I want to send my application before Christmas. It still needs a little work. But there's no guarantee they'll accept me, and I won't know until summer."

"So let's put it all in the basement for now," Kehuan suggested. "It's clean and dry, I checked."

And that was what they did. The funny side effect was that if anyone wanted to admire Niki's works now, the place to go was Kehuan's bedroom. But he was sure it was just a temporary situation because Niki never stayed idle for long.

And indeed, just a few days later, when he entered her room to propose making dinner together, he found her bent over the small desk and drawing something on a sheet of paper. Several pencil drafts were already spread on the bed behind her, for the lack of space. Not a desk for an artist, this one.

"What are you doing?" Kehuan asked curiously.

"Sketching a new scene for my comic," Niki answered abstractedly.

"Really?" he asked, pleased and even more interested now. "I haven't seen any new episodes lately." Well, duh, genius.

"I was kind of busy..." she started ironically, but then suddenly whirled round to look at him. "You knew about the comic?"

"I watched it practically from the start," he admitted. "When I was in Taipei, I checked your website every day."

Niki was silent for a moment.

"It's just a thing for kids," she said at last, looking abashed. "For fun."

"It's brilliant," Kehuan assured her. "Don't you know it?"

"Maybe," she said, looking away. "But it's really nothing important..."

It didn't sound right. In the past, Niki had always been confident in her work, and he'd never heard her downplay or diminish it.

"Can I watch you draw?" he asked, studying her carefully.

"Why?" she sounded even more embarrassed now, and a little anguished. "It's such a waste of your time."

Kehuan wondered who might've put such notions in her head, and the answer was depressingly obvious.

He thought for a moment. How to explain it to her?

"You know, myself, I'm kind of a dud when it comes to art," he confessed at last. "All thumbs with all these crayons and brushes, and no inspiration whatsoever. The only thing I've been ever good at was finding you more pebbles or shells. Oh, and maybe cleaning your tools."

Niki was still staring at the sheet of paper in front of her, fiddling with her pencil.

"Truth be told, I've always loved watching you work, and doing some simple tasks for you," Kehuan told her sincerely. "It made me feel like I had a little part in creating all those wonderful things."

"Really?" she asked quietly.

"Yes."

She raised her head finally and studied his face with her CGI eyes. Kehuan hadn't seen them for so long that he'd lost all immunity, and every time she stared at him now, especially at close quarters, he felt as if his heart was practicing somersaults.

"All right, you can watch," she decided. "And if you don't mind, you could scan the drawings later, and upload them on the website."

"Done," he promised. "And I'll order some takeout."

* * *

He meditated about this conversation a lot later.

That she'd thought this way was a shocker, and he'd had no idea. They hadn't really talked for more than half a year, and only now did he start to realize how many things might've gone wrong in such a long time.

What other venomous thoughts had Anna managed to plant in Niki's head? What effect on her could this rotten affair with Anna's lover have? What hurtful things could other people have said or done to her in all those months when he'd been away, killing time?

There was no way to know, and Kehuan had no illusion that she'd simply open up, start talking, and conveniently list all such issues for him to tackle at once. The relations between them seemed to have returned to that old routine of quasi-siblings, at least on the surface, and he wasn't happy with it at all, but now he realized that it might yet turn out even that was just appearances, and they'd fallen much more apart than he'd ever suspected.

And it was all his own doing.

* * *

Chen Xiao came to Poland again for Christmas break, as promised, and took them both on a trip to the mountains, where Kehuan and Niki had a lot of fun trying downhill skiing for the first time in their life.

It looked so deceptively easy on TV, but it turned out to be a total sham. Niki had it easier, since she'd already done quite a lot of cross-country skiing in Finland, and maybe skating helped somewhat as well, but Kehuan ate more snow than he cared for, and he swore and laughed in turns the entire time the torture devices stayed attached to his legs. But he got a kick out of it all the same, and besides, it was the first new and entertaining thing they'd done together for a long time, and he was very grateful to

Chen Xiao for coming up with the idea of the trip in the first place.

Their relations with Niki were still strained. Most of the time things seemed to be all right between them, if not great, but then suddenly she'd get tense and edgy again. He often thought he'd love to know what was going on in her head at such moments, but never dared ask. She might tell him there was no sense to go on like that and to get lost and leave her alone already, and then what would he do?

Thank goodness he could at least talk about her without such qualms. Chen Xiao truly loved his distant daughter in his calm, unshowy way, and liked to chat about her, and Kehuan discovered that he enjoyed it as well.

And so they talked, and these conversations often veered in different interesting directions, like the one that started with his announcement.

"If Niki gets accepted to the university in Canada, I'm transferring as well," Kehuan told his mentor one day. "I've already started the procedure. Just so you know."

He wanted to make things clear, so there wouldn't be any misunderstandings between them in the future.

"I gathered," Chen Xiao answered wryly. "I'm starting to think she has no chance of ever shaking you off, whatever I do."

"Wouldn't you be happy to have both of us there?" Kehuan asked with a certain dose of irony.

In the past, Chen Xiao told him many times that if he ever chose to move to Vancouver, he had a permanent job at his software company guaranteed. Not that Kehuan really needed such favors.

"I would, actually," Chen Xiao answered now, smiling. "You might even consider getting Canadian citizenship."

"Do you have it?" Kehuan asked. He'd never thought about it before.

"I was born in Vancouver," Chen Xiao said. "So I became a citizen automatically."

"So you've got dual citizenship, like Niki," Kehuan mused. "I had no idea. But in that case, why did you get her Taiwanese passport back then, and not Canadian?"

"Because it seemed easier. Taiwan has *Ius sanguinis*, and besides, your father agreed to back me up. He still had some clout in diplomatic circles then."

"So do you really feel Canadian, or Taiwanese?" Kehuan asked, curious.

"Both, I guess," Chen Xiao answered unperturbably. "What about you?"

"When we were in high school, Soeng Taejin used to pester me about it all the time. He wanted me to declare myself, and my allegiance, as he called it." Kehuan smirked, remembering some of those discussions. "But what allegiance can I have?"

"Your mother was Korean, right?"

"Yes, and I was born in Seoul, but I don't remember Korea at all. We left when I was two."

"You speak the language, though," Chen Xiao noticed.

"That's just because of the Soengs," Kehuan answered, shrugging. "I think I would've forgotten it completely by now otherwise. My first tongue is Mandarin, anyway."

"What about Taiwan, then?"

"Ah, Taiwan," said Kehuan dryly, remembering these last months he'd spent there, going more insane every day, and also that first summer in Taipei long ago, when he was six. "Not so special for me."

"Poland?"

"It's Niki's country, and her people, and language," Kehuan answered. "And I've lived here for so many years. I guess it's more home than any other place, but I wouldn't call myself Polish."

"Vancouver's not a bad city for someone like you," Chan Xiao remarked. "It's a proper mix of cultures, don't you think?"

"Perhaps," Kehuan answered noncommittally. "But world is big. There are many other places out there."

And who knew where the cat would want to roam in the future.

The way he grew up meant Kehuan really didn't identify himself with any particular place, or people, or culture. Even his language was just one of several modes of communication he used, the default one and obviously the easiest, but not precious to him in any way. And if that made him incomplete, or crippled somehow in other people's eyes, so be it.

But it didn't mean he had no sense of belonging. Quite the opposite. And while the trouble with belonging was that it limited your options, that was also the beauty of it. Kehuan didn't have to concern himself with deliberating where he was going to live in the future. His professional skills could be utilized practically anywhere, and he didn't need any special place to pursue his interests, either, and so it was very simple: wherever Niki wanted to go, he would go with her, as always.

* * *

In the middle of January Chen Xiao returned to Canada, and Niki started to study in earnest. She had her finals in May, and because of the whole affair with Anna and the creep she'd had no chance to put enough time and effort into her schoolwork in the fall and was lagging behind again.

Luckily, she had Kamila, who came around almost every day now, and they both crammed like possessed. Though it was mostly parallel effort rather than joined one, since they were going in different directions with their university plans, and needed to take exams on different subjects.

Niki had flummoxed everybody when she announced she hadn't applied to the university for the visual arts program, but for interdisciplinary studies.

"I don't know why you are all so surprised," she told Kamila. "I want to study languages as well, and different cultures. I've been always interested in such things."

"True," Kamil admitted. "But aren't you an artist at heart, first and most?"

"Perhaps," Niki agreed. "And I'm going to include some art courses in my program, of course. But you know, one doesn't have to study art to be an artist. Just saying."

"But one has to study medicine to be a medicine doctor," Kamila noted with a sigh. "Life isn't fair."

Since the exams were her priority, Niki wasn't originally going to take part in any extra-curricular activities anymore. The way such events as concerts, plays, or exhibitions were treated at the international school, it was a rare case when students of the last grade were engaged; Chris Morton, who'd been the president of the music club during his final year, had been one of the few exceptions to the rule.

But Chris was no longer at the school, and the music club had been taken over by the younger generation, namely by the very same gaggle of Niki's ducklings who used to follow her around back when they were still cute little first- and second-graders. They were all in the last year of primary now, a new crowd of teen music enthusiasts, buoyant, self-confident, and full of unorthodox ideas. Niki loved them all to bits, and when they approached her one day and asked if she'd agree to sing with them in one last concert at the end of the year, she had a real problem with telling them no.

"We know you're busy," cajoled Kate, one of Niki's favorite ducklings. "We really won't bother you much. All will be organized without your involvement, and the band will practice on their own. You'll just need to come to one or two rehearsals. Please?"

"You know very well it doesn't work like that," Niki said, half-amused and half-annoyed with this blatant manipulation. "If we are to perform together, we need to practice together, and more than once or twice."

"But it's our last chance," chimed in Piotr, another of the ducklings, currently taller than Niki by about ten centimeters, and probably heavier by some fifteen kilos. "We originally planned to let you be for now, and to ask you to sing with us again next year, even if you're out of school then, but Taerim Soeng told us you're going to Canada."

"Come on, Niki," Kate implored again. "You wouldn't do that to us, would you? Leave without a proper goodbye?"

And since Niki had always been a strong opponent of leaving without a goodbye, she said yes in the end, and started attending the meetings of the music club again twice a week. She now felt like a Methuselah there and spent most of the time sitting on the side with Ms. Mazur, listening to the rehearsals and giggling with the teacher at all the raucous discussions, impracticable ideas, and inevitable personality clashes.

"Were we as funny as them before?" she asked the teacher once, wiping tears of laughter from her eyes. "When we were their age?"

"You must be joking," Ms. Mazur answered with glee. "Mauricio and you, and Kehuan? Sori and Jason? Ridhaan and Kamila, and the twins? You were even funnier."

Niki snickered again, and they sat for a moment in companionable silence before the teacher spoke again.

"That's why I love this job," she said with an affectionate smile. "Keeps me feeling young."

Niki was ultimately very happy that she'd agreed to the whole affair, however time-consuming it was, and chatting with Ms. Mazur was certainly one of its upsides. The downside was that she didn't have much free time left for skating, but she still went to the ice-rink once a week, and Kehuan often came along, just to watch. The first time he'd seen her practice her new routine, he'd been caught totally off guard.

"When did you learn to skate like that, Niki?" he asked with awe, and Niki felt all warm inside.

"Last summer," she told him truthfully. "Everybody went away, and I had nothing better to do but draw comics and rollerblade for hours every day. It's not that different from ice-skating."

Kehuan fell silent at that, obviously upset with her words.

"I'm so sorry I left you alone with Anna," he burst suddenly. "I must've been really muddled—"

"It's not your fault," Niki interrupted. "At the time you left she was acting—normal, I guess. Our relations were okay, and she even started working... Everything seemed all right. You couldn't have predicted it'd go this way."

"I could've, and I should've," Kehuan refuted bleakly. "She's unbalanced, and I knew it."

"I pity her, you know," Niki confessed. "Even now."

"Give it a rest," Kehuan told her firmly. "She doesn't deserve any compassion from you."

But Niki shook her head. "I don't think Anna was so bad at the beginning, you know?" she said ruefully. "I think she had good intentions. But we were both really difficult children, and your father was a terrible husband, honestly speaking."

"Can't deny that," Kehuan admitted. "Still. She hurt you so many times I can't even count. And I let her hurt you again, even worse. I'm so sorry, Niki."

Niki knew he meant all of that, just as she knew he beat himself for not being there to protect her from Dominik, and she really wanted to tell him that she wasn't angry and that all was good, only it wasn't true.

She was still upset, and she was still angry. Not for these things with Anna, and certainly not for Dominik; none of that was Kehuan's fault. She didn't know exactly why she was so mad at him, and it was doing her head in.

Niki wanted them to be good again. She missed Kehuan very much, every day, and wanted things to return to the way they'd been before he left in the spring, but it somehow didn't work this way. There was a barrier between them now, and even if a big part of that barrier was the time they'd spent separately, and all those nasty things that happened then, at its core was something else, that elusive reason why she felt unable to simply let it go.

Niki talked about it a few times with Kamila, but it didn't help much. Besides, Kamila had her own reasons to feel down.

The twins were leaving Poland in the summer, and Niki was going to Canada, if all went well. They were all going to split, and Niki was sad already just thinking about it. But she suspected Kamila felt much worse because her parting with the Soengs looked like it might be a permanent thing.

One day during the long recess, Niki noticed her alone with Taerim in the secluded part of the school grounds. He looked uncharacteristically solemn, speaking to the redhead in an urgent manner. Then they seemed to argue for a while before going separate ways.

"Did I see it right?" Niki asked later, feeling a little hopeful, though not too much. If Kamila wanted it, it would've happened ages ago. "Has one of them finally made a move?"

"Something like that," Kamila admitted. "But forget it."

"Why? Did you turn him down?"

"Sure I did."

"I've always hoped you'd be interested, you know," said Niki honestly, since it was the best way of speaking with her friend. "And it looked a little like that, too."

"Please," Kamila scoffed. "I respect my bacterial flora more than that. I don't have a notebook thick enough to catalog all the girls those two have slept with."

This was a charge hard to rebut, and Niki had to laugh a little.

"Anyway, they are leaving," Kamila added after a moment. "No point in complicating things at the end."

Niki was actually quite sure that both twins would fight to stay if their foxy only said a word, but she suspected this was exactly the reason why her friend hadn't, and wouldn't.

Unless some genius scientist came up with an immediate idea how to clone Kamila on the spot, this problem was unsolvable.

* * *

In February Niki had the winter break at school, and once again went for a week to Lahti at the invitation of her friendly Finnish family.

Kehuan wasn't happy about parting with her again when they'd only just got back together, but what bothered him more was that she hadn't even asked for his opinion this time. At first, he simply concluded that she must've been still mad. But later, when he was alone, he started meditating about Niki and other people, and also about himself and other people, and came to a different conclusion.

Kehuan was well aware of his own reclusive tendencies and lack of social skills, but it had never troubled him before. He thought he didn't really need other people; he had Niki, and that was enough.

But she was different. Niki liked people and was interested in them, and it worked the other way round, too. She might've been detached and withdrawn when she was younger, but even then complete strangers wanted to befriend and protect her as soon as they met, and it never changed. He'd seen it happen so many times over the years. Take the twins, who'd adopted her as their triplet practically from the first day, or Kim Hana and Yoon Sori, who so often included her in their private little world, or Mauricio and Jason, or the Finnish family. Even, unbelievably, the whole gang of the ex-nazi boys, who now seemed to be of the opinion that Niki was their bosom buddy, and called regularly to invite her to their futsal matches.

Kehuan had rather mixed feelings about it. On the one hand, there was no denying that he was jealous because in his head Niki was his, and that was that. But on the other hand, he was very glad there were other people around who'd been willing to pick up his slack, and to help her, and keep her company when he'd been away.

And then this train of thoughts brought him to the realization that maybe it wasn't right, or even fair, to cling to her so much. She needed space to breathe, after all, and some time to spend with her friends. Maybe that was why she went to Finland without discussing it with him first. And maybe it was also a signal to him to practice his underdeveloped social skills a little bit as well and to put some effort into maintaining relations with those few people who still cared for him.

On that note, he called Soeng Taejin, and found out that his cousin and Yoon Sori were just having a short break after the midterms. So he packed a small bag and took the train to Cracow, to check if there was anything left to salvage from their friendship.

On his arrival, he learned that Taejin had taken a day off at work on his account. His cousin and Sori had decided to take him on a three-day-long skiing trip, since they'd already heard from Niki about their Christmas outing. Cracow was located close to the mountains, and skiing had recently become their favorite weekend pastime.

Kehuan thought it had to be some form of revenge on their part for all his past offenses and wrongdoings, willful or not. They could ski quite well, especially Sori, who regularly went on winter holidays with her all-sports mum. But Taejin wasn't bad either. He'd learned the basics as a child back in Korea and later had a chance to improve during two winter camps his parents had sent him to in middle school. As a result, they had a riot watching him struggle, and both cackled like crazy every time he lost balance and tumbled down, which happened rather a lot.

Kehuan approached the whole thing philosophically. The weather was splendid, the views of the snow-covered mountains sparkling in the sun breathtaking, and skiing was fun. He could tell he was making quick progress, too, even if his efforts looked abysmal for now. And if a little laugh at his expense helped Taejin come to terms with the situation between them, and made him feel better, well. Kehuan certainly could swallow a dollop of indignity, and bear a few handfuls of snow in his underwear.

On Saturday, some college friends of Taejin and Sori came from Cracow to join them, and in the evening they all went to a bar for a few drinks. Kehuan still wasn't a great fan of alcohol, but in the spirit of reconciliation, he drank a beer and two shots of vodka, and he was already feeling a bit fuzzy when his cousin suddenly decided it was time to clear the air between them.

"Y'know, I had it all figured out," said Taejin self-mockingly, turning to him with a slushy smile. "I was gonna marry your li'l cousin, and you'd marry my li'l cousin, and then we'd all be...one big happy family."

Yoon Sori, who also was also sitting at the bar, right behind Taejin, and chatting with her friends, turned around with a dismayed expression on her face, but Taejin waved at her pacifyingly.

"It was all my phantasies, y'see. I thought you were the brother and I'd be the boyfriend, but it turned out in her head it was all...kind of...the other way round."

"You saw Niki's comic," Kehuan guessed. His logical thinking wasn't impaired that much by the alcohol yet, and it wasn't rocket science.

Taejin nodded several times in an exaggerated manner.

"Sori showed it to me," he admitted melancholically. "And what can you do? If she says I'm the big brother, I have to be the big brother. She called me that many times, too, y'know? Only I didn't listen properly. Stupid."

"Stupid," Kehuan agreed. "We don't need to intermarry to be a family.

We already are one big family, you doofus. You're my cousin, and Sori's your cousin."

"But what about Niki?" Taejin asked anxiously, waving at the barman to order another round of drinks.

"Niki got adopted by your brothers as their triplet at the age of six," Kehuan reminded him. "And didn't you say it a minute ago? She's your little sis, too."

They clinked their glasses and drank the beer, and then the shots.

"But do you know, it's the first time I heard you admit it of your own accord," Taejin noted.

"Admit what?" Kehuan asked. The room was getting somewhat blurred around the edges.

"That we're family."

Kehuan rolled his eyes, which wasn't the best idea. "Isn't it obvious?" he asked drily, shaking his head to get rid of the double vision.

"Even so, it's good to hear," Taejin told him with a happy, delirious smile, and put an arm around his shoulders. "Sometimes you need to…state the obvious. Let's drink some more to celebrate it, li'l brother."

* * *

The next day Kehuan had the mother of all hangovers, and Taejin didn't fare much better, despite having much more practice in excessive drinking. But Yoon Sori still kicked them out of bed at some ungodly hour and dragged them to the slope, which was completely heartless and barbaric of her, as they broodily agreed.

In the afternoon they returned to Cracow, and it wasn't until Taejin summoned him to the common kitchen in their student apartment, and Sori put a small round cake on the table that Kehuan realized it was his birthday.

And Niki hadn't called.

He'd never paid much attention to birthdays and some such, but in the past, she'd always bought or made him a present, or at least called him if they'd been apart. Had she forgotten?

But she hadn't, as it turned out. At about nine in the evening, his phone rang.

"Happy birthday, Kehuan," she said, and added the Polish wishes, "All the best for you."

"Thanks," Kehuan answered, relieved. "Did you have a good time over there? I'm picking you up at the airport at five tomorrow, right?"

"No," Niki answered. "That's another reason why I'm calling. The Heikkinens asked me to stay a few days longer, so I've changed my reservation."

Kehuan's good humor vanished at once. "So when are you coming back?" he asked morosely.

Niki stayed silent for a moment. "Do you know how many times I asked you this question last year?" she asked at last. "And never got an answer."

"Niki—"

"I'll be back next Saturday," she cut him off. "I'll text you the time."

Kehuan returned to Warsaw on Monday, as planned, and busied himself with work, but he still spent a significant amount of time during the next few days thinking about what she'd said because it almost sounded as if... But it wasn't possible, was it?

Lately, the more he'd thought about the previous year, the more he couldn't believe he'd really acquiesced to that insanity, and the way he'd dealt with the whole situation later made him squirm with mortification and regret. But she must've known that one thing at least.

It was eating at him now, the question, and when he finally saw her walk out of the arrivals on Saturday, dragging her suitcase behind her, it was the first thing that went out of his mouth.

"Niki, you knew I'd come back, didn't you?"

Niki looked surprised for a moment, and then she bore into him with her alien eyes.

"How could I have known?" she asked, her voice low and angry.

"I said so, didn't I?" Kehuan asked nervously, seeing quagmire all around. "In June."

"And after that, you returned to Taiwan, and didn't call me again until my birthday," Niki reminded him. "And even then, you didn't say ..." She stopped, and looked away, blinking rapidly.

"But you must have known..." he was lost for words. "How could I not come back?"

Sometimes you need to state the obvious, he heard Taejin say in his head.

"I should've said it every time we talked," he realized, feeling helpless. All too late now. "Is that why you're so angry at me? Still?"

"You left me," Niki answered, glancing at him, and turned her head away again. But he had enough time to catch the betrayed look in her eyes, and heard the way her voice wavered. "You just left. I told you not to, but you still did."

"I didn't want to leave, Niki. I had to."

"Everybody leaves. When I was little, mum left, and Chen Xiao..."

"You're not being fair. Alina didn't leave you, and neither did Chen Xiao."

"Not voluntarily, no. You're right. But one day they both suddenly disappeared, and I was alone."

Hard to argue with that. It was the truth, from her point of view.

"Then your father left, too. Then Mauricio. Sori. Taejin. Even the twins are leaving soon." Her voice trembled again, so she stopped speaking, and kept quiet for a moment. "People have their own lives, and so they leave all the time," she continued, looking at him with somber eyes. "But you were this one person who was supposed to stay."

Kehuan felt more wretched with every word she said, and more scared, too. But he'd been scared shitless in the past on quite a few occasions already, and they'd all had to do with this impossible cat. And they'd got over it then, so they'd get over it now as well.

"Niki," he said, pushing the word out through what felt like a wad of cottonwool stuck in his throat. "I really didn't want to leave. I had to."

"You had to," she repeated dispassionately. "I guess it's no problem then."

He'd thought about it so many times. Had it really been unavoidable? It'd seemed like there had been no other choice back then, but if he'd tried harder, and if he'd known the consequences... But that was the beauty of the hindsight, of course.

“I thought I had to,” Kehuan corrected himself. “But I won’t do it again, ever. You know I don’t make the same mistake twice.”

“You don’t?” she asked in a peculiar tone, and Kehuan knew at once what she was referring to. Their two wondrous nights of lovemaking.

“That wasn’t a mistake,” he assured her, beyond certain in this matter. “It was just the time that was wrong.” He had a vague feeling he was quoting some love song right now, but so what. Love songs were there for a reason.

He hoped she’d ask if now the time was right, but Niki inquired instead, “What if you think again that you have to leave?”

“I won’t leave anyway,” Kehuan declared without hesitation. “I’ll assume I’m wrong, and I’ll look for a different solution to the problem.”

She seemed to consider his answer for a while.

“All right,” she said finally, sounding tired. “Let’s go home.”

They were still standing in the middle of the arrival hall, amidst people walking in all directions, some engrossed in their own matters, some in a hurry, and some looking at them curiously.

So Kehuan took over the handle of the suitcase and grasped Niki’s slim hand, and then they walked out of the airport, got on a bus, and went home.

* * *

That conversation let him look into her head a little, and now he finally understood what he’d done so wrong: he’d broken her trust in him.

Niki usually gave people big credit of trust. She was an open-minded and optimistic person at heart, and never thought badly of anybody until they proved her wrong, but if they did, she didn’t forgive easily. And Kehuan had been given the biggest credit of trust of all, and he’d screwed up royally.

The worst thing about it was that broken trust wasn’t something that could be mended overnight. An apology wouldn’t work, even if he repeated it every day, and neither would any words of convincing, nor an immediate act, like going into a fight for her, or cutting his hair. The only thing that could fix it was time, and staying by her side no matter what, and even then, there was no guarantee they'd return to what they used to be before. But there was really no other way.

He could tell that Niki didn't want to dwell on it anymore. After that conversation at the airport, they reached an understanding of sorts. They were more at ease with each other now, but things between them were really at a standstill, waiting to be resolved at some undefined later moment when they weren't so raw and painful anymore.

Right now, Niki's exams at school were getting close, so she concentrated on practical issues, and Kehuan had no choice but to do the same. She spent her days cramming, and he spent his working, and if she didn't invite him to accompany her when she took a break and went ice-skating, and then rollerblading when the days got warmer, he just visited his old martial arts club instead, to vent out some of his frustration, or played basketball again with Jason and Marcin, and some other guys. He noticed that a few of Marcin's boys liked to come to the park from time to time and watch Niki rollerblade. Apparently, they were hell-bent on keeping the status of the bane of his existence to the very last day of his stay in this city.

During the week preceding the finals, Niki got very nervous. Kehuan wasn't really surprised when he woke up in the middle of the night before the first day of the exams and saw her sitting in the beanbag near the window, staring away at the river and the downtown behind it.

"Niki," he said quietly, and she turned her head in his direction. "Did you have a nightmare?"

"Yes," she answered. "It's the stress. I don't normally have them anymore."

"I know," he said. He could see she didn't put any blanket over herself, nor a sweater, so he asked, "Aren't you cold?"

"A little," Niki admitted, and Kehuan hesitated.

The situation looked like an almost exact copy of that setup from over a year ago which led to their first night together, and he was sure she recognized it as well. But everything was different now.

"Come here," he said, moving aside and making space for her in his bed.

It was her turn to hesitate. "I don't think…" she started quietly and stopped.

"I know," Kehuan promised, and he really did know.

He'd observed her for months. All the contusions had healed long ago, and she was eating again, so she felt and looked much better now. In other words, she was back to absolutely lovely, and also back to driving him crazy. Kehuan couldn't pretend to himself that he didn't want her like stupid, or that he didn't hope desperately that she'd want him again, too. But some switch got flipped off in Niki, and at least in this one matter he'd been right before: she didn't even have to tell him no, it was enough that she stopped sending him yes, and he knew to keep his distance.

He'd wondered many times if it was his fault as well, or if it rather had something to do with the rat, and every time this suspicion came to his head, he felt tempted to go and find Anna's creep, and disfigure him once again for tainting for her something that should only be beautiful and exciting.

So when she finally stood up now and came closer to his bed, he didn't try anything funny, despite the one hundred or so ideas that flashed in his brain all at once. He just caught her hand and pulled at it until she sat at the edge of the bed, and then lay down next to him. He spread the blanket over both of them and gathered her to himself with both arms.

She went rigid for a moment, but he whispered, "Shh, it's all right, just sleep," and pulled her closer still, kissing the top of her head.

And wonder of wonders, five minutes later she really was asleep. Kehuan's body rebelled against this outcome, but his heart swelled with gratification, and he felt immensely pleased with himself.

Because just think about it. It turned out there was something he could do for her now that he hadn't been able to do in the past.

Wasn't it awesome?

* * *

At the beginning of June, the exams were finally over, and Niki could participate in the last hectic rehearsals for the end of the year concert. The ducklings chose a motive of summer and holidays for this year's event, and Niki loved their choice of songs, and the arrangements, too. They were so good. She was as proud of them as any mama duck could be.

She was doing backing vocals in a few pieces, and solo in just one song at the finale of the concert. Even the ducklings knew she was a fan of oldies, and they presented her with a choice of several classics. Niki picked one of her favorite Polish songs, which she remembered singing with her mum when she was a child, though it had been ancient even then.

It was just a few days before the concert when she received a phone call from Yoon Sori.

“Niki, you won’t believe it,” her big sis chirped excitedly. “Guess who’s coming for a visit.”

Niki thought for a moment. Who could’ve put Sori in such high spirits?

“Don’t say,” she breathed with joyous disbelief. “Mauricio?!”

“Mauricio and Ridhaan, both of them!” Sori confirmed, bursting with excitement. “They’ve coordinated to come at the same time and hatched this plan to go on holiday together. It’s a bit out of the blue, but I’m in, and so is Jason. Taejin still needs to check if he’ll get the time off at work. Would you like to come as well?”

“Sure I would,” Niki answered at once. An impromptu holiday trip with some of her favorite people, who’d say no to it?

“What about Kehuan?” Sori asked.

“I’ll ask him, and Kamila as well. The twins?”

“Already talked to them. Now we only need to convince aunt to let them go. But don’t worry, it’ll be done,” Sori promised, sounding like a SWAT trooper preparing for a mission, and Niki snorted happily. Whoever underestimated Yoon Sori because of her cute looks, girly style, and super nice manners made a serious mistake.

“But where are we going?” she asked, feeling thrilled already.

“The lake district. But there are some competing ideas. Biking or kayaking? What do you say?”

“Oh gosh,” Niki laughed. “Never done much of any.”

“Don’t fret, it’ll be great,” Sori assured her, and Niki snickered again, thinking that Sori probably didn’t realize how much like her mum she sounded in certain situations.

"But I can't go yet," she remembered suddenly. "I've still got the concert at school next Friday."

"Oh, we know," Sori assured her airily. "We're all coming to listen."

Niki didn't feel any desire anymore to say it was a waste of their time. She got over that one already, thanks to Kehuan, and was determined to resolve her other issues as well. She just needed a little more time.

* * *

"What's up?" asked Mauricio, smiling at Kehuan a little ironically. "I heard you've been seriously testing your luck."

"Yeah," Kehuan admitted. "But I've come to my senses already."

"Good," Mauricio approved. "So is everything back on track?"

"Not yet," Kehuan told him ruefully. "I've messed up so many things I need a schedule to put them all to rights again."

"Oh boy," Mauricio answered, upset. "Do it fast, pretty please. If you two don't make it, I don't know what hope there is for the rest of us."

They were sitting in the international school assembly hall, and Kehuan felt somewhat nostalgic. He hadn't visited this place for two years already, if not longer. He probably wouldn't even consider coming to a school event again, but he wanted to hear Niki sing.

The concert began a few minutes later, and it was quite good. He didn't recognize any of the kids on the stage, but he knew they were Niki's charges, so he was glad all went well. And then the final song started, and he recognized the opening chords with what felt like a sudden stab to his gut. He'd heard it so many times in the past.

It was as if Kehuan was watching his own private video clip. The melody and the lyrics, and Niki's magical voice conjured up image after image, scene after scene, some of them long forgotten and now suddenly summoned back from the depths of time and his memory. And each of these snapshots from the past seemed to bring up the same question. Can we be this again?

"I really missed hearing her sing," Mauricio commented wistfully when it was over. "What was the title of that song?"

"'So much sun in the city'," answered Kehuan in a strangled voice.

"Great piece, and decently arranged, too," Mauricio said, "but I didn't get much of the lyrics. My Polish got rusty. What was it about?"

But Kehuan didn't think he could answer that question without making a total wimp out of himself.

* * *

In the end, they split the holiday trip into two parts, and did some kayaking first, along a lovely river winding through the dense forests of the Masurian lake district. Then they rented the bikes in a small bustling tourist town, and rode them along local roads and sandy forest tracks, up and down the wooded hills, and around the lakes dotted with white triangular sails.

They slept in tents and had to disassemble and pack up their small camp every day in the morning, to set it up again in a different place in the evening, and it was a pain and a lot of fun at the same time. Niki couldn't remember laughing so much during any vacations, but of course, it was mainly the company. She supposed they could all sit around and play chess for a week, and she'd still love it. Though not as much.

On the last but one day they ended up on a middle-sized camping site with a facility building in the middle, which apart from the bathrooms and the common kitchen sported also a big room dedicated to some undefined social functions. And surprise, surprise, there was a piano and an acoustic guitar in it. The piano was totally out of tune, making poor Mauricio wince every thirty seconds or so, and the guitar wasn't great either, but they still managed to put together quite a nice jam session. The highlight of the whole shindig was Ridhaan beating out the rhythms on a few bowls, a metal bucket, and a small wooden barrel in lieu of drums. By midnight there was a huge crowd of people inside the room, and a second one outside its opened door, listening, cheering and clapping, and singing many of the songs along.

When they were leaving the next day in the morning, complete strangers waved at them and called out their goodbyes and good wishes, and Niki really hoped it wouldn't be the last time they all had such a fantastic time together.

* * *

Around noon on that last day, they encountered an obstacle on the way, in the middle of the forest. A small wooden bridge spanning a river had been damaged in a gale several weeks earlier, and the foresters closed the access to it by boarding it off, to prevent accidents.

They all got off their bikes and started debating what to do. The water looked shallow, but the river was broad near the bridge, and the bikes had a lot of luggage on them. Carrying them across as they were wasn't going to be easy, but on the other hand, unstrapping the bags and moving them separately would take much more time.

"We'll go first," Soeng Taejin decided, motioning to Kehuan. "You all wait here."

Fording the river turned out to be a laborious task. The current was quite strong and the bottom uneven, and at some places, where it dropped suddenly, the level of water reached Kehuan's thighs, which wasn't good news for the shorter people in their group. It was easy to fall and go under if one wasn't careful.

"I think the guys will have to get all the bikes across, and maybe we should give the girls the piggyback ride, too," Kehuan said to his cousin after he'd put down his bike on the other side of the river, sighing with relief.

Taejin nodded, winded as well. "Let's go back," he said, and they waded through the water again, carefully testing the route and trying to remember the deep places and the eddies.

The whole process took almost an hour. The guys carried their own bikes first, and as Kehuan watched them, he wondered if he should've offered to help Mauricio, who was the smallest and the slightest of the boys and struggled a lot under the weight of his bike. But he suspected the offer would've been rejected anyway. Mauricio had a lot of pride.

Finally, the guys were back, and it was time to sort out the question of female transportation.

Sori immediately climbed on her cousin's back, and they started the crossing. Jason followed after them, carrying her bike.

The twins looked at Kamila expectantly.

"I don't need anybody to lug me around, thank you very much," she announced haughtily. "I've got legs long enough."

"Nobody dares say otherwise, foxy," Taeyeon assured her in a silky voice. "But are you sure? The current's strong."

"Just take my bike," she ordered, entering the river, and he obeyed without further discussion while his twin took care of Niki's steed.

Niki, a little concerned, observed her friend push forward through the water, but the redhead was doing well. She was quite tall for a girl and really did have long legs.

"Get on my back, Niki," Kehuan said.

She did, and he breathed deeply, putting his arms under her legs and hitching her higher up. They hadn't slept in one bed again after that one time or touched in any significant way, and it felt so good to feel her body pressed to his. She put her arms around his neck, taking care not to strangle him, and Kehuan walked in the river. He could feel his heart hammering in his chest, but he could also feel Niki's, who seemed to be just as affected as himself.

"Niki," he said finally, stepping carefully on the uneven riverbed. "I really miss you."

"I miss you, too," she answered quietly.

They were now near a small islet of sand in the middle of the stream, so Kehuan took a turn to it. Niki jumped down as soon as they were out of the water, and they stood eyeing each other for a moment before someone started calling from the other shore. Kehuan turned and saw Kamila at the edge of the water, looking in their direction with her hands on her hips. He made a gesture for time, and she simply nodded and said something to the others, and everybody started to settle around and take out food supplies from their bags.

He turned back to Niki.

"I really want to make up for all of it, you know," he said imploringly. "I know I screwed up. Just tell me what I need to do."

Niki stayed silent for a moment, deep in thought.

"Why did you even think you had to leave back then?" she finally asked. "I never got it, really. There must've been some special reason." She looked up at his face. "Don't tell me it was just because of the sex and the age gap."

"Well, it was because of that, mostly," Kehuan answered, perplexed.

"You could've moved out," she said, "and we could've made a deal to meet only in public places for the time being."

It sounded very logical, but Kehuan doubted it would've worked. There was this sense of inescapable necessity he'd always felt with Niki, and honestly speaking, he knew he'd have done his best to circumvent any obstacles and to be with her again and again. So he didn't comment.

"But there was also this matter of giving you time and space," he said instead, quoting Chen Xiao. "To finally let you make your own choices. Because you'd always lived with me, and never had a chance to be on your own, and to consider what you really wanted."

"Is that what Chen Xiao said?" Niki asked in a disgusted tone.

"Yes."

"And you believed it."

"Yes..."

"You are both fools," she declared disdainfully. "You make it sound as if you found me in the streets like some homeless pet and then kept me out of the goodness of your heart, and I had no part in this decision at all."

"Not like that—"

"You forget it was me who found you first," said Niki, and Kehuan had a sudden flashback of the tiny child with enormous bright eyes, holding out an insulated cup in her outstretched hand.

"That's true," he admitted.

"Of course it's true. You were so cold and lonely that I had to take pity on you. And I kept finding you many times later because you were so dim you never knew where I was," she continued irritably, and he could only stare because that was true as well.

"And when I really needed time and space for myself, I never had any problems with ditching you," she added, and he was dumbstruck.

True, true, and true once again.

But Niki wasn't done yet.

"I touched you first. I kissed you first. I always knew what I wanted," she went on angrily. "I loved you, and you treated me like a delusional child."

Kehuan felt as if she'd hit him with a crowbar. Everything she said was so reasonable and logical, and it turned out he'd really been just an arrogant fool. And she was mad again. What now?

Sometimes you need to state the obvious, he remembered suddenly.

And in the end, there was only one thing left to say, this truly, really obvious thing, and here's hoping it would save him, and save them.

"I love you, Niki," he told her, putting all his sincerity in the words, and years of absolute confidence in this one matter. "I always have, and I don't think I can ever stop. Please forgive me. I'm sorry I hurt you. I'm sorry you got hurt even more by other people because of me. It's my fault, too, whatever you say."

She stood still now, watching him with wide eyes. He wasn't sure she was even breathing anymore.

"I'm sorry you were alone again and felt abandoned. I never meant to abandon you, I swear. How could I? You're everything I have."

There was another moment of stunned silence.

"People can't have other people anymore," Niki spoke finally, coming alive again. Her voice sounded much warmer now, and there was a trace of humor underneath the words. "These days everybody belongs to themselves."

"I don't know about it," Kehuan disagreed. "I belong to you, for example."

She examined his face up close, and he could see every golden and dark blue stripe in her crystal eyes.

"Really?" she asked softly, sounding very young and hopeful. "You do?"

"Yes," he answered. There had never been any doubt about that. "You have me, Niki. You have me."

He had to have uttered some right words during this overlong speech, finally, because she sighed, stepped closer, and snuggled up to him, putting her arms around his waist and her head against his chest.

Kehuan breathed deeply and hugged her tight as well. And as he kissed the top of her head, closing his eyes for a moment, he thought with a deep sense of relief that it seemed they'd finally dug themselves out of that hole and started moving forward at last.

* * *

"Niki, we need to go," Kehuan called out.

She was skating at her new favorite spot, earbuds in place, and he'd been standing there for a long time, reluctant to put a stop to it. He loved watching her move in graceful loops to the music only she could hear, spinning, gliding forward and backward, and performing crossovers and turns. But they still had a lot of unpacking to do, and she had an orientation meeting at the campus later in the evening, and he thought it'd be a good idea to eat something in the meantime, too.

"It's so beautiful here," she said, sitting down on the bench next to him and glancing over the water at the mountains in the north. She started to unstrap her rollerblades. "And yet I miss Warsaw."

"I know," Kehuan admitted. "At least it doesn't rain so much over there."

Niki snorted at that, but then she turned serious again.

"Maybe it's because mum always wanted us to live in Poland," she said after a moment, sounding wistful.

"We can go back whenever you want," Kehuan assured her.

"Nah, it's all right," Niki answered. "I'm just a little homesick, but it'll pass. And besides, we have to go to Taipei first."

"Why? There's nothing interesting in Taipei."

"There are tones of interesting things, you dummy," she chided. "I've done a lot of research on the net. And I still have the Taiwanese passport, you know. Have to finally go and see my first country."

"If you say so."

"Besides, your father's there. Don't you miss him?"

"I talk to him every week," Kehuan answered. "We're good."

Niki shook her head and laughed. "You are impossible," she told him, and Kehuan felt happy, which didn't make much sense. It seemed like everything she said or did made him happy these days. Mush for the brain, seriously.

She stood up, he took the rollerblades from her, and they started walking back home, to their new apartment.

Originally, Niki had intended to stay for some time at Chen Xiao's place, but as soon as Kehuan realized that, he launched a blitzkrieg campaign against this inconvenient idea. It happened during the last week in Warsaw.

"Did you have time to look at those student apartments?" he asked her two days before their departure. "I've sent you the link."

"Not yet," Niki replied. "We can do it when we're already there, can't we? There's no hurry. Chen Xiao isn't going to kick us out of the house."

"But we shouldn't pester him for too long," Kehuan suggested sneakily. "He has a boyfriend, after all."

"You're kidding!" she exclaimed. "Whom?"

"Some architect guy," Kehuan answered indifferently. "I met him last year."

"Wow. That's really great!" Niki thought for a moment. "Okay, I'll take a look at the apartments in the evening," she promised, and Kehuan smiled covertly, feeling smug. They reserved their own place in Vancouver on the same day.

On the way home now, they discussed their plans for the week. Kehuan wanted to look for some second-hand piano again, as the old one had stayed in Warsaw. He'd offered it to Ms. Mazur for some talented scholarship student, to her great delight. Niki had given away many of her works, too, but the rest, together with Kehuan's library, had arrived a week ago and needed to finally get unpacked. At the weekend she wanted to go hiking, together with some new friends she'd met at the campus, and Kehuan agreed it was an excellent idea. He didn't even mind the friends too much.

They entered the building, and what do you know, the elevator wasn't working again. Damn. So they started climbing up the stairs and were just one level below their fifth floor when Niki suddenly stopped and turned around.

"I wanted to ask you something," she said, giving him a slanted look. "We aren't going to give Chen Xiao the satisfaction of having his way, are we?"

"What do you mean?" he asked, curious and a little entertained. The cat was obviously up to something.

"You aren't really waiting until I turn eighteen, are you?" she clarified, looking him straight in the eyes.

Kehuan hadn't been much winded before, but now he suddenly felt there wasn't enough air in this staircase. It was really hot, too. His breathing accelerated rapidly, and his heart started pumping blood at double speed, making him dizzy.

Niki walked down one step and threw both arms around his neck.

"Come here," she murmured, and Kehuan's feet moved forward before he made a conscious decision.

Ah yes, the magnet. Absolutely failproof.

She put her forehead against his, closing her eyes, and when their lips touched as well, Kehuan felt as if he got zapped. His fingers let go of the straps, and the rollerblades fell to the floor with a loud thud while he grabbed her head with both hands and started kissing her as if his life depended on it.

"Niki," he whispered against her lips after a moment, needing to check and make it absolutely clear because things were slipping out of his control rather fast. "Are we going to…?"

"Yes," she told him, already flushed and breathless, even as her lovely eyes sparkled with laughter. "Though maybe let's go inside first."

And so they did.

A word from the author

Dear Reader,

Thank you for reading Kehuan and Niki's story. I hope you enjoyed it and will want to meet some of the characters again on the pages of my next books.

I would appreciate it very much if you expressed your opinion in a short review. If you don't feel like writing anything, you can just rate the book. To quickly access the "rate or/and review" page on Amazon, please scan the QR code from the next page or type in your browser the link:

https://tinyurl.com/ttwb-hc-review

Your opinion is important to me, and I value all feedback. I also believe ratings and reviews are very useful for the whole community of readers. Leaving a review, you are making a difference.

Thank you for your time. Till we meet again!

Yours,
Magdalena Stanhoff

About the author

Magdalena Stanhoff writes contemporary novels about third culture people. She loves traveling and is vividly interested in how diverse cultures coexist, clash and mix, and how it influences people's life. Her novels explore romantic love, family bonds, and friendship in their various forms and shades, and since the author is also an incurable dreamer, they always end with the HEA.

Visit **www.magdalenastanhoff.com**

Printed in Poland
by Amazon Fulfillment
Poland Sp. z o.o., Wrocław
13 December 2022

748d800d-7b9d-4099-8f47-ccd7a4a49262R01